Unleashed

A Defiant Dragons Novel

Aria Glazki

Anika Press

Cover design by Danielle Fine
Author avatar by Alex M.

ISBN: 978-1-943572-20-5
Copyright registration number:
TX0009325801

To Jim,

Thank you for everything

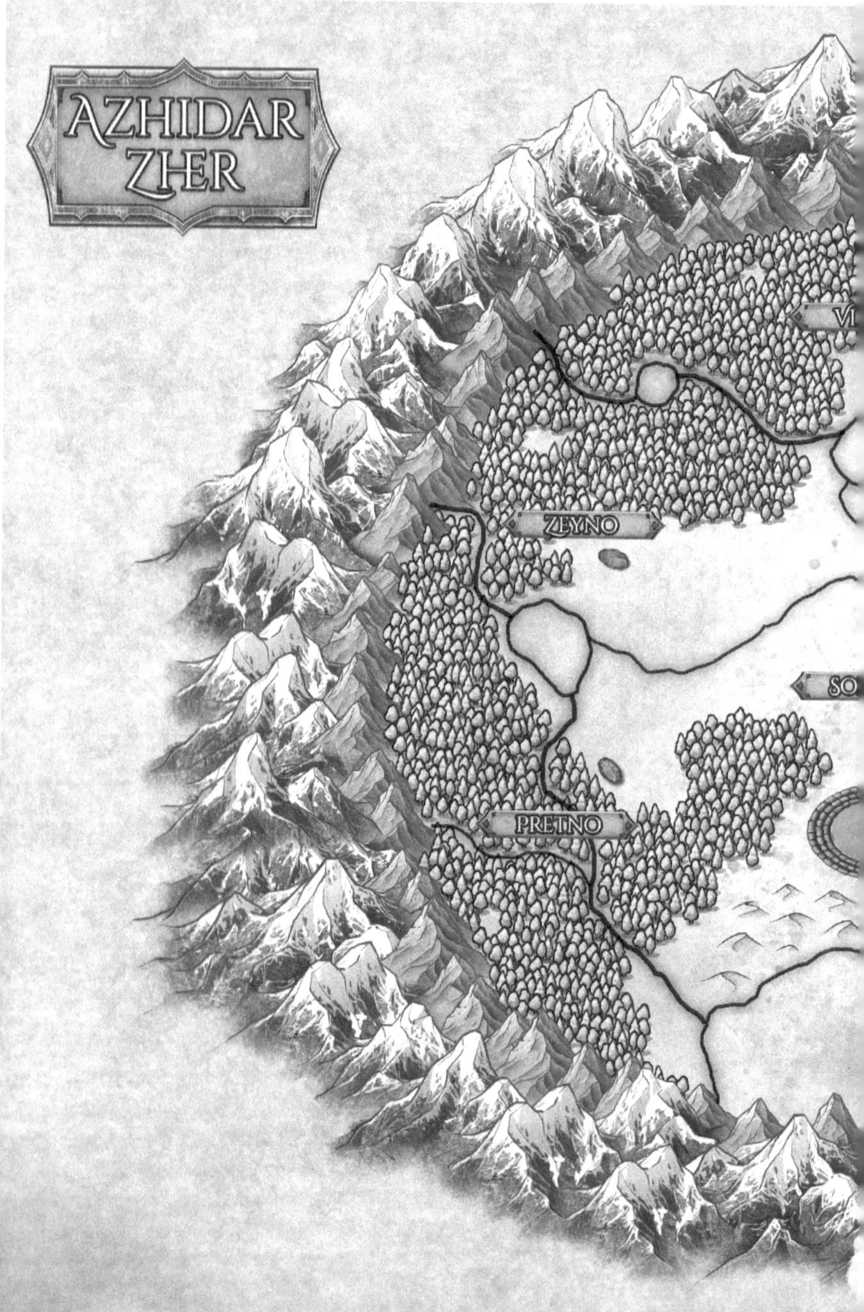

AZHIDAR ZHER
VI
ZEYNO
SO
PRETNO

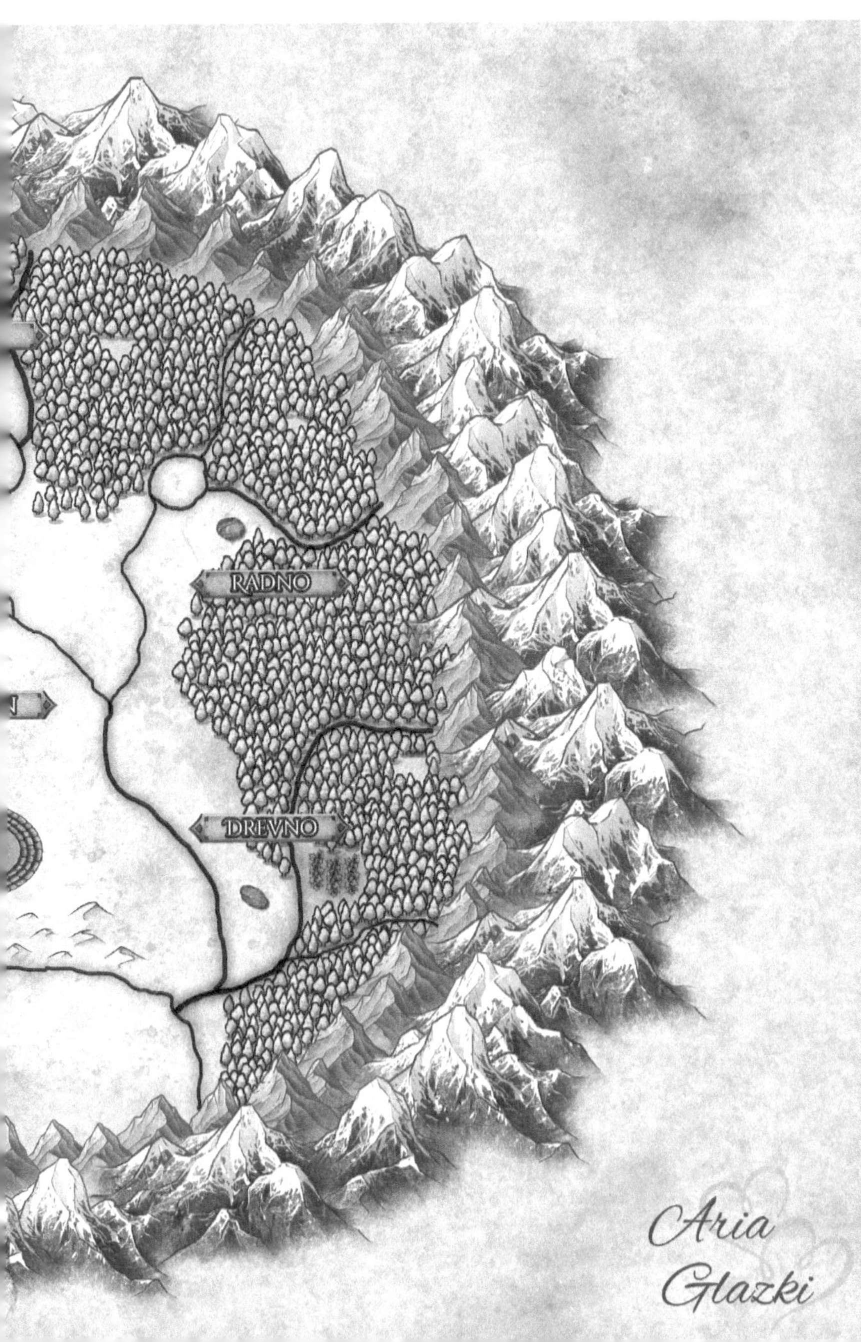

RADNO
DREVNO
Aria Glazki

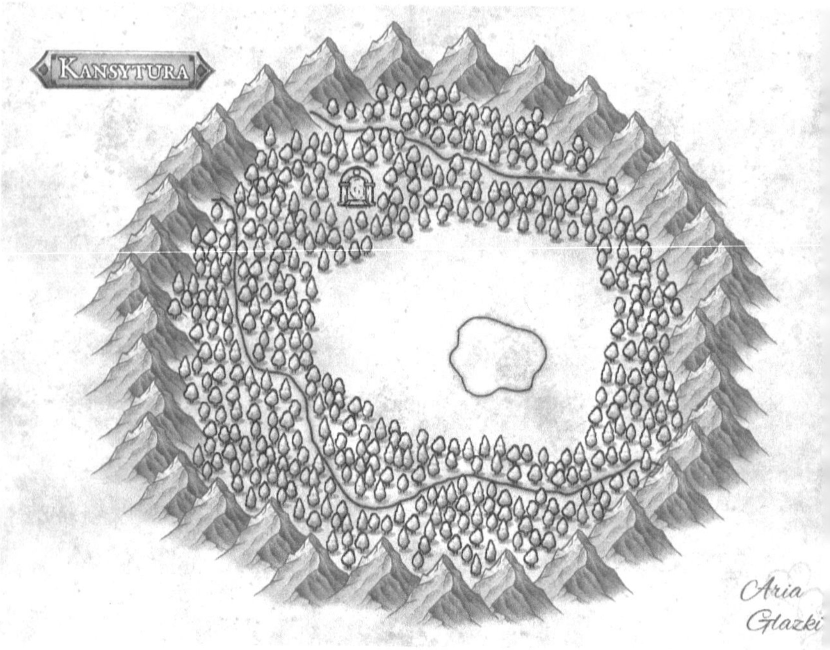

High-resolution full color versions of both maps
are available at patreon.com/AriaGlazki

Dear Reader,

This is a sizzling dragon shifter fantasy romance. Please be aware that it includes content some readers will find distressing, such as discussions of sexual violence, abduction and captivity, minimal torture, post-traumatic stress disorder, and violence resulting in death.

Read at your own discretion, and please prioritize your mental health.

For a more detailed list, please visit:
content.ariaglazki.com

If you're looking for steam, I advise patience. This story may be a slow burn, but it definitely brings the heat.

Thank you for reading!

Aria

Chapter 1

THE PRESENCE OF ANOTHER DRAGON TINGLED OVER THE skin of Tia's human form, and she twisted in her seat to observe the newcomer loping down the stairs to the front of the lecture hall. If he felt her too, she'd have to run.

She should have run anyway, but it had been nearly a century since she'd seen another of her kind. Young dragons visited the mortal realm to learn how to survive in it, but there weren't that many of them. Encountering one was rare. It had been so long.

Older dragons occasionally popped by as well, maintaining their connections to human society, but as this realm's population grew ever denser, more and more preferred to stay with their own kind. Unless they were hunting someone. Meaning her.

This dragon paid no attention to her, shuffling papers at the front of the hall. Bronzed terra-cotta skin and burnished dark-brown hair hinted at the coloring of his true form. He looked up, scanning the smattering of students, but his gaze didn't linger on her. Tia shut her eyes, giving in to the sensation of being even this close.

"Power nap?" Naiara asked, plopping into the seat beside Tia's. She slipped her messenger bag over her head, dislodging her short hair enough to reveal the new magenta hiding under the black. She'd changed her nose ring to a matching stud as well, a tiny pink stone glinting when she moved.

"Cute color," Tia said, still tracking the newcomer at the front.

Naiara grinned. "Discreet, right?"

"Totally professional," Tia agreed.

"Yeah. Wish I had a boss as chill as yours." Naiara's boss at the campus coffee shop was considered old-fashioned nowadays, insisting employees stuck with hair colors that occurred naturally—in humans—and kept any body art covered.

But as human technology and aesthetics advanced, blending in became much easier for Tia. No need to use glamour when colored contacts could hide her amethyst eyes. No more hiding the swirls of color on her torso when they could pass for abstract tattoos, if anyone did catch a glimpse. No relying on toxic compounds to mask the bright blues and purples of her own hair. Though today it likely helped that her hair was twisted up, tucked close to her head. She may never have met the dragon who'd settled in to the TA chair, but her coloring was distinctive. If he even suspected...

The smart call would have been to leave, not just the room but Pennsylvania. Bordeaux, Tokyo, Buenos Aires, Florence— Tia had plenty of options. And she'd started over plenty of times before, unable to settle anywhere longer than about a decade, sometimes fifteen years before mortals caught on that she wasn't aging like them. Glamour helped, but it drained too much energy to keep up constantly. Still she'd only been in Pennsylvania a couple years this time around. Her fast, easy friendship with Naiara was only one reason abandoning her current life early would, frankly, suck.

"Who's the hottie?" Naiara murmured as the professor called the class to order.

Good question. Had curiosity about the mortals brought him to their realm? Or was he searching for her? Tia wasn't even registered for this class, auditing it because Naiara wanted the company. So if the unnamed dragon had somehow discovered her current mortal identity, he still wouldn't have had a reason to look for her here.

Could it be a coincidence? Maybe then she could stay. Find an excuse to drop the class and never cross paths with him again. As much as she missed her kind, her body begging to curl up next to him, keeping her distance wasn't merely the smart call. It was a matter of life and death.

Azar doodled on a pad of paper as the human professor droned on about the course syllabus. He'd enjoyed his previous time in the mortal realm, but over a century had passed. So much had changed.

Already he'd heard students tittering about his preference for paper and pen instead of the complex devices of various sizes many had placed before them, tapping away with their fingertips. He had one such device in his pocket, set up for him as this employment had been by Laisren. Since this wasn't Azar's first foray into this realm, it had been easy to position him as an expert in Victorian England and the literature of the time.

Under different circumstances he may even have enjoyed spending time around vivacious young humans eager to learn in and out of the classroom. The mission superseded such frivolity.

The Peran Estate had been flagged as potentially being owned by an unknown dragon. It was rarely inhabited by a mysterious owner with seemingly endless financial resources. There was at least some possibility it could lead to his quarry, unlikely as that was.

His post at the university was merely the means to ensure his own livelihood among the humans. Not all dragon lines managed mortal resources with an eye to the future, cultivating properties and riches, crafting the identities necessary to retain their fortunes through the centuries. Nowadays, few could venture in and out of the human realm. Azar's mission depended on the foresight and connections of Laisren. The small sum he'd saved from his time in England would help, but it wouldn't last long. He had to gain entry into the Peran Estate, to meet the owner and eliminate them from contention.

He wasn't presumptuous enough to believe he'd be the one to find the missing heir, but if every one of them worked in conjunction with Laisren's plan, it would only be a matter of time. Failure was no longer an option.

As the lecture neared its close, Tia sent Naiara a quick message.

Gotta run. See you later?

Naiara frowned but let Tia sneak past her, out of their row and up the couple of steps to the exit. The head start meant the TA wouldn't have a chance to follow her.

The humanities quad was quiet, a few students dotting the benches and the stone outcropping. The slight breeze and late-morning sunlight did little to calm the bite of adrenaline that had jittered through her body ever since the other dragon—introduced by the professor as Azar—had casually upended her life.

Tia could withdraw from the semester, citing a personal emergency or some mental health issues. Disappear for a few months and hope by next semester he'd be gone.

She shook her head as she unchained her bike from the rack. Mortal thinking had infected hers, if she believed even for a moment that a few months was enough time for Azar to move on. Dragons felt time differently. They were patient. Even if his presence was unrelated to her, most visits to this realm lasted years, sometimes decades.

She didn't want to leave, but the grief of departure was familiar. She'd tried at times to stay in contact with the friends she hadn't wanted to abandon, writing letters or later taking advantage of the telephone. But faking a life she wasn't leading, falsifying everything that came with human aging, was more like crafting fiction than maintaining true relationships. As travel became easier, some old friends had attempted to track her down. A few times she'd pretended to be her own daughter. The resemblance was "uncanny."

It was less painful to disappear. Pick one of her many identities, move to one of her other properties.

Her phone vibrated against her hip as she rode up the gentle slope leading to the Peran Estate. Contemporary technology meant this time she could stay in touch, for a while at least. Keep tabs on Azar through Naiara. Since he hadn't noticed her in the lecture hall, he may not know anything about this identity. She could move but not disappear, not yet.

Inside, Tia plopped onto an overstuffed couch in the living room, fingering the chain around her neck. A few days ago she'd had some classmates over for brunch, the adjacent casual dining room filled with their laughter and camaraderie. She was just starting to build a new community here.

But as tired as Tia was of being alone, it was preferable to the alternative. This was the life she'd signed up for when she ran from Azhidar Zher. She might risk staying for a few more days, withdrawing officially and saying her goodbyes. Making new arrangements for the care of the property.

Ultimately, though, leaving was the only choice.

Chapter 2

ET YOU A REFILL?" A YOUNG WOMAN IN A GREEN APRON asked, pausing by Azar's little glass-topped table. A flicker of recognition warmed her expression. "Hey, you're the TA for Professor Weston, right?"

He let the pad on which he'd been sketching his surroundings drift down to the tabletop. Forging connections with the students was precisely why he was spending his evening in this little coffee shop at the edge of the university. "Azar," he said, nodding at her.

"Nice to meet you." She smiled then leaned down, nudging his sketch to see it better. She was close enough for him to feel the heat of her body, pick out the blend of coffee and apricot on her skin from the assault of scents around him. He was still adjusting to the new social norms that allowed such unabashed proximity. The human's hair fell forward, revealing a bright color in the hidden strands. A pink stone glinted in her nose. "Wow, you're pretty good. Why aren't you in the art program?"

"This is simply a hobby."

She nodded, straightening. One hand landed on the hip that jutted to the side. "Some hobby." Her head tilted to the opposite side as she ran her eyes over him in appraisal. "Been in town long?"

"No." He gestured to the second chair near his table. "Would you like to join me?"

"Mmm, I can't." She fingered her apron as if to explain, then straightened and picked up his empty coffee cup. "But maybe I could show you around sometime? Give you the lay of the land."

For all the ways the mortal realm had changed, humans, ultimately, did not. The appreciation in her hazel eyes was unmistakable.

"Ever been to the Peran Estate?" Azar asked. If she were offering him a tour of the local sights, perhaps he could do some proper reconnaissance.

She frowned, eyes narrowing suspiciously. "Why?"

Azar shifted his shoulders casually. "I've heard it has some spectacular architecture, beautiful lands." He tapped his sketch. "Could be interesting to draw."

She hummed in response, the suspicion not quite disappearing. "Where'd you land on that refill?"

He'd pushed her too far. Mortals may be far more direct than he was used to, but their openness seemed to have unknown boundaries. "I'd appreciate one," he said.

She had started a conversation with him; perhaps someone else would as well. He had to be seen engaging in this community, earning their trust. The future of the dragons depended on Laisren's plan, and Azar would do everything in his power to help. Even if that meant biding his time, sitting here, sketching while the days slipped away.

He flipped to a new sheet as the woman placed a fresh cappuccino on his table.

"Here," she said, plucking the pencil from his lax grip. She scribbled her name and a series of numbers on the new page. "Text me sometime."

She walked away before he could respond, but Azar smiled to himself. Integrating into human society was the first step. Someone here would know something about the owner of the nearby estate. Once he learned how to utilize the "portable telephone" in his possession, he could start making progress. For all their sakes.

"We can agree you owe me, right?" Naiara said, leaning on the marble island in the butler's pantry. "For bailing on that class," she clarified at Tia's arched brow.

Tia shoved aside the pang of guilt. She hadn't brought up yet that she was leaving entirely. She had no illusions about Naiara's ability to move on with her life, but first Tia would be in for a pretty serious guilt trip. "Sure," she said, keeping their conversation light. This night should be about silly gossip, the gooey pizza sitting between them, and the rather nice Viognier she was pouring.

"It's the first weekend of the semester," Naiara pointed out, sliding a thick slice onto her plate then licking the sauce off her fingers.

"So?" Tia carried the wine glasses to the table in the casual dining room and returned for the pizza box and her plate. After all the years spent among humans, she'd grown accustomed to having her meals at a table, not in the fields—or standing at a counter. Even without the formal place settings and multiple courses of the past, sharing food remained one of the core bonding activities for humans. Sitting together at the table facilitated that. Or maybe after these last centuries, she was stuck in her ways.

Naiara grabbed her plate and joined Tia. "So we should have a party. Well, you should have a party. This place is amazing. You open the doors here, and you could compete with the Greek parties."

"I'm a glorified house sitter, remember?" The lie explained how a college student with no obvious connection to the owner could live in a mansion. "No big parties allowed."

"Oh, please, when's the last time the owner was here? I'm not talking anything crazy." She hummed around a bite of pizza, her eyes widening as an idea struck. "We could have a dinner party. Get Josh to help us cook. Dozen people, tops. And no one ever has to know."

"Why does this feel like a trap?" Tia teased. If she didn't go back to the university, she would probably be safe staying for two more days. A farewell dinner wasn't the worst idea. She did enjoy entertaining, and this place was certainly built for it.

Besides, needing to say a proper goodbye was one of the reasons she was still there. "Okay, fine," she relented.

Naiara squealed and pulled out her phone.

"A *small* dinner party," Tia reminded.

"Definitely," her friend agreed with a mischievous smile. "Keep it intimate."

Azar paused before the large double doors of the Peran Estate and flared out his power. He'd barely believed it when Naiara had invited him here, especially given her earlier suspicion. He wasn't worried about escaping if this turned out to be a trap of some sort, but there was no point in being reckless. The property was large, and his power could only reach so far, but nothing inside pushed back against him.

A pair of humans waved as they exited their vehicle, parked amid several others on the intricate stone pattern of the front drive. Azar lifted his hand in return.

Though none of them had knocked, one half of the carved double doors swung open. "Welcome, welcome!" Naiara stepped back and swept a hand inside.

The mortal couple exclaimed at the two-story entrance with its marble flooring, double curved stairway, and currently extinguished chandelier. The manor was easily as grand as the finest he'd served in during his time in England. Electric wall sconces lit their way as Naiara turned to the left, the path to the right remaining in shadow.

"We're doing appetizers on the deck before dinner," she explained as she deftly ushered the three of them down the hall, through an entryway into an informal dining space, then through another open entryway and across a casual sitting room. Pausing by the French doors as the others stepped through, she turned to Azar. "So what do you think?"

He took a moment to look out beyond the deck, his eyes letting him see far more than humans could. Even so, he was mostly guessing when he said, "It's beautiful." The grounds were expansive, though he knew that from his research. In different times, soaring above the lush greenery whose scent he could make out underlying the foods being offered would not have been unpleasant.

"I didn't know you lived here," he added, gesturing so she would precede him onto the deck. If she could host an event here, she had to know the owner.

"Oh, I don't. Can you imagine?" She walked him over to join the others by a plush seating area. "Tia's the property manager, and we are totally taking advantage." A chorus of cheers met the statement.

Naiara introduced all the humans on the deck, but Azar missed the names, waiting to hear the only one that mattered. He absently accepted a crystal flute of a drink identified only as *bubbly*. Where was this Tia?

"Here we go!" a broad-framed man in a navy chef's coat stepped out onto the deck, carrying two platters of food.

The humans exclaimed again, their jovial mood pleasant enough but distracting. The woman who followed the chef jolted when she saw Azar. Certain humans were somewhat more aware of what they considered the supernatural, able to feel power they couldn't fully comprehend. They were remarkably good at ignoring all the signs, however, explaining them away or simply pretending they hadn't felt anything.

"A toast to Tia!" Naiara suggested, and the woman resumed moving as if the moment hadn't happened.

She smiled and laughed with her friends, accepting the crystal flute they pressed on her. Her hair flowed out behind her, a vibrant blend of colors that once would have marked her as magic. But the hair closest to her scalp was a pale gold, a sign of the new human practice of dyeing their hair as they did cloth. He'd seen it all around the university. Still, she was beautiful.

Most importantly, she was the woman he sought. Or rather, the next step in reaching the owner. The Fates must have been on his side. On *their* side, for this all to happen so quickly. The sooner he could ascertain that the owner was merely another human, the more resources could be devoted elsewhere.

Azar lifted his glass with the others, toasting the woman who was his hostess for the evening, and his next challenge. She had the information he needed, so he would persuade her to share it. Knowledge gleaned during his younger years spent among the humans would help.

The fastest way to gain a mortal's trust? Seduction.

Chapter 3

"O H YOU TOOK YOUR CONTACTS OUT. BOO." NAIARA POUTED briefly but soon tossed a mac and cheese ball into her mouth.

"They were bugging my eyes," Tia lied. Technically, she'd just glamoured her eyes to look brown, but putting *in* her brown contacts was high on her list. The less power she used around the other dragon, the better, though it wasn't like she could actually bleach her roots in the middle of a party she never should have agreed to. The moment she'd felt the dragon on her deck, she'd damped the non-mortal elements of her appearance. It seemed, so far, that he hadn't noticed. At least, he wasn't treating her any differently than he did the humans.

"What made you invite the TA?" she asked, stacking the empty platters on one of the twin islands in an attempt to keep the kitchen moderately organized.

"He's *hot*," Naiara said, as if that explained everything. Which, under any other circumstances, it would have. She twirled out of Josh's way, ignoring his irritated frown.

"Need help, Josh?" Tia asked as he started shelling shrimp.

"Please. I knew what I was getting myself into." He threw another annoyed glance at Naiara.

"I'm helping!" she protested, picking up a wooden spoon to stir the risotto.

"And he *is* hot," Josh said. He shoed Naiara away from the stove, easily juggling whatever was happening in the three pans. The blend of garlic, rosemary, caramelizing onions, and buttery mushrooms permeating the air was literally mouthwatering.

"Plus he wanted to see the mansion," Naiara added.

Tia stiffened. "He did?"

"Everybody does," her friend confirmed absently. She moved into the butler's pantry to pick up a platter with a tear-and-share spanakopita. "That's why they're here. Relax! No one's being graded, he's here to have fun." She cocked her head in the direction of the deck.

"Be there in a sec," Tia assured with a smile she wasn't quite feeling. After verifying Josh wasn't feeling too taken advantage of, she grabbed a couple more bottles of wine, but then snuck upstairs to her bathroom to put in those contacts. Even though Azar had already seen her, she twisted her hair up to deemphasize its coloring. At least her eyebrows were bleached to a very mortal blond. Her fingers double-checked that the clasp at her neck was holding strong. After a few deep breaths, Tia made her way back down and out to the others. She couldn't disappear in the middle of her own party.

And Naiara was right: the newcomer *was* hot.

Maybe Tia wouldn't have noticed if she hadn't been isolated for so long. But Azar's nearness tingled all over, a caress coaxing her to let her guard down. It wasn't like she had remained chaste all these years. Far from it, but being with humans was different. And there he was, a handful of steps away, sending her an easy smile as he lifted his glass in her direction.

She pulled herself away to set the fresh bottles on the outdoor bar. Even with her back turned, she felt him moving closer. Her teeth clamped down on her bottom lip to stop the shiver working its way through her insides. If she reacted to his power, he'd know. As it was, she'd be leaving this place behind as soon as the humans had gone. So much for saying goodbye. Naiara might never forgive her.

"Your home is lovely," he said above her ear. Deft motions mixed a drink in a fresh crystal tumbler. He spoke with a smooth British accent, perhaps choosing it to stand out. Flirting with mortals was a novelty—until it wasn't. Or perhaps a previous visit to this realm had landed him in the UK, and he'd simply picked up the regional English dialect. Tia'd worked hard to modify her accent to blend in as she moved around over the decades.

"Thanks, but it isn't actually mine." She offered him a bland smile. Her heart may be pounding, her body screaming at her to close the meager gap between her and the dragon within reach, but her survival instinct was louder, stronger. If he even *suspected...*

"No?" Azar asked, turning to survey the grounds behind the house. On her first trip to the mortal realm, when she'd purchased this estate, these lands had been sufficient to enjoy in her real form, to soar freely above them or play in the little lake secluded at the back corner of the property. Of course, that was before the humans had become so populous, and cameras inescapable.

"Just house-sitting. How do you know Naiara?" she added, testing to see if he'd noticed her in class three days ago after all.

"We crossed paths at the coffee shop at the university. She was kind enough to take me under her wing, as it were, offering to introduce me around."

Was he toying with her, hoping she'd react to the choice of words? Tia'd been hiding far too long to fall for a maneuver as transparent as that. "Shouldn't be keeping you all to myself, then. Please." She swept a hand toward the others, indicating he should join them.

All she had to do was keep his interest directed elsewhere for a few hours, until decorum would force him to leave with the others. As long as he believed her to be human, that shouldn't be too difficult.

Then Tia could do what she should have the moment she'd seen him: run.

"Don't you get creeped out, living here alone?" that evening's chef asked as they all lounged around the fireplace in one corner of the hexagonal sitting room with digestifs and dessert. "I mean, that kitchen's amazing, but all those empty bedrooms?" An exaggerated shudder made the others laugh.

Azar chuckled too, keeping up with the conversation even as his focus remained on their hostess.

"You get used to it," she demurred. Delicate hands cradled a glass of sherry in her lap.

"Sure you don't need any help looking after this place?" Laura joked. "I could use a break on the rent."

"Or it'd be perfect for a sleepover," Naiara said. She lay half-entwined with another of his "students" on a small sofa.

No one appeared too concerned by the impropriety of his presence, and Azar certainly wasn't going to point it out. He sat on the larger, angled couch, directly beside the overlarge arm-chair-esque end on which Tia had settled.

"I'd get fired," she pointed out, directing her comment to anyone but him. It had been like that most of the evening, with her never crossing the line into outright rudeness but purpose-fully avoiding him as much as was possible in such a small gath-ering. He clearly unsettled her, confirming his hunch that she was one of the more sensitive humans.

The hunter within him was thrilled. She wouldn't be quite that easy a target. And despite the metaphorical ticking clock hanging over him, echoed by his own steady heartbeat, he did have *some* time to win her over. All he needed tonight was to find a reason, a way to see her again. If that didn't work out, he would find her on campus. At the very least, the multicolored strands of her hair were bound to stand out. Even with the bulk pinned out of sight, a purple curl had fallen free, emphasizing the pale curve of her neck. Despite his impatience to do his duty, seducing her would be no hardship.

"Your last day, then," Naiara persisted. "Besides, we'd all help you clean up."

"Like you are tonight?" Tia pointed out with a wry smile.

Naiara's nose wrinkled, and she let out a soft groan. "No, tonight, I am passing out right here."

"Hey, we were promised a tour." Yoni threw his hand around his partner's shoulders. "And we're not leaving until we get one."

"We'll stay here all night if we have to," his partner chimed in, setting off another round of satiated laughs.

Tia shook her head at the teasing, a touch of sadness or perhaps loneliness shading her smile.

"That settles it," Naiara announced. "Tia gives the tour, Josh makes some coffee, and we'll stay right here. Can't leave the fire unattended." She smirked, sinking deeper into the cushions.

"You are so lazy," Josh said, swatting at her legs from his seat on a pile of pillows beside the low upholstered table with the remaining desserts.

"You're the one who stuffed us full of that amazing food," she countered, kicking lightly in his direction.

"That's her way of saying 'thank you,'" Tia said pointedly, lifting her sherry.

The rest of them joined in with murmurs of assent. Josh waved off the compliments, his face flushing beneath his close-cropped beard. It was all so simple, so casual, as if none of them in that moment had a single care in the world. Their ability to set any of their concerns aside and enjoy the moment was enviable. The meal had been skillfully prepared, the atmosphere remained light, and yet Azar couldn't forget that he was there for one sole purpose.

"I'd be interested in a tour as well, if we wouldn't be putting you out," he said for Tia's ears alone as the others continued their jokes.

"Make sure to show them the solarium," Naiara said, overhearing. The others fell quiet. "Oh, and those paintings in the *salon.*" Reverence with a healthy dose of sarcasm inflected the word. "Azar's really into art."

"Perhaps we could help you clear up first," he offered, tightening the trap of the polite hostess a touch more. Whatever light she could shed on the history of the manor would certainly be useful.

"Not necessary," Tia murmured. She scooted forward on the generous cushion and stood. "Well, then. The last tour of the evening will begin in approximately thirty seconds." A self-deprecating smile accompanied the words, and the satisfaction of success thrummed in Azar's chest.

Perhaps he was celebrating too quickly, but thus far everything about this mission had turned out far easier than expected. If his associates' missions were proceeding as smoothly? Perhaps what remained of the dragons could be saved.

Chapter 4

AND THROUGH HERE IS THE SOLARIUM," TIA EXPLAINED, "but Naiara forgot it's dark out, so there isn't much to see." She'd rushed through the tour, trying to seem bored when really she was impatient for the evening to be over so everyone would leave. She'd allowed herself to luxuriate in Azar's presence throughout dinner, more or less safe among the humans. He'd shown an interest in her—enough that Naiara had decided sleeping with her TA wouldn't be the smartest call after all—but nothing that indicated he recognized Tia as another of their kind.

Still, she had a long night ahead, packing up enough to make it clear Tia-the-grad-student wouldn't be coming back, writing out goodbye notes to Naiara and Josh, emailing to withdraw from her courses. She had duplicates of anything she may truly need in each of her main properties, and the resources to buy anything she overlooked in the rush, but she'd learned if she truly disappeared without a word, the humans were *more* likely to search for her.

The handful of mortals who had elected to explore the mansion peeked inside the solarium, but only Azar wandered in.

"Guess you'll have to have us over again when it's light out," Yoni joked.

"Rude!" Rin whispered sharply.

"No, this was fun," Tia said. "I'd love to have you over again sometime." The truth of the statement lay bittersweet at the back of her throat. She'd likely exchange some emails with Naiara but would probably never see any of the others again.

"I think Azar got lost," Marisa said, peering into the dark room.

"Azar?" Tia called, hoping he'd wander back out on his own. When he didn't answer, she hesitated, glancing at the humans. Being alone with him was a terrible idea.

"Maybe he wants you to find him," Laura suggested with a smile.

"Yeah, we can find our way back," Yoni said, ushering the others away. They'd all made it back into the adjoining study before she could respond. Calling them back would be childish.

"Azar," Tia repeated, stepping into the glass-enclosed room.

"It's a beautiful view," he said quietly. He stood with his back to her, nearly centered in the segmented curve of glass that looked out onto the back of the property. With no lights on outside, moonlight caressed the gentle slopes of abundant greenery as it did his hair, his shoulders.

But human eyes wouldn't see the detail they could.

"It's dark," she said. "How can you tell?"

"Depends on where you look." He glanced at her over his shoulder before dropping his head back to look up through the glass roof.

Tia moved forward, drawn closer for the exact reason she should have stayed away. She stopped near his side, and he turned to face her. Soaking in as much as she could feel of his proximity, she forced her gaze up and to the stars, as if she really had never enjoyed the beauty of the skies above her property in the darkness.

When she let her gaze drift back down, he was still watching her. If he'd known she wasn't mortal, surely he would have made that clear before now. There was no reason for Azar to stall, unless he was attempting to lull her into a false sense of security.

Or else, he didn't know, the protection charm holding steady.

"You're quite beautiful as well," he said, moving closer until she had to tilt her head back up to meet his gaze. His fingers hovered by her face a moment before lightly nudging a curl that had come loose behind her ear. The faint touch would have made her jump out of her skin if not for the iron grip she maintained on her control.

What was he playing at? With the humans nearby and surrounded by glass, he couldn't risk shifting any more than she could.

But then, if the contact had been a test, his hand wouldn't still be lingering, fingertips tracing the skin below her ear.

And if he *didn't* know, what was the harm in taking a few moments to enjoy his touch? The mortals had a term for this ache for closeness with her own kind: skin hunger. Well, she was ravenous.

When she didn't move away, Azar dipped his head, pausing at her sharp inhale with his lips mere millimeters from hers. Gold-flecked brown eyes watched her calmly, as if it didn't matter to him whether they would kiss. But it mattered to her. In a few hours at most, she'd be gone. Away from here, yes, but also far from him or any other dragon. As it had to be.

But maybe not right now. Tia'd barely moved before he caught her lips, his fingers cupping her head, angling it for his kiss. The same charm that kept her safe from his detection dulled the full sensation of his caress, keeping everything she craved just out of reach. But the heat swirling from her lips through her core was more than she should have allowed herself. Being there with him was playing with fire.

Good thing Tia was a dragon.

Her fingers dug into the cotton covering his flesh as she pressed herself closer, succumbing to the taste of home.

Azar slid his fingers through Tia's hair until he found the clip that held it up. Softer than he'd expected, it tumbled down her back as he coaxed her lips open. The faintest hum of power clung to her, not unlike the seer he'd crossed paths with centuries ago. Did she know her potential? Maybe once he ruled out the estate's owner, he could help Tia explore, steer her into learning about her innate abilities. It would take Laisren time to organize things so Azar's absence soon after the start of the semester wouldn't arouse unnecessary suspicion.

Shaking off the weight of his mission, he focused on this moment. Seducing Tia may be a calculated decision, but she deserved his undivided attention. Her hands pulled him closer, body pressing up into him, lips melding with his as if she were trying to drink him in. Light pressure on a fistful of her hair broke their kiss. The rasp of her exhales filled the secluded room, her skin impossibly luminous in the moonlight. Her tongue flicked over her lower lip.

"Where'd you say those bedrooms were?" Azar asked. Had they been alone in the manor, one of the plush seats nestled along the glass walls would have served plenty well. But the privacy of a bedroom would likely help her relax and enjoy their time together.

The question seemed to remind Tia of the others as well. She twisted back to look at the faint golden glow seeping through the partially open door to the music room, her grip on him easing.

Azar dipped his head to her neck, nuzzling the tender skin. "Your friends will understand." If there was one thing humans always understood, it was desire.

She didn't respond, but she didn't move away, either. If one kiss was all she was ready for, Azar could wait, coax her to see him again. As she thought, he nibbled along her clavicle, nudging the collar of her loose top out of his way. He caught the exact moment she chose, the tension of indecision dropping from her frame with a long exhale. He touched his tongue to the pulsing vein at the base of her neck, lingering over the delicate scent of lilac on her skin.

"Upstairs," she breathed, stepping back.

Azar trailed her silently back the way they'd come. She didn't rush, but neither did she hesitate, moving confidently through the music room, the study, the library, then up a helical staircase, her hair swaying along to the swish of her hips. She veered into the first doorway by the landing, not bothering to turn on any light in the upstairs hall. The bedroom was impeccably neat, a large bed standing against the wall to their left, a generous seating area before them. With the moon on the other side of the manor, only soft ambient light filtered through the windows.

Near the center of the room, Tia turned to face him. Anticipation had brought swaths of rose to her cheeks. Even without his power, he could have easily dominated her petite frame, but still she tilted her chin up in challenge. He pushed the door closed with a quiet swish.

Undaunted, Tia stripped off her gauzy blouse, revealing black lace cupping her breasts and a long chain that disappeared teasingly between them, ending in a dark pendant lying at the top of her abdomen. It glinted red when it caught a bit of light.

Azar moved toward her until his hand found the soft curve of her waist. Her palm skimmed up his chest, and he briefly wished he could use his power to dissipate the fabric. Disposing of it the mortal way would have to be fast enough. He let go to strip off his shirt, then recaptured her lips.

His grip on her ribcage tensed, and she reacted instantly, pressing up off the floor to land with her legs clasped around him. Strands of her hair teased his shoulders as her tongue swiped his. That faint hum of power tickled his palms. Did she feel that too?

Her thighs tightened around him, and she broke their kiss, arching backward with her inhale as if serving up her breasts for his pleasure. True, Azar had a job to do. But to use the modern parlance, this part? It didn't suck.

Tia sucked down air, forcing her mind to work well enough to commit every piece of this to memory. Azar's lips trailed down her sternum, and he hitched her up higher to lick along the edge of her bra. She clutched his shoulders for balance, relishing the strength in his muscles, the light bite of his power blanketing her.

She'd never tested the limits of the charm that protected her, not this close to another dragon, and definitely not skin to skin. Could he feel the suppressed remnants of her own magic beating against the protective cage? Would he notice? Would the glamour concealing her markings hold?

Azar's teeth pressed into the flesh of her breast, and she forgot to care. He snapped open the clasp of her bra, and the fabric drooped, a strap slipping down her shoulder. He didn't give her time to strip it off before his tongue found a tight peak. Tia's hips bucked, but she wanted more than this hurried half-dressed impatience.

She dropped her legs, hanging a moment off the floor until he lowered her to her feet.

"What's wrong?" he asked, breathing not quite as hard as she was, his hands roaming over her back. "Are you all right?"

Tia trailed her fingers over the sharply defined lines of his torso before stepping away. Moving toward the bed, she let the bra fall to the floor. A quiet growl sounded in the air behind her. She bent more than was strictly necessary as she slipped off her pants, and suddenly she could feel him at her back. The sheer heat radiating off him made her sway back against him, revealing that he'd lost his pants too.

His fingers caught her hair close to her scalp, his other arm a band wrapped around her ribs, both holding her in place as the proof of his arousal jutted against her. He rotated them slightly so the faint light from outside hit her breasts, and another growl rumbled from his chest into her. The combination of his touch and his magic, even muted as it was, was nearly enough to undo her. Had touch always been this overwhelming with another of her kind? It had been *so* long.

"You're nearly vibrating," he said by her ear, cupping a breast as his thumb and index finger pinched her nipple. "We have all night."

Tia stiffened at the reminder, reality dousing her need. She had an hour, two at the most. And then how long would it be before she came across another of her kind? The longer the better.

He caught the change in her, the tug on her hair turning into a gentle massage as his other hand trailed down her abs, landing low on her belly. "We can stop," he offered. As if he couldn't help himself, he nuzzled her temple.

Tia turned to face him squarely, and his hands dropped to her hips. Far less light filtered in through this room's windows than in the solarium downstairs, but it was still enough to highlight his face. She'd snuck glances at him all night, telling herself she was verifying he hadn't somehow discovered her. But at least some part of her was drawn to the sharp cheekbones, the perfect cupid's bow of his lips, the measured control underlying the serene look in his gold-flecked eyes.

"Absolutely not," she breathed, pulling his head down.

He kissed her chastely, as if they weren't standing there practically naked, but one fingertip trailed up and down her spine in reminder. His mouth brushed hers lazily, and now it was her impatience that brought her closer, rising on tiptoes as her tongue flicked out. He caught her ribcage, keeping her from pressing into him, allowing only the contact of her hands clasped at his neck and her nipples grazing his hairless chest. She would have moaned her frustration if not for the suspicion each of his moves was calculated. Tia wasn't one to beg.

Nipping at his bottom lip, she let her hands drift down his torso to the band encircling his hips. The faintest hint of a smile touched his eyes a fraction of a second before she was flying through the air, aimed perfectly for the mound of pillows on the bed. A laugh escaped her on impact, but the humor fled as he stalked toward her. Their time together might be limited, muted, overshadowed by the prison of her reality, but Tia suddenly had no doubt he'd provide enough fodder to feed her fantasies for many, many years to come.

Chapter 5

AZAR HUFFED OUT A BREATH AS HIS HEARTBEAT SETTLED, bracing on his elbows so he wouldn't crush Tia. Her limbs languidly untwined from around him. He twisted to the side, landing beside her.

"Bathroom?" he murmured. He would have gathered her close, but the contraceptive device she'd provided was less than comfortable. His kind couldn't conceive with humans anyway, but she had insisted.

She gestured to the doorway nearest to the bed. He skimmed his lips at her temple once more, then made his way to the modern water closet. The ubiquity of indoor plumbing had made this sojourn to the mortal realm more pleasant than his last. The overcrowded humans didn't have the magic of Azhidar Zher to handle their waste, so they'd created their own, ridding the air of the previously pervasive stench.

Azar cleaned up quickly, leaving the light on and door ajar to provide some mild illumination for Tia's eyes.

"This place really is quite incredible," he said, returning to the bedchamber. "You're fortunate to live here."

"I am." She sat up, holding the sheet loosely to her chest. Her eyes swept down his body as if she was weighing whether to propose a second go-round.

He certainly wouldn't have minded, but this was the time to focus. "Is the owner nice?" he asked.

She tensed almost imperceptibly, trying to cover by shifting to the foot of the bed, letting her legs drop over the edge. "She's not around much."

So the owner was female. Azar's heart sped. "You must have met her, though," he prodded.

"Yep." Tia stood, looking around for something on the floor. Her clothing, perhaps.

Azar came closer and scooped up her brassiere, holding it out for her.

A wave of power hit him. Tia gasped, and he met her eyes. Those dark eyes that had helped fool him. But almost all the other imperfections of humanity had disappeared in the wash of her power. Her pale skin glowed, as did her hair, no longer dulled by whatever trick she'd used, the purples and blues echoed in the swirls over her ribcage, reaching around toward her back. Something still masked her eyes and her brows, but there was no question. It was *her.*

Azar fell to his knees, bowing as she reigned in her power. "Tasuna," he breathed, switching to Drakonazyk. How could he have spent these hours with her—*lain* with her—and not even suspected? Had whatever kept the majority of her power masked also prevented her from recognizing him as one of their kind?

The questions whirling through his mind ceased as the points of an invisible claw surrounded his torso. Azar froze.

One false move and she could easily spear him with her power, end him not far from the bed that still held both their scents.

"Who is it you think I am?" she demanded, also in their native tongue.

He'd never expected to be the one to come face-to-face with her, but Azar had been sent for a reason. Despite the sharp points threatening to skewer him, he lifted his head to meet her gaze. She'd let the sheet fall away, materializing a loose white dress embellished with her purples and blues. If not for the threat of her claw, he would have materialized clothing as well, out of respect. Seemed wiser not to risk it.

Her eyes snapped at him, but the effect was muted by whatever still hid their true color.

The magnitude of the moment hit him. He had found her.

Now he had to bring her back.

"Seraphina Ig—"

That invisible claw tightened, the talon on his neck threatening to break skin if he breathed too deeply. "Don't," she growled.

Azar dropped his head, bowing as low as her grip would allow. Was he insane to think it was fear bringing that breathlessness to her voice?

This wasn't happening. It *couldn't* be happening. But there he was, bowing before her. Speaking her name. And there her pendant lay, glinting atop the crumpled sheet. The chain must have come loose at some point, sliding off her when she stood. All of which meant he knew. There was no taking it back.

She could kill him. It was the smartest choice, the only way to ensure no one else found out where she was. Even if she escaped him, how long would it be before more dragons descended upon the estate, searching for any clue to her new whereabouts? She could change her appearance more drastically, pick a brand new name out of the pile, but she didn't want to abandon the identity that owned this estate, or the property itself. Besides, how long before magical assistance helped them find the secrets within the walls?

Even now, she had to decide whether to pick up the amulet, shielding her power once more but sacrificing the strength that held Azar in place. Another dilemma that would have been solved with his death.

"Tasuna, please," he said, speaking the language whose sounds she'd missed nearly as much as the feel of dragonkind. Rooted in many of the ancient mortal tongues, it had evolved along its own branch once the dragons had resettled together. While some pieces remained here and there in human languages, nothing quite compared to Drakonazyk.

Tia eased her grip. The full rush of her power had been almost more pleasurable than the orgasm he'd just given her. But remaining unshielded now was no more safe than setting Azar free.

In a final flex of her power, she released him and scooped up the amulet, all without moving her human form. She palmed the stone. If Azar didn't behave, she should be able to drop it quickly enough.

He remained on his knees but wrapped himself in a short-sleeved tunic and pants.

"Get up," she snapped, her fingers digging into the stone Rhea had enchanted for her.

He stood cautiously, keeping his head bowed, not meeting her gaze. Her lips twisted bitterly. She should have run the moment she'd seen him in that lecture hall. It was Tia's own recklessness that had landed her here. She'd been so careful for so long. The temptation of closeness with another of her kind had been too great, but it sure as hell wouldn't be her downfall.

"What are you doing here?" she asked.

"Hoping to meet the owner of this estate." A thread of defiance underlay his words. So he bowed out of ingrained tradition, not out of any respect for her.

"Why?" she bit out.

His shoulders rose and fell a couple times with his breath, as if he was taking the time to choose his words. Finally he lifted his gaze, determination straightening his posture. "The dragons need you."

She scoffed. How many times had those same words been repeated before she'd first run? "It's an old, unnecessary ritual. You've all been fine the last few centuries without the maros."

His jaw clenched, but otherwise he hid his irritation at her refusal to submit. She wasn't about to make this easy on him— or to return to her kind. She did have to decide what to do.

She'd been weak, allowing him this close, capitulating to her need. Many would call her weak for not killing him on the spot. She couldn't think with him staring at her, but she knew better than to turn her back.

"Please, hear me out," he said, his voice careful, as if worried she would snap and slaughter him after all.

"What exactly do you think you can say that would convince me, considering you want me dead?"

That was what it all boiled down to. At the death of her father, she and her brother had been expected to participate in a ritual that was barely more than a sacrifice. A battle to the death, the victor becoming zubir—sovereign over all dragons. At least there were only two of them. Even if their parents had borne more, the ceremonial battles weaned the heirs down to one. Many believed the victor absorbed the power of the rest.

Shortly after her father had passed on, Tia had run. Ever since, dragons pursued her, determined for the maros to happen. Why couldn't they simply accept Nahash and move on? Everyone expected him to triumph over her, and for centuries now he'd been their zubir—exactly as they wanted.

"You're wrong," Azar said.

"And you're overly bold." How quickly all the affectations of her rank returned.

She didn't recognize Azar. Had he even been alive when she'd left? Not that she'd known every dragon back then.

"I don't want your death," he claimed, still holding her gaze as if eye contact would make him more believable. "*We* don't want your death."

Tia wasn't about to fall for it. The handful of dragons who'd managed to reach her through complex networks of magical creatures had also attempted trickery to lure her back. It all came down to the same thing: participating in the maros.

Maybe it was that he was the first dragon she'd been this close to in centuries. Maybe that her skin hunger had gotten a taste, and it wasn't anywhere near enough despite the adrenaline and fear dominating her body now. Something made her hesitate at the determined earnestness in Azar's voice as he said, "We need you to save us."

"Five minutes," she allowed, striding past him to the window seat. At least she could plan while he talked.

Azar took a moment to center himself as the one they'd all been searching for crossed the room and settled perfectly framed in front of the window. Now that her true identity had been revealed, she even moved regally, nothing like the graduate student she'd been impersonating. Anger churned in his gut at her disinterested selfishness, but that wouldn't serve any of them now. If she wouldn't care about everything else happening among the dragons, she would care about the danger stalking her. She may have remained hidden these last centuries, but that was when only the most fanatical of dragons had cared to search the mortal world. As things grew worse, more and more believed her to be critical to their salvation, one way or another.

"There are three factions searching for you," he began.

She didn't even blink, watching him from her seat with that zubiran indifference. True, he'd been using Tia-the-house-sitter, but he'd liked her well enough. The gracious, welcoming hostess who'd joked with the mortals and then shivered under his touch had little in common with the Zubir's sister.

"The first believes the problems facing the dragons stem from the incomplete maros, that the Zubir needs to absorb your power."

"To kill me, you mean," she corrected, her voice even.

He, too, didn't flinch from that truth. "Yes. They believe without the maros, without your death, the Zubir will never be…"

He hesitated, searching for a circumspect way to describe her brother. "At his best."

Predictably, she didn't comment. No one closed ranks like ruling families. It had been the same during his time among the humans.

"The second," Azar said, stepping closer, "believes the maros to be unnecessary."

One delicate blond brow arched.

"They believe your death is sufficient, even without the ceremony."

Something inscrutable passed in the depths of her unsettlingly miscolored eyes. "And which do you agree with?"

"The third."

"Well please," she said drily, "don't keep me in suspense."

"We want the maros to happen," he admitted. "We simply want you to win."

Chapter 6

WELL AT LEAST THAT MEANT HE DID WANT HER ALIVE. IF he was telling the truth, anyway. "Out of the question," she said. "I won't participate in the maros."

"I understand you're scared," he said, approaching with one palm reaching toward her.

He stopped at her smirk, the hand dropping, fingers curling like claws at his side. "You've been among the mortals a long time, but we can help you prepare."

"We?" She rose, stalking toward him. "You won't be informing anyone you've found me."

He swallowed nervously despite the difference in their sizes. Bitter satisfaction seared her gut.

"We're leaving as soon as I gather a few things," she announced. With him along, she couldn't rely on her normal escape plan, but there were plenty of contingencies in place. She simply had to decide where to go. And who to be.

"Why would I accompany you if you refuse to return?" he challenged, passion for his cause or perhaps simply youth making him brave. "For that matter, why leave at all?"

"I'm leaving for the safety of the humans still scattered about downstairs." Not to mention her own. On the plus side, the advent of Wi-Fi meant she could make arrangements for the care of the estate and withdraw Tia Davies from the university while on the road, before dumping the cell phone associated with this identity. Maybe Naiara could move in, with the double benefit of her saving on rent and her presence complicating things for any more dragons who came sniffing around.

Unless the dragons had resumed killing humans. Tia would have asked Azar, but she needed to maintain the upper hand with him while she figured out her next steps. She couldn't control him—and ensure his silence—indefinitely.

"And you"—she smiled humorlessly up at him—"don't want to be the dragon who let me get away."

His eyes widened with a flash of panic.

Good. Let him suffer for blowing up her life. She might have been the one to stupidly let her guard down, but he was the one *hunting* her, even if he claimed he was going the "catch and release" route.

He followed her as she moved still barefoot through the halls, past the open air of the two-story ballroom at the center of her home and into her suite on the opposite end.

"Where are you planning to go?" he asked.

"I imagine you don't have a passport," she said, switching back to English, "so it will have to be somewhere in the United States."

"'Tasuna."

She spun on him where he'd stalled near the door to her bedroom. "*Don't* call me that."

He bowed his head, though it seemed more like a way to hide his irritation than true deference. "I don't understand," he told the floor tightly.

She didn't have time for this. "What?" she asked, tucking the amulet under her chin to hold it close while reconnecting the chain. If Azar decided he wanted to attack her after all, maybe she would just let him.

He looked up, unable to pull off that false subservience for long. "Why would we need human paperwork when we could fly?"

"We will be flying,"—she needed to get him somewhere remote as quickly as possible—"in an airplane."

He blanched but tried to cover, smoothing his features into a courteous blankness. "Why bother with mortal machinery?"

"'Cause I don't feel much like walking." She stepped into the closet to start packing, tossing clothing directly into a waiting suitcase. She could pull off minor glamour while the amulet was on, but even materializing a simple tee shirt was beyond her. Forget shifting to her true form, even if they could fly through modern skies undetected. The ubiquity of cameras, not to mention detailed satellite imagery, made that impossible. Not that she would have risked shifting and calling the attention of any others hunting her.

"There must be an alternative," he insisted from his new spot across from the doorway to her walk-in closet.

She would have been irritated by his insistence on keeping her in sight if it hadn't been damned convenient for her. "Don't worry, I'll pay." He may not have spent enough time among the humans to have the resources, but money was the least of her worries.

"Tia—"

"*Don't.*"

His brow furrowed at the bite in her tone.

"That's not my name anymore," she said as dispassionately as she could. She'd used many over the years, rotating them as necessary. But she could never use that one again. Who knew what he'd already reported back to whomever led his faction about the student "house-sitting" the estate he'd clearly been sent to scope out. He'd stolen that name from her. He certainly didn't get to say it now.

Something akin to concern filtered into his expression.

She stalked away to switch out her contacts in the bathroom. She grabbed some basic toiletries and extra lenses, then tossed those on top of the clothes. Since leaving it would be considered suspicious, she added her laptop, too. She'd "forget" it at the airport, after performing a factory reboot for the layer of anonymity that would provide.

What was she forgetting now? The private study held plenty of documents, but the most important ones were safely elsewhere, and nowadays practically everything she would need was accessible online. She could have the maid service she occasionally used stop by to clean up after the party, and she'd call a taxi to take the two of them to the airport tonight. Not one of the new driving apps, so she could pay with cash. Azar may not be fond of technology, but if the leader of his faction had any brains, there'd be someone more familiar with the modern world and computers working with them. It had gotten harder to hide in the digital age, but she had the benefit of having completed several degrees in computer science, keeping up as the technology developed. Plus, she'd had to do something with her time.

"Did you drive here?" she asked, heading into the private sitting room directly above the living room where mere hours ago everything had been fine. She'd been planning to leave, yes, but not like this.

"No." Azar followed to the open entryway. He peered into the perpendicular opening into the study.

She paused by the large sectional sofa. "Turn around." When he hesitated, her head tipped in that subtle but commanding way that had once been second nature to her. It had served her well for her early centuries among the humans, no one questioning her nobility even if they couldn't quite pinpoint her family lines. Gold finding the right hands hadn't hurt.

With a soft dip of the chin, he obeyed, turning to face back into the bedroom. "Please don't run," he said quietly. If he'd been human, she would have called the words a prayer.

Keeping an eye on him, she moved to the large fireplace in the corner. She placed her palm on the third stone above the mantel on the right side, pulsing a tiny bit of her power into it to open the hidden compartment. Packets of new identities lay inside, along with cash and even gold for good measure. This wasn't even her largest repository. Humans weren't entirely wrong about dragons hoarding treasure.

She flipped through the options, weighing the names, their appearances. She'd have to pick up hair dye when she could. Even that bit of glamour was draining with the charm around her neck.

A few options she quickly discarded, the names variations on ones she'd used too recently. She tried to stick with ones similar enough to her own name that training herself to respond wouldn't be quite as difficult. Since she'd be discarding this new identity as soon as she figured out what to do with Azar, she chose the simplest one, grabbing a stack of cash as well.

Simple as that, she was someone new. As soon as she changed into something more comfortable for flying than the—albeit lovely—dress she'd materialized on autopilot, they'd be all set to go to her cabin, safely off the grid in the Sierra Nevada mountains.

"What will the mortals call you now?" Azar asked, at her insistence pulling on the more modern shirt he'd been wearing earlier. She'd tucked what appeared to be a new identification card into the back pocket of her pants before returning them to the other end of the mansion and into the previous bedroom. He hadn't missed the generous stack of currency she'd casually placed inside her handbag.

She barely glanced up at him, her eyes now sheltered behind green rather than brown. "Inna."

A simple, pretty name. And admittedly clever, using the final syllables of her own. Had she not been clever, she never could have avoided the dragons seeking her this long.

She scooped up his discarded pants, taking out his portable telephone and wallet. She flipped open the latter, pulling out the plastic card that now also signified currency before tossing him the leather. She made quick work of disassembling the telephone into several smaller pieces before disappearing into the adjoining washroom. The device didn't reappear with her.

"Guess we're all set," she said, surveying the room, ignoring the rumpled bed.

"You don't have to leave," Azar reasoned. "We can keep you safe."

The skepticism in every line of her face spoke volumes.

"If I informed the others where you are, you'd immediately have a small army at your side."

"That's a pretty way of saying 'keeping me prisoner until I did what you wanted.'" She strode to the travel bag waiting in the doorway.

He reached her a moment later. "Allow me."

She frowned but didn't protest him carrying the bag.

"We would help you prepare," he persisted, following her down the staircase. No one in their faction wanted to harm their last hope.

"Enough," she whispered roughly, spearing him with her gaze. "You say you want me to be zubir? Then obey me. You will tell absolutely no one."

Yes, Tasuna, he thought, testing her ability to maintain psychic communication despite the blood-red amulet that was her true prison. When she didn't react, he added, "As you wish."

A tiny chuckle cracked the severity of her expression. "Nowadays, that phrase has connotations you don't mean."

"Understood." With the tension between them lessened a tiny bit, he ventured, "Perhaps you might consider an alternate mode of transportation?"

She sighed, heading toward the center of the manor. "Airplanes really aren't all that scary. And they're the most efficient option."

"I'm not frightened," he insisted, walking a step behind. Why should being crammed into a contraption made by mortals as it traveled thousands of feet in the air, with no ability to escape even by shifting, frighten him? "If you aren't able to shift for fear of detection, I'm certain we could find something that would allow me to carry you."

She scoffed. "So many reasons that won't be happening."

They both fell silent as they crossed through the grand entryway and down the hall back to the open area she had called the butler's pantry during the tour. After dashing off a quick note he didn't presume to read, she returned her attention to him. "I know the mortal world so much better than you. You want to protect me from what you call the other factions? Getting on a plane is the best way you can keep me safe."

She didn't wait for his response, heading back to the room where the remaining mortals now slept, sprawled on her furniture. She slipped the note under the pillow Naiara was using and checked the remnants of the fire. Back in the informal dining room, "Inna's" hair turned into a pale blond. Like that, no one who happened to glimpse the two of them leaving the estate in the middle of the night would think this woman was the brown-eyed graduate student with the distinctive hair as opposed to merely another of the guests.

Was this another benefit of the amulet? With it damping her power and a touch more magic to alter the delicate bone structure of her face, she could have even fooled him from afar. Azar had no doubt she could have run again, stayed hidden for months if not years more. There was some reason she was keeping him close. But as long as she did, he had a chance to plead the dragons' case, to awaken any hidden empathy she may have or find a way to sway her with logic.

The weight of his kind's future lay heavy on his shoulders, a responsibility that never should have been his to bear. But the Fates must have steered him to finding her for a reason. If he couldn't convince her to return, then wherever they ended up, he'd find a way to contact someone who would.

Chapter 7

INNA GRIT HER TEETH, TRYING TO FINISH RESERVING A RENTAL car and run through her mental checklist of everything else that needed to get done while Azar nearly pulsated with impatience, pacing in small circles around the little food court table she'd chosen at the airport. They still had hours to kill before the flight she'd found, but that was fine since her computer needed time to be reset. Or it would have been fine, if his tall, muscled form hadn't been attracting all the attention she really needed to avoid. As it was, human security protocols meant it wouldn't take all that long for someone searching to find Azar's name on a flight manifest. She was banking on it taking a while for anyone to even start looking.

Either way that was a problem for later, unlike the wariness that peppered the appreciative glances thrown his way. Inna sighed and stood. Azar immediately stilled, channeling his inner bodyguard as if he expected the smattering of humans surrounding them to attack at any moment.

Just hours ago they'd been exchanging bodily fluids, but still it felt weird to settle a calming hand on his upper arm. "You need to relax," she murmured in Drakonazyk. Anyone who managed to overhear should dismiss the sounds as one of the myriad human languages. "Before the humans start wondering if you're this nervous because you're an evildoer"—Drakonazyk had no word for *terrorist*—"about to blow them up." The combination of his skin tone and mortal racism didn't help.

His scent made her skin hunger clench deep in her torso, but he shuddered at her touch, as if he couldn't stand having her so close. *Tough.* They were stuck with each other until she figured out a plan beyond holing up in her cabin.

Still she let go. "If something does go wrong, you can always jump out and shift midair, okay?" She offered a smirk for good measure.

His shoulders dropped with his rough exhale, a small twitch of his lats bringing to mind the flare of wings.

The desire-driven part of her brain protested loudly as she stepped away from his radiating warmth and plopped back into her chair.

The grate of a nearby coffee shop rolled up loudly as it opened for the day, and Azar glanced over. "Would you care for a coffee?" he offered in English, likely because the dragons also had no word for the human beverage.

"I'll come with you," she said instantly but frowned when a glance at the computer revealed it needed more time. Though it wouldn't be hers for much longer, she couldn't risk leaving it behind with the data even partially intact. And she couldn't let Azar out of her sight, either.

For the first time since they'd arrived, he lowered to one of the other chairs beside her. "What if I promise I don't have any poisons or magical potions on me?" he asked wryly. The implication must have caught up with him, because he frowned too. "Ignore that." He leaned forward on the table, lacing his fingers together. "I won't be dragging you back kicking and screaming, *Inna*. You'd simply run again."

He straightened with a deep breath, looking more comfortable in his skin than he had since she'd first mentioned airplanes, as if the subject of the maros grounded him. Was his belief tipping the scales to fanaticism? "To win, you have to want to win."

"Never gonna happen."

His head wove subtly on his neck, not quite fully becoming a headshake, as he stood once more. "So, coffee?"

"Sure," she said. Besides, the shop wasn't so far away she couldn't watch him. "Do you need cash?"

His cheek twitched. "I think I can cover it."

She shrugged, settling as comfortably as was possible in her chair. "Airport markup."

Concern quirked his brow as he hesitated.

"I was kidding," Inna assured. The price gouging was bad, but his wallet had held bills along with the debit card she'd tossed.

He nodded curtly and walked away, all that earlier tension returning to his posture.

When he reappeared with the drinks, he also set a little bag with chocolate croissants beside her. Under normal circumstances, the gesture would have made her smile. But she knew now any kindness he showed her came with a dragon's hoard of ulterior motives.

✧ ✧ ✧

Imitating the mortals pressing close around them, Azar lifted the travel bag into one of the compartments above the rows of squished seats. He gestured for dragonkind's last hope to precede him into the row so she could sit beside the window, his body separating her from the mortal who'd be sitting near the aisle. Aside from convincing her to live up to her duties and save dragonkind, he also had a responsibility to keep her safe.

She mirrored his gesture, indicating he should enter first. "I'm smaller," she explained. "I'll take the middle."

He nodded and obeyed. It was an odd line to straddle, needing her to listen to him, to allow him to train her, and yet deferring to the authority custom proclaimed she wielded as a member of the zubiran family, even if in voluntary exile.

For a moment there, when she'd offered him the simple comfort of her touch, he'd been tempted to forget his mission, to take her back to bed and let the others sort themselves out like she'd left them to do. But there were too many depending on him.

And in any case, "Inna's" disregard for all the consequences their kind faced would have quickly overshadowed any pleasure they found together.

Cramped in the small space, Azar focused on his breathing as the humans slowly found their designated places and the small screens on the back of every seat played a film regarding emergency safety measures. If he lost control of his power, what kind of damage would it do?

He curled his fingers into fists as the engines rumbled and the metal cage of the airplane began to move.

"Here," Inna said, reaching out a pair of small rounded contraptions. Similar to those he'd seen around the university campus, nestled in students' ears. "Put these in your ears," she instructed, confirming his impression.

Once again he obeyed, jaw clenched tight. There was no need for any of this. In the time they had spent waiting in the airport, he likely could have flown them to their destination.

He startled as the delicate melody of a violin sounded in his ears, turning his head to find Inna watching him.

"Technology isn't always as bad as you think," she said. "Just close your eyes and listen."

She turned away, refocusing on the handheld device she'd used for practically everything thus far, including purchasing their passage.

With a deep breath and an orchestra in his ears, Azar obeyed a third time. As wondrous as this private concert was, it was the gesture that simultaneously helped him relax and strengthened his resolve. If she was capable of this small kindness, perhaps he could get her to care about them all.

"We're alone, you know," Azar said hours later as Inna squinted out the front window of the automobile. Streaks of purple and blue had started showing through the blond of her braid, as if maintaining the illusion required energy she could no longer spare.

"And?" Fatigue lined her face and stooped her shoulders.

"No need to maintain the concealment." If he'd known how to control the machine, he would have offered to take over. Not that she would have agreed.

She shot him a bleary-eyed look. "Oh, right." The blond fell away, leaving her natural colors to gleam in the sporadic beams of light from other vehicles. She leaned forward slightly as they maneuvered the curves in the road, climbing higher into the mountains.

Bags of food and other supplies she'd purchased near the start of this drive filled the seats behind them. Azar had largely tried to remain unobtrusive as she'd navigated the market, loading a rattling metal cart. Aside from when they'd ordered a meal, consumed sitting in the lot beside the shop, they hadn't said much to each other since the airplane had ascended into the sky. He'd even held his tongue as she rattled off a selection of meats to the human butcher, though his stomach seized at the luxury of choice lying behind the glass, refrigerated as it was.

"Maybe we should stop so you can rest," he suggested now.

"I'm fine," she answered, not even glancing at him this time. "We're almost there."

A half hour of winding turns later, she stopped before an isolated wooden cabin. Her hair returned to blond before she got out. She left the vehicle's lights on as she briefly disappeared, an outdoor lamp lighting when she stepped back out. So at least one modern convenience was available to them here, wherever that was.

Azar got out and opened the rear door to pick up a few of the bags. "I can bring everything in," he offered when she did the same on the other side.

She ignored him, leading the way into the cabin. Inside, the rounded logs became smooth planks of cherry wood illuminated by the golden glow of a modest electric chandelier. She moved purposefully past the seating area to the adjacent open kitchen, setting her bags onto the dining table before passing him to head back outside for more. Azar followed suit. They passed each other several more times before everything was inside, covering all the available surfaces in the kitchen area. Her travel bag waited on the floor.

"How can I help?" he asked as she began unpacking.

She hesitated with several cuts of meat in her hands. Her eyes ran over the far less precious supplies, finally settling on a bag near him. "Why don't you take things into the bathroom. Door on your right, once you turn around."

It didn't take him long to organize the soap, toilet paper, and other things she'd purchased within the bathing room, which did sport modern plumbing. Azar paused to wash his hands, the flow of water refreshing after their tense drive.

"I'll sort out the rest tomorrow," Inna said once he'd rejoined her. "If you get hungry, help yourself to anything." She frowned, her head tipping to one side. "Do you know how to cook? If not," she added before he could respond, "try to stick to the prepared stuff tonight so you don't burn the place down."

She tilted her travel bag on its little wheels and moved to the twin doors perpendicular to the one leading into the bathroom. Pointing to the left one, she said, "Your bedroom." She opened the second door enough to roll her bag inside. "My bedroom." Her hand ran over her face. "What am I forgetting?"

Azar waited mutely.

"There should be towels in the small cabinet in the bathroom, but if not, they'll be in the trunk in your room." Her gaze sharpened on him despite her obvious fatigue. "No leaving or contacting anyone. I'll figure the rest out tomorrow."

At his nod, she entered the room designated as hers, the door swiftly shutting behind her.

The cabin was silent, though nightlife teemed in the forest around them. The smooth wood of the main rooms continued in the room she'd pointed out to him, with a large bed centered before a latticed window in the far wall. A second window overlooked the porch, covered only by a thin gauzy curtain, so there was no need for him to worry about any additional lighting. Azar stripped off his man-made clothes and lay down on the bed.

I'll figure the rest out tomorrow, she'd said. Which meant he had the whole night to devise his strategy. Tomorrow he would start the work of convincing her to do her duty.

Chapter 8

INNA UNPACKED ONLY ENOUGH TO CHANGE INTO SOFT SHORTS and a tee shirt, then went into the bathroom to wash the airplane off her. And *finally* remove her contacts. She should have thought to grab eye drops while they were at the store, but if that was the only thing she'd forgotten, she'd get over the dry burn in her eyes.

Tomorrow she would deal with the new laptop and burner phone that she'd kept stashed in the carry-on. Some days she'd felt paranoid, keeping her primary properties stocked with regularly updated "go bags." But the last however many hours had proven paranoia could come in handy. She'd taken care of everything she could using the plane's Wi-Fi, and now her old phone was continuing its trip in a random seatback pocket, wiping itself clean as it went.

Inna grabbed a bag of plantain chips from the dining table and double-checked the lock on the front door before shutting off the great room light. Under normal circumstances, she loved this cozy little cabin. Now she'd probably have to end up selling it.

She tore open the bag on her way back to her bedroom. Azar had kept the door to his cracked open, but as long as he didn't betray her before morning, she could get some sleep.

Cuddled under the blanket, she popped another salty chip in her mouth, letting herself relax into the whisper of power that flowed from the second bedroom. Even now, her body begged her to get up, nudge open his door, and snuggle up next to him. She hadn't even gotten to cuddle with all that beautiful sensation of male dragon before her safety had been shattered. But Inna was far too old to expect the world to be fair.

Didn't mean she couldn't indulge her imagination, remembering the feel of him pressed against her, of wrapping herself around him as she came as close to sinking into his power as her amulet would allow. In her mind, though, nothing stood between them.

His mouth trailed lazily down her body as his hand molded her breast, fingers teasing its peak. In a flash, he had her straddling his lap, her back pressed to his chest as she lowered onto him, gasping as he bit her shoulder. The sting of the bite disappeared when his fingers slipped between her legs. She swam in a haze of pleasure when somehow his mouth replaced his fingers, and she was on her back, clutching his head closer.

She whimpered when he stilled, those gold-flecked eyes meeting hers, his mouth still out of sight as he whispered, "Seraphina."

She jolted awake at the name, early-morning light bathing the bedroom. A dull ache persisted between her legs, but she shoved her need aside. A long exhale flowed out of her lungs as she sat up, the chip bag crinkling with her movements. Apparently exhaustion had beaten out hunger last night. One kind of hunger, anyway.

That tingle on her skin meant Azar hadn't left, or at least hadn't gone far. She palmed the amulet, tugging on it to check that the clasp held. The To Do list she couldn't quite put her finger on yet pricked at her brain, but it would have to wait until she had some breakfast.

She slipped from her bedroom right into the bathroom. At least indoors she didn't have to mask her identity, so she could skip the contacts. She'd bought bleach and hair dye, but Azar knew who she was, and she wasn't planning on leaving until she figured out what to do about that. So for now she just made herself moderately presentable then changed into a simple black blouse and jeans.

When she made it out into the main area of the cabin, Azar was standing near the counter, staring at one of the steaks she'd packed into the meat drawer last night.

"I know it's not as fresh as you're used to," she said, and his shoulders tensed. "But it's still pretty good, or you could sear it with some spices."

She rummaged through the paper bags still waiting to be unpacked and pulled out a box of muffins. It took her a few tries to find a saucer and knife—not like she memorized the layout of every kitchen she owned.

As she sliced the muffin, he wrapped the meat back up, nudging it away from himself on the counter. "I apologize," he said in Drakonazyk, his head bowed. "I should have asked."

She hid her frown by turning away to stick her plate into the compact toaster oven in the corner. "I told you," she said, sticking to English, "help yourself to anything."

He still hadn't moved when she turned back around.

She leaned against the counter, drumming her fingers on the edge. "The cabin's remote, but if we're here long enough to run out of food, it's easy enough to make a supply run." When he still didn't say anything, she added, "You need to eat."

His head seemed to bow even further, though his shoulders remained ramrod straight. "Thank you, Tasuna." Resentment colored his voice despite the words.

She shot up to her full height, even if that was still at least a foot shorter than him. This time, she matched his use of Drakonazyk. "I told you, don't call me that."

His head rose slowly, the movement predatory enough that mortals or even lesser dragons would have instantly reclassified themselves as prey. But amulet or no, Inna was at the top of this particular food chain. The toaster oven dinged as their eyes snapped at each other, his jaw stubbornly set.

His rough exhale broke the silent standoff. "You can't have it both ways."

Inna's eyebrows twitched with her irritation. "Meaning?" she asked through clenched teeth.

Azar took a step forward, knowing full well she wouldn't retreat from him. But he'd been thrown off by the lure of the meat stocked in the modern icebox, then knocked further off balance by finally seeing the natural amethyst of her eyes. He had his own share of irritation to deal with. "You can't refuse to be zubir, refuse to fulfill your role, and still command me as if the hierarchy remains."

Recognition passed in the depths of those eyes, and her posture eased. "Fine," she said, switching back to the English she seemed to prefer, "you're right." Unperturbed, she moved away to retrieve the pastry she'd warmed, then stepped around him to reach the icebox. "Do whatever you want."

She brought out a package labeled as butter then settled at the table, shoving aside the bags still covering it to make some space. Deftly she placed thin slices of butter on each segment of the pastry, the creamy pieces melting into the brown swirled with white.

Azar forced his own muscles to unclench. Hunger wasn't helping his patience, and he needed all the patience he could find to get through to her. He moved some of the bags over to the countertop, then hesitated back at the table. "May I?"

A glare was his only answer.

He remained where he was, ingrained and oft-reinforced deference for the zubiran family winning out.

She sighed, shaking her head slightly. "This is the third and final time I'm telling you to help yourself."

He held back the automatic thanks and lowered to a chair on the diagonal from her. For the sake of ease, he took a pastry from the same transparent box as her. She twisted up out of her chair, and he froze. But she merely set a small plate before him, replaced the cut of meat in the icebox, then brought filled water glasses for them both. Finally she slid a spoon into her warmed breakfast.

Azar tore off a chocolaty piece as well, mulling over the easy consideration so at odds with his understanding of the ruling family. Then again, she had claimed she would ignore the difference in their status. The change was peculiarly effortless for her.

"The cabin is quite isolated," he ventured in English when she was about halfway done with her meal. If she preferred the language, that was an easy enough way to accommodate her.

"That's the idea," she muttered.

"Perhaps, while we're here," he said, choosing each word carefully, "we could set aside that our goals are, it would seem, at cross-purposes."

Amethyst irises found him.

"Hear each other out?" he suggested. If reason could convince her, it was the simplest place to start.

His breath stayed trapped in his lungs as she considered.

"Fine," she said, standing though her food was unfinished. "But first I'm making coffee."

Arguments flew around his head as she withdrew a new machine and set it going. As it hissed and gurgled, the rich scent of the beans permeating the air, she unpacked the remaining bags into the tall cabinet beside the icebox. Perhaps he shouldn't have been surprised at this point when she placed a filled cup beside him, settling back at the table with a similar one.

The courtesy or the weight of the moment knocked all the complex thoughts out of his mind, leaving him only with, "The dragons are dying."

She was unmoved. "We're not actually immortal. Dragons die with age."

"They're starving," he persisted.

"Impossible," she dismissed. "We live in a— *You*, and they, live in a pocket paradise created for the dragons," she explained as if he were a misinformed child. "There's plenty of prey for hunting."

"There *was*," Azar corrected, pushing his anger at her sheltered ignorance into a tight ball of fire this form wasn't meant to contain. He had to stay calm, rational. "Things have changed, resembling more the old mortal ways. The herd animals have been corralled into livestock, closely controlled. Those in favor with the Zubir eat well." They gorged themselves, charring the meat they couldn't consume to prevent others from having it. "The rest struggle to get enough." Even the boars had been over-hunted to near extinction.

That seemed to make an impression, grooves forming between her eyebrows, around her mouth. "Nahash is honest, and reasonable, and kind. He wouldn't tolerate a system like that."

"Perhaps he was," Azar said as respectfully as he could. "If so, he's changed in the centuries you've been gone." Her eyes narrowed distrustfully on him, so he added, "Haven't you?"

She took a deep breath, resolve transforming her posture and her expression. "All right. Then I'll find a way to speak to my brother, explain the impact this is having. Convince him to free the herds, or find a compromise. This doesn't require a coup."

Abandoning her coffee, she began clearing up, setting dishes into the sink before wiping down the already clean countertop.

Azar stood as well. "Many wouldn't consider completing the maros a coup."

Her head snapped to him, the look in her eyes nearly as sharp as her talons. "It's *not* happening," she said, over-enunciating.

He stifled the urge to argue that point. She had shown concern for the dragons, more easily than he could have dreamed. Providing her a clear picture of their reality had to be his focus. "It may be too late for an alternative."

She stopped wiping at nothing and turned around, letting her weight lean somehow imperiously into the counter behind her, her arms crossing in challenge.

As she was still listening, Azar explained, "Some consider the situation desperate enough that their only choice is to kill the Zubir." There was much more he hadn't yet shared.

"Well, then, problem solved, right?" Sarcasm dripped from every syllable like acid. "If one of them succeeds, you'll force Nahash's children to go through the maros, and one of them becomes the new zubir you all want."

The realization dunked Azar in ice. The problem perhaps wasn't that she was callous or selfish, running from responsibility. "You don't know."

Clearly discomfited by the change in him, she straightened, arms dropping to her sides. "Know what?"

"The Zubir is childless. And so are the dragons."

Chapter 9

"I MPOSSIBLE," INNA REPEATED, BUT THE PROTEST SOUNDED thinner this time.

Sadness had replaced the calculated combativeness in Azar. "I hatched a few years before you left," he said, confirming all her suspicions of his youth. "And there are only three dragons younger, all hatched the first decade of your absence."

Disbelief turned her breathing ragged. Staring into Azar's grim face wasn't helping, so she yanked open the door to the back deck and strode outside, remembering to make her hair appear blond a few seconds too late. Inhaling the fresh mountain air, she bent her head over the railing, curling her fingers around the wood.

It was a *myth* that the health and power of the dragons depended on the zubir, a legend started with calculated shrewdness to explain the supposed necessity of her family line. There had to be some other explanation. If she found a way to speak with her brother, everything could be resolved, even if he was still among those determined for the maros to take place.

But it was the realization of *why* Azar and his cohorts wanted her back that clawed at the inside of her throat. If not for the pendant strangling her power, the beams below her hands would have been torn to shreds, her rage roaring through the forest.

She spun on him the moment he ventured out onto the deck. "So that's why you want me as zubir? So I'd win then start popping out baby dragons?"

"That's not how—"

"I know how it works," she snarled. To think he'd actually been about to explain dragons were hatched, not born! "I'm talking about the associated *tradition*"—she spat the word out—"of ensuring fertility with a female zubir." How ironic that she'd already slept with him.

He shook his head, playing the part of clueless messenger well. "I don't understand. I'm not aware of any such traditions."

She laughed mirthlessly. "How young you are," she taunted, but he didn't react. "Well, then, let me educate you." Her nails dug into her palms, but she kept her posture as regal as centuries in corsets had trained her to be. "Three zubirim ago, well four, now. Before my brother, my father, and his father, we had a female zubir. It doesn't happen often." The bigger males with their larger wingspans often triumphed in the maros, naturally favored in a fight. "After she took the title, the zoval dictated she had to prove she wasn't barren." Funny how the council of nettakim had never raised such a concern with the males. "So she was forced to mate with every male who wanted a go until 'the spark of life' was seen within her, making that male her bira."

Understandably she had been traumatized, and it was really her forced mate who ruled until her relatively early death.

Azar's head shook again. "Zubirim pick their own mates. All dragons do."

"Unless the zubir's female. And then she's repeatedly raped by a succession of males. All under the guise of *duty* and *tradition.*"

He stalked toward her, stopping near enough that the anger he was trying to contain bit along her skin. "I would kill anyone who dares try."

The fight seeped out of her, replaced with the fatigue of experience in the face of his ideological naiveté. "And here I thought the point was to stop dragons dying."

His arm lifted as if to find her shoulder, but she stepped out of reach. "You don't get to have it both ways either."

The hand dropped, his brows lowering.

"You want to speak for dragonkind? Represent them in an attempt to 'reason' with me? You don't get to pretend your concern is for me." Not that she wasn't worried about what he'd revealed. One more piece of the puzzle for her to figure out—*without* returning.

Defeated, at least for the moment, Azar sank onto one of the outdoor chairs, despite the layer of debris covering everything out here. He slumped over the table, speaking more to it than to her. "There has to be a way for you to win without that price."

Inna sagged into the railing at her back. It must have seemed so simple to him before: find her, save the dragons. Pity for his harsh disillusionment prompted her to say, "*If* I ever became zubir, I'd make sure all the dragons knew not to touch me without permission." She would have ensured they'd be too scared to try. "But the point is moot."

His despondent gaze shifted from the dead pile of leaves on the table to her. "There's more I haven't told you."

"And yet, I think I'm done for today," she said, passing him to head back inside.

Her To Do list had ballooned, but right now the twin pair of denial and procrastination ruled, decreeing decisions could wait for the duration of a bath.

Azar leafed through a leather-bound tome of Elizabeth Barrett Browning's collective works, too distracted to read. A soft breeze floated the earthy scent of the forest into the bright main room of the cabin. The whole structure could have fit into Inna's manor at least ten times over.

Under other circumstances, he may have enjoyed holing up here, taking occasional flights over the mountains and sunning himself on the deck. Especially with the company of a dragon as beautiful as Inna. True, he had yet to see her other form, but he could imagine.

He understood now, why she'd left. The maros demanded strength and sacrifice, the one price of being born to the zubiran line. But what Inna had told him was unimaginable. Caught between death and the consequence of prevailing, she'd found another path. Clearly, she wasn't the self-absorbed coward he'd expected.

Still there had to be a way to help the dragons without risking her in that way.

When the door to the bathroom finally opened, Azar froze on the couch. Lying down, he couldn't see her, but the bedroom door shutting spurred him into motion. He set the book carefully on the low table centered within the seating area and went into the kitchen portion of the open space.

By the time he knocked on her door, Inna had dressed, though her hair remained damp as if she didn't want to, or couldn't, expend the power to dry it fully. How much did the amulet hinder her abilities?

Her gaze fell to the board he'd prepared, with thick slices of beef, salted crackers, even cuts of two different cheeses, and a small bowl of marinated olives.

"I didn't know," Azar said quietly as she blinked at the food.

Her lashes lifted, and those startling amethyst eyes met his. Her lips twitched faintly. "Neither did I."

Some measure of understanding passed between them, loosening the block in his chest.

Then she sighed, glancing at the food once more. "Why don't you give me a couple of minutes, and I'll join you out there."

He nodded mutely, heading back to the dining table when she let the door drift shut. He should have realized the food wouldn't signify much. Not only had she provided all the food in the cabin, but this selection had also barely made a dent. Food clearly wasn't as meaningful to her. It made sense, since even in the mortal realm, it was enormously simpler to obtain now than in England of centuries past. Admittedly, Azar had indulged a bit upon his arrival, taking the edge off his hunger. He might prefer aurochs to cattle, but still on his first visit to the market, the abundance had been staggering, though he'd been careful to ration the funds Laisren had supplied.

"How about some wine?" Inna offered some minutes later, moving past him to the tallest cabinet along the wall. That hint of her power whispered along his skin, much harder to ignore now that he could no longer convince himself it was her selfish inaction that was responsible for dragonkind's difficulties. She turned with the bottle and two glasses in hand. Her eyes flicked to the meager selection he'd prepared, then over to the seating area, and back up to him in silent question.

It would be a less formal choice than the dining table. Either way this seemed a turning point of sorts. "Wherever you'd prefer," he said.

She veered to her left, settling on one of the armchairs beneath the windows he'd opened. Azar lifted the board and returned to his earlier spot on the sofa that demarcated the living and dining segments of the space, facing its twin that sat under another pair of windows, which looked out onto the porch.

Inna jumped up when he set the board on the edge of the low table nearest her. She returned almost as swiftly with a corkscrew, a pair of small plates, and the paper napkins common to the time.

With those items balanced on her lap, she said, "That was kind of you."

"You need to eat," he said, echoing her comment from that morning.

Wry humor lightened her expression.

He held his hand out for the corkscrew. "May I?"

She passed it over without so much as an arched brow, setting the plates aside. Remnants of Tia the carefree grad student showed through in how she curled her legs under herself, relaxing barefoot into the soft cushions as he opened the wine and poured.

Yet when he looked up, the depths of her eyes appeared haunted, her expression grim.

"The situation is urgent," Azar said, unwilling to downplay the reality and risk additional misunderstandings, "but perhaps further discussion, any decisions, would be best served by a new day." He hadn't even been among the mortals for a full two weeks. No one had dreamt they'd find her this quickly. And in truth, a handful of mortal hours weren't likely to impact dragonkind as much as space for Inna to process might.

"Whatever shall we do with ourselves in the meanwhile?" she asked, the sarcasm more teasing than unkind. She leaned forward to set some morsels on her plate, leaving the bulk of the meat.

That simple consideration made him wish momentarily they could be two humans passing the time in this cabin, that nothing stood in the way of them coming together in pleasure as they had the night they'd met.

Despite the temporary moratorium on more serious topics, that wouldn't be possible. Neither would ignore the reality of their positions.

"I could read to you," he offered instead. The book he'd perused was one of many set neatly on the two short shelves separating the seating area from the entryway. The shelves in the room where he'd slept held even more, in a variety of human languages.

Her nose wrinkled in distaste. "The books'll get dirty. Or they would"—she shot the second plate a pointed look—"if you were planning on eating."

He was indeed hungry, and the coppery, tangy scent of the meat had pooled saliva around his tongue.

"Cards?" she suggested as he remedied the plate's emptiness.

"Wouldn't they end up equally dirty?"

"Sure, but they cost maybe a dollar. The books would be much harder to replace."

Azar nodded, swallowing a chunk of meat. They were both tacitly agreeing to find a distraction, but it didn't much matter how they filled the time of this tentative truce. Any way he could find to connect with Inna emotionally may help him convince her to do her duty, for the sake of them all.

Chapter 10

AFTER WINNING AT YET ANOTHER HAND OF SPEED, INNA gathered the cards, setting them in a neat stack beside the now empty cutting board Azar had used as a platter. They'd both ended up on the floor, to be within easy reach of the low coffee table. To an outsider, it would have looked intimate.

But despite the lighthearted card games, a string of tension thrummed between them, that awareness of reality weighing on them both.

She'd ignored that push for too long as it was. "I have some things I need to take care of," she said, rising to her knees, and Azar's smile dropped.

"Of course." He nodded curtly, also shifting to rise. He gathered their small plates and dirty napkins. "I'll clear up."

That quickly, reality rebuilt all the barriers between them. She could have stopped him, taken care of cleaning up herself. In some bizarre way, he was her guest. But even pretending the hierarchy didn't exist, that he didn't owe her any form of deference, she could accept the offer of help. She had enough to do. So she simply thanked him and went to collect her laptop. By the time she brought it back out to the dining table, Azar had already started rinsing the dishes.

She checked first on the responses to Tia's abrupt withdrawal from school. The messages were mostly well-wishes and condolences, along with instructions for some paperwork she'd need to fill out. The maid service had confirmed they'd cleared up after the party and the remnants of her tryst in the guest suite. Naiara was demanding details, understandably offering to take over Tia's "house-sitting" gig, and suggesting a video chat whenever Tia had a moment.

The smartest call would be to sell the Peran Estate, but even if all the artwork, furniture, and personal artifacts could be gathered up and placed into storage, Inna couldn't get rid of the property until she emptied out the hidden vault and sealed the other secrets. She'd have to find a way to return, but first she needed to decide what to do about the dragon standing near the opposite corner of the dining table.

When she looked up, he asked, "Would you mind if I stepped outside?"

Of course not, she wanted to say. But that would be sloppy. "Actually, I need you to log in to your university email. To explain your absence," she added when his brows quirked in confusion.

"Of course," he murmured, rounding the table to sit at the chair perpendicular to hers.

She used the VPN spoofer to change the superficial location information attributed to the open incognito window and navigated to the university login page before nudging the laptop around to face him. She stood, watching over his shoulder as he hunted for the right keys to enter his username.

"You don't trust me," he said, nevertheless typing in his password, one slow key at a time. Whoever had trained him in contemporary mortal life hadn't been especially thorough.

"We hardly know each other. And as you said, ultimately our goals are at odds. You shouldn't trust me either."

His torso twisted so he could look at her. "I believed you ran because you were scared, and stayed away despite everything happening because you were selfish." He said it matter-of-factly, as if he weren't insulting her.

Inna blinked slowly, imitating boredom—a trick she'd picked up centuries ago.

"In the days we've known each other," Azar continued, "I've learned you're kind, compassionate, generous. Thoughtful, intelligent, deliberate." He stood as if his next point deserved the gravitas of a more dignified position. "I do plan to convince you to return, but I would never do anything to harm you."

Something lonely and primal in her wanted to believe that. But even if he meant the words, that didn't necessarily make them true. As it was, she was trusting him more than she would have liked. With the amulet around her neck, he could overpower her in an instant.

"We may not be each other's chosen confidants," he said, interrupting her thoughts, "but I do trust you."

If *that* was true, she could use him. Guilt chipped at her soul that she'd even thought it. But just because she wouldn't be fixing it his way didn't mean she'd ignore the troubling things Azar had shared about what was happening in Azhidar Zher.

Using him in the process would still give him exactly what he wanted, and that would have to be good enough.

Focusing on her current To Do list, and ignoring his overstuffed inbox, she sat and opened a fresh message. "Who were your professors aside from Weston?"

He frowned at the name, but the surprise quickly drained away. "That's right, Naiara is in that class."

So he hadn't noticed her. It was sheer dumb luck—or maybe sheer animal attraction—that Naiara had invited him to Tia's. The human couldn't have predicted the consequences. And if *Tia* hadn't given in to her need, she still might have escaped undetected. She wouldn't be making mistakes like that again.

"Right," Inna murmured. "Who are the others?"

As he listed the names, she looked up each one in the university directory, adding their emails to her message. She typed a quick note about a family emergency forcing him to withdraw for the semester. If for some reason he wanted to return after all this was over, whoever had set him up at the university could help him figure it out.

"Why are you contacting them?" Azar asked. He moved his chair a little ways away, as if not to crowd her, but also clearly showing he didn't feel the need to read over her shoulder.

"You abruptly disappearing would raise questions. Humans tend to worry nowadays."

"I see."

Inna sent the message and exhaled. One more thing taken care of. Only about a million to go, but she didn't need Azar around for them.

Dropping her hands from the laptop, she asked sternly in Drakonazyk. "Are you planning to contact anyone?"

Dispirited humor quirked his lips. "Is that a test, or an offer?" When she didn't answer, he sighed. "No, I am not planning to find some forest nymph or fairy to pass along any messages."

"And if you happen to come across one?"

His expression grew even more grim. "No."

"Then all right." She switched back to English. "The deck's all yours."

He rose to his feet as she turned back to the computer, closing out the window before opening a fresh incognito one and again spoofing the VPN.

"Feel free to choose a book, if you'd like." She may not trust his promise not to contact anyone, but the books were harmless in that sense. While she had plenty of classics as well, many of the books here were likely to be new to him.

"Thank you," he said, almost automatically. He hovered by her side until she looked up from the screen. "Do you by chance have some paper and a pencil?"

"Uhm, maybe." She rose slowly. Where would something like that be? The kitchen was out, and the display cabinet near the fridge held mostly larger or fancier food-related items, like the samovar with its cylindrical glass cups in their wrought-metal holders. The cabinet in the corner had a few DVDs, chess and backgammon sets, and some other things she couldn't remember, so she headed there.

Azar started to protest her taking time to search, but an annoyed look quickly shut him up. It took some rummaging, but she finally found a pad of blank pages and some fresh pencils in the top drawer of the buffet.

As she searched for a sharpener, he said, "I could use a knife."

"Right, sure." It was possible he planned to write a message and somehow get it to the other dragons, but she couldn't actually lock him up and control his every movement. He had claimed he wouldn't be passing any messages, and he had spent that one class doodling. Inna handed over the supplies. Murmuring his thanks, Azar made his way out onto the deck.

She settled back at the laptop, slipping a debit card from her back pocket. She'd plant some seeds to throw off anyone looking for them, then respond to Naiara, and get in touch with the firm currently responsible for managing things like the taxes on her U.S. properties. As much as modern technology made it more difficult to disappear, it did also simplify overseeing all her estates and accounts. All she needed to do was remember various login combinations, and she could be any of her core identities with no glamour involved, allowing Tia to send a resignation email to the owner of the Peran Estate and for the owner to re-spond, all without Inna moving from her seat. So even if someone looked very closely at Tia's university email account, they wouldn't have cause to suspect she was anyone other than who she'd pretended to be.

Figuring out what to do about the dragons would be much harder. She could try to contact Nahash, but she needed more information first. Azar seemed willing to provide that, but he also wasn't being entirely honest with her.

Ultimately, she would need to find a way to speak to her brother without revealing her location. There was every possibility he, too, believed it was her failure to participate in the maros that harmed the dragons, weakened his rule. She wouldn't let him learn how far from true that was.

Chapter 11

WHEN AZAR FINISHED BATHING THE FOLLOWING MORNING, Inna stood in the kitchen with bags of frozen fruit and a new machine on the kitchen counter. Last night she'd made and shared a dish she called "lazy lasagna." Despite the tenuous détente between them, they hadn't eaten the mix of pillowy ravioli, sauce, ground meat, and cheese together. She'd disappeared into her bedroom soon after pulling the dish out of the oven, taking with her the device she'd been using to communicate with the outside world.

She considered him somberly now before turning back to her supplies. "I'm making a smoothie, would you like one?"

He would have answered had he known how to. She was so comfortable with everything in the mortal world, it made him feel out of place. Which was absurd, since this *wasn't* his place. It wasn't hers either.

She glanced over her shoulder, that multicolored hair that should have immediately given her away swaying with her movement. "Do you know what a smoothie is?"

Gritting his teeth at his ignorance, he shook his head.

Her whole torso sighed, and she twisted to lean back on the counter. "It's a blended, er, sort of pulverized mix of fruit. Well, some people use vegetables, but I'm sticking with fruit."

He would have preferred some of the meat in the refrigerator. Fruit did little to satisfy a dragon, though this form didn't require as much sustenance. One of the reasons even those who weren't forced to had spent recent decades primarily in these bodies, to stave off the hunger. But among the mortals, they ate as the humans did, so Azar simply nodded. "Thank you."

Several minutes later, Inna poured the results from the machine with the spinning blades into two tall glasses. She set one on the table beside where he stood, but rather than consuming her portion, she began to clear up.

When she noticed he hadn't tried the *smoothie*, she arched an eyebrow. "It's not poisoned," she said, echoing his comment from the airport.

"Never crossed my mind." Azar picked up the chill glass with the pink goop.

She sidled over to her own glass, watching him as she sipped pointedly. A bit of the mixture clung to her top lip, and she swiped it off with a deft movement of her tongue.

Dragging his attention back to the issue at hand, Azar followed her example, swallowing the cold mix that tasted much better than it looked. Tart and fresh, it slid over his taste buds and down his throat. Catching her gaze again, he repeated, "Thank you."

She rolled her eyes and walked over toward the sofas.

"I thought perhaps…" Her posture stiffened, and he trailed off. He'd spent the prior evening sketching, but also strategizing. Staring at each other, trapped in this cabin, while discussing everything that needed to be said wouldn't be productive, the walls around them only reinforcing the ones between them. "Perhaps we could go for a walk."

Her eyes narrowed as she tried to suss out the trap that didn't exist. Moving, surrounded by the freedom of the forest, should defuse her animosity somewhat, giving her a target for her anger aside from him. He sipped the fruit mix while she considered.

"Fine," she said finally, and it felt like a victory. When she learned the full truth about the Zubir—the plight of the dragons—the compassion he'd discovered in her would convince her to help. Even if they had to figure out how to protect her after the maros, there would be plenty of time to do that while training her to win. They couldn't risk her going up against the Zubir unprepared. How long had it been since she'd even taken her true form?

They finished their breakfast in silence, but soon Inna was leading him to a trail that rose in a gentle incline and curved into the woods. Skin-tight bottoms clung to the supple muscles in her legs before disappearing beneath the hem of a loose tunic that didn't quite cover the swell of her ass. Azar had fashioned a tunic today as well, but it didn't compare to the way hers looked on her. She had also transformed the color of her eyes and hair again.

"Are you concerned we may be observed?" he asked, letting the sense of the forest envelop him before diving into the more difficult topics that lay ahead. He would have preferred to shift, to soar above the trees bathed in the early sunlight, but walking in the dappled light would have to do.

"You never know nowadays," she answered cryptically.

"It must be difficult," he ventured next, "altering your identity constantly. Growing accustomed to a new name."

"I usually have more warning." Her frown said everything about whom she blamed for her hasty departure. Though since they meant her no harm, there was no reason she couldn't have remained in Pennsylvania. "But at this point, I'm used to it."

"You've done it before?"

She shot him an indecipherable look. "You've spent time among the humans before. Around when?"

"Eighteen hundreds." Much as life here had changed since then, a walk in nature was essentially the same. Even if back then, she would have worn a gown that accentuated her waist and plumped her breasts like an offering. She also likely wouldn't have been seen speaking to him. He'd worked in stables, in alehouses, as a footman. She would have undoubtedly remained among the nobility.

She nodded, her pace remaining even as she scanned the woods surrounding them. "And what did you do after ten, fifteen years?"

"Changed locations." But he hadn't changed his name.

A leisurely breath expanded her ribcage, her frame small enough that the movement was obvious even beneath her formless clothing. "Yeah, back then, you could do that, depending on your rank, how far you went. Whether anyone would go looking. Identification papers have grown ever more complex, and with the internet, pretty much everything, all the official information about every human being in most countries, can be shared in seconds."

The trail they were following forked, but she veered to the right without hesitation. "And don't forget, it wasn't only humans looking for me. They wouldn't have troubled themselves too much, but if someone gave them reason to try harder…"

Not having a response, Azar let the rhythm of their footsteps fill his silence. Mere minutes later, Inna paused at a small overlook, a faint smile touching her lips and lighting her eyes as she took in the view. Lush green mountains and the darker dips of their valleys lay spread before them. Again he wished he could shift, this view a mere echo of the one that would be afforded them by flight.

Longing replaced the moment of peace on Inna's face, as if she'd had the same thought.

"How did you learn to conceal your appearance?" he asked to distract her. And because he was curious. If it was a skill that could be acquired, not an effect of her amulet or some other object of power, he could find a way to learn.

She answered absently, still staring at the trees below them. "Glamour's a common power among the—" She spun on him, her gaze sharpening. "It's a *common* power," she repeated more slowly, "among the dragons."

Azar frowned as Inna's mind spun, trying to work out the implications of his question.

"You never learned?" she asked. Not every dragon mastered the ability, which seemed tied to one's overall strength, but even with him in this form, it was clear Azar wasn't weak.

"No." He paused, but ostensibly his entire purpose was to fill her in on what had been happening in her absence, so he soon continued. "I've never seen another dragon use it."

"Well they wouldn't, really, back home." He probably hadn't spent time with other dragons while among the humans. That would explain it. Even if none of the young dragons had learned, many of the older ones had long ago mastered that power.

His mouth opened to speak, but he shut it in frustration, his frown deepening the lines in his face. If he had been mortal, he would have wrinkled by now.

"Let's back up." She led the way back to the trail. She'd wanted to visit the vista point one more time, but she didn't want the weight of everything that had gone wrong to overshadow the memories she had of this place.

"You said Nahash is childless," she said when Azar caught up. "He hasn't chosen a bira?"

"He…has."

There was something odd in his voice, so she prodded, "She's infertile?" Inna had stopped believing dragonkind depended on the zubir—or the zubiran couple—long before her father had died. Waiting out of respect was entirely too mortal a concept, especially since birth control definitely didn't exist in a species that rarely procreated as it was. Besides, it had been hundreds of years. Could it be something psychosomatic? The conviction that their fertility depended on the zubiran couple impacting dragonkind's ability to produce children?

Azar still seemed at a loss for words, so Inna stopped, facing him on the trail, and voiced the only other option. "*He's* infertile?"

Obviously torn between the need to catch her up and fear of her reaction, he still didn't answer.

"Whatever it is, just tell me."

He shoulders rose and fell as he took two deep breaths, staring into her eyes as if they offered some kind of lifeline. "The Zubir's mate…isn't a dragon."

Inna scoffed, but with the words out, Azar grew more somber, his grim expression and solid stance making him look almost severe. In mortal form, dragons could be physically intimate with other creatures, but those pairings couldn't produce offspring. If her brother's chosen mate wasn't a dragon, he would *never* have children. And apparently the dragons believed that meant neither would they.

She leaned against the thick trunk of one of the old trees nearby, sliding down until she was seated on the ground. "What is she?" Inna asked, mostly out of curiosity. Tradition may dictate the zubiran family had two immutable responsibilities—the maros and procreation—but since she'd run from one, she couldn't really begrudge her brother shirking the other for love.

Azar remained standing, his head framed from this angle by the tops of the trees, like an ancient wreath. "A siren."

Well, that possibly changed things. "You think his affection isn't genuine?"

The question seemed to help Azar finally find his voice. "Whether it is doesn't change anything. If the Zubir's being manipulated, he's not strong enough to lead the dragons. If he isn't, his decisions are on the verge of destroying us."

"You keep saying that. Are the situation with the herd and lack of new hatchlings the only problems?" The hunger—insufficient nutrition—could also be responsible for the lack of reproduction. It would take some time to arrange, but she would find a way to discuss the food issue with Nahash. And a siren's power was limited by proximity, right? So Inna would insist on them speaking in private, to try to suss out that relationship.

"As I mentioned, the Zubir has pushed us to become more like the humans." Azar frowned again, but this time it was like he was puzzling something out for himself. "Or, that of centuries ago here. A class system, a feudal lord. Pens corralling the animals at the sobran and in each tribe's territory, overseen by zubiran delegates, always from another tribe.

"A requisite number of dragons from each tribe are sent into service, weaving and dyeing cloth, cleaning, even plowing fields for crops brought from the mortals. Tithes of gold and jewels are required, hoarded at the sobran or bestowed upon those the Zubir favors. More ornamentation can mean more food." Anger made his breathing grow deeper. "None in 'neutral' lands or skies are allowed to be in their natural form, not without special dispensation. Dragons *selected* into service at the sobran are rarely allowed to leave. Some haven't for decades or more, never allowed to shift."

"Why?" The question escaped in his pause. She certainly knew the ache of not being able to shift, to fly, to live in her true form.

Azar's voice was even, but resentment punctuated every syllable. "Because the Zubir deems it so. Even he is rarely seen in true form, though occasionally he flies his mate above those toiling below."

Unable to remain still, Inna rose to pace back and forth along the trail. "None of this makes sense."

Azhidar Zher had been created when the growing population of humans had butted up against dragonkind, infringing on their lands. Dragons could blend in with the mortals, of course, but with the standing decree not to allow humans true knowledge of magical creatures, it became nearly impossible for dragonkind to live as themselves here on Earth. The nettakim of the time had brought the plight to the High Council of the Fae, leading to the creation of a small separate realm, a beautiful space with plenty of land and prey for them to hunt. All so the dragons could live in peace.

Or, in as much peace as a species that solved even minor issues through violence could. The whole point of their home was for dragons to be dragons.

A zubir had been selected through battle from the five tribes' nettakim. Even then the dragons had seen the wisdom in leaving their strongest, wisest members alive, each fight lasting only until one yielded. Her ancestor had bested all the others.

The new zubir represented the dragons in their new High Council seat and ostensibly kept the dragons in line, defusing any serious unrest. Lore had started—likely from the words of the first zubir himself, not that Inna could prove it—that the dragons' power came from the zubir. The tekkess, the tribes' tradition of selecting a new netta with fights similar to the one that had chosen the original zubir, had morphed into the maros. The claim that the winner absorbed the others' power fed the myth of the zubir's unparalleled strength and the dragons' reliance on that power. And since the maros showcased ruthless brutality, even toward one's kin, dragons rarely challenged the zubir. Certainly she had never found mention of such challenge in the archives.

"What else?" Inna asked, turning back to Azar.

He had remained rooted to the spot, like her agitation had made him calm. "Does there need to be more?" he tested.

She drew herself up as regally as she could under the circumstances, forcing herself to remain still as well. Perhaps he had no reason to give her the benefit of the doubt, but his misconceptions didn't define her. She wouldn't be jumping through his hoops. "You keep saying the dragons are *dying*. From hunger, or something else?"

Chapter 12

THEIR LAST HOPE HAD SWITCHED IN A BLINK OF AN EYE FROM spiraling to single-minded, her attention focused on him and the information he still hadn't shared. Despite all their pretenses that rank had been forgotten between them, she'd pulled herself up straight, managing to look down on him even though he stood taller. They both knew that with that stone about her neck, he could easily overtake her, and still she behaved with ingrained assurance that he would never even try to attack her. Azar wasn't foolish enough to believe that it stemmed from trust rather than the inflated confidence of her position. Even if she hadn't told him point blank she didn't trust him.

"The elders from hunger," he admitted. "The strongest try to sacrifice for those weaker, or at least ours do." He had limited knowledge of other tribes.

Her head tilted with her assessment. "Including you."

His teeth ground into each other. He forced his jaw open. "What makes you think I'm not one of the weaker ones, benefitting from their protection?" Maybe if he'd been stronger, he would have been able to do more.

"What else?" she repeated rather than answer.

"When the Zeyan Netta passed, the Zubir presided over the tekkess."

The faintest shrug softened the intensity of her scrutiny.

"He announced some adjustments," Azar said, still easing her in. Or maybe giving himself time.

The selection of a new netta was traditionally a time of celebration. Or so he'd been told. It was a rare occasion, when tribes came together at the sobran to watch the ceremonial fights. They were always ruthless, dragons battling for the right and responsibility of leadership.

"What adjustments?" Impatience laced Inna's voice.

"No one outside tribal lands can take true form," he repeated, still buying time. He itched to turn away so he wouldn't have to face her reaction. Instead he rooted his stance firmly, standing strong like the tall trees around them. "Not many made the trip to the sobran for that tekkess, though I'm told in the past nearly every dragon did."

Unlike the vapid, self-centered princess he'd expected before finding her, Inna was shrewd. Her lips pursed, her gaze remaining sharp as she waited for his revelation.

Azar swallowed, taking a moment's refuge in the determination on her face. How different she looked now from the soft, pliable woman who'd kissed him under the twinkling night sky. It was a relief, seeing her ready to defend their kind.

Still, regret lay bitter on the back of his tongue. How much easier would it have been to forget the others? To set aside what he had to say in favor of kissing her again, erasing all the harshness from her features.

But he wasn't here for himself. He had a job to do, and he had to trust she wouldn't turn her back on the dragons. Especially not after learning this.

"The Zubir announced the named prospects wouldn't be allowed to withdraw." Every netta made a short list of sorts for the next one, even if historically all dragons from the tribe could choose to participate, and prospects had been allowed to bow out. Still, it was the other change that had shocked them all and finally convinced Azar to join Laisren's search. "And that tekkess matchups would be to the death."

Terror flashed in Inna's eyes before she masked it as effectively as she did their true color. Nettakim made their list of prospects over time, not waiting until death was imminent. The names of those participating in that tekkess had been known for decades, even centuries in some cases. And the Zubir's word had killed all but one. The grief of the Zeyno had been felt by them all.

Well, most, some dragons relishing their new privileged positions too much to care.

"He's gone mad," Inna breathed. Her ribcage shifted erratically with her emotion. "That's what you were trying to tell me. He's gone completely off the rails."

Azar would have preferred to gather her in his arms and recant, to protect her from the knowledge that weighed on him, on them all. Instead he nodded sharply.

She spun away, her breathing now audible as she stared at the trees.

"Koritza will die soon," he said, and she jerked back around to him. The Drevan Netta was old enough Inna would know her name.

A breathy, humorless chuckle escaped her lips. "You're meant to fight."

"No," he corrected quickly, though he would have been named if not for the harsh reality of the Zeyan tekkess. Respect for the passing of a fellow netta had kept Koritza from naming Azar when planned. Coincidence had spared him to come find Inna. Or perhaps the Fates had intervened even back then.

Her eyebrow crooked imperiously. She clearly knew that correction had also been an omission.

"But the best of the Drevno. My teachers, friends," Azar admitted. All now marked.

An eerie acceptance had washed over Inna. "So you came to convince me to take the same risk from which you want to spare them." She nodded faintly as she spoke. "Don't worry, I understand. I'm nothing but a stranger." A bitter smile tensed her cheeks.

"That isn't it. I care for my tribe." But that wasn't the point. Frustration made his growl trickle into his voice. "Even before the change to the tekkess, dragons were at risk, hurting. The Zeyno lost nearly a dozen of their strongest. The Drevno stand to lose almost as many. Over and over as nettakim die, we will be forced to destroy one another until your brother is no longer in power. And there will be no heirs to take his place. If there are any dragons still alive by then."

The pain and hopelessness in her expression helped him regain control. She may not want the responsibility of her birthright, but wishing things could be otherwise wouldn't help anyone.

"You are our best chance," he said. If those planning to kill the Zubir succeeded, the dragons could easily fall into a war from the uncertainty, the tribes fighting against those who'd helped the Zubir oppress them, against each other, against the notion of another zubir, around the question of who it should be. They'd slaughter each other out of revenge, yes, but also from the combination of anger and frustration and grief.

"I know you're concerned regarding the maros, but I can help you train, prepare. And meanwhile, we can find a solution to…that other…"

She scoffed, turning and stalking down the trail. "How exactly do you propose to 'train' me?" she asked when he caught up. "I can't shift here, and for that matter, neither can you. What's this brilliant plan of yours?"

Exposing themselves to mortals was an offense punishable at the discretion of the Zubir. It was true that Azar wouldn't want to find himself at Nahash's mercy. Especially since many now believed it was the siren he'd picked as mate who truly made the decisions. Little else explained the shift to mimicking the mortal world.

Nevertheless… "Surely we are isolated enough here that the mortals wouldn't notice, perhaps at night."

"Welcome to the modern world, Azar. The humans surveil every inch of their planet at all times. We might not be noticed in all that footage, but we could be. And even still, they aren't the reason I won't shift."

While he'd only understood part of what she said, he grasped the point that mattered most. "We can protect you from the other factions," he insisted as they neared her cabin.

She paused at the base of the short stairway up to the deck. "My *request* that you not contact anyone stands. I will figure out my next steps, how to fix this. And if you ever want me to return to the dragons, you will give me the space to do that."

He bowed his head in response. No part of what she'd said had been a request. Worry ate away at his insides, but he clung to the fact that she did care enough to save them from her brother. All Azar had to do now was get her to admit there was only one way to do that.

Chapter 13

INNA STALKED INTO HER CABIN, AND FOR A BLISSFUL HALF A second before Azar followed, she was actually alone and could pretend she hadn't heard all of that. Everyone had wanted Nahash as the new zubir, no one expecting her to win the maros. Some bitter, dark part of her wanted to leave them to deal with the consequences. Most of them probably blamed her for escaping before the maros, for not "ceding" her power to her brother. Why should she clean up the disaster they'd all asked for?

Except it wasn't all of them. And no one could have seen any of this coming. The whole point of their new home was for dragons to live as dragons. *How* could he be forcing them into mortal bodies, mortal mistakes? Forcing them to kill one another.

The maros might have its justifications, keeping their family tree a strong "proud" line rather than a mess of branches that could lead to infighting. Plus it bolstered the mythology of the zubir's power. Inna may not support it, but it was understandable.

But decimating the elite of the tribes? The Zeyno might have killed one another, but none of them would have risked going against their Zubir. Even if he had lost his mind. Nahash would have simply killed them himself, in deed as easily as he had in word.

She didn't know whether to start throwing breakables or curl up in a ball and sob. The damn amulet around her neck wouldn't let her shift and roar all her emotions over these mountains.

"You could hit me."

She spun to face Azar who still stood by the open door to the deck. "What?"

"I can take it," he said, stepping closer.

"Oh, I get it." She crossed her arms to hide the fists she couldn't unclench. "The insanity's contagious." With her power muted, he'd barely feel it if she hit him. Regardless, it wasn't going to happen.

He shrugged, though on him the movement looked sinewy, like he'd flared out a wing that wasn't there to resettle it. "However I can help."

"Didn't we just cover this?" A couple more breaths stuffed her emotions down behind a practiced veneer of calm. "You did what you came here to do. I know now."

She should have known before it got this far. She'd done too good a job cutting off all communication with any of the creatures who could have found her, warned her. Now the mess might be too big to clean up, but either way, it was on her shoulders. No matter how the two of them had briefly pretended they could ignore her rank, the implications of what Azar had revealed changed everything. "I will figure out what to do. If for some reason you're a part of my plan, I'll let you know."

Temper flashed in those gold-flecked eyes, but like her, he pushed his irritation aside. "I can help," he repeated, emphasizing each word.

"How?" Her arms dropped with the question, swinging out with the force of the movement or maybe the oomph of her exasperation.

"Strategy." With calm deliberation, he turned back and shut the door before moving closer to the living area. "It seems as though…"

Inna's jaw shifted with her impatience at his prevaricating.

Azar stilled, then his shoulders straightened even though they'd seemed straight before. But suddenly he looked like he might actually be one of the strongest fighters the Drevno had. "I know him better than you do now," he said bluntly.

"Oh?" she challenged, even as something other than irritation stirred low in her belly. She'd seen glimpses of this version of him before. A confidence filled out his stance, as if he finally knew what he had to offer in a way he hadn't even when he'd suggested he could "train" her.

"I know he always lilts to the left—"

"Before swooping down to the right," Inna finished for him, that stirring of attraction doused in an ice bath. How incompetent did he think she was? She'd grown up observing Nahash, had been meant to fight him to the death, and Azar thought she hadn't noticed something that basic?

"I know his mate's name," Azar persisted.

Inna sighed, the dissipating adrenaline leaving her more empty than annoyed. "And you'll tell me, to help save the dragons. Just like anything else you know that could be of use."

His teeth ground into each other, jaw clenching at the truth in her words. "All right. Let's start with the fact that you're incapable of being around other dragons."

Her eyes narrowed. "Meaning?" The growl in her voice should have warned him off.

Instead this newly confident Azar smirked.

She choked on a gasp as the sense of his power changed from a tingle to a flood. It tried to pull her under, but even the deepest parts of her body reveled in the sensation, entirely willing to drown, resenting the stone that kept her tethered to the surface. Under just about any other circumstances, Inna would have jumped him, needing his touch along with the embrace of his power, letting herself forget everything else but the feel of him between her thighs, against her skin.

He reigned his power back in, resignation aging his eyes. "If you're distracted by that, what will happen when you're surrounded by the dragons watching you fight? Not damping their power for humans' sake?"

"The maros isn't happening," Inna insisted. Though he did have a point otherwise.

She'd nearly gotten used to the prickle of his proximity, but that was nothing like the full lushness of him simply not holding back. With hundreds of dragons doing the same?

"You're right," she said. "I do need to grow reaccustomed to being around dragonkind." And he clearly wanted to feel helpful. If humoring him would make him more amenable, it was a small price to pay. "So stop acting like I'm human."

Unlike the last time when he'd been trying to make a point, Azar let his tight control on his power ease out. Inna swallowed visibly but otherwise managed to hide her response. The impact of his unrestrained power had already washed away her glamour, revealing the true beauty of her hair, those amethyst eyes that trained stubbornly on him. At least she'd admitted that the feel of their kind would be a distraction for her right now. Shocked as she'd been by all that he'd revealed, her disbelief hadn't made her unreasonable.

Now he needed her to understand he could be useful. There was too much at stake for her to return to the dragons unprepared. Her trepidation was understandable. But sooner or later, she'd recognize the maros was the only choice. Azar had to make sure it was sooner, and that she would be ready to win. He also couldn't risk pushing her too far, too fast.

"I need to think," she said now, turning away toward the bedrooms.

"Take your time," he said with practiced deference.

Her head jerked toward him, eyes narrowed, seeing through his politesse.

Azar flared out a little more power, going a touch beyond his natural uncontained state. It was a petty move, wanting to see her react to him.

Inna rolled her eyes as she turned away, entering her bedroom, but he could have sworn there'd been a flash of heat in her gaze. Like the first time, when her lips had parted, those eyes growing wide as if he'd caressed her.

He knew it wasn't personal. How long had it been since she'd felt the full presence of another dragon? Though trapped in their human form, the dragons at the sobran didn't quell their power the way they all had to here on Earth. Inna had been isolated from even that sense of others. That was the only reason his presence impacted her so strongly.

Azar walked over to the couch, toeing off his shoes and dematerializing his shirt. Would she notice even that small use of power? Surrounded by it as their kind constantly was, they learned to tune it out. To say Inna was out of practice would be an understatement. If she was so easily distracted, she'd never triumph over the Zubir.

Still, simply being the one that reacquainted her with the proximity of dragonkind, like some sort of inoculation, wasn't all Azar was good for. Her dismissiveness pricked his pride. He may never be her equal, but something pushed him to want her respect, even if she hadn't yet entirely earned his. A wise leader knew when to rely on their allies—something she obstinately refused to do.

One short message would be enough to bring all the dragons Laisren had placed among the mortals to this cabin, to help her train and plan. To protect her from anyone sent by the other factions who might discover her. She was ignoring the resources available to her.

Perhaps he wasn't being fair. She'd only learned the truth minutes ago. Once she internalized it all, would it be enough to change her mind? She'd clearly understood the danger of leaving her brother as zubir. Whatever strategy she may be concocting, she would need Azar at her side. And when she reemerged, he'd help her see that. For now, there wasn't much he could do but wait.

Chapter 14

INNA STRIPPED OFF HER HOODIE, TAKING HER TOP WITH IT. Azar's presence seemed to fill every millimeter of the cabin now, making her skin too sensitive for even the lightest fabric. She stripped down to only her bra and panties and lay down on the bed, fighting the impulse to take those off as well.

She should have been thinking exclusively about everything he'd finally revealed. Her body had its own ideas, leaving her torn between taking the edge off the need his power stoked and facing the horror of her brother's rule.

Rationally, an orgasm should help her focus, removing the distraction of her unwanted arousal. Even the soft lace of her lingerie felt too abrasive now, scraping against all her hypersensitive parts. Inna slipped off the straps of her bra and palmed her breasts under the cups. Her hips writhed involuntarily against the quilted coverlet. Even with the amulet insulating her, Azar's power was nearly as effective as his touch had been.

Her hands fell away at the reminder of him beyond the door. A pulse of need made her shiver, her breath coming in gasps as she wrestled with her desire.

If he hadn't been in the living room, she would have snuck into the bathroom for a cold shower. A dip in a chill lake would have felt even better. As it was, Inna blew her breath out in a slow, controlled stream. Then again.

The amulet lay cool and heavy on her abdomen, a weight she'd briefly forgotten. She gripped it, sitting up. Dragons were dying, spiritually and literally. Aside from freeing the herds and abolishing whatever decrees kept them imprisoned in mortal bodies like she was, she'd have to find a way to restore the tribes' sense of community.

Her skin still tingling, Inna replaced her bra with a soft tee shirt and opened her laptop to start formulating a plan.

Peace had been tenuous at first in the new realm, dragons too used to fighting for their territory, their food. By the time the High Council had intervened, limited space among the humans had meant all the dragons had coalesced into five main tribes, the Radno, Virno, Pretno, Drevno, and Zeyno. Each tribe was primarily made up of dragons in one family of colors: reds, whites, blacks, browns, and greens, respectively. Though others remained, they'd mostly been absorbed, showing up as little variations or splashes of color, like her blues and Azar's gold, assuming he was telling the truth about being incapable of glamour. The purples had been wiped out entirely, their memory only occasionally cropping up in dragons like her, though it remained strong in the eyes of the zubiran line.

The five tribes had divvied up the new realm, but the Viran dragon who'd become zubir—her ancestor—had had the wisdom to bring them together for each tekkess and other events of significance. That strengthened the ties among the tribes, allowing for a general peace.

Did Nahash understand how his decisions had destroyed that? Making travel to the sobran more difficult, ensuring fewer dragons attended. Turning the tekkess itself into a gruesome slaughter rather than a showcase of strength and cunning. Forcing dragons into what sounded like slave labor, and controlling food through delegates.

The brother she remembered would never have allowed this, much less been the instigator. Had he indeed gone mad? If so, why wouldn't the Fae Council have informed her? They could have found her, even if her precautions had prevented others from doing so.

If only she could talk to Rhea, the friend who'd helped Inna escape and happened to have a seat on said council. But there was no easy way to contact her from this cabin.

Which left Azar as Inna's only real source of information about Azhidar Zher. And about the siren at the center of it all.

Like when it came to most creatures, Inna's knowledge of sirens stemmed primarily from human sources, which tended to be hit or miss when it came to accuracy. She'd certainly never met one. Was Nahash's mate simply in love? Could ignorance be at the root of all the dragons' problems?

No, that was disregarding all the malicious changes causing dragonkind to be destroyed, much like they would have been had they remained among the humans.

Inna procrastinated awhile, checking her email and mentally circling the challenge in front of her. She'd assured Azar she would find a solution because like it or not, this *was* on her.

Yesterday's naïve spurt of protectiveness, those glimpses of understanding between them, couldn't change that.

Still, she needed more information. So when delaying started to feel more like hiding, she got dressed again and strode purposefully into the kitchen.

"Have you eaten?" she asked, taking out the leftovers of her lazy lasagna.

"Yes," said Azar, who'd risen from the couch at her reappearance and materialized a shirt to cover his terracotta skin. For once, he didn't thank her.

Inna kept her eyes on the bowl of pasta. Sprinkling grated cheese on top, she said, "Tell me about the siren."

"No," Azar said.

Inna glanced over her shoulder, something like curiosity flickering in her eyes. "No?" she echoed, resuming preparing her food.

She wasn't the only one who'd done some thinking, planning. In merely days, the seemingly insurmountable obstacles of finding the Zubir's sister and convincing her to listen had been overcome. The next challenge before him was to prepare her, and that meant convincing her to value his opinions. He needed her, yes, since no one else could challenge the Zubir, much less be accepted as the new one. But he couldn't blindly let her call all the shots, either, playing the obedient lackey.

"Yesterday you said our goals are at odds," he began.

"You claimed that first," she corrected, not turning around even though her bowl now stood in the miniature electric oven on the counter.

Azar mentally ran through bits of their conversations. "Indeed. You see now we were both wrong?" He failed to keep the question from his voice. Her brother was the only member of the zubiran family Azar had ever known, and Nahash's displeasure was vicious. Even knowing there was no way Inna could physically harm him, certainly not while she insisted on smothering her power, the ingrained deference was difficult to abandon, especially when she'd resumed behaving in accordance with their roles.

"Oh?" came the dry reply.

"Maros aside, we both want to save the dragons."

Her entire body sighed as she finally turned, her weight resting on the counter behind her. "I thought we covered this. The way you do that now is by answering my questions."

Because he couldn't stand still any longer and wouldn't retreat, Azar stepped closer. "Our goals are aligned, and yet you do not treat me as an ally."

She snorted, her derision a chilling echo of her brother's, and straightened, ignoring the chime behind her. "Because you aren't. You're a resource, sure."

She stalked toward him, and suddenly he was grateful for the table between them despite the stone hanging below her breasts. "But you're not an ally," she said, baring her teeth, "you're my *responsibility*."

Her demeanor changed in an instant, the anger replaced by bored dismissiveness. Following her moods would give him whiplash.

She turned away to get her food. "You don't want to tell me what you know? Fine. I'll find another way." She shrugged as she settled at the table. "Or I won't."

Her eyes found him, still frozen between the dining table and the sofa. "And your whole sojourn to the mortal realm will have been a waste."

Chapter 15

THE THREAT WAS WORSE THAN A BLOW TO THE HEAD, SCAT-tering his thoughts, his determination. Every time he thought he'd found an inroad, she swatted him away as if he were nothing more than a minor nuisance. He should have rejoiced that she considered the dragons her responsibility, and him among them.

But damn it, she was his responsibility, too. Since she would not allow him to inform the others of her location, *he* had to coax her back. *He* had to ensure she was prepared. That she would prevail rather than dying, along with any hope for the future. That all of this wasn't for nothing.

He mimicked her trick from the mansion, an invisible talon landing on her breastbone. "Everything else ahead, you really want to fight me, too?"

With a deep breath, she settled her full fork back in the bowl. A slow, bored blink followed. "If you could have done this without me, you would have," she said, calmly calling his bluff.

She leaned forward slightly, and he drew his power back automatically before catching himself. Still, that small movement had destroyed whatever he'd hoped to accomplish. Azar let the invisible claw dissipate.

Inna's head tilted as her eyes ran over him. "If you can't do something as simple as answer my questions, then stay out of my way." She picked up her fork, swirling it around the bowl. "Before I ask you do something you really don't want to do."

She didn't wait for him to respond, resuming her meal as if nothing of consequence had passed between them.

Azar lowered stiffly into the nearest seat. "What do you want to know?" he asked, conceding. Perhaps he was out of his depth, but that didn't mean he was out of options.

Inna swallowed the pasta that had become tasteless. She'd won their little battle of bluffs, centuries of added experience and the incontestable reality of their roles giving her the advantage. Her irritability at the effect of his power had probably helped, too. Mostly it had been simple fact. Azar *was* her responsibility now, as were they all.

She had no intention of making an enemy of him, but she also couldn't allow him to believe they had equal skin in this game. He'd been right that this wouldn't be a coup. There'd be no army to gather, no willing soldiers standing strong at her back. Whatever happened, it would come down to her and her brother. The fate of the dragons depended on *her.* Another thing Azar had been right about in the beginning, even if he seemed to be willfully ignoring it now.

"Let's start with her name," Inna said. Though she changed her human identity often, she hadn't forgotten the significance of a name among the fae, many of whom had populated the Earth long before the humans had taken it over. It was part of why she'd stopped Azar from completing hers, not knowing who might have heard and how.

"Jadokari," he said, sullenly not elaborating.

She stifled her sigh. "This part is only as difficult as you want to make it."

Compassionate and *intelligent* he'd called her just yesterday. She'd seen the hope in his eyes as he filled her in, even if it had been mixed with a deep sadness. As if he regretted disillusioning her.

Maybe it was even admirable in a sense, his desire to shoulder more of the responsibility. Even if it did stem from some naïve belief that if he just tried hard enough, everything would turn out all right. That she'd win or lose in the maros he was so intent on seeing happen based on *his* effectiveness.

Actually, put that way, it was more insulting than admirable.

"I'll answer any questions you have," he said. "But I can do more to help you."

"If I free the dragons from my brother's—from what's happening, you'll be seen as the one who made it happen. Isn't that enough for you?"

He flinched almost imperceptibly, but his expression softened. "You think I'm concerned about being lauded?"

"No. I do believe you care about the wellbeing of dragonkind."

"And yours." His hand moved forward on the tabletop as if to reach for her, though that wasn't physically possible with how they were sitting. Catching the movement, he drew the limb back.

"Sure," she murmured. "As the only weapon in your arsenal." Or perhaps to garner favor with what he saw as his next zubir. "Let's get back to what matters."

"You matter," he countered, and the part of her that still wanted to curl around him gained the upper hand for a moment.

Reason regained control about the same time as he added, "I've clearly done a clumsy job expressing it, but—"

"Stop. We keep going in circles. You want me to be your next zubir? Do what I ask. You want to help? Do what I ask. Are you seeing a common theme here? We've covered this: you can't have it both ways." She sighed. "Neither of us can." He couldn't be her fun sexy distraction, or her source of comfort, or anything other than a resource for her to use and then protect. And she couldn't be anything other than the daughter of a zubir.

His frustration huffed out his nostrils. No doubt in his true form, the noise would have been accompanied by tendrils of smoke.

"Start at the beginning," Inna directed, nudging her leftovers out of the way. "What do you know about Jadokari?"

"She doesn't like to be around us in our natural form." He shook his head, his fingers curling into fists. "Reconnaissance isn't what I'm good at."

"You're the one here." Something was tapping at the edges of her mind, impatient for her to piece it together. "She's mated to a dragon but doesn't like dragons?"

"I'm not sure sirens mate like we do," he pointed out.

It was a good point, but not relevant to whatever was on the tip of her mental tongue. "How does she communicate?"

Confusion threw off Azar's sullenness. "What do you mean?"

"Does she speak?"

"Yes, of course."

"Telepathically?" As dragons did. Most retained that ability in human form, too, only the amulet blocking that in Inna's case as part of its protection. The crucial point was they *couldn't* speak aloud in their natural form. Was that the root of the siren's objection?

"I don't know," he admitted, this small failing weighing far too heavily on his shoulders. "I'm sorry."

"It's fine," she assured absently. She'd have to find out somehow. "I'll be right back."

She returned quickly with her laptop, opening a fresh document for notes alongside the Wikipedia entry for sirens. Human mythology might not be the most reliable source, but it was a good jumping off point to guide her questions. Maybe between it and Azar, she could get a decent idea of how everything had become so messed up. "Where were we?"

Relief felt strangely like nausea, strong enough to keep him awake long after Inna had gone to bed. They'd spent hours going over what he knew about the Zubir, the siren, and the situation at the sobran. Now he sat on his bed with the same sketchpad he'd doodled in the day before, flipping through his sketches of the dragons' savior.

He'd bungled things with her. He'd tried sheltering her, attempting to preemptively manage her reactions, and he'd tried challenging her. Neither had gone over especially well, each new revelation pushing her to look further inward rather than relying on him. After his scattered, tentative approach to conveying the problems they faced, he wouldn't have trusted him as an ally, an advisor, either. Perhaps that was the true reason Koritza had reconsidered naming him as a prospect for the tekkess.

Azar shook the thought away, flipping to a fresh page. Exhaustion and stress were wearing on him, which always muddled his thinking. He'd feel more clear in the morning, but first he had to disengage from the tornado of thoughts about his inadequacy in representing the dragons, preparing Inna for what was to come.

Sketching normally helped, even in Azhidar Zher, though after running out of mortal paper, he'd mostly had to rely on smooth stone and cavern walls. Now, though, no matter how he started a sketch, it ended up including the dragon presumably sleeping in the room next door. He'd yet to get her quite right, his mediocre skills incapable of capturing the complex reality of her on paper.

At least while she'd been in the bathroom, he'd managed to send a quick message seeking Laisren's advice. Unlike her, Azar knew when to ask for help, even if he had refrained from describing their location in deference to her unease. The Fates might have had their reasons for letting him be the one to find her, but that didn't mean he couldn't rely on the others. Laisren had known her, before all this happened. He would know how best to get through to her.

Then maybe she would recognize the wisdom in relying on the other dragons intent on seeing her succeed, all eager to help her. Inna may be used to being alone, so accustomed to hiding that she was wary of any dragon's motivation. But Azar knew whom to trust, even if he hadn't known the history of their last female zubir. Laisren being one of the oldest Drevno would help there as well. She couldn't dismiss his counsel on the basis of youth.

Inna soared over familiar landmarks, the thrum of dragon-kind's particular flavor of power reminding her she wasn't alone. Leisurely but not directionless, the flight wasted neither time nor energy. It had been a long time since she'd dreamt of flight. Though she knew where this was headed, Inna lingered in the air, feeling her wings, stretching her neck, expelling flickers of flame that sparred with the dusk.

When she landed at the edge of the hot spring, it was with bare feet and in human form, the secluded pool not large enough for dragons. Her sigh was carried off by a warm gust of wind. Even here in her mind, she couldn't indulge fully in her true form.

Still she sank into the heat, sweeping her arms through the water. The sound of some creature scurrying into the rocks turned her head, this dream less fuzzy in its surroundings than most others. But then, it had her memories to play with.

Inna dipped her head back, allowing the warmth to seep into her scalp. Another sound had her straightening, materializing clothing as she sought its source.

The dream weaver's face seared itself into her mind in the half second he took to ponder her. His breath puffed glittering dust onto her skin. The edges of the dream faded, the water swirling around her, mud sucking at her feet. The weaver watched as Inna fought, clawing her way out, but the amulet had reappeared around her neck, sapping her of strength.

"What are you doing?" a familiar voice asked in Drakon-azyk.

No matter how her throat worked to explain she was trying to escape, the words wouldn't come.

"What we must," a gravelly voice she couldn't place answered instead of her.

The water dried up, leaving her trapped to her waist in the ground. She twisted every which way she could, but the weaver had disappeared, his task complete.

"You did well," the second voice assured. "You found her, for all our sakes."

Above her, the stars winked out one by one. Her last flash of flame became an exhale of dust.

Almost too quiet to hear, the familiar voice said, "I don't understand."

Oh, but she did.

She woke in chains. Well, only her arms were shackled above her head, though the real manacle lay in its usual place, on a far more delicate chain around her neck. She kept her muscles lax so whoever had abducted her didn't realize quite yet that the weaver's dust had worn off.

Still in the soft tee shirt and shorts she'd worn to bed, she didn't know how long it had been. She didn't know where she was, though all indications pointed to a cave. She had no way of knowing in which realm, human, dragon, or otherwise. She also didn't know who had captured her, or what they wanted.

But she did know one thing: Everyone responsible would die.

Chapter 16

With that certainty fixed in her mind, Seraphina Ignatia opened her eyes, planted her feet firmly in the rough dirt floor, and lifted her head to face her captors.

"So the pirha rejoins us at last," the gravelly voice from her dream said in Drakonazyk from somewhere to the left of the cave's bright entrance. Wherever they were, it was daytime. And this cave wasn't big enough for his other form.

Seraphina didn't respond to the insult, standing with as much strength as the awkward position allowed. Her muscles already smarted from her having been hung by the wrists while unconscious. If Laisren thought a little physical discomfort would break her, let him.

She hadn't recognized his voice in the dream, but she did place it now. One of the oldest Drevno, he'd been disqualified in their last tekkess by her father, deemed unfit to lead. Apparently he'd never gotten over it.

With a shadowy movement of his arm, he directed his lackeys to tighten her chains, stretching her until her toes barely brushed the earth. Since he could communicate telepathically with the dragons foolish enough to do his bidding, the gesture must have been for her benefit.

Seraphina didn't allow him the pleasure of seeing her react. Her fingers wrapped around the thick metal coils, arms supporting her weight. An inhale re-centered her, a measured exhale blowing out the ache in her muscles. Another intentional breath followed as the males who'd chained her came to stand in full view. She recognized neither, but she wouldn't forget them now any more than she would the weaver who'd been enlisted to help.

She would survive this. They would not. The reminder played in her head like a mantra.

Laisren moseyed forward and stopped with the two others dramatically at his back. The invisible extension of his claw lifted her pendant, a derisive grimace contorting his face. "How kind of you to weaken yourself for us," he said, allowing the stone to drop back into place.

The pinpricks of his talons settled around her, tight enough that each breath pushed her flesh into the sharp points. But he wouldn't kill her here.

No, if he'd simply wanted her dead, he could have killed her in the cabin and saved himself the trouble. He wanted something more from her, her death probably planned as a public spectacle. Whether he intended to use it for a coup or to garner favor with her brother, he'd be disappointed.

Sure, the amulet limited her options, but with calm and vigilance, she would find a way.

Anger flashed in Laisren's muddy-brown eyes, and he sliced through the cloth of her shirt, leaving it in tatters. The greedy gazes of the other dragons traced the revealed skin as if they'd never seen a female this close.

"As Tasuna"—Laisren bent in a sarcastic half bow—"refuses to speak, I suppose we'll let actions speak for us as well."

A sharp point dug briefly into her shoulder before slicing down her arm, the fabric of her tee swinging away to hang from the other shoulder. Seraphina wrapped herself in glamour, which didn't stop him from tearing away whatever remained of her shirt but did prevent any of her captors from seeing her exposed.

Her satisfaction from thwarting him in this small way may have been petty, except that the eagerness in the other dragons' eyes was disgusting. And just a smidge disconcerting while she remained chained.

Laisren's expression held only derision and loathing as he sliced into her hip when cutting away her shorts. She couldn't stop the blood from dripping down her leg, but she let the pain fuel her resolve. All he got for his trouble was her perfected slow blink.

With another searing swipe across her abdomen, he spun away. His henchmen eyed her, confused gazes moving from the glamoured burlap sack draping her from shoulder to knee, to the scraps of cloth by her feet. The sickly warm trickle of her blood probably dotted the fabric. Throwing uneasy glances over their shoulders, the pair nevertheless followed Laisren to the mouth of the cave.

"She'll wear herself out quickly," he said, neither lowering his voice nor using telepathy. He *wanted* her to hear.

Seraphina pulled herself up on the chains then slowly lowered as close to the ground as she could get. The shackles bit into her wrists, but the balls of her feet now grazed the dirt.

"A power she *stole* from us all," Laisren announced, obviously in response to something. "All you have to do is watch her. Don't get too close."

"What if she, you know…" The taller of the two henchmen threw another worried glance over his shoulder. In the light from the entrance, his brown skin had a tinge of green, as if somewhere in his line the tribes had mixed. It wasn't common, but neither was it unordinary. He threw a disgusted look back at her.

Laisren met her gaze, satisfaction tightening his cheeks. Apparently some things were worth keeping private among them.

Ignoring the hesitation of his lackeys, he took a few steps out of the cave. His true bulk shadowed the entrance before he flew off. So they weren't in the mortal realm.

The lackeys huddled together, throwing glances her way but not speaking aloud. Seraphina inhaled past the stinging ache of the slashes on her abs and hip, exhaling as she pulled herself up on the chains again to change which muscles were pained by her position. The amulet didn't make her quite as weak as a human, but it was close. She needed to act while she could to ease the strain on her body. As it was, the glamour was draining her, but there was no way she was giving it up. Not yet, anyway.

With the lackeys distracted, she repeated the movement several more times until the links eased enough that the balls of her feet landed solidly on the ground. Her breath caught with her relief, and the shorter lackey's head jerked toward her. Seraphina swallowed roughly, holding her breath until he was satisfied she hadn't somehow freed herself and refocused on his coconspirator.

Seraphina shifted her shoulders to ease the burning in the tight muscles. Standing on her tiptoes for however long she'd be chained wasn't her idea of a good time, but it was a serious improvement.

The flunkies with a ticking clock over their heads kept shooting her furtive looks from the shadows, but as long as they stayed there, she could lose herself to imagining their gruesome deaths. For all that she'd abandoned their brutality, she was still a dragon.

Chapter 17

CURSING HIS HELPLESSNESS, AZAR PACED THE SMALL CABIN for hours after Laisren and the others disappeared with Inna. How had they found this place? He certainly hadn't expected them to show up and carry her off, all his protests ignored. They'd had an easy time of it, with her rendered unconscious by a creature barely the size of his palm.

"You did well," Laisren had claimed, as if Azar's part in the fight to save the dragons was over.

He should have felt relieved. The whole point had been to find the Zubir's sister and bring her back. But not like this. They'd *said* they would do whatever was necessary, but abducting her in her sleep? He didn't even know where they'd taken her. Wherever it was, she would be far less inclined to help when she awoke.

Azar had expected Laisren to know how to get through to her, and maybe the old dragon would. Maybe she was fine—

safe and sound and formulating a plan with the help of Laisren and the others he considered his comrades in arms.

The roiling in Azar's gut contested that possibility. It had felt so right contacting them, exactly like he'd been supposed to.

But nothing about how they'd stolen her in the middle of the night was right. Especially when Laisren declared there was no reason for Azar to go with them.

Nausea climbing up his throat, he deviated from the path he'd been following around the great room to make it outside to the deck. His legs rushed him down the short staircase to the path they'd taken together just the day before. Staring at the trees and vines around him, Azar fell to his knees.

"Please," he said aloud, unsure if any of the creatures she'd been concerned he'd find out here were telepathic. "Please, help me help her. If any of you can hear me, if you know In—" He swallowed, already used to the alias, but it wasn't her true name. "If you know Seraphina Ignatia, if you care for her, or you know what she means to the dragons. Please help me."

Predictably, there was no response.

He sank back onto his heels, dipping his head back to stare at the unblemished blue sky, his lungs working overtime. "Please," he whispered.

On his own, he couldn't even return home to talk to his contacts, try to convince them to reveal her whereabouts. *He* was the one who'd found her, but that didn't change that he was trapped here now. Besides, there was no way he could take on all the dragons working with Laisren on his own.

And if he did free her—and he was growing more certain by the minute that she needed to be freed—where would they even go? They couldn't safely hide in Azhidar Zher, and taking her to the sobran to escape through the portal risked forcing her to face her brother before she was ready. Besides, he didn't have her resources to conceal them in the mortal realm again.

His shoulders bent, head dropping as he held back the screams or sobs building into an aching ball of pressure in his torso.

She would hate him for not listening to her. For thinking he knew better. For trusting Laisren. For not finding a way to remove the amulet that hindered her before they'd taken her complacent body.

For not shifting and stopping them, consequences be damned.

Azar pounded his fist into the ground, the echo of his claws slicing furrows into the dirt. Clumps flung through the air, spraying back to the ground.

He had to *act*. But how?

Lifting his face to the tree line, he repeated, "Please. Help me help her." For hours, his mouth dry and voice going hoarse, he beseeched the air and whatever creatures might stumble upon him. "If you know Seraphina Ignatia, blood sister of the dragons' Zubir, please help me. Help me save her."

Shortly after darkness fell, a new face for her list replaced the two who'd spent the day watching her.

Hours before, the greener one had approached warily with a wide bowl of sorts. Noting the fire in her eyes, he'd warned, "You try and kick me, I'll knock you out."

It wasn't a threat so much as a guarantee. He probably wasn't one of the strongest Drevno, but compared to her weakened state, he'd barely have to try to render her unconscious. And she had to stay awake, alert. Not only did losing consciousness mean being unable to maintain the glamour that shielded her body from their eyes, but it also meant an intolerable helplessness, with no way to know who did what to her.

So she hadn't moved as he'd quickly positioned the bowl between her feet.

She also hadn't used it, though her bladder wasn't especially pleased with that decision despite the thirst sucking all the moisture from her throat. She simply couldn't bring herself to do it, the humiliation winning out. That shame was exactly what Laisren wanted her to feel, hoping to break her, which was the main thing preventing her from kicking the bowl into the cavern wall.

The two torches lit on either side of her were there for the same reason, none of the dragons needing the light to see. But keeping her illuminated meant she had more reason to keep the glamour firmly in place, and it left her jailors in shadow.

Or it would, if the night guard hadn't wandered into the pool of light, sipping casually from a leather skin. "Want some?" he taunted, holding it out toward her with a smug grin. "Oh, I forgot. Tasuna can't move."

He sauntered closer, dematerializing his tunic to reveal the rich burnt sienna that was wasted on him. He tilted the skin, still out of reach, obviously hoping she'd strain for the liquid within. When she didn't move, malice flashed in his eyes. "Fine," he said, letting red fluid dribble onto the dirt. "Waste my generosity."

He turned his back, walking beyond the light so she couldn't quite make him out in the shadows. His steps stalked around her in circles, eyes presumably on her. Seraphina fixed her gaze on the blackness of the cave's entrance, tracking his moving shadow with her peripheral vision.

The gashes from earlier had eventually stopped bleeding, but the muscles in her legs were already shaking, ready to give out. Her arms and shoulders burned. Still she wrapped her fingers more firmly around the chains, gritting her teeth as she pulled her weight up enough to give her legs a few seconds of rest.

She would survive. She wouldn't allow Laisren or his flunkies to break her. She would not cry, no matter how the part of her brain feeling every way her body hurt wanted to.

She couldn't afford to lose the liquid, anyway, as each of the new lackey's loud slurps reminded her.

"Well, there goes the wine," he said eventually, tossing the skin aside as the torch to her right burned out, deepening the shadows. He stalked slowly toward her. The second torch illuminated the mix of entitlement, lust, and anticipation on his face.

Still he was wise enough to stop too far for her legs to lash out effectively. One hand cupped his crotch.

Seraphina forced calm into her expression. There were many things she'd learned among the humans, including the psychology of rapists. She wouldn't play into his fantasy of dominating a member of the zubiran line. Or maybe, any female.

"Tell you what," he said, his hand moving along the front of his pants, "I'll loosen the chains. Let you down on your knees if you suck me off like the humans do." He snorted. "Get some fluid in you."

Her stomach clenched at the idea, bile climbing her throat.

Would it be smarter to agree? The moment he loosened the chains enough for her hands to move, she could tear the pendant from her neck. With her full power, she could fight him, yank the chains free. Heal.

Would she be fast enough? He'd have to move to the wall to loosen the chains, but if he noticed her trying to get rid of the amulet, he could jerk them even more taut than they were now. If he was strong enough to wield his other form with pure power, his claws could force her to be still as he worked the chains, leaving her no chance. And no choice, once he'd literally forced her to her knees.

But there was one option still available to her.

Steeling herself, she focused a fresh deep breath on relaxing the necessary muscles. It was the right call, the best option.

Despite the logic, it took a few breaths before she succeeded, finally relieving the pressure in her bladder.

With a roar of disgust, he jerked forward long enough to backhand her across the face. Her ears ringing, she barely made out his steps moving away.

Blood trickled into her mouth, and his cursing filled the cavern. Her fingers spasmed weakly around the chains as she clung to consciousness. Still, Seraphina smiled.

Chapter 18

RIT WAS AN INTERESTING WORD. THE GRIT SCRATCHING AT Seraphina's eyes with every blink, coating her tongue and teeth, choking her every attempt at swallowing? That grit was bad.

The grit that let her stay upright despite the pain stabbing through her nerves, and even keep glamour shielding her body? That grit was good.

Gritting her jaw as she fought the pain probably fell into the *bad* category. Especially since it worsened the throbbing in her face.

Seraphina inhaled past the blood burbling in her nose, running through the growing list of dragons who would, one way or another, face her wrath. Yesterday's shorter Drevan had returned for the day shift, replacing the one from the night before, who'd decided to stay away until the sun rose. A red female appeared throughout the day to exchange silent words with Seraphina's equally silent guard, always handing him a full wineskin as if the reminder of water would be enough to destroy her. But the quiet simply let her alternate between planning her revenge and mentally listening to every Broadway number she could remember. "Raise a Little Hell" cycled through her head a few times.

It wasn't until sunset colored the field outside her cell that the red dragon approached, swinging a skin that was still half full. Had Laisren persuaded a Radan to join his cause, or was she one of those rare dragons living in a tribe outside their coloring?

Her lip curled as her eyes ran over the glamoured burlap, growing thin in carefully chosen places.

Seraphina's swollen lips protested as she parted them to ask, "What did he tell you?" The words were as dry as her mouth, barely audible. "To make you hate me like this."

The red, whose coloring was really more the kind of magenta mortals would have deemed unnatural, was tall enough that she needed to look down to meet Seraphina's eyes. "Your family ruined us," she said under her breath, her lips twitching with rage.

"But the Zubir loves waste." Anger twisted into warped satisfaction as she upended the wineskin. The liquid flowed into the dirt, stray droplets spraying Seraphina's legs. "There's your water." Her shoulders rose and fell with ragged breaths, her fingers digging into the emptied skin as if she were fighting to keep herself under control. "Be grateful Laisren has plans for you. Or I would tear into that pampered waste of a body right here."

"Jillianne," the daytime guard called. He'd been joined by another brown, this one with magenta streaks in his chestnut hair and the same black eyes as the red female. Seraphina would have easily bet one of her fortunes they were related.

Granted, right now, she would have readily spent that fortune on a sip of water. She blew out a breath shaky with the tears she wouldn't allow. Information mattered more, no matter how she grieved the wasted droplets turned to mud.

The new dragon threw Seraphina a glance before peering outside the cave. If he hadn't kept looking back over his shoulder, she would have forced her muscles to lift, to try to pry off the amulet.

She probably would have failed. In all her decades among the mortals, her magically hindered body hadn't felt this weak.

When he was satisfied the others had left, her newest guard swung his own bulging skin off his shoulder. He walked toward her confidently but not smugly, stopping short of the mud with a frown. He stared at it awhile, forehead furrowed like he was wrestling whatever remained of his conscience.

Then his black eyes, with their tiny red flecks that glinted in the torchlight, met hers. "Don't try anything, and I'll give you water."

Was this Laisren's next attempt at getting to her? "Why?" she croaked.

He shrugged, finally coming up with, "Laisren wants you alive."

Something she already knew. Either this was someone who followed every order to the letter, trying to rectify the female going off script, or this show of kindness was a trap. "You first," Seraphina rasped out.

Confusion startled him back a bit, but he caught himself before retreating too far. The exact moment he understood her request was written all over his features. He uncapped the skin and held it above his lips, letting her see the water pour from its neck into his mouth. So unless they'd thought to give him the antidote beforehand, it likely wasn't poisoned. Probably worth the risk.

When he met her eyes again, Seraphina nodded. He warily took a step forward. When she didn't kick out at him—not that she could have done much damage at this point—he moved closer, lifting the skin close to her lips but still low enough that she would have had to strain, bow her head to reach it. He frowned again when she wouldn't submit.

Then his expression cleared, his eyes almost gentle as he re-positioned the skin more comfortably for her. She would have liked to ask what he was doing there, lacking both the animosity and the blind obedience of the others. But after the betrayal that had landed her here, she knew better than to trust what she saw in these dragons' eyes. And she wouldn't risk a flash of temper stealing her water again.

She parted her lips, closing the remaining distance between her and the relief of cool water flowing over her tongue, down her scratchy throat, easing at least that much of her discomfort. He waited as she gulped down nearly half the skin, finally stopping to catch her breath.

The water hovered between them like he didn't know what to do next.

Seraphina licked over the cut in her swollen lip. "You could let me go, you know." It was worth a shot. Some part of her didn't want him on her list.

The words spurred him into action, his feet ushering him back beyond the limited reach of her legs. Something close to regret crossed his features before they resettled into determined stone. "Whatever it takes to save the dragons."

He spun away, walking toward the cave's entrance to take up the previous guard's spot, eyes trained firmly but blankly on her, watching for movement but no longer seeing *her*. Just the mission, whatever the hell that was. This one was as convinced as Azar had been that following Laisren's plan was the sole path to salvation. That plan was seeming more and more like an outright coup, killing her and somehow taking out her brother as well.

Despite Laisren's undeniable ability to convince others to obey his orders, he'd made at least one mistake that would corrode the very foundation of that plan. Seraphina's line had self-selected for generations for the strongest, arguably most brutal, among them. Her bloodline might have landed her here, but her heritage meant she would survive.

And take her revenge.

Chapter 19

A S DUSK TRANSITIONED TO TRUE NIGHTTIME, AZAR LANDED softly on the edge of the clearing where Laisren had for decades now gathered those intent on finding Seraphina to save dragonkind. Dragons Azar had planned with, trained with, even, in some cases, considered friends.

Several of them now sat in small clusters, all in human form. They'd all gotten into the habit to fend off the persistent hunger of never having enough to fill a dragon's belly.

Azar stifled the pang of guilt as he shifted back into human form as well. The frozen meat he'd taken from the cabin and stashed among the gnarled roots of an oak belonged to Seraphina. If he was wrong and she was fine, she could choose to share. Likely would.

In truth, it made little sense for her to be anything other than fine. From everything Laisren had told Azar before sending him to the mortal realm, she should be training for the maros. Remaining out of sight of most dragons, certainly, but perfectly healthy.

Except then why abduct her as she slept?

No one paid him much attention as he strode up to join the gathering. Seraphina wasn't among them, despite the fact that none but those working together with Laisren would come here. Like several of the oldest dragons, he had claimed a small amount of land at the edge of the Drevan territory as his.

He stood now from his throne-like seat made of stumps covered in hides. *What are you doing back?* he asked mind to mind.

Azar didn't approach. There was no need when telepathic communication could be kept between only them. *I'm not expected back at the university. I came to help with whatever's next.* He didn't elaborate on how he'd managed to return without an item of power doled out by the dragon he'd foolishly trusted.

Laisren's eyes narrowed shrewdly on him. *We have it well in hand. Go. I'll let you know if you're needed.*

I want to help, Azar insisted. *I found her for you, like you wanted.* And he may never forgive himself for it. *I can help her ready for the maros.*

Laisren lowered casually back to his seat. The dragons between them paid them no mind, likely having their own silent conversations as they gnawed on bones nearly picked clean.

We work as a collective here, he said. *There's no room for individual agendas. You've clearly grown attached to the Zubir's sister. If you're no longer ready to do what it takes...*

That sense of foreboding grew into a sucking pit in Azar's gut. *My goals are the same as they've always been.* Though now it seemed those goals weren't actually aligned with Laisren's, even though the older dragon had cultivated them. Still Azar repeated the mantra by which they'd all lived. *Whatever it takes to save the dragons.*

As I said, Laisren responded, unyielding, *I'll let you know.* He smiled magnanimously, gesturing to an empty space not far from Azar. *Meanwhile, as the humans say, take a load off.*

With a sharp nod, Azar obeyed, striding over to a cluster that included Tapio and Gonsal. Both had been at the cabin. Exchanging greetings, he lowered to the ground and was instantly handed a leather skin filled with the fermented grape juice the Drevno enjoyed, even if it paled in comparison to the wines of the humans.

Since there was a limit to how much the dragons could physically bring with them from that realm, and they didn't on the whole attempt to emulate the humans, the tools mortals had developed weren't available in Azhidar Zher. Generally, the dragons had no need, even if they sometimes enjoyed indulging. This lightly fermented juice had mostly been a whim of the first Drevan netta to live in this realm, who'd brought over a treasured grape plant, which now grew unkempt on a piece of their lands. Tradition kept it harvested and processed. Tradition and the variety it offered from their pure water.

"And here's the guy responsible!" Neske clapped him on the shoulder, speaking aloud so their entire cluster could hear. The more dragons involved, the more power it took to speak mind to mind.

Azar choked down his guilt with a sip from the wineskin. He grinned modestly, acting the part of one who had accomplished what they'd all wanted, and passed the skin back to Gonsal. Did the others know where Seraphina was? Had they known what would happen to her once she was found?

"How'd you get the pirha to trust you?" asked Spirula, Tapio's mate who'd always rubbed Azar the wrong way for some reason he'd never bothered to pinpoint.

He lay back onto his elbows, as if there were nothing more important than recounting his exploits for the others' praise. "Told her what she needed to hear," he said aloud for Laisren's benefit. The older dragon still watched Azar, who watched him in turn out of the corner of his eye.

Tapio leaned closer. "Did you hear what she did to Egill?" He jerked upright, throwing a glance over at Laisren as if he'd been directed not to share that particular tidbit. It sounded as though Seraphina was fighting back.

"Anyone know where Koios is?" Azar redirected. Of all the dragons in their faction, Koios was the only one Azar had considered a friend before joining their cause. Since he wasn't here, he could have been pretty much anywhere in Azhidar Zher, even if he would have avoided the sobran if at all possible. He would also easily share anything he knew about Seraphina, and Laisren's plans.

"Guard duty." Neske snorted. "Probably pissed *himself* by now," she added, making the others laugh, even as she earned a growl from Laisren.

Azar sat up, frowning at her. "He's one of us."

Gonsal muttered, "Some of us are more useful than others."

"He's doing his duty while we're loafing around here," Azar pointed out. *Guard duty* didn't sound good. But everyone knew he and Koios were friends. It would be only natural for Azar to seek him out now that he'd returned.

"And I was stuck in that cave all day," Tapio grumbled. "While you were, what? Playing with the humans?"

"My reward for a job well done," Azar countered, fighting every instinct to leap up and head straight to the mountainside filled with caverns and crannies. Laisren could have scouted any one of them for his more secret business. Azar couldn't leave so abruptly without arousing suspicion. More likely being stopped on Laisren's orders and ending up somewhere needing to be "guarded" himself.

Besides, he needed time to contact the mysterious ally who'd gifted him the charmed stone that allowed his return home. And to formulate a plan for escaping with Seraphina. Patience was his friend, but he would find her, even if he had to check every single cave in the Drevan territory.

Laisren might very well have some complex plan in place to save the dragons. But the only thing Azar cared about now was saving *her*.

Chapter 20

"THERE YOU ARE," SAID A VOICE SHE NEVER WANTED TO HEAR again.

The newbie guard stiffened, standing up straight from the cave wall he'd been leaning against.

Seraphina's fingers tightened on the chains, her jaw clenching as a trickle of adrenaline tried its best to revive her.

The dragon who'd betrayed her barely spared her a glance before turning his back, but she could have sworn it had been hatred in his eyes. Maybe all she saw was a reflection of hers.

In his carelessness, he'd stepped in front of her guard, leaving her free from both their gazes.

Seraphina let the glamour she'd been clinging to drop. She gasped in relief of saving even that bit of energy, then bit her lip—and winced at the stab of pain. Still, the renewed flow of air into her lungs couldn't risk calling the attention of the dragons at the entrance.

"You're not supposed to be here," the Drevan she didn't entirely want to kill said under his breath.

The other didn't answer aloud. From the netted bag slung across his torso, he withdrew a bottle of beer. Seraphina would have rolled her eyes if her eyelids hadn't already felt like sandpaper.

His carefree laugh slammed against her carefully erected defenses, overwhelming her with the urge to rage against her chains despite the damage that would do to her. She'd very nearly *trusted* him, believed those false promises falling from his lips.

She should have killed him back at the mansion.

As the newbie guard took the bottle, his hand drifted down, resettling the bag behind his hip. He patted it twice, and little sparks of light flew out. Seraphina's eyes narrowed on the flickers as she forced fresh glamour into place.

The differently colored lights sped across the cave, two zipping into her hair as a pink-and-yellow one hovered briefly in front of her, a delicate finger placed to impishly curved lips.

Seraphina held still, ignoring the tugs on her scalp as the third one joined its friends. "The amulet," she breathed, far too quietly for the other dragons to hear. If the sprites undid the clasp, she could get out of here. Regroup and plan her next moves.

"Not yet," a little voice whispered back.

The guard dragon shuffled out from behind the other, though he barely glanced her way, content to see her unmoved.

"You won't believe the taste," Azar said aloud.

Anticipation clear on his face, the guard undid the stopper in the bottle, lifting it toward his comrade before taking a swig.

Surprise rounded his eyes as he turned the bottle to check out the label. "That's spectacular," he said, a genuine grin on his face.

"Thought you'd like it. Come find me when you're done here." Azar sauntered out without a backward glance.

The guard took another swig of the beer, then shot her a guilty glance. Shaking himself out of some internal argument, he resumed his previous post, occasionally lifting the bottle to his lips. Still the sprites didn't move, even their minimal extra weight an added layer of pain pulling on her head, her neck. But with his eyes glued to her, she couldn't risk asking them anything.

Had that glimmer of hope been nothing more than calculated manipulation?

As the night wore on, she contemplated shaking the little creatures from her hair. The guard's eyelids drooped, and he jerked himself out of the desire to sleep, rewarding himself with more beer. Little giggles floated around her ears.

"Soon now," that tinkling voice murmured to her. "Matera said the amulet stays on or they'll catch you."

Hearing her friend's formal title, knowing a true ally was involved, almost brought Seraphina to tears.

But this could all still be a trick. Even if it wasn't, she would need all of her energy, all the focus she could muster to do whatever was needed next.

When the guard slumped against the cave wall, sliding down until he landed on his butt, the beer bottle lax in his hand, two sprites flew out of her hair and up to her wrists. As nimble fingers worked to undo the restraints, the third returned to her place in front of Seraphina's face.

"Thank you," Seraphina mouthed.

The sprite nodded, then flew to her ear. "Follow us," she whispered as for the first time in days Seraphina's arms fell to her sides, her weight fully on her feet.

Every cell in her body screamed at the pain, the unhealed gashes in her torso protesting the loudest. She hissed in as quiet a breath as she could but obeyed, stumbling her way out of the cave.

She would have paused to embrace the fresh air, to rest for the briefest moment against the side of the mountain, but the sprites urged her on, tiny fingers and flutters of wing pushing at her shoulders.

So on raw feet, her body intolerably sore, the wound at her hip reopening to bleed anew, she staggered, clutching the plants and rock rising to her right for balance. When the little creatures ducked into a new cave, she steeled herself against the hope that there, finally, she could tear off the charm that bound her to this weakness.

Instead of safety, she found Azar.

With a scrap of parchment in one hand and charcoal in the other, he sighed in obvious, erroneous relief.

Seraphina's lip curled as the coal finished a pattern on the cavern wall.

When he looked back to her, Azar's hope melted into blankness. "We don't have much time."

"You sure as hell don't," she managed through her dry throat, her raw lips.

The sprites zipped into a floating triangle between them. Their leader did a nervous little twirl in the air, her hands spread out as if to call for peace. With her focus back on Seraphina, she said, "The Mother of Muses said to take him with you."

The old, unused title got Seraphina's attention, as it was meant to. She nodded, limping closer to the symbols he'd drawn, the sprites flitting out of her way.

With a mumble more so than an incantation, Azar read from the directions in his hands, opening a hazy wall of fog where the cavern wall used to be. He watched her, but she turned back to the sprites. Muscles fought her as she tried to lift her hand in acknowledgment, thanks, and goodbye all in one.

As one, the three dipped in the air, their wings fanning air onto her hand as they passed their own fingers over the raw wounds, easing that bit of pain before winking out of sight.

"How—" Azar asked, but her angry look cut him off. "Please," he murmured instead, gesturing to the opening.

"You first," she countered. Azar may be too young to know about the Mother of Muses, but Laisren wasn't. Seraphina's desperation to find safety couldn't overtake her reason. She couldn't afford to let her guard down again.

Surprise or confusion or something she was too worn out to interpret flowed across his expression before he nodded and stepped into the mist. Huffing through gritted teeth, Seraphina wrapped her fingers around the amulet, ready for whatever waited on the other side.

Chapter 21

AZAR BARELY HAD TIME TO GET HIS BEARINGS BEFORE Seraphina, thankfully, appeared beside him in the lush, empty field. He turned toward her, materializing a cloak and pulling it off to cover her body in place of her fading glamour. "I'm so sorry." The apology died on his lips as she spared a derisive glance for his cloak before refocusing her fury on him.

He dropped to his knees in the high grass seconds before her amulet fell to the ground, freeing her power. Instantly her legs were hidden behind a loose white skirt, the raw skin on her wrists healed. He didn't dare look up to see more, bowing his head lower. He couldn't imagine what she thought of him now.

Or rather he could, but didn't want to.

The moment he'd seen her strung up in chains, the entire side of her face a mess of purples unnatural even for her, his own fury had burned through him. Had anyone else been guarding her, Azar may have forgotten any reason or strategy and slain the other dragon on the spot. How could any of them have condoned that kind of treatment, of *anyone* much less the one dragon capable of saving them all?

After this, he wouldn't blame her if she turned her back on the dragons and never looked back. He was tempted to do the same.

How could Laisren have had this planned all along, even as he'd convinced Azar all he wanted was to save their kind? To find her, reason with her. Help her triumph in the maros. It had been all the older dragon talked about, thought about.

"I didn't know," Azar breathed to the ground, hating himself for his blindness. Had he been the only one who hadn't seen the truth? Those he'd spoken with beside the fire had seemed to know what had been done, had even helped to make it happen. Even Koios had participated…

How could they have let this happen?

How could he—

Seraphina leapt into the air and dove into the lake beside them, jolting him from his thoughts. Long moments later, she surfaced in her true form, flaring her wings out with twin sprays of water. Edged in her stunning purples and blues, those wings settled briefly at her sides before her body was propelled once more through the air. She landed elegantly in front of him.

Azar gaped at the splashes of color kissing her brilliant white, the lovely line of her neck. He zeroed in on the pink slashes marring her scales, and the pit of guilt within him yawned larger.

She snarled at him, a lick of flame coming to her lips.

He dropped his gaze back to the ground. *My deepest apologies*, he repeated. *I never meant—*

Enough. I don't need your lies.

He deepened his bow even further. *I found you as quickly as I could.* Still his chest ached with his failure, that he'd gotten her captured in the first place.

Oh yeah? she countered. *Which time?*

Azar's consternation pressed against Seraphina's mind as his spun in response to her question. He didn't move from his low bow, so she shut her eyes, taking just one moment for herself.

Even with the amulet off, finally back in her true form, her body remained sore. Not for long. She could feel the gashes from Laisren's claws knitting closed as she stood under the warm sun. Normally, those swipes wouldn't have left scars at all, but her healing had been delayed too long. At least the rest of her injuries had become nothing but a gradually lightening ache, demanding less attention now than her exhaustion.

Here in this miniature realm, her dehydration abated by a deep gulp from the same lake that had eased her pain, all she wanted was to cry or sleep or both. She could do neither until she was safe.

With Azar there, she still wasn't.

For all her anger and resentment, she had to think strategically. She could make him tell her everything he knew, about the dragons in general, but more importantly about Laisren's plans. Even if Azar were telling the truth about being kept out of the loop, there would be useful information in what he shared.

So once again, she was stuck with him until she made up her mind on how to dispose of him.

He crouched on the ground, bent nearly in half, as if that display of subservience would change anything. *Tasuna, please,* he said in Drakonazyk, and for once she didn't correct him. *I didn't know he'd—*

Quiet. She was so sick of him claiming he didn't know something. His ignorance—at best—had led to her being strung up in chains. To a night spent practically powerless with her would-be rapist lurking in the dark.

Seraphina pushed back the memory. There would be time to process and feel it all later, once she was safely alone.

Get up, she growled to the dragon cowering before her, smoke curling at her lips with her irritation.

He hesitated then unbent gradually, as if expecting her to attack at any moment. Even standing straight, in his mortal form his size was hardly comparable to hers. Still he met her gaze head on, filling his expression with sorrow and guilt. As if that would make her forget the threat he posed.

Tell me everything, she commanded.

I don't know what happened. He shook his head, his eyes dancing around unevenly. "Years," he said aloud, refocusing on her. "*Years* he spent convincing us... Or, me. That finding you was the key to saving the dragons."

A faint whiff of meat distracted her from Azar's bewilderment, her hunger finally overtaking her rage. All the energy healing required had left her ravenous. But there was no meat, no animal life at all in this secret little realm.

And if he hadn't lied about *everything* before, the rest of the dragons had been living with hunger for decades at least...

She dragged her attention back to Azar, but he'd stopped speaking. Realization sparked in his eyes. *You're hungry.*

No shit, Sherlock, she thought, careful to shield the response from him. A frustrated growl escaped her nonetheless.

His hands came up as if to pacify her, reminding her of humans faced with guns. She was far more dangerous. But then, so was he.

"I didn't know," he said, "what happened to you after— I didn't know if you'd be…" He stopped, gathered himself, and finally said, *I brought you meat.*

His hand dipped into the bag that had carried the means of her escape, slowly reappearing along with some of the steaks from her fridge.

She scoffed, and it came out like a huffing snort. *Poisoned like the beer?* It was the only explanation for why her guard had passed out. Certainly the alcohol content wouldn't have sufficed.

Azar startled at the accusation. "No, I—" A flicker of his own fire squared his shoulders and his jaw. *I was worried about you. I didn't know, but after what happened at the cabin, I was worried they would—* He lifted the steaks in offering rather than finish the thought, as if whatever he would say could be worse than living through it. *I took the frozen ones, so they should still be fresh enough.*

The steaks were generous in size, but not compared to her current form. Without the amulet, she could hold her own against him, whatever form she was in. Seraphina shifted, wrapping herself in a soft sweater and loose pants that shouldn't irritate her skin too much.

Azar's arm dropped as he looked down into her face. "I'm so sorry," he breathed.

She ignored the empty words, unwrapping one of the steaks and tearing into it. A deep, dark part of her didn't even care if the meat was poisoned, if this was the moment she died.

But that capitulation was at least in part a trick of her mind, spurred on by her hunger. So she kept chewing, kept swallowing.

Unwrapping a second thick cut of beef, she instructed, *Continue. For decades he brainwashed you. And then?*

That expedient concern of his faded into a blank determination. "I sent him a message from your device," he admitted, choosing to use his voice perhaps so his heavy sigh could punctuate the words. "I asked for his counsel, didn't say anything about where we were."

I don't care, she interrupted as her jaw worked, juices from the not entirely defrosted meat coating her fingers, trickling down her chin. His words confirmed Laisren worked with someone skilled at tracking via human technology, but she had been working under that assumption anyway. The question remained how they managed to communicate between the realms. Yet another to add to her list and figure out later.

"I don't know why he would—" Azar swallowed roughly, his head shaking. *Please understand,* he continued, his words a mix of telepathy and voice, "I have no idea why after all that he would, *any* of them would… All I've heard for *years* is how critical you are to our survival, and I believe that." *I believed him.* Rough exhales added texture to his voice. "Over and over, he told us that the most important thing was finding the lost heir, convincing you that—"

"*What* did you just say?" Seraphina interrupted, forgetting the meat she hadn't consumed yet.

Azar gaped at her, bewildered by her vehemence.

"The most important thing was…" she prompted impatiently.

"Finding the lost heir, the key to saving the dragons."

The laugh bubbling up out of her throat sounded vaguely hysterical to her ears, but Seraphina couldn't stop it. It morphed into something manic, then disappeared into the unadulterated silence around them.

He wants to find the lost heir, she repeated slowly. "And because you're a *child*," she snarled, advancing on the confused Drevan, "you thought he meant me."

"Who else could he mean?" Azar asked.

Before the last word had fallen from his lips, Seraphina was flying toward the tree line, all her fury and exhaustion and pain pouring out in a torrent of flame.

Chapter 22

CONFUSION SLOWED AZAR'S RESPONSE AT FIRST AS SERAPHINA flew off. Then wonder and appreciation for her beauty and might held him in place as her fire filled the sky, stopping carefully short of the trees. Her pain echoed under the rage of her roar, and still she was magnificent.

He knew nothing of this place, except for some unnerving sense he hadn't had a chance to piece together. It was neither Earth nor Azhidar Zher. The Mother of Muses hadn't bothered to inform him how they would leave, saying something cryptic about him figuring it out if he deserved to. She had sworn Seraphina would be safe here.

Nevertheless Azar shifted, winging after her. Keeping his distance, he tracked her, alert for any sign of trouble. Laisren might have intentionally misled him, the "lost heir" a misdirection Azar didn't understand, but he knew with an unshakeable certainty that Seraphina mattered. To the future of the dragons, but also to him in a way he hadn't had time to consider ever since she'd been stolen from her bed and he'd been unable to do much more than watch.

He'd failed her once, but he'd never fail her again. Whatever it took, he would keep her safe.

Back off, she commanded.

Azar slowed, circling low over the field with the lake. What lay beyond the trees?

Seraphina flew higher, neck outstretched and wings moving in sure, even strokes, strong despite what she'd suffered. But if she faltered at this height, the fall could be catastrophic. Azar climbed after her, positioning himself to catch her should fatigue or injury overtake her body. Smaller than him, she was still big enough to take them both down, but he could at least ease her fall.

Fire snaked out her throat, singeing the air between them. *I know you heard me.*

He adjusted his trajectory, keeping pace with her but not climbing higher. He deserved all her anger and more, but with her not at full strength, her current flight was reckless.

Beneath all that fury, she was pragmatic and reasonable. So perhaps he could redirect it by offering the problem he hadn't yet solved. *Are you seeking a way out?*

This high, he could see the trees ringing the field lay like a thick but patchy carpet until they reached the foothills of an oval of low mountains. Haze lay beyond them, but every pocket of land obscured by the trees may hold the secret to returning to one of the realms they knew. The winding gaps that likely signified a pair of streams might be a good place to start.

When he didn't hear a response, Azar sped up to fly closer in case the distance between them had grown too great.

Last warning. Even in his head, he could hear the growl in the words.

I wasn't sure you—

Her neck swiveled so she had him in her sights, and her body wrenched sharply around in the air. Her wings seemed to shimmer in the sun as she maintained her position.

Azar veered off his course so he wouldn't be heading straight for her. *Tasuna, please. You may not believe it right now, but my only aim is to protect you.* There may be plenty he didn't know—undeniably more than he'd realized—but he trusted his body, his agility, his strength.

She dove for him with a roar. The draft from her wings caught him as he jerked away. He twisted to face her, instinct taking over, muscles relishing the exercise. He had far more practice handling physical attacks than the roiling masses of her fury and his guilt.

Her smaller body hovered slightly higher than his, taking the strategic position, amethyst eyes snapping. Smoke curled out of her nostrils. Her claws twitched, betraying her intent to attack toward his head. Azar swiveled away.

His left wing caught in one of hers. The signal he'd read—a feint! Tightening her wing in a sort of spiral movement around the joint of his, immobilizing it, she dove, propelling them both toward the ground.

He craned his neck back. His free wing fought fruitlessly to slow their drop. A vicious blast of flame had him ducking, losing focus for precious seconds.

Did she realize his greater bulk meant he needed more time to reverse course? If she didn't let go soon, let him come out of the dive, he'd be the one with catastrophic injuries—at best.

Panic sharpened his senses, every blade of grass a distinct point of color against the russet earth. *Tasuna, please.*

She didn't react, the ground rushing at them.

Please don't do this, he begged, pulse pounding. A strikingly clear image of his body destroyed by the impact, blood painting the grass, crystalized in his mind. He yanked on their joined wings, to no effect. *Please, Seraphina…*

With one quick motion, her wing unwound from his.

Still he almost crashed, the shock of her mercy making him nearly too late to react.

Adrenaline and relief coursing through him in equal measure, he shifted the moment he landed, falling to his knees not far from the lake where they'd started out. His muscles trembled as he fought to settle his breath.

She landed, too, seeming to shift midair and touch the ground already in human form. Before meeting her, he would have considered the trick impossible. The amulet he hadn't noticed her retrieving swung from her fingers as she stalked toward him. Azar bent until his forehead nearly touched the earth. The long blades of grass mimicked him, bending away from the force of her stride.

The stone dropped in front of him, catching the light of the sun. Its blood-red glint was menacing, but not as menacing as her command. *Pick it up.*

Swallowing, he unclenched one fist. He reached for the amulet slowly, willing control into the limb so it wouldn't waver. The moment his fingers closed around the stone, the world went dull. The charm was a crushing weight and a sucking force at once, leaving behind only helpless emptiness that threatened to collapse.

And she'd worn it for *centuries*.

"Look at me," she ordered, and he jerked his head back in trembling degrees, hardly able to force his body to obey.

He kept his gaze low, on her chin rather than her eyes. Her impatience rumbled through the air, and he rolled his eyes higher to find a steely resolve.

"Don't ever underestimate me again. I didn't kill you for your betrayal, but make no mistake"—she pried the enchanted stone from his fingers—"I will kill each and every one of them."

Azar's throat convulsed around his inhale, the flood of his power returning nearly bowling him over with its force.

Ignoring his wheezing gasps, she added, "And I sure as hell won't need your help to do it."

Chapter 23

Seraphina's breath huffed out as she spun away, her hair and skirt swaying in unison. Azar remained on the ground, flexing the power of his claws to help himself balance. Piecing together bits jangling around in his head, his brain tentatively resumed functioning.

Everything around them remained unnaturally immobile. Or maybe it only seemed that way to him, his nerves still jittering.

One realization pounded against his skull, insistent to the point of pain. "You could have won," he said on an exhale.

Weakened, not fully healed, undoubtedly still hungry, and yet it had taken her mere minutes to overpower him, a dragon nearly one and a half times her size. Azar had no delusions of being as strong as the Zubir, but if she could subdue him that quickly, she would have at least had a reasonable chance of triumphing against her brother.

She turned back to him, hostility sharpening her features. *What.* The syllable whispered in his mind, a nearly silent warning.

Overrun by all the stress and anxiety of the last several days, he couldn't hold back the question. *Why would you run?*

She'd brought up the obscure tradition threatening a victorious female, yet even then, she had seemed more resentful than scared. He'd assumed it was her refusal to return, her certainty she'd never face that threat. But she'd told him even then. *I'd make sure the dragons knew not to touch me.* Through zubiran decree or sheer force, she could have ensured none dared try, tradition or no.

A bitter, breathy chuckle deflated Seraphina's posture. Disappointed resignation transformed her features, world-weariness he'd seen at the cabin weighing down her shoulders despite the unyielding, captivating core that remained. "All those factions searching for me, everyone hating me for not submitting to the maros, labeling me weak. How is it not one of you misogynistic morons ever realized I left"—aggravation progressively colored her voice—"because I didn't want to *kill* my *brother.*"

Surprise played openly over Azar's expression, as if he'd truly never considered that that was what he'd been asking her to do. Kill not merely the mad Zubir, but her own flesh and blood.

Dragon siblings were rarely born in the same century, so they didn't grow up together in the way of the humans. And nevertheless, she'd lived her life with the presence of her older brother, even enjoyed his company as she'd aged.

Her first foray to live among the humans had undoubtedly altered her perspective on the maros as well, making it seem less like a necessity or an inevitability.

Except now apparently it was both.

The enormity of what she'd been through and had yet to face pushed against her skin from the inside as if she'd soon explode. There was only so long she could hold back the gathering torrent of tears. She needed to get out of here.

You don't know how to leave? she asked the dragon whose mere presence still fed that incendiary anger within her.

His head drooped with his regret, answering even before he'd said, *I don't.*

Good. Stay here. She started to turn away, but the mean, resentful part of her added, "Maybe I'll come back for you. But if you're not in sight of the lake when that happens, maybe I'll just leave you here."

He gaped at her, the dread of being abandoned overshadowing even his confusion.

She flew off before she could either double down or take it back, leaving behind the amulet he now knew better than to touch. She needed this time without it, and where she was going, it wouldn't be necessary.

Chapter 24

RHEA'S RECEPTION HALL WAS GRAND AND IMPOSING, MADE of white marble with undertones of pink and peach and yellow helping it seem warm. The pixies and nymphs flitting about the outer hall enhanced the sense of brimming life so at odds with the gleaming stone.

Wrapped in a softly draped floor-length white gown shot through with her purple and blue, Seraphina strode purposefully through the massive space. Unhesitating, she entered the inner receiving area and lowered to one knee before the verdant throne on which Matera rested. Gratitude and respect bowed Seraphina's head.

"Glad to see you safe, zubir's daughter," the ageless voice said.

"My sincerest gratitude for the role you played," Seraphina responded, equally formal.

"Leave us," Rhea commanded to the curious creatures surrounding them. Seconds later, only the two of them remained.

Seraphina raised her face to the ancient, timeless leader of the fae, who also dropped to her knees in the rich earth, despite her exalted station. A cool hand caressed Seraphina's face, her eyes prickling as the dam threatened to break. Here she was truly safe. Finally.

"Oh, Seraphina," her old friend said, a world of compassion in those words.

Before she knew it, Seraphina was sobbing, held up only by the solid grip encircling her, keeping her together. All the pain and terror of waking in chains, the threat of rape, the uncertainty of how she'd survive it all tore out of her throat, echoing off Rhea's enclosed inner sanctum. Time lost meaning, marked only by the cacophony of desperate sobs and ragged breaths.

When finally Seraphina's cries had settled into uneven gasps, Rhea maneuvered them onto the deceptively comfortable seat of plants that had woven itself wider. Her friend's hands came to Seraphina's cheeks, cradling them as her lungs struggled to find a smooth rhythm.

With the edge of her grief dulled, a riotous swirl of complexity remained. And yet, at last, it was easier to breathe.

Rhea's hands fell away, one clasping Seraphina's in her lap. If the space hadn't been magically soundproofed, the raw sounds of moments ago would have undoubtedly terrified the creatures remaining outside the grand doors. They'd terrified the part of Seraphina that had been cogent enough to hear them.

"Thank you for helping me. Again," she said, squeezing the fingers keeping her tethered. After a final calming breath, she let go, wiping at the tear tracks on her face before smoothing her skirts.

"You should thank the young dragon." At Seraphina's frown, Rhea added, "You aren't truly planning to abandon him."

"So much for privacy in Kansytura," Seraphina half joked. When she had left behind the dragon realm, it had been Rhea's network of loyal creatures that had created the amulet which had kept Seraphina safe for so long. Somehow, Rhea had also manifested the petite pocket realm in which Azar waited, a place for Seraphina to escape from the human world, for emergencies but also to have somewhere she could be her true self. Or more accurately, Rhea had had it created, since her own powers weren't that vast despite her seat on the High Council of the Fae.

Thousands of years old already when Seraphina and her brother had been introduced in preparation for filling the dragons' seat, the leader of the fae had found Seraphina refreshing, or amusing. The two had since formed one of the closest, and certainly most enduring, friendships of Seraphina's life.

"I can see it in your guilt," Rhea corrected now with that unflappable patience. Any strong emotion was transparent to her.

"Of course I won't." Nothing lived in Kansytura. Leaving Azar there would mean condemning him to die of starvation. Angry as she was, she had enough mercy left to offer a quicker death than that.

"I just needed some time, away from him," she confessed, rising to pace in the literally incomparable garden growing and changing according to Rhea's whim.

"You're angry with him."

"He betrayed me." She wouldn't have gone through any of that if not for his revealing her location to Laisren. Though if she went down that path, she never would have been put in that position if she'd simply left Pennsylvania as soon as she'd seen Azar.

But then she still wouldn't know what was happening with the dragons. With her brother.

"He's the reason you're free."

Seraphina paused, facing the one being she could truly rely on. "You're the reason I'm free."

Rhea's head tipped, her expression conveying volumes. It was the one she wore whenever Seraphina was, to her mind, acting younger than her years. With Azar around, she had fresh perspective on Rhea's side of that experience. Still she remained stubbornly silent, unable to feel anything beyond the anger and, yes, hurt.

"You think it was easy for him, to contact me? Hours he spent on his knees, begging the air for help. He would have spent hours more if Celestine hadn't heard a rumor from a tree nymph who loves to gossip."

What were those hours compared to the ones Seraphina had spent chained?

With a wave of her hand, Rhea materialized a stool right behind Seraphina, who lowered down onto it. The vines and leaves grew around her to create a molded seat.

"He is young," her friend admitted. "There is much he has yet to learn. Yet he also knows things you do not."

Seraphina's mouth opened to protest.

"Like when to ask for help," Rhea said pointedly. "He is right there, waiting, willing to do anything to help you."

"To help the dragons," she corrected.

"Yes and no. He cares for dragonkind. Do you fault him for that?"

Seraphina sighed, trailing her fingers through the small purple blooms growing on the arm of the new chair. "Why ask the question when you know the answer."

"So you would know it," Rhea said with her indulgent little smile.

"Did you know what's happening with the dragons?" Seraphina redirected. She would need to figure out what to do about Azar, but her main priority was no different than his: helping dragonkind. Her second was taking out Laisren and his lackeys. Azar was closely entwined with both, but he wasn't why she'd come.

"I see you're worried, hesitant to confront your brother." Curiosity meant Rhea allowed the change of subject. In her existence, it was rare not to know what was happening, but the dragons were an independent race. Anything not brought before the High Council was outside their purview, and none of her usual sources—no nymphs or muses or other creatures— were involved with dragons, either. Usually, anyway.

At some point, Seraphina would need to track down the dream weaver who'd enabled her abduction. And to thank the sprites who had helped free her.

"Nahash's rule has been catastrophic. From what I'm told."

Rhea waited silently, not bothering to point out Azar had no possible reason to lie. No reason to seek Seraphina out if he hadn't spoken the truth. Unless he'd somehow been misled about all of this, too. But then the magenta female had made similar references to Nahash's shortcomings.

Seraphina passed a hand over her face to wipe away her frown. "Apparently, Nahash has mated with a siren. I have no idea if it's a genuine connection or some manipulation on the siren's part."

Her consternation was echoed in Rhea's expression, which only fueled the whirl of anxiety in Seraphina's gut.

"Maybe you know something about her?" she added. "Her name is Jadokari."

Rhea rose in a smooth, even motion that might as well have been her shooting up off the throne and to the vaulted ceiling. The leader of the fae was imperturbable, yet now confusion and concern met in the lines of her usually flawless face.

"What is it?" Seraphina asked, standing as well and steeling herself for the answer.

"Jadokari isn't a siren, Seraphina," Rhea said, the many colors of her eyes swirling with her agitation. "She's a succubus."

Chapter 25

HOURS MUST HAVE PASSED SINCE SERAPHINA HAD GONE, but the light hadn't changed one bit, making tracking time impossible. This was what it would be like to be left here to die. Waiting by the lake in the flawless false sunshine as his body incrementally wasted away.

Azar had finally figured out what felt off about this pocket realm—the quiet. There were no hoofbeats, nor rustle of insects. Not even the whisper of leaves in the preternaturally still air. Aside from his own breath and the gentle gurgle of water in the distance—so soft as to possibly be a figment of imagination— there was no sound at all. Neither mortal nor fae lived here. He was entirely alone. The place they'd come to free Seraphina had become his prison.

He lay curled by the lake, wings and tail tucked close to his body. If he was going to die here, he'd do it in his true form.

Except he didn't actually think Seraphina would abandon him here to starve. She would have called him naïve, at best, for that belief. But if she'd truly wanted him dead, she could have simply killed him and been done with it. The more he thought about the moment she'd spared him, playing on an endless loop in his mind, the more it seemed she'd always planned for him to survive. Not only had she steered the steep dive close enough to the lake that the water could have saved him, but the parting movement of her wing had also nudged him higher, added precious time to ensure his safety.

Or perhaps he'd been trapped longer than he realized, and the solitude had already begun to warp his mind, his memory. It didn't seem likely. While hunger tugged at his insides, it wasn't yet the sucking pit of need he'd experienced many times before. So he couldn't have been here too long.

Guilt poked at him in the silence. Everything Seraphina had been put through was his fault. Plus there were whatever consequences Koios would face for her escape. If Azar hadn't taken Laisren at his word, if he hadn't dismissed Seraphina's caution as paranoia, neither of them would have suffered for his decisions.

A few hours or days of isolation, of battling back that niggling uncertainty of whether she'd return, was no more than he deserved.

It was also an opportunity to take stock. Despite everything, Azar was certain Seraphina was critical to helping the dragons. No matter how justified, it wasn't likely she would turn her back on them all.

While she would almost certainly destroy those who had tormented her, she wasn't cruel. Her reluctance to harm her brother, despite the allure of becoming zubir and all the power that conferred, underscored that.

Azar's guilt found stronger purchase. How could he not have recognized the sacrifice they'd all been expecting her to make? He'd personally pressured her to kill her kin, seeing the Zubir merely as the one responsible for the dragons' suffering. But even if she'd lived her life aware of the impending maros, she would also have spent centuries with a brother not yet corrupted by power.

Azar's determination had made him blind in so many ways. Even setting aside the most obvious consequences of her abduction, all his revelations—his very presence—had been nothing but added burdens on Seraphina's shoulders. No matter his intentions, his appearance had literally destroyed the life she had built for herself among the mortals.

Perhaps if he hadn't been trying to manage her reactions, to sway her behavior, everything would have turned out differently. He'd been alternately too confident in his own strength, his knowledge that had proved far from reliable, and too overwhelmed by the reality of who she was. Even that glimpse of the true extent of her power, back at the Peran Estate, had been like nothing he'd ever felt before.

It could have been the mark of the zubiran line, a bite to the power any dragon would recognize, but it seemed to go beyond that. Aside from the Zeyan tekkess, he hadn't spent much time around the Zubir. But even then, he hadn't sensed anything remotely like Seraphina's power. She was special.

And since she seemed to have no immediate plans to kill him, Azar would do anything he could to serve her, however she required. If she would let him.

A breeze in this painfully still place signified the presence of someone other than him, and Azar's head lifted. Catching sight of Seraphina's purple-edged white, he shifted to his human form. When she landed beside the lake, he dropped to one knee.

Please, get up, she said, sounding entirely worn out. This wasn't the royal whose anger had lashed out at him, but the kinder, more approachable dragon from the cabin.

By the time Azar had come to his feet, she had shifted as well, leaving him to face her troubled frown.

Still relief was a sliver of light sneaking through all the darkness of the last few days. "You came back."

Guilt over the empty threat she'd voiced before leaving was the least of Seraphina's problems, but still it made itself known. She sighed. "I shouldn't have done that. Shouldn't have suggested I'd leave you here, and I shouldn't have attacked you like that. I'm sorry."

She may not trust Azar after everything, despite Rhea's unsubtle nudging, but she did need his knowledge of the dragons' current affairs, of Laisren's plans. And it was far easier to get someone to help voluntarily than through force. Whatever else she could say about Azar, he seemed committed to the idea that she was the savior he'd wanted to find.

Everything else could wait for later, despite how her body had resumed craving his nearness. Funny how none of the other dragons she'd been around lately had that effect on her. Then again she had been starved, dehydrated, beaten, and oh yes, chained at the time. So maybe it was simply that falling apart in Rhea's arms had allowed Seraphina to resume feeling anything at all beneath the anger and fear.

Regardless, she wouldn't be giving in to her body again, no matter how Azar's power tugged at her. He could be useful; that was all that mattered.

"Thank you," he said, acknowledging her apology, wary surprise in his eyes.

"I need information."

"Every detail I know," he agreed instantly.

"There were others sent to find me. Where?" She needed to know where it was safest to return in the mortal realm. Aside from the fact that they'd both need to eat, she craved a hot shower. A bath may be too dangerous a waste of time, but the heat of a steamy shower would be a suitable compromise to help ease the residual aches in her body. She'd become spoiled by human luxuries.

Concentration creased between Azar's brows. "All over. India, China…"

"More specifically?"

"Beijing. Erm, London, Buenos Aires, Paris. St. Petersburg. But not everywhere was tethered to a specific location like the Peran Estate." A smidge of confidence returned to his posture and voice as she listened. "India was a traveling mission, days or at most weeks spent in one area then moving on somewhere new, trying to find something that connected to you." His own guilt flashed across his features, but he buried it and kept going. "Similarly with Northern Africa."

"Canada?" she prompted.

He hesitated, the lines in his face deepening as he tried to remember. "I don't think so."

A slow smile stretched her cheeks. "Perfect." Everyone always forgot Canada. The country didn't deserve it, but right now, its neglect would prove exceedingly useful. "I'll be back," she assured as she picked up the amulet she'd have to resume wearing soon, wrapping it in a few layers of materialized cloth. Her teeth ground into each other at the thought of putting it back on, leaving herself weak again.

Tasuna? The word was a whisper in her mind, as if he'd hardly meant for her to hear it.

She turned back in time to catch the panic he tried to hide. "While we're here," she said with a sigh, "please don't call me that." This realm had been meant to be her refuge, not a reminder of all the responsibilities she'd have to shoulder, the unfair decisions she would soon be forced to make.

He hardly reacted to the request. "I could perhaps join you, serve as backup," he said, though it was clear the offer stemmed at least in part from the desire not to be left here again.

Logically, it was the smart call. The pendant would hinder her power, and if Azar were truly on her side, his ability to remain at full strength without the same risk of discovery would be helpful. It was a big *if*. Self-preservation instincts egged on by her recent trauma resisted the idea of showing him how to leave, giving him that access to every connected property where the portal led.

But Rhea, who could read emotions and intent regardless of how someone wanted to hide them, had trusted Azar's desire to help Seraphina. And this show of faith on her part could also deepen his loyalty.

It was manipulative, but she couldn't afford to consider anything other than tactics. With all the implications of what Rhea had revealed… Seraphina didn't have the emotional bandwidth for anything beyond cold strategy. One foot in front of the other, as the humans said.

Fine, she agreed, already shifting for the flight to the touch-stones that led to the exit. *Let's go.*

Chapter 26

*W*HAT IS THIS PLACE? AZAR ASKED WHEN THEY STOOD IN-side the midway portal. He cautiously ran his eyes over the half circle of verdant archways, then glanced behind himself to the smaller clearing they'd landed in moments prior.

Seraphina's fingers clenched around the amulet's chain as she clipped it back around her neck. For centuries she had accepted its necessity, but now she couldn't help flashing back to the cave, to her captors' eagerness to degrade and subjugate her. It wasn't strategy but hatred driving them.

Forcing her breathing to slow, she chanted to herself, *It will keep you safe. It will keep you safe.*

The whole reason she'd ever worn it was to help avoid detection while in the mortal realm. And they wouldn't be there long.

She hadn't realized she'd closed her eyes until she opened them to find Azar hovering nearby, concern painted on his face. "Are you all right?" he asked.

"This one," she said, stepping away toward the third archway from the left, "leads to the Peran Estate." She moved past the glowing centered entrance to Rhea's receiving rooms, stopping in front of the second to last archway. "And this is where we're going."

Not all of Seraphina's properties were linked here, but those that were had ample emergency supplies, from cash to identification, which she regularly restocked. If she hadn't had Azar with her, leaving the mansion behind would have taken her minutes rather than a full day, with no human paperwork required. Back then, she hadn't wanted to trust him with this secret—still wouldn't have if there'd been any other choice.

But they needed sustenance and supplies. If they didn't use noticeable amounts of electricity or otherwise make their presence known, there'd be no reason Laisren or his cronies would suspect this property was where the two of them had popped up, even if they did manage to track it to the identity they now knew.

Seraphina allowed herself the time for two more deep breaths, then stepped through, leaving the Drevan the choice of whether to follow.

When Seraphina disappeared through the archway, Azar considered the one she'd designated as leading to the property where they'd met. It was clearly a test, presenting him with the option of returning to Pennsylvania. But there was nothing waiting for him there. Certainly nothing more important than being at Seraphina's side, whatever she chose to do.

A cool sensation enveloped him as he passed through the portal, quickly dissipating when he stepped out into a space with a built-in cabinet to his right, a sliding door to his left, and an open entryway revealing a large bedroom before him.

Seraphina hadn't turned on any lights, but the golden glow of outside illumination filtered in through the bedroom's high windows. She stood leafing through mortal paperwork, a stack of currency already in her hands.

"What shall I call you here?"

She waited to answer until she'd slid one identification card out of the pack. "Natalia, but we shouldn't be here long enough for it to matter." She sighed, looking out into the darkened bedroom. "I'd hoped it would be day. No lights," she instructed, meeting his gaze. "But feel free to take a shower, behind you, or get some rest."

"What about you?"

Her lips tightened, not quite frowning. "I'm going to check the kitchen then get to work. I'll let you know if I find anything edible."

"I can help." Not with her work, but searching the kitchen he could certainly handle.

Her jaw clenched as if fighting back words, but finally she nodded. He followed her a few steps further into the bedroom.

She gestured to the double doors now evident to his right. "Turn left, then left again. No lights," she admonished a second time.

"No lights," he repeated. He knew better now than to question her precautions.

With a final reluctant nod, she moved past him back into the in-between area where they'd arrived. Another set of double doors faced the bedroom's, but Azar followed directions, going left, down a couple steps, then left again, which took him directly into the kitchen. A small nook with a round table for four was situated beyond a large kitchen island, with a larger dining area past a second island to his right. Like her other properties, this one had ample windows and an open layout to welcome the light.

He searched the refrigerator first, which didn't take long. It was empty aside from some frozen bars of butter and two packs of frozen vegetable mixes. Neither of them would be satisfied with greens.

The pantry nestled behind the refrigerator proved to be a bit more of a challenge, as it was mostly blocked off from the windows' light. That would mean its light would also be protected from view, but still he obeyed her restrictions. There wasn't much to sort through here either. Some jars of pickled vegetables, a few bags of crisped and salted vegetables, a few more with chocolate-covered indulgences, and a couple tins of fish. Those were an improvement of sorts, but the tiny containers would hardly make a dent in either of their hungers.

When he found a bag of dried beef labeled *jerky*, his stomach seized around its emptiness. Dried meat wasn't his first choice, but it was still meat.

Seraphina waited where they'd started, sitting on the floor against the outcropped wall, with a small computer illuminating her face. From what he'd seen of this home, remaining here did seem like a smart choice to ensure the dim light would not be noticed from the outside.

Or perhaps she was being overly cautious after what she'd been through, overestimating Laisren's reach in the mortal world. Azar shoved aside his guilt and held the bag out in front of her. "Best I could find."

Disappointment pinched her features. "Go for it." Her eyes flicked back down to the computer. "The butcher will be open soon enough."

Her fingers tapped the keys for several more seconds before she closed the device and stood. "I'm going to take a shower." She hesitated mid-step, considering him.

"You have my word I won't contact anyone, or do anything," he assured. He would find somewhere to wait that would ensure his invisibility to any potential prying eyes.

Her shoulders dropped with her exhale, as if she'd been holding the breath, and she entered the room beyond the sliding door, which turned out to be an expansive closet. She emerged with a stack of clothing, added a couple towels from the cabinet, then passed into the bathing room. Since it connected to the area where he stood with merely a door-less opening, Azar moved away into the bedroom to give her greater privacy.

Her suggestion about getting rest had vaguely implied the bed was his to use, but he would leave that for her. He wouldn't be sleeping anyway. The two plush chairs across from the foot of the bed weren't optimal in terms of remaining out of sight of the windows.

In that sense, the best place he'd seen thus far was the landing between the two opposing sets of double doors, so that was where he went. As the shower turned on, he leaned against the doors to the unknown room, stretching his legs out in front of him. Under normal circumstances, he never would have chosen a dark indoor space over the beautiful pocket realm he'd left. But after the uncountable hours of eerily unchanging light and silence, the dark was soothing.

And here, he wasn't alone.

Chapter 27

SHE HAD RINSED OFF IN THE LAKE AND MATERIALIZED FRESH outfits numerous times, and yet it wasn't until the citrusy soap coated her skin that Seraphina began to feel clean. She scrubbed her whole body three times and washed her hair twice before lowering to the steam shower's seat to let the conditioner set, though really to allow herself a couple extra minutes before facing everything that lay ahead.

Her scars had healed into thin, slightly puckered slashes of white that would likely never leave her, but they served as reminders of the promise she'd made to herself. And to keep that promise, she had to keep moving forward.

Among anticipated official notices from the university, a string of anxious messages from Naiara had been waiting in Tia's email. The human had understandably put together that Tia and Azar had disappeared at the same time. When she hadn't immediately heard back, she'd threatened to contact the police. That kind of attention to one of her identities was the last thing

Seraphina needed to add to her overflowing plate. It was a good thing she had checked that account. It was less good that she'd been honestly able to reply her brother was dying.

One way or another, Nahash wouldn't come out of this alive. Seraphina knew only a little about succubi, but enough to know his "mate" had likely pursued him for his power, not his personality. His odd behavior and inability to appreciate the impact he was having could also potentially be traced to her leeching off him. But even if that were the case, the damage was done. There was no way the dragons would trust Nahash to lead again. So either the succubus would eventually drain him dry, or Seraphina would have to face him in the maros. She didn't see another way.

Hopefully there would be something in all the research she'd quickly downloaded to the laptop. Internet may not exist in Kansytura, but the battery should probably work just fine. First things first, though: getting food.

By the time she'd made it out of the shower and gotten dressed, dawn was lightening the sky outside the bedroom's windows. One thing was conspicuously missing from the primary suite, however.

"Azar?" she called. She didn't raise her voice, but anywhere in the house, his dragon ears should have been able to hear her.

There was no response.

Fear inexplicably gripped Seraphina's throat, sending her pulse racing. A million reasons could explain his silence. None came to mind, and yet she was overwhelmingly sure each one could only be bad.

Fingers wrapped around the amulet so she could yank it off her neck if needed, Seraphina slowly opened the bedroom door.

She spun back and away from the opening, leaning against the wall to quiet her gasping breath. Her hand fell away from the pendant, and she sunk to the floor, hugging her knees to her chest until the trembling eased.

She had to get ahold of herself. Logically, she knew her panic was baseless, a reaction to the surge of adrenaline triggered by her trauma. But logic and understanding only went so far.

If her body hadn't jumped to panic, she would have realized she could still feel that tingle of his presence that had so recently felt unignorable. Indeed, Azar had simply fallen asleep, leaning against the door to the den, his hand still on the bag of beef jerky.

That pesky logic dictated that she should sleep, too. It would help her recover, body and mind. But buying food and heading back to Kansytura was more important, so Seraphina pushed herself up off the floor and collected the cross-body purse with her new ID and cash.

Downtown Victoria wasn't far, and normally she would have simply ridden a bike over or even walked. Who knew in what condition the bicycle stored in the garage was, and either way, the quantity she'd be purchasing would overwhelm its little basket. So she would have to hope one of the cars was in good enough shape for the drive there and back.

She hesitated on the landing where Azar slept. Waking him only to tell him to move to a bed didn't make much sense. On the other hand, if he woke to find her gone, he might do something drastic like go searching for her.

Palming the amulet so it wouldn't smack him in the face— *not* because she felt the urge to be at full strength to be around him—she bent to nudge him on the shoulder.

He woke instantly, fingers catching her wrist.

He let go almost as quickly, and she straightened, fighting the instinct to back away from him. The landing wasn't small, and with him up on his feet now too, there was plenty of space between them.

"Sorry—" he started to say, but she waved off the words.

"I'm heading out. I should be back in an hour or so. There are plenty of beds," she added, heading toward the stairs by the front door. Three bedrooms upstairs and another downstairs, in addition to the primary on this level, meant him sleeping on the floor was absurd. Even if his comfort wasn't her priority.

He trailed her to the stairs. "I could come with you."

He might have intended it as helpful, but the offer still came across as presumptuous—as if she couldn't protect *herself*. With the amulet on, maybe she couldn't, but she'd survived in the mortal world for hundreds of years without a bodyguard. The point was moot, anyway.

"I'm less recognizable alone," she explained, heading down to the garage. "Anyone looking would expect to see the two of us together, and you can't change your coloring." To underscore her point, she glamoured her hair and eyes into the dull brown on "Natalia's" ID.

He didn't argue, but when she reached the garage door, he said, "Perhaps…"

She turned, lifting an eyebrow.

"If you're able," he said carefully, "changing the shape of your face would do even more to obscure your identity."

The point was irrefutable. And if for some reason she needed to show her ID, she could drop that part of the glamour. Humans would never believe her face had changed shapes before their eyes, undoubtedly convincing themselves they'd been mistaken in their first impression, if it came to that.

"That's a good idea, thank you," Seraphina admitted. She focused on adjusting the shape of her jaw, making it more square and her lips wider to match. As a bonus, she made her nose turn up at the end. Since there was no mirror around, she asked, "How's this?"

"Incredible," he murmured like he was marveling at some discovery. Humans peered at new technology in much the same way. At some point, she'd have to dig deeper into why he'd never been taught glamour.

For now, she simply gestured to the door set perpendicular to the garage's. "There's another bed through there."

"Thank you," he said but didn't make a move toward it.

Seraphina had more important things to do than playing hostess. So she turned away, grabbing the keys from a dedicated box mounted on the wall.

When the car started, she breathed a little prayer of relief, her stomach already composing a list of everything she'd buy at the butcher's.

Azar woke to a rumbling like the one that had signified Seraphina leaving. He'd debated trying to stay awake, but getting as close to full strength as possible was the most important thing he could do since Seraphina hadn't wanted him with her.

As the rumbling repeated, he opened the door she'd gone through. She was standing at the open back compartment of her car. He could already smell the meat inside, despite its packaging.

He strode over to help, and she stepped toward the house without a word, paler than usual due to hunger or exhaustion or both. He picked up as many bags as he could grasp, which was still only about half. More covered the back seat. Saliva pooled around his tongue.

Though he knew the way back up to the kitchen, Seraphina had stopped in the hallway that led to the stairs.

"In here," she said, pressing her shoulder into the sliding doors to create an opening she widened with her hand.

Aside from the bedroom where he'd napped, Azar hadn't explored this lower level. The room she led him into was vast, practically the same size as the one that housed the two automobiles, with a spot empty for a third. She crossed the space to the compact corner kitchen at its far end, sighing when she set down the bags she'd carried as if their weight had been too much.

The soft sound spurred him back into action, and he'd placed everything he held onto the countertop before she made it halfway back across the room. They managed to empty the car with only one more trip, though many of these bags were relegated to the floor.

Seraphina packed several at random into the empty refrigerator, then washed her hands. Unwrapping a cow's liver, she said, "Dig in."

Azar's mind stuttered at the luxury of choice, the scent of fresh meat surrounding them nearly overwhelming. The selection was astounding, including several whole birds. Those wouldn't be his first choice, too different from the land-bound prey of Azhidar Zher, but he'd grown used to eating whatever was available. Now that there *was* a choice, he didn't know where to even start. Did she have a preference for what should be left to her?

She didn't comment on his hesitation until she'd crumpled the empty wrapping from the liver. A touch of pink filled her cheeks now that she'd eaten. "I'm not playing the hostess versus guest game again," she said, picking up one of the bags and moving to the little table set beside the kitchen space. "Eat, or don't eat, but stop staring at the food as if you're Oliver and I'm Mr. Bumble."

The message was clear. Azar washed his hands as well and chose a bag filled with smaller packages. He hesitated again when his mind caught up to the fact that he'd been about to join her at the table as if they were equals.

She didn't react, focused on the pile of carefully wrapped cuts of meat she was devouring. The light sucking sensation in his stomach convinced him to risk sitting with her, and she didn't lash out or do anything but keep eating. So finally he bit into a juicy cut of lamb, the light sweetness of the meat flooding his taste buds.

When their human-sized stomachs were filled, they took the remaining bags upstairs. Seraphina lined a larger version of the traveling bag she'd taken to the cabin with some kind of frozen blocks then instructed him to fill the bag "with as much as you can carry, literally." A smaller bag of supplies she'd gathered waited by the portal entrance when he brought the cache of food over. The cuts that remained she packed into the freezer in the primary kitchen. It wasn't even midday on Earth before they had returned to the solitary realm.

Seraphina shifted immediately back to mortal form once they landed beside the lake once more. Despite satisfying her hunger, she swayed slightly on her feet as she removed the computer from the second bag she'd carried.

Azar shifted back too, materializing a warm cloak that he spread on the ground. Like with any creature, there were limitations to dragons' powers. They could only materialize clothing made from natural fibers, only on their own bodies, and only in their own individual colors. Still, dragons were resourceful, and they had long ago found workarounds such as this one, materializing items of clothing with multiple uses. Azar laid a second cloak atop the first for extra comfort.

"What are you doing?" she asked, even her voice exhausted.

Had she slept since—

Since being abducted. The realization dunked him in ice. "You need to rest," he said as evenly as he could.

"Here I thought I'd made it clear I can take care of myself."

"Yes, but you aren't." Even here, where of all places she should feel safe, she wouldn't let herself sleep. Instinct urged him to pull her under his wing or even take her into his arms, but too much damage stood between them.

Because to her, he was part of the problem.

The observation earned him a sharp glance. She straightened from their supplies. "I am not your obligation. All you need to worry about is answering my questions."

"I don't feel obligated," he countered, "I feel—"

Despite the challenge that appeared in her eyes, her brows rising pointedly, Azar stopped holding back the unfiltered truth. After everything that had happened, he had nothing left to offer her, and no energy to pretend otherwise.

Jaw clenched, he admitted, *I feel broken.*

Chapter 28

THE PAINED HONESTY OF THE ADMISSION CRACKED SOME-thing inside her, but Seraphina didn't respond.

"I know what you went through is exponentially worse," he continued aloud. "I don't even fully understand how you're up-right right now. But everything I believed, all the hope I had that kept me going, searching for you… The certainty that I was do-ing the right thing to help us all…" He trailed off a second time, collecting his thoughts.

The emotional honesty was startling. Human or dragon, few would expose their internal wounds like this. Was this some sort of manipulation, to earn her sympathy? Though Seraphina couldn't read emotions like Rhea could, to her his confession felt raw, sincere.

"Meanwhile all I was is a naïve pawn he'd manipulated to do his bidding. To hurt you. I still don't understand why," Azar added almost as an aside. His torso shifting noticeably with his rough breaths, he continued, "I am concerned for your welfare, and I would choose to help you in any way I could. But I'm also simply…broken. And too drained to pretend otherwise."

Later she could blame her soul-deep exhaustion, but really it was her honesty answering his when she breathed, "Me too."

If only she could give in to that pull of his presence, to forget every reason she couldn't fall into his arms, hold on to him as the one shelter in the storm of her emotions. If only she could believe the alluring lie that there could be safety in his embrace.

"Seraphina," he said, his voice pitched low.

He moved closer, stopping perhaps a foot in front of her. Even now with their admissions hanging in the air between them, she refused to retreat.

I'm so sorry, he repeated, a world of guilt and regret in his eyes.

Or maybe she was projecting what she yearned to see.

His hand rose, hovering tentatively by her face, tempting her to succumb like an echo of that fateful moment in the moonlit sunroom. His fingers curled, the hand dropping away. "You need to sleep," he murmured, head bending not in a bow but as if his lips were drawn to hers.

"Last time I slept, I woke up—" She clamped her mouth shut. She couldn't let herself go there.

"What do you need to feel safe here?"

She scoffed. "You're the one scared of me, not the other way around." Another reason she wouldn't touch him that way again. The obvious power imbalance meant any contact was more like sexual harassment. She may have lived through numerous lifetimes of humans dismissing or even accepting such behavior, but she would never be the perpetrator.

"I'm not scared of you," Azar stated, his brows quirking briefly. He shifted even closer, still not touching her, though the combination of his body heat and power felt like a caress. "I'm in awe of you. Your compassion, and resilience. Your unshakeable conviction, and your ability to admit wrongdoing." The smallest smile tugged up one corner of his lips. "If not your weaknesses."

Seraphina didn't respond to the attempt at teasing or to the rest, her mind still struggling to pull the pieces together enough to process the implications of his words.

"You're more knowledgeable than I am," Azar said without any apparent resentment, "and you're stronger than I am. But I'm not scared of you," he repeated. "And despite all that, you still need rest."

With a determined exhale, he stepped back. She almost leaned into the motion, digging her nails into her palms to stand her ground and not follow his pull. Pesky logic reminded he was right: sleep wasn't optional. Besides the undeniable physical necessity, it should have as positive an impact on her ability to recover from the trauma as cuddling theoretically would. Her skin hunger hadn't gone anywhere, even if that need was now overtaken by everything else.

"We're alone here," Azar pointed out.

A sarcastic response died within her, requiring too much energy to express.

"So I can stand watch, or you can tie me to a tree or something. Tell me what you need."

There it was. He knew she didn't—couldn't—trust him enough to be unconscious around him. Kansytura was secure, isolated, and impenetrable aside from the portals in her properties. Still her subconscious couldn't let her truly rest to the point of helplessness with him around.

He chuckled with some realization, but it was a resigned, humorless sound. "I know what will work." His teeth ground into each other, muscles in his arms bulging as his fingers clenched into fists. *I'll wear the amulet.*

"No," she said aloud and telepathically at once. She'd intended to make a point, telling him to touch it, and she had. He'd barely been able to breathe holding the stone she'd worn all those centuries. He would survive wearing it, and he'd be incapable of hurting her while he did, almost certainly incapable of taking it off on his own. She would be safe enough to relax except for the conscience that would torture her. Nearly the same way she would be torturing him.

Had offering been a calculated move? She was too rundown to keep searching out the hidden intentions behind his every action. There was so much she still had to unravel. Would it really be foolish to let her guard down a little bit, here where he was literally the only risk? To believe he'd made the suggestion out of concern for her wellbeing, even if only because he needed her to fix the situation with the dragons?

Even if she convinced her conscious mind, there was that instinct that fought closing her eyes. The panic she could feel waiting for an opportunity to pounce.

"Or," he said, halting her deliberations, "you could shift." In his eagerness at the idea, he stepped closer again, quickly moving backward when she stiffened, in an absurd parody of an old dance. "Consider, in that form, you'll know with certainty the amulet isn't on, cannot be used against you. We both know you can take me down in minutes at most, so you wouldn't need to worry about being overpowered somehow. And I won't shift anyway," he assured.

The eagerness in his expression or maybe the suggestion itself eased the whirl in her mind. Like coming up for air after being buffeted under stormy waves. "Another good idea," she admitted.

His lips quirked. "It's that nap I took."

Seraphina bent to unzip the exterior pocket on the carry-on she'd filled with the inedible supplies. "I can take you down, yet you aren't scared of me?" she prodded.

"I respect your strength. But I will not give you cause to use it against me. And I also respect your reason and your mercy. So no, I'm not scared of you."

She might have been safer if he had been, but something that felt oddly like satisfaction unfurled in her chest at the confirmation that he wasn't. She handed him the pad of paper and set of pencils she'd bought at an art store near the butcher.

Emotions she'd have to decipher later played across his expression, far too intense for the simple tools she'd purchased. He would have to be occupied *somehow* while she made her plans. Though given the two helpful suggestions he'd made today, maybe he would have something to contribute beyond intel. Something to consider later.

She shifted and settled a few dragon-sized paces away from Azar and their supplies. She might still not be able to sleep, but she could rest her eyes, try to shut off her brain for a few minutes. In this realm with no insects or animals to cover the sounds of his movement, she'd be able to hear him and react swiftly if necessary.

All Azar did was flip open the sketchpad, running his fingers almost reverently along the pencils before selecting one. To the rhythm of his pencil strokes, Seraphina's eyelids drifted shut. A sigh eased out as the smooth scratching sounds continued, varying in length and pressure almost like music lulling her to sleep.

Chapter 29

H E'D MEANT EVERY WORD HE SAID TO SERAPHINA. AND YET, it was the gifts that drove the point home inside him, transforming the traits he'd enumerated from abstractly observed to deeply personal. She couldn't have materialized these, so she would have had to think of them before, back in the mortal realm. Starving and exhausted, wounded emotionally even if the physical injuries she'd suffered had healed, she'd still been considerate enough to remember his enjoyment of drawing and purchase these materials.

Azar paused in fiddling with the shading and held the pad up to compare his sketch to the incomparable dragon finally sleeping, bathed in the perfect light as if intentionally for him to draw. He'd drawn her before, back at the cabin. But whether human or dragon form, his attempts didn't come close to capturing her.

Nevertheless he flipped to a fresh page. He kept drawing until the pencils grew dull, then opted for a swim in the pristine lake. Still Seraphina slept, undoubtedly needing the time to recover from whatever Laisren had done to her in that cave. Azar swam in circles, propelling himself through the water to help burn off his anger and frustration. The memory of his helplessness.

But she was safe now. Right there, in sight, body moving steadily with her breath.

Azar strode as carefully from the water as he had into it, trying not to make any unnecessary noise that may startle her. With no chance of being unexpectedly discovered, he didn't bother materializing clothing, letting his skin soak up the light as he lay back on the waiting cloaks. His head fell to the side to keep Seraphina in view. With the picture of her at rest constant before his eyes, he too drifted off.

When he woke, minutes or hours later, she still slept. The softest little snorts accompanied the flow of her breath, making him smile. How simple it could have been if it were merely the two of them, apart from the politics and intrigue of the dragons. They could relax in the sun, take their time becoming acquainted with one another, enjoy each other's company and, if they wanted, their bodies. Without hierarchy, obligation, or past miscalculations between them.

There were some indications Seraphina wanted that too. Her preference he not use her title. The thoughtfulness of her gift. Caring about his impression of her. Even her insistence that they treat the food she provided equitably.

Despite his regret, and the guilt that wouldn't leave him until long after the haunted look left her eyes, Azar couldn't continue to grovel before her. It didn't serve either of them, and he truly wasn't scared of her. She was stronger than him, but he was stronger than most dragons he'd met. Alone she was still more vulnerable than with him at her side. Something she would never believe if he kept vacillating between self-assurance and behaving like a cowering, barely coherent fool intimidated by her rank. Consistency was imperative in a trusted soldier, or advisor—whichever she needed him to be.

He was aware now of how little he knew, but she had asked him to be forthcoming, not omniscient. In all their interactions, she'd seemed to respect him most when he expressed himself freely and honestly, without trying to package the information in a way that may be most palatable to her. Her exhaustion had perhaps made her more receptive to his recent suggestions, but when she woke, she would undoubtedly remain convinced of their wisdom.

That was what she needed from him—dependable perspective. He had to show her she could rely on him. That he wouldn't foist his responsibilities unto others and thereby endanger her again. He would do his utmost to help her shoulder the burdens of everything that was to come.

To start, he'd keep his word and stay in human form and near her side as she slept, even if he would have enjoyed a flight. Instead Azar rose to retrieve the sketching materials he'd left atop the travel case that held the meat. He flipped the pad open, only giving the previous sketches a cursory glance as he found a blank page.

How long have I been asleep? Seraphina asked, and he spun around to face her, materializing pants out of respect. She lifted her head, stretching up on her front legs, shaking off the stillness of sleep.

Awhile, he said. *It's difficult to track time here.*

Of course. She answered and shifted at once, soon striding toward him in loose pants but a tight, short-sleeved top.

He forced his eyes up above her collarbone.

Unperturbed, she sat cross-legged beside their supplies and withdrew the computer from the smaller bag. She frowned when the screen lit up. *Almost a day.*

You needed the rest.

She sighed, frowning now at him.

Thank you for these, he said, gesturing with the art supplies. He'd been too surprised before to express his gratitude. *It was extraordinarily considerate of you.*

She shrugged off the statement, dropping her eyes. "Are you hungry?" she redirected.

"I wouldn't object," he said, voicing the words aloud as she had.

She shut the computer again. "You didn't have to wait."

As she unzipped the stockpile of meat, Azar lowered to the ground nearby. "It hadn't crossed my mind." He'd gone longer than a single day between meals before. Besides, sharing food fostered intimacy, and they could certainly stand to have more of that.

Removing the top layer of cold packs, she asked, "What are you in the mood for?" The question was almost lighthearted, and tension seeped from his shoulders. Sleeping had truly done her some good.

"What's on the menu?" he teased, earning him a quick twitch of her lips.

Their eyes met as she tossed him a white packet, and Azar didn't duck or look away. They settled into a silent meal, the tentative détente a turning point that did even more than the meat to fill the pit in his stomach.

Azar paced in a tight semicircle as he answered Seraphina's questions. With his back turned, she let her eyes linger on his ass, unable to shake the memory of the muscled line of his nude body that had greeted her upon waking. Sure, they'd already slept together, but that had been in the dark, with the amulet dulling every sensation. It didn't compare to seeing his bronzed combination of browns unabashedly exposed to the sun.

She wouldn't have objected to him remaining naked now. But that would definitely count as sexual harassment. Besides, she needed to focus.

"How many dragons at the sobran now?" she asked.

"A couple hundred."

"Forty from each tribe?" The number was staggering. Rarely did dragons spend that much time at their central meeting place aside from major events, the tribes still leading largely independent lives. A couple hundred would hardly register for humans, but none of the tribes were especially populous. Their numbers weren't equal, either, since no external force directed their reproduction. Hatchings were simply rare, and with no new dragons in hundreds of years…

"At a minimum," Azar confirmed as she squinted at the screen, skimming the research she'd found on succubi.

"How much do you know about Jadokari?"

"Not much more than I've already shared."

"How long has she been there?" Seraphina pressed. "How did they meet?"

He stopped pacing to face her. "I don't know how they met. Rumors that the Zubir had developed a relationship with someone began before my first visit to the mortal realm. Back then, some found favor bringing back the gifts he would present to her, but no one thought twice about it. It wasn't this compulsory hoarding of treasure. There were grumblings, nothing solid. And I was young…" Frustrated, he brushed his hand through his hair, disheveling it in a way that only made him more attractive.

Seraphina flung the thought away. Sleep had definitely done her good. She felt more in control of herself, that jittery panic that had seemed just under the surface now fainter, easier to suppress. Apparently with its needs for food and sleep satisfied, her body had moved on to the next one in line: sex. Or maybe more accurately, the cuddling she'd denied it before. Closeness.

None of which were going to happen. She had to make a battle plan, not fantasize about something she could never have.

"But it doesn't matter," Azar said, approaching. "The siren isn't the problem. Your brother is."

Seated on the ground with her legs crossed, the laptop balanced on her thighs, she had to crane her head back to keep her eyes on his face. The significance of what she was about to share demolished any traces of desire. "I should tell you something."

There hadn't been much opportunity since Rhea's revelation, but if Azar were going to support a coup of sorts, he deserved to know the reality of what they were facing. In truth, he could choose not to continue helping her, not to risk his own life if she did lose in the maros. He could simply stay here while Seraphina tried to sort out the dragons.

He sank to the ground, stoic concern seeming to age him, which was silly since he wouldn't show marks of age for hundreds more years.

Seraphina set the laptop aside on the ground. "Jadokari isn't a siren. She's a succubus."

Azar's lips turned down. "I don't understand the implications," he admitted.

"From what I've been reading, a succubus uses sex to steal her target's life force, or power. Leading to their physical and mental deterioration." She swallowed past the lump that had grown in her throat. Apparently she'd been more accurate than she'd realized when accusing Nahash of losing his mind. Only technically, maybe it wasn't his fault.

Azar paled, rearing back. "And through the Zubir's power, she can access the rest of the dragons."

"That's a myth." At least half of Seraphina's research was myth, too, but on the plus side, human academics had aggregated various sources for her to sort through.

"Perhaps," Azar interjected into her thoughts, the single loaded word sufficient for him to reclaim her full attention. "But a myth believed by an entire society for generations spanning thousands of years…"

Breath froze in her lungs as she gaped at him. In all her disenchantment with her family's history, how could she not have realized this? A sufficient number of humans believing the same thing for long enough could theoretically impact reality, though more likely it would be some of the magical creatures still intertwined in their realm helping things along.

But the dragons were… "A *telepathic* society," she whispered.

Which meant not only had she been wrong about how much the zubir's wellbeing impacted the rest of the dragons, but there was also every chance she'd been wrong about the importance of the maros. If she'd gone up against her brother and lost, would he have truly been infused with her power? Ended up strong enough to withstand the succubus's influence?

All those dragons starved, pressed into servitude, and trapped in human form... *Dead.*

A warm hand landed on her shoulder, squeezing gently. Azar's face blurred a little before her eyes. "Seraphina," he said as she blinked him into focus. "You're not alone in this."

"It's all my fault," she exhaled, tears gathering as the panic resurged, pressing against the inside of her skin like it wanted to scrape its way out.

"Hey." Azar shifted closer, his hands cupping her jaw, a thumb skimming over her cheek. "No, it is not."

The little flecks of gold in his eyes lay like a slightly abstract sunflower around his irises. "Seraphina," he repeated, only his voice and his touch keeping her tethered. "The siren—*succubus*. In all likelihood she targeted the Zubir because of his connection to the dragons. It would be"—his head shook lightly as the magnitude hit him—"the ultimate triumph."

"If I hadn't left, he might have been strong enough—"

"*If* you had lost, he may have still fallen for her. We may have ended up precisely where we are. Only you wouldn't be around to save us." His fingers tugged on her earlobe as his hands dropped.

"You can't do glamour," she said, the thought floating to the top of the mess within her mind, some realization still out of reach.

He shook his head rather than answer.

Seraphina looked away from the distraction of him to the lake with its pristine surface. "None of you can do glamour," she said, the pieces coming together.

"No," he confirmed.

"Because she's already drained all the dragons of significant amounts of power." That had to be true, but it wasn't the main thing pricking at her mind. "That's why he needed you," she finally realized.

Confusion replaced Azar's concern. "What? Who?"

"Laisren. He needed dragons who could blend in without glamour." The Radno, the Zeyno, even many of the Drevno, Virno, and Pretno with mixed heritage wouldn't be able to mix with the humans without suspicion if they couldn't hide their coloring, the visible hints of their ancestry that would now be considered unnatural on Earth. It explained why there'd been so few dragons simply visiting that realm, the rare ones she'd encountered all hunting her.

Azar's jaw clenched. "Makes sense."

And yet all these tidbits that had been explained weren't what she should have been focusing on. "Jadokari's been feeding on the dragons for centuries." How powerful did that make her? What was she capable of aside from leeching power through sex with her victims? "I haven't found anything about killing or even trapping a succubus. They keep draining a victim until they... die." If Jadokari killed Nahash, would every single dragon die with him?

If Seraphina did kill him in the maros, would that suffice to sever the succubus' connection to the others? Was there *any* way for her to save her brother?

Azar's hand landed back on her shoulder, his thumb now tracing her skin at the edge of the tee shirt's collar. "You'll figure this out," he said, endless certainty in his eyes. "And I will do anything in my power to help."

She leaned into the touch for the duration of a blink, wishing fruitlessly yet again that things between them could be simple enough for her to find comfort in his arms. Then she pulled away. "You need to stop touching me."

His hand instantly fell away, leaving behind a gaping hole in her gut.

Don't be ridiculous, she told herself. That sucking emptiness had everything to do with the unknown enemy Seraphina would soon have to face, and nothing to do with never feeling Azar's touch again.

Chapter 30

"Why?" He shouldn't have asked, should have listened and let it go. But the pull to hold her wouldn't be so easily assuaged. The reminder that Laisren had manipulated him hadn't helped, making Azar want to bury his guilt by snuggling close, to let the feel of her replace all the recent horror and fear, if only for a while.

He would have understood if Seraphina recoiled from his touch, if she didn't seem to want it in the same way he did. But that wasn't the case. She was making this decision due to some kind of logic. Some reason holding her back that wasn't clear to him.

"Why what?" she asked, her chin tipping up as her expression shuttered.

"Why shouldn't I touch you?" he clarified though they both knew what he meant.

She sighed, that world-weariness overtaking her attempt to close herself off from him. "Because there have to be limits, to what you would do to *help*." When he didn't respond, she continued, "Whether you feel you're fulfilling some need you perceive me to have or trying to curry favor or I don't know what, you don't need to use your body that way. I won't—"

"Stop."

Seraphina's beautiful but tormented eyes widened at the severe syllable.

"You think I'm, what, whoring myself out for the cause?"

"You've said many times you'd do anything to help save the dragons. I'm just saying you don't—"

"Does it feel good when I touch you?" he interrupted. Anger roiled through his core, though she hadn't truly done anything to deserve it.

"That's not the point," she said with deliberate patience, as if explaining something to a child.

"It should be the only point."

A hint of uncertainty broke through, piercing something deep within him but also urging him on.

"When I touch you, it isn't because I'm trying to 'service' you." Azar sighed. "I understand there's an insurmountable amount of damage between us now." All the regret in the world wouldn't change that. "But here we are in a realm that's literally a pause from reality, a place where even time has no meaning. Your rank doesn't have to exist here, and neither does the future." As he spoke, his anger boiled itself out into a longing echoed in her eyes. "We're here, entirely alone," he reminded. "Why can't we take comfort in each other?"

He lifted his hand to the curl draped over her shoulder but stopped shy of running it through his fingers. "If there's some other reason, something real, why you don't want me to touch you, please say so." He scooted closer, taking the risk of feeling the silk of her hair. *Because otherwise I'm going to kiss you.*

He caught the anticipation that flickered through her expression, but still he hesitated, mouth centimeters from hers.

"It doesn't mean anything," she said, the puff of her air caressing his lips.

"A moment between time," he confirmed. They were both too emotionally raw to put much stock in something as simple as touch.

Her spine straightened as she sought his mouth, tentatively brushing his lips. Azar slipped his hand through her hair to cup her head, letting the kiss stay soft, a delicate rhythm of their lips catching and releasing.

The cloaks he'd materialized before hadn't gone anywhere, but they were too far away, so he created a new one. He paused their kiss to untie it from around his neck and spread it out beside them.

Her wary gaze fell on the rectangle of material. He climbed onto it and lay on his side, propping one hand under his head and reaching the other out to her. She hesitated. If she decided against it now, he could never let her see how much of a fool he felt, thinking she could at least temporarily look past all the history and politics standing between them.

But she crawled to his side instead, and finally his arms were closing around her. Her nails dug into his shirt, and her lungs expanded roughly like only now was she truly able to breathe. He held her, stroking her hair as the desperate inhales turned into sporadic ragged breaths that gradually evened out into calm. The tension in her fingers released as well, becoming the faint glide of her palms.

Tracing the curve of her ear, he let his lips brush the top of her head and his eyelids fall shut, memorizing the feel of her nestled against him.

After some time measured only in breaths he hadn't counted, Seraphina pulled back, her hair fanning around her on the cloak. Azar braced above her, his lips brushing hers once more. But like the rest of her expression, they remained tight.

"This still feels a bit like sexual harassment." Before he could voice his lack of familiarity with the term, she explained, "Like I'm taking advantage of your desire or sense of obligation to…do what you think I want. Not even because of my position, but because of what I'm going to have to do."

He raised up higher, adding distance between their bodies. Her hands slipped from his back but one still rested on his side, like she couldn't bring herself to let go entirely. "Am I taking advantage?" he countered. "Of your need for touch. Your desire to be near your own kind." He would have been fine with being a tool she used to fulfill her needs. That was entirely different from preying on the way those needs may cloud her decisions.

"No," she said quickly. Still, disquietude passed in her eyes. "No, of course not," she said with more certainty.

"Neither are you," he assured, leaning closer. *We both want this*, he added, nuzzling her lips until she stretched up into the kiss, pulling him closer.

They kept the kiss light, nearly chaste. And when it ended, the thread of tension running through her body hadn't quite disappeared.

"What is it?" he asked, skimming his knuckles down her cheek.

"I'm wasting time." She frowned, pushing him away though still not too far, her fingers curving into his flesh. "I should be focusing, finding a way…" The agony of responsibility floated to the surface of the mix of emotions in her eyes. "It's already been hundreds of years, the dragons are starving—"

"It *has* been hundreds of years." Azar trailed his fingertips over the curve of her ear again, and her eyes drifted shut awhile as if she couldn't help herself. "So an hour, a day, they won't make much difference. You can take the time you need. For yourself, and for planning."

Finally a deeper breath expelled that tension with her exhale. Her ease unlocked a realization he should have had much sooner.

"We could also shift," he said. When was the last time she had curled close to another dragon?

Shock greeted the suggestion, quickly followed by the glistening of gathering tears. Azar froze. He'd expected her to miss the sensation of being hide to hide with another of their kind, tails curved around each other, one under the other's wing. But whatever emotions were playing over her face, inside her head, he couldn't decipher them.

"Or not," he quickly corrected. His hand hovered near her. Would touch help or harm at this point? "Talk to me."

Seraphina swallowed a lump that wasn't there, her breaths coming fast and shallow. Less violent than the flood at Rhea's, the emotions buffeting her now were no more controllable. A tear leaked out the corner of her eye, and still she tried to contain the incomprehensible mass whirling within her.

"That was…considerate of you," she managed, to allay Azar's unmistakable apprehension.

"Seraphina," he murmured. The hand hovering by her face dropped to run through her hair, that gentle tug like the barest caress. "You're safe," he added, and her breath caught. "Whether you need to cry or scream… Let go, let yourself simply be."

He rolled them, gathering her close so she lay partially atop him. His shirt dematerialized with the movement, his palm landing on her back below her tee, the feel of his skin on hers nearly enough to shove her over the edge into pure need.

If she dropped her head now, her mouth would land at his neck, an intimacy usually only mated dragons allowed each other, letting their powerful jaws near somewhere so catastrophically vulnerable. A liberty she hadn't taken even when he'd believed her human.

"You're safe," Azar repeated, his palm traveling in a soothing pattern over her back.

She collapsed onto him, turning her head to face his shoulder. He held her through cries that were barely more than whimpers, as emotions she couldn't name trembled their way out of her body. His lips turned into her hair, but he remained silent, undemanding. When she got rid of her pants, he followed suit, dematerializing the majority of his so he was left with odd little cutoff boxers to match her boy shorts. Legs tangling with his, she huddled close, letting the skin-to-skin contact heal what it could until an inhale no longer felt like a battle.

He didn't protest as she sprawled atop him, her lungs finding a rhythm inverse to his. Lulled by the sun and his touch, she considered letting her top dissipate too. Since the hesitation meant reason had overtaken need and instinct, she sat up instead, steeling herself against whatever she would see now in Azar's eyes.

He followed her lead here, too. Concern and compassion lay over a touch of guilt, but she could find neither pity nor condemnation for her weakness. That realization threatened to unleash another wave of emotions, but this time Seraphina retained control.

"I should get back to work," she said, looking toward the discarded laptop. It would tell her how much time had been lost.

Humans would argue her mini breakdown hadn't been a waste, allowing her to process a little more of the trauma and anxiety building up within her, to take some comfort where she could find it. None of them had the future of an entire species on their shoulders. She had to create a battle plan.

"We," Azar said, reclaiming her attention. "You are not alone," he repeated. His hand landed on hers, long fingers reaching up past her wrist. "We will figure this out. And there's nothing that says we can't be touching while we do."

She slipped her hand out from under his enough to lace their fingers together. A small smile curved his lips, his shoulders loosening a little. *Sera*— she caught in his mind. Since neither had meant for her to hear it, she didn't respond.

"Where are we starting?" he asked aloud. "Do you need the computer?"

It had all her research, but there was plenty more she could learn from him. And knowing how much time had passed wouldn't help it go more slowly. So for now, the laptop could conserve battery. Still she sighed. "What do you know about the lost heir?"

Chapter 31

AGITATION REACHED EVEN THE FINGERS TWINED WITH HERS, tensing them like a curling claw. "Nothing. He'd talk about the Zubir's sister and the lost heir, and I thought both meant you. Who is it really?"

She'd never doubted his ignorance was genuine. Nevertheless, Laisren must have let something slip when discussing his plans. He might not be as big a concern right now as the succubus, but Seraphina had to account for any ways he might undermine her. She settled more comfortably on the rectangle of fabric filled with all of Azar's browns. Disentangling her fingers from his, she tugged her bunched tee shirt back into place, elongating the hem to cover her hips like a tunic.

"The first zubir was chosen by tekkess from among the nettakim. So why not the second?" she asked.

Azar's head shook at the history he hadn't had cause to question. "The maros…"

"The first zubir was the most powerful among the nettakim, and so he was established as the most powerful of all dragons living in the new realm. Within decades, the claim that every dragon in Azhidar Zher depended on the zubir's power began appearing in written history. If the zubir was so exalted, only stands to reason his offspring would be more powerful than other dragons as well, right?" Azar frowned, but she pressed on. "Why then select from among the tribes at all? The zubiran offspring would do. So when the first zubir died, his sons underwent a tekkess."

"Not a maros," Azar clarified.

"Not yet. As they had been aware of the growing rumors and perfectly happy to feed them, it seems the brothers agreed the loser would disappear from view and, so as not to repeat the mistakes of warring humans who contested distant bloodlines, never breed. It's not entirely clear if he was exiled back to the human realm or hid in a piece of the new one that hadn't been settled.

"At some point, with the rumors of zubiran power growing but also memories of his brother casting doubt that the second zubir was as strong as the first, he decided his children would participate not in a tekkess but in a maros. With time passing and his brother nowhere in sight, he seemed to have convinced enough dragons that the maros had been the way for him as well, the ceremonial murder of the brother leaving the original zubir's full power intact." As luck would have it, none of his three children had bred before his death, and so that particular limitation had been placed on all future zubiran offspring: no children before the maros. Thus not a single zubir had ever met their grandchildren.

"But the brother didn't keep his word?"

"How dare you impugn the ancestor of the lost heir?" she asked, her bitterness coming out as sarcasm. "It is believed by some the brother of the second zubir had, unbeknownst to him of course, bred before the 'maros.'" She crooked her fingers for emphasis. "Maybe the timing even did work out that way, who knows. Those who believe think that there's a living descendant of the brother, who has the right to participate in the maros that occurs during their lifetime. Some claim that said descendant 'stole' some of the zubir's rightful power and is obligated to return it into the mix by participating." Somehow no one realized there could be more than one of these descendants by now. Or even none at all, if the line hadn't continued.

Like most myths, interpretations varied. Seraphina might have been wrong about the way current reality had been shaped by millennia of belief in the lies of the first two zubirim, but originally it had all been rumor and myth. Or more accurately: propaganda.

"How could anyone find a lost heir from whispers and untracked lineage? If one even exists."

Pivoting from the past to the future, she said, "You tell me."

Azar sat straighter, exasperation marring the lines of his lips. "I told you, I don't know."

"Yes, you do. I need to know everything you have ever heard Laisren say about finding the lost heir. You might have thought he meant me, but you said yourself, that was the term he used. You spent years listening."

He nodded thoughtfully, then fell back on the cloak with a resigned sigh. "This might take us a while."

✧ ✧ ✧

The grooves in Seraphina's face grew progressively deeper the longer she stared at the device she'd brought from the human realm, her shoulders hunched. She'd asked for space to read through the gathered information, but whatever she was learning seemed to weigh her down more.

Azar set aside the sketch of the Peran Estate he'd been working on from memory. Not that he'd grown tired of drawing her. But this worn and worried version didn't much warrant commemorating. He took a few moments to re-sharpen the pencils with the clever little device she'd handed him before burying herself in the computer. Her thoughtfulness only strengthened his resolve.

"You should take a break," he said.

All the irritation she'd been channeling at the device turned on him. "I don't need a caretaker."

"Perhaps you do," he countered. Someone to occupy themselves with her needs while she was engrossed with worrying about everyone else's didn't seem like the worst idea.

A low growl rumbled in his head, but she spoke aloud. "And here I thought I'd made myself clear. The last thing I am is weak."

Seraphina...

Her lips pinched, her chin notching up as her jaw shifted.

Undeterred, Azar moved closer until he sat on his heels beside her. "I care about you. I'm concerned for your wellbeing. That has nothing to do with considering you weak."

Uncertainty appeared in the deepest shadows of her eyes. Recently enough, she'd been curled in his arms, taking the comfort she needed, yet still she worried he was seeking out weaknesses to exploit.

He palmed the back of her wrist, trailing his thumb over the soft skin in the front. Her fingers curled into a fist, the tension in her body only growing tauter. But she didn't pull away.

"When's the last time you allowed someone to care for you?" Azar asked softly.

She tugged her hand from his lax grip. "I had friends in Pennsylvania before all this, if you recall."

Friends she would have had to abandon in a decade at most, even if he hadn't come along. How many humans had she similarly grown to care for then been forced to leave behind? "But when did you last let anyone close enough to know the truth of you, to see you vulnerable?"

Anger sharpened her gaze, but he could see beyond it now to the longing and fear.

"That isn't the same thing as weak," he preempted.

"They're synonyms."

His lips tugged up. "You're being contrary on purpose."

A soft exhale drained that vibrating tension from her posture.

"I don't think you're weak," Azar said to drive the point home. "But I won't stop being concerned with your welfare, even when you aren't. Especially when you aren't. And not because you're the Savior of Dragons," he added, inflecting lightness into the unofficial title. "Because you matter to me."

Something stronger than guilt over her abduction and hope for the dragons' future compelled him to care about her being free from harm.

Trepidation warred in her expression with a desire to believe him, until finally both were shuttered behind a wary acceptance. "Where did all that emotional intelligence come from?"

"Maybe I'm born with it."

With a tiny chuckle, she murmured, "Maybe it's Maybelline."

Azar hesitated. He didn't want to douse the glimmer of light that had appeared in her expression. Or to admit his ignorance, yet again.

"Human joke," she filled in, noticing. Was it only the lack of distractions in this realm that had them both so attuned to the other?

In any case, his initial point still needed addressing. "Eat something," he suggested. "Then come for a flight with me." They could both benefit from giving all their muscles a chance to work.

He caught the capitulation in her expression before she sighed and shifted the computer off her lap. She stretched toward the bag with the meat, rising up onto her knees when she couldn't quite reach. She'd lengthened her earlier shirt into a tunic, but still the motion revealed the strong lines of her bare legs, the purple fabric hugging her ass.

He almost didn't catch the parcel she tossed at his head, but he didn't miss the arch in her eyebrow. Or the light blush on the crests of her cheeks.

Or that even when she settled with her own meal, she didn't materialize anything to clothe her legs. A light frown returned to her face as she contemplated the large round of meat she'd unwrapped. Easy enough to consume for a dragon; less so for a human, especially one as petite as her. She used an invisible talon to slice through it.

"I know it sounds indulgent," she said as he unwrapped his own meal, "but I wish I'd brought some herbs or something, for some variety. Humans aren't wrong that food should be enjoyed, savored. Not merely consumed."

Azar nodded, also slicing through the cold muscle. "When I was younger, before the animals were corralled, I remember enjoying the hunt. The chase, the fresh kill."

"I guess I forgot what that's like," Seraphina mused sadly, a chunk of meat suspended by her mouth, also forgotten.

"But you're right," Azar added, "the humans certainly are inventive with their food." Even the Zubir's idea of cultivating plants brought from Earth, allowing more variety in the dragons' meals, wouldn't have been a bad one—if it hadn't required what amounted to slave labor.

Soured on the idea of sitting here, filling his stomach—if only the human-sized one—when so many others were still struggling under the Zubir's rules, Azar suddenly itched to *move*. "Why don't we shift, swallow these, and go for that flight?" he suggested, even though it went against everything she'd been saying about savoring their meals.

Seraphina eyed the hunks they held, each nearly the size of one of his thighs. "Hardly enough to satisfy a dragon."

Something in his mind whispered that he could satisfy her better than any cold chunk of meat ever could.

Thankfully before he could speak, she'd flipped open the travel bag to take out their remaining food. "Help me unwrap these."

She wasn't wrong about their unfulfilled dragons' appetites. Nevertheless, caution and the inescapable memory of hunger made him ask, "All of it?"

"I can pick up more when I go to charge the laptop," she said, already working to unwrap and lay out the various cuts she'd purchased, each a slightly different color with a unique scent.

Azar buried the instinct to hoard all the meat, safeguard it aside from small rations to keep them alive. "I could go," he offered instead, picking up one of the packages. Gathering the similar white parcels and whole birds stuffed into her freezer would be easy enough.

"No, you couldn't."

She said it absently, but Azar's hands stilled with the steaks only partially unwrapped. "You still don't trust me."

She stilled too, for the barest moment, then her head swiveled toward him. "Do you know how to charge a laptop?" It wasn't a true question.

"No," he admitted. The ache somewhere beneath his hunger remained.

"It should only take a couple hours."

"I could go with you." Knowing the exit made the possibility of staying here alone more palatable, but he didn't want to let her out of his sight. How would he even know if something had gone wrong?

"There's less risk if it's only one of us," she insisted.

"With the amulet on, there's less risk if I am at your side."

They'd had nearly the same exchange the last time. Still she bristled at the reminder of the stone.

Azar tossed the parcel he held aside and moved nearer so he could lay his hand on her shoulder. "If we stay inside, there's hardly any risk at all."

"You're right," she breathed, forcing her lips to curve in an unnatural smile.

He moved even closer, letting his hand slip under the fall of her hair to her other shoulder and bringing his other hand up to meet it in a sort of awkward perpendicular embrace. She stiffened with her inhale but then sagged into him, bringing one hand up to rest on his arm. Her head twisted so she could meet his eyes, a glimpse of that true vulnerability reflected in hers.

Azar eased the clumsy embrace to cup her jaw. "It's not all bad," he said. "You could take a bath." She seemed to enjoy them, and they relaxed her.

To be fair, heated baths had made it to Azhidar Zher as well, at least to the Drevno and, according to Koios, the Radno. Since flame was hardly a problem for them, it had been easy enough to create dedicated stone pools that were heated as needed.

Seraphina's cheek tensed under his palm with her reluctant, yet far more natural, smile. "We should eat," she said, pulling away.

Without a word, he moved a few strides away and shifted. Unimpressed, she watched him as her fingers nimbly finished unwrapping the packet he'd set aside earlier. Azar bent close to another waiting parcel and released a light flick of fire. It burned away the paper, barely browning the meat. With a taunting huff, he snatched up the result, swallowing down the piece that hardly registered in his larger form.

Willingly rising to the bait, Seraphina moved back and also shifted. *Show off*, she grumbled, choosing one of the unwrapped hunks.

Azar laughed, plopping down on his stomach before consuming the piece he'd started on at first. This one was big enough it actually required chewing.

A breath of flame passed along the unopened parcels, stopping just shy of his muzzle, jerking his head up. Mischief glinted in the perfect amethyst orbs of her eyes as she tossed a hunk of meat in the air, her neck elongating as she stretched back to catch it.

So beautiful, he thought to himself. Her gaze speared him as if she'd heard.

An instant later she was in the air, winging toward the trees. *You coming?*

Chapter 32

Seraphina, Azar called behind her as she flew for the farthest part of the oval tree line.

Hmm? She didn't slow for him, not pushing herself but rather enjoying the sensation of the air around her, her wings propelling her forward. She'd have to put the amulet back on soon, but Azar was right about taking a few minutes to stretch her wings.

You heard that? he asked.

Seraphina fought the impulse to check how far away he was. A dragon's ability to be heard stemmed from their own power, not that of those listening, but there were some secrets she'd kept even before leaving Azhidar Zher.

So instead of answering him, she asked, *Can't keep up?* Let him think the hum he'd heard before was his imagination.

To get a sense of where he was, she did a simple flip in the air. Then, because it was fun and he'd only just left the lake, she added a twisting flip. As Azar gained on her, she floated lazily toward the trees, then dove to snatch one leaf in her teeth, angling her body up from the canopy without disturbing any others. She released the leaf, shooting a tiny bubble of flame to incinerate it midair. One of many exercises she'd devised to keep herself sharp during the countless time she'd spent here alone.

She wasn't alone now, Azar hovering near her position above the trees. Awe wasn't easy to read on a dragon's face, but that was what his expression reminded her of. Or maybe she was getting too full of herself.

Race you, she said, taking off across the open field. Alone she'd circled the tree line, marking her spot based on the lake, counting the seconds of the flight. She'd ducked and woven out of the grasp of imaginary foes, challenged herself to navigate along the rivers, among the trees. One particularly bad day, she'd torn out some smaller trees by their roots, tossing them into the air, dirt and rocks and branches pummeling her. She'd healed fast, and Kansytura, created to be an idyll, had appeared untouched on her return.

Seraphina pushed the memory away as Azar gained on her. His larger body mass was accompanied by larger wings, so she worked her own wings harder, focusing on the furthest point of the trees. They could fly beyond them to the little mountain range that served as boundary for this island of existence, but there wasn't much to do on those barren hills.

Azar nipped at her tail, reminding her of his proximity. *What do I get if I win?*

Her amusement came out as a snort. His presumptuousness only spurred her to fly faster, pushing herself in that way that let her feel every muscle working, past any stiffness or discomfort until all that was left was the whoosh of the air sliding along her body, her target in sight. She added a little twist to the last length of their race, pulling up out of it and around to face Azar not far behind her.

He swerved to avoid her, his larger frame not as nimble, and satisfaction pulsed through her. She dropped down to circle lazily above the trees, her talons skimming through the leaves. Azar swung in a larger circle a bit higher than her, not daring to touch the treetops.

He did dare to let one wingtip brush along hers. Seraphina swung her neck around to find his eyes fixed on her. And why not? Nothing stood in their way, no unexpected obstacles awaiting them in the air. Still she turned away to watch the unchanging landscape below.

Displaced air warned that Azar had flown higher, reclaiming her attention. He did a sort of vertical corkscrew twist before falling backward into a loop to come around and face her again. His neck lengthened, bringing the blunt edge of his muzzle toward her at an angle that allowed him to nuzzle along her jaw. Seraphina pressed into the warmth of his scales but soon swerved away.

He swooped down and around her, caging her forelegs in his claws, a swift downward sweep of his wings propelling the two of them higher. Her wings matched his rhythm as their necks and faces rubbed against each other, their bodies growing nearer.

Seraphina's wings faltered as she melted into the inferno coming to life between them. Azar's sure movements compensated, keeping them aloft as she burrowed into the soft scales of his neck.

No, she moaned as their tails twisted around each other.

Azar's head pulled back so they could look one another in the eyes, but he didn't let go. He nudged her muzzle almost like a kiss.

Since she refused to whimper aloud, every cell in her body did instead. It was like she could hear that body cursing her as she disentangled herself from his embrace. *We have to stop*, she told him, dipping into a measured dive to the ground, needing the solidity as desire fluttered through her. The sensation too much in her current form, she shifted back to human, but even the slide of the cotton she materialized shot fresh flares of need through her.

Why? he asked, landing a safe distance away and also shifting, clothing himself in tight brown pants but forgoing a shirt. Purposeful strides moved him closer.

She closed her eyes as the reminder of the risk tipped the scales from desire to reason.

Azar's fingers brushed her hair back, swept over her ear, snapping her eyes back open. "Why do we *have* to?" he murmured, his power pulsing against her with his heartbeat. Or maybe that was her heartbeat, her body reacting to the warmth of his proximity even if it was only an echo of his true form's heat.

"I won't fight while pregnant," Seraphina explained. She may have rejected the other limitations of her so-called birthright, but this was one risk she couldn't stomach. She took a deliberate step back from him. "And I *have* to fight."

Patience with a condescending undertone accompanied him pointing out, "With your brother as zubir, the dragons are barren."

"The dragons are a lot of things I'm not." Dragonkind having children was rare, the risk so minimal as to be laughable. Except her finding herself "in the family way" at the worst time possible seemed like precisely the kind of cruel twist the Fates would throw her way. Pregnancy had never been a concern with her human partners, but even one unprotected time with Azar was too big a risk.

His head cocked. "Why do you think that is?"

"I don't know," she said on a heavy sigh. Though it was an important question. "Maybe because I stopped believing long ago."

"No, that doesn't make sense," he mused, pulling her into his arms before she could think to protest. And she didn't want to, so she laid her head on the supple muscles of his chest. "Not like the rest of us are all fooling ourselves. Millennia of belief made it *true*."

Another piece of the puzzle to figure out. Maybe it didn't matter. It wouldn't change what she had to do.

"By the way," Azar murmured into her hair, "there are alternatives, in our current forms. Ones that don't risk you breeding. I'd be more than happy to—"

"What?" she asked, pulling away, though his arms didn't let her go far. Still she finished acerbically, "Service me?"

An assured smirk slanted his lips. "As many times as you can bear."

Everything inside her clenched at the promise in his eyes.

Reason prevailed, and she tugged out of his grip again.

"Seraphina…" he said, humor threading through his exasperation as he caught at her arms.

Her chin tipped up, jaw clenching to keep her body under the control of her will.

"So there is no ambiguity, I would enjoy sex with you in any form, whenever you may be interested." He chuckled mirthlessly to himself, skimming his palms up her arms as he closed the distance between them. "In fact, I already did, even when the amulet hid your identity."

Something clicked. Had the amulet protected her somehow from the succubus's influence, sheltered Seraphina's power from that interference as it had from detection?

"What is it?" Azar asked, sensing the change in her mood.

She shook the question off, turning toward the other side of the field where their supplies lay waiting. "We should get going," she redirected, heading in that direction to get enough distance to shift.

A low, frustrated growl followed, tightening parts of her that didn't give a damn about all the logic in the world—this one or others. Taking off into the air once more, Seraphina made a mental note to check the Victoria house for condoms.

Chapter 33

S o I was thinking," Seraphina said after they'd crossed back into the empty home with her stash of frozen meat, "while we're here, *Natalia* can go pick up some takeout. If you're interested in trying any more mortal foods."

Sunlight filled both the bedroom and bathing room on either side of them like it had when they'd left. If not for the slightly different cast of the light, it would have seemed like no time had passed at all.

"If you'd like." Azar followed her into the large bedroom, where she dealt with the computer and its cords, attaching one end to the wall. He didn't bother suggesting he could run the errand in her place.

"The computer needs an hour or two, probably. Feel free to sleep or shower… Or, want to watch a movie?" She winced as her eyes fell on the bag he still held, and she started to slide off the bed, saying, "Oh, but the ice packs need to go in the freezer."

"I can handle it," he assured.

For once, she actually listened. "The downstairs freezer has more room," she said, her attention already back on the computer she'd opened.

When he returned upstairs, she was settled with her back against the headboard, the device balanced on her lap. "So, movie?" she asked with an absent smile, tapping blindly on the small keys in front of her.

"Or I could help you plan."

Her fingers froze, a heavy sigh accompanying her knees flattening to the bed. "There isn't much to plan. I show up, the maros happens. I kill my brother, hope that destroys the succubus's connection to the dragons…" Her head lolled to the side as she looked out the far window.

Azar moved forward, dropping to his knees beside the bed. "I'd kill him for you, you know."

Seraphina's head jerked back, her gaze sharpening on him.

"If it was only about severing that connection, if the maros didn't matter, I would kill him so you didn't have to." Even thinking it was treason. Azar wasn't foolish enough to think he could best the Zubir in a fight, but whether through poison or deception, he would have done it to spare Seraphina the pain.

But if they'd learned anything, it was that the maros *did* matter. The Zubir's power *did* impact all the dragons. Which meant the burden of this rested entirely on her.

"And your friends? If I asked, would you kill them, too?"

She scoffed at his hesitation and shoved the computer off her lap, scooting along the bed to get around him.

He rose to block her path. "Sera—"

Her glare severed the name. "I'm going to take a bath, and you're going to get out of my way."

An ache balled in his chest, at the pain she'd suffered, the role he'd played, the lingering disbelief that dragons he'd trusted could have treated her that way. The niggling voice saying he'd known what their anger made them capable of inflated that ball further with every breath. "I will kill anyone who hurt you," he promised, staring into her beautiful, determined face, "unless you would rather do it yourself."

"But?" she prompted through gritted teeth.

Azar's breath huffed out. He'd betrayed Koios to save her, had seen the other dragon's involvement firsthand, and still he couldn't reconcile his friend's participation with the dragon who'd never wanted to join Laisren's faction in the first place. "Koios, did he…"

A measure of understanding—or was it misunderstanding?—softened her stance. "They didn't exactly introduce themselves," she said, her voice a seething, terrifying quiet.

"The one I"—*poisoned*—"gave the ale to," Azar explained. The one he'd ultimately convinced to join the cause. Koios was older, but Azar was stronger, more assured. Before all this, anyway. Clearly he shouldn't have been. His mistakes, his overconfidence had cost both his friend and Seraphina.

"What are you asking me," she said now that she knew whom he'd meant. "If he unchained me? Stood up to the others and let me go?"

They both knew he hadn't. He would have been too scared, not only of Laisren but of his own mother. Azar agreeing to join had tipped Koios over the edge, but his mother's alternating insistence and negligence would have badgered him into it eventually.

"Did he—" Azar swallowed the hard lump that blocked the question whose answer he didn't want to face. "Did he hurt you?"

Clearly fed up with the impasse between them, Seraphina twisted away, walking around the bed.

"I know he didn't help," Azar continued, pleading the case of someone he had to believe deserved it. Someone who might have already been dead, killed for Azar's meddling by Laisren or even Jillianne. "He's a follower, he wouldn't have gone against them on his own. But did he—"

"No." Her shoulders lifted and fell with her breath before she turned back around to face him from her spot in front of the window. Evening light blanketed her like a protective bubble.

A measure of relief let Azar breathe as well. So he hadn't been wrong about at least this one thing. "Then please." He'd extended a hand to her before even realizing it, reaching for her though in this moment she was much further from his grasp than the mere meters between them. "Have mercy on him. Given the chance, he'll follow me rather than Laisren. He'll follow you."

Her derisive scoff bisected his train of thought. "After you tossed him to the wolves?"

Regret dipped Azar's head until his chin nearly brushed his chest. If time had been on his side, maybe he would have reasoned with Koios instead. But his priority had been saving Seraphina. Would he even have the chance to make amends to the friend who'd only been caught up in all of this because of him?

"You drugged your friend to get me out of there," Seraphina said in that measured voice that meant all her emotions had been stuffed beneath the regal veneer. She took equally measured steps back toward Azar, the quiet footsteps stopping when her bare feet reached this side of the bed. "Will you kill him if I tell you to?" she asked, the lightness in her tone belying the topic, signaling a trap.

Azar searched her face, but everything about the Seraphina he knew was lost behind that implacable façade. Even knowing the question was a test, all he could offer her was truth. "I'd beg you for your mercy." His breath sounded louder than normal as the world narrowed only to this moment, the future zubir standing before him, and the answer he couldn't force himself to give. Instead he admitted, "Then I would take his place."

In a personal grievance between dragons, those involved would fight until satisfaction, a netta, the zubir, or death stopped them. But in an official execution, one could volunteer to replace a dragon whose life they found worth saving. Koios could do better, given the right influence and the chance. Azar's influence had taken that chance from him, but he could give it right back.

"I know that isn't what you wanted to hear," he said, cursing the yawning chasm that had reappeared between them when not long ago they'd found a measure of intimacy. At least physically, though it had seemed more than that. "I care about you. But it's my fault he was there to start with—"

"Enough," she interrupted wearily, the mask slipping. "It's not a bad thing to be loyal," she said to the floor. "In any case, my brother comes first, as the Zubir must."

"Please, tell me what you're thinking." He had to widen the crack in that unapproachable shell.

"That none of us has much choice in the part we play," she said cryptically, striding past him back toward the bathing room. Water soon gushed into the large tub.

Dumbfounded, Azar nevertheless followed cautiously, ready to spin away were he to find her undressed. Ridiculous as that was, given the knowledge he already had of her body.

She didn't react to his joining her on the marble floor that delineated the bathing area.

Seraphina, he thought, but aloud he said the part of her name he could. "Nat."

Her head turned so her profile was illuminated by the high windows that flooded the space with light without allowing the outside easy view.

"What can I do?"

"To save him?" she asked without rancor.

"To span this reappearing rift between us." How could all the barriers and pitfalls between them have resurfaced so quickly?

"I don't know."

Because she looked rather small and lonely with the regal walls stripped away, Azar moved forward, stopping short of wrapping his arms around her. "You are my priority," he murmured above her ear. "I will help you plan and fight at your side, and comfort you when you let me." He paused, the erratic beat of his heart warning him not to say the next aloud. "But I will not follow you blindly."

A sigh rippled through her muscles, easing her stance as she turned around. "You shouldn't. Like he shouldn't have." Resignation weighed down her features. "And if I win the maros, the dragons should rally behind me because they want a better life, not because tradition declares it their duty. Blind obedience never led to anything good."

"You didn't want me to say I would kill him." The realization was quickly followed by the certainty that she remained disappointed by his answer.

A mirthless chuckle twitched her cheeks. "Have you ever killed anyone?"

For all the viciousness of the dragons, with no hatchings and so many weakened, they hardly ever killed their own now. In his first hundred years, it had been different. Nevertheless, until the Zubir had lost control, dragon deaths of any cause had been rare.

"No," Azar admitted, "I've never killed anyone." He also hadn't lived his life knowing he would have to. Unsure what answer he hoped to hear, he countered, "Have you?"

Chapter 34

S TILL QUESTIONING WHETHER I'M CAPABLE?" SERAPHINA asked, shunting aside the part of her that mourned the intimacy they'd so recently shared, the taste of peace in his embrace.

"I'm not that foolish."

Behind her, hot water rushed into the tub large enough to easily fit them both, and suddenly the drain of these two flip-flopping sides to their interactions was too much. She'd fallen apart in his arms, only to be left questioning when and how he might use that against her.

Seraphina turned away. "Go," she dismissed.

He hesitated, the faint shadow of his power pulsing closer before his footsteps carried him away. A glance over her shoulder revealed he'd stopped a couple steps past the opening to the bathroom, his back turned. How stupid was she that she felt protected, rather than trapped?

Huffing at her own foolishness, she stripped off her clothes and folded one of the towels she'd grabbed to prop it under her neck. With her hair clipped up and out of the way, she bent over the tub to shut off the water, acutely aware of the visual Azar would have gotten if he turned around. She knew he wouldn't.

So finally, she sank into the hot water, reclining against the sloped edge. She hadn't bothered to look for bubble bath or to check whether the tiny bottle of fragranced oil she'd noticed last time had anything left. Her "bodyguard" might have gotten the wrong idea if she scented the water. The heat would have to suffice to ease the tension running through her.

She'd meant it about preferring the dragons rally around her not out of blind obedience, though pragmatically she shouldn't care why, at first at least, as long as they did. The truth was she didn't want them rallying around her at all.

She didn't want to kill her brother, but she also simply didn't want to lead. There would be so much damage to unravel, to earn back the trust of dragons who'd do their duty while resenting the very existence of a zubir. A position that had never been meant to have such extensive influence over their everyday lives.

And regardless, Seraphina had spent nearly two thirds of her life among the mortals. She wanted freedom from the pendant weighing on her abdomen, but leaving her entire existence here behind, indefinitely?

Her head dropped back to the cushion of folded towel, fingers trailing slowly through the water, displacing the surface like the softest wind. She should have remembered to turn on music or something, but Azar had thrown her off, leaving her with nothing but her thoughts.

She knew the broad strokes of what she had to do, like she'd told him. Announce her presence, prevail in the maros. Hope for the best. There had to be a better way to ensure the dragons were freed of the succubus even if Seraphina failed. Died.

And if she lived, she'd have to figure out how to actually lead.

Water lapped at her skin, and on autopilot she shifted to displace the sensation, succeeding only in agitating the water further, its slide along the tops of her breasts an infuriatingly insufficient caress. Her nipples had beaded from the combination of lingering desire and the heated promise of the bath. Her body forgot the impasse between her and Azar far more easily than her mind could.

Still her head drifted to the side, eyes finding the broad shoulders guarding her from unanticipated, nonexistent intruders. Seraphina palmed her breasts, as if hiding her nipples from view and from that persistent slide of water would somehow lessen the tight need. Maybe if her hands had stayed still, it would have worked. Her body knew what it wanted, and hot water wasn't nearly enough.

Her teeth sank into her bottom lip as one hand let go to find its way down her torso, the other moving in widening circles before skimming the ridges of her closed fingers across the taut tip of her breast.

Despite the unobstructed clarity of the water, Azar couldn't see her from where he stood. Not unless he turned his head just enough to glimpse the reflection in the mirrors above the sink. Even then, he'd mostly see the far side of the tub, where her legs rested, fighting the urge to rub together. Because even if he couldn't see, he could hear. If she made too much noise, he might be tempted to turn and check on her. Or he'd guess exactly what she was doing.

The thought speared heat through her. Vestiges of reason reminded that later, *after*, his knowledge would feel humiliating, not hot.

With the faintest of sighs she forced her hands away, up to the edge of the tub, watching his shoulders for any twitch of recognition. Could she send him somewhere without giving herself away? Was one orgasm really too much to ask?

As many times as you can bear whispered through her mind. Seraphina slapped one hand against the water.

Azar jerked, his head twisting a few degrees toward her. "Are you all right?"

Seraphina clenched her jaw tight against the moan building behind her breastbone. She refused to let it out, no matter the unbearable sensitivity of her unsatisfied need. So much for a relaxing bath.

Memories of Azar's hands and tongue, undeniably adept, weren't helping. If she could have felt his mouth on her without the blood-red cage around her neck, she might have instantly come undone.

The reminder of the catch-22 was like a gut punch, curling her shoulders in around her torso. The dragon in her couldn't indulge in the pleasure he could offer for all the complex politics and loyalties between them, and the human her would always know what she was missing because of the same charm that kept her safe. Well, safe-ish.

"Tell me you're okay," Azar said, his voice tight, ready to spring into action.

"I'm fine," she told her thighs, wavering beneath the settling surface of the bathwater.

"No, you're not," he said, his voice closer. He'd taken a few steps backward, angling his body away from the pair of sinks and the mirrors above them. Maintaining the charade of privacy. "Does the computer need to be monitored?"

The unexpected question knocked the desire aside for a moment. "What? Not particularly."

"We could call a truce." Was she imagining the huskiness in his voice? "Return to…whatever it's called. Stop letting everything else get in the way, and simply enjoy each other."

Her lips parted in a silent moan. In either realm, they kept finding themselves here. The laptop was password-protected. Letting it charge while they recharged almost seemed like the responsible choice, getting this distraction that kept rearing its head out of the way.

It was the perfect excuse, except she knew that was all it was.

Water rushed off her body as she stood, unbearably loud to her ears.

"Is that a yes?" he double-checked.

The small towel she'd propped beneath her head slid slowly down the smooth slope of the tub and plopped into the water. Its larger counterpart waited on the nearest edge of the sink, easily within reach. She could come to her senses, wrap it around her body, and return to the ridiculous number of emails she had yet to sort through. Stifle her desire by ordering a decadent amount of takeout.

Or they could work up a real appetite.

So instead she said, "Hand me the towel."

Chapter 35

T HE MOMENT THEY CROSSED INTO KANSYTURA, SERAPHINA pulled the amulet up over her head. She paused to hang it on a visible branch, letting her towel drop. The wash of her power only augmented the need pulsing in her core.

A slow groaning exhale sounded in her head, followed by Azar's voice behind her. "You aren't even trying to be fair."

Her lips curved as she veered off toward the stream, walking barefoot over the unrealistically soft forest floor, only a structured strapless bustier that plumped up her breasts and lacy boy shorts between her skin and the dappled sunlight. "Seems to me you're the one still fully dressed."

"Not anymore."

The words coiled in a tight spiral low in her belly, but Seraphina refused to give him the satisfaction of looking back. The unchanging prickle of his power proved he was keeping pace with her. She strode to the stream's edge, wading directly into its cool waters before turning around.

Azar had stopped several steps back, his broad shoulders and muscled torso kissed by the unimpeded sunlight in the open air near the stream. Eyes locked on his, she lifted a hand to the clip still on her head, releasing it then shaking out the heavy fall of her hair. The edges of his jaw grew even sharper as it tightened with his swallow. With exaggerated care, she ran her fingers under the bottom edge of the lace hugging her ass, arching into the motion. Though he couldn't see that side of her, his cheeks flushed.

The tip of an invisible talon hooked under the bustier, dead center between her breasts, stealing all color from the world.

"No, don't," she gasped.

Instantly his power withdrew, the faint pressure disappearing. Her hands dropped, her breath coming loud and ragged as her muscles spasmed, disrupting the stream's gentle flow.

Sera— "What's happened, are you all right?" He started moving toward her, drawing up short when she jerked backward.

Her teeth ground into each other, and she tipped her chin up, fighting through the unwarranted panic flooding her system again.

Azar stepped backward as if to give her space. *Come out of the water*, he suggested gently. When she didn't move, he added, "You know we don't have to do this, do anything you don't want to do."

I could say the same to you. Had lust clouded her thinking so much she *had* crossed the line into taking advantage?

A smirk flashed then disappeared. "I've wanted you since I thought you were human."

How could that of all things have been the perfect thing to say? But her eyes found his again, a smoother breath expanding her lungs. Relief followed, the panic receding as quickly as it had overtaken her.

His eyes assessing, Azar moved forward, stopping on the bank with a hand outstretched. Her footsteps splashed through the water, her legs still a little unsteady, which was the only reason she slid her hand in his. His thumb swept over her skin, and he tugged her closer even after she'd made it onto dry ground.

"What happened?" he asked with his arms loosely linked around her.

"Turns out I have triggers."

"Triggers?"

"A human term. Reminders that take someone back to…" The word *trauma* got stuck crosswise in her throat.

Azar's lips pinched even as they turned down at the corners. "I'm so sorry about what happened to you." His hand skimmed up her back, tucking her in closer. At the same time, he sank down, shifting her to his lap in one smooth motion so her butt wouldn't hit the ground.

With a sigh, Seraphina let her head drop to his shoulder. Azar held her wordlessly, the stream's faint babble the only sound or movement.

The trouble with triggers was you couldn't know what they were until they'd hit you. In hindsight, it was completely reasonable that a dragon slicing off her clothes would scream *danger* to her mind now. But she hadn't exactly thought through every possible touch or scenario ahead of time. She hadn't been thinking much at all.

She didn't especially want to be thinking now, wrapped in Azar's arms and his power and his concern for her. Her lips brushed the warm skin nearest them, and immediately he dropped a matching kiss to the top of her head.

Still Seraphina said, "We should get back." As his hands obediently slid away, she straightened. The thin layer of dried mud on her feet broke off when she stood.

The lingering tingle of desire in her breasts made itself known, and Seraphina hesitated. There was a reason she'd gone along with Azar's suggestion of returning here for what amounted to a quickie, even if she didn't want anything about it to be quick. She didn't have the whole plan worked out, but it would be pretty soon, and then they—or she, but it wasn't likely Azar would stay behind—would be returning to Azhidar Zher. This could very well be her last chance to sleep with him, without the amulet in the way this time. And much as she told herself it was good to remove the distraction so she could focus on everything that would have to be done, there was no denying she wanted this.

"Everything okay?" Azar asked, already a few feet closer to the portals that led back to the responsibility of reality.

With reason only a hairsbreadth away, Seraphina didn't want to tempt the Fates to stop this yet again by talking. So she did the next best thing to make herself clear.

Chapter 36

ONE MOMENT SERAPHINA WAS STANDING IN FRONT OF HIM with a contemplative look on her face and that incredibly alluring white-and-blue band cupping her breasts as if offering them up to him. A blink later, the top had disappeared, leaving her bare aside from the long strands of her hair playing peeka-boo with her nipples. The impact was like the most pleasant punch to the gut imaginable.

Still Azar held himself back. *Are you sure you want this?*

Her head tilted, shifting the fall of her hair. *Are you?*

Damn it, Seraphina, you're going to have to actually give me a straight answer this time. Especially after what had happened mere minutes ago. He could handle something making her change her mind, but at least when they started, she had to be sure.

"Yes," she over-enunciated, and a heartbeat later he was back at her side, hands slipping under her hair, down to her ribs as their lips met. The kiss was soft for about a breath and a half before giving way to their pent-up lust. Seraphina's arms wrapped around his shoulders, clutching him closer. Her breasts pushed into him, her hair sliding between them like silk.

Groaning his need, Azar lifted her so their mouths were on the same level. Her legs wrapped around his hips, one of his arms encircling her so his freed hand could palm the delicate lace she'd created specifically to tease him. Quite successfully. Her hips arched back into his touch, their lips and tongues never lightening the ferocity of their kiss.

Seraphina ground lower in his grip, her body wanting what they still couldn't risk. Azar hitched her higher, stepping them toward the line of trees. *Cloak*, he directed as his fingers skimmed over the heat between her legs.

She gasped, breaking their kiss to catch her breath, every exhale puffing against his lips. But a soft drape of cloth appeared over her back, letting him press her into a thick, textured tree trunk. Both his hands returned to grip her ribcage.

He trailed his lips along her jaw toward her ear, flicking his tongue out for a taste of her soft skin before dropping respectfully to her collar. His mouth traveled down along her sternum. Her legs grew slack as he lifted her higher. He licked the spot between her breasts, and her thighs tightened around his ribs.

A faint frustrated sound accompanied her hand sliding into his hair, nudging him toward one side. Tempting as the straining peak—both, either—was, Azar forced himself to slow, alternating soft kisses and swirls of his tongue on her skin as her chest pulsed with the force of her breath.

A quick glance up revealed her head had fallen back against the tree. Her fingers curled against his scalp, into his shoulder, as he continued the measured path up to the top of her breast and over the lush mound, nudging aside a strand of her hair along the way.

He paused to gather himself, pushing his own need aside as she arched to bring the taut knot of her nipple closer to his lips. His breath streamed out, and a faint, impatient *Oh, come on* he likely wasn't supposed to hear followed.

Azar smiled at the sign she was losing that impenetrable control and exhaled against the tip, intentionally this time. A prolonged swipe of his tongue followed, before he caught her nipple gently between his teeth. Her breath hitched, and she froze. A delicate puffed exhale accompanied each time he flicked his tongue over the bud.

When her legs quivered around him, he replaced teeth with lips, sucking her more fully into his mouth. A whimper of relief and need escaped her, her calves pulling him closer as her hips writhed against his torso.

Relying on that contact to keep her pressed up against the trunk, he used one hand to free her other breast from the veil of her hair as he lifted his head away, baring both mounds of temptation to the light. He would have loved to draw her like this, one breast glistening from his mouth, the other waiting for its turn, her lips parted, expression pleading the way she wouldn't with words.

Since she was in no danger of falling, his free hand palmed the neglected breast, massaging with light pressure in small circles.

"Azar," she moaned when he pinched the tip.

And because she rarely used his name, he gave in, swiping his tongue over her nipple before sucking at it. His fingers drifted down over her abs, dipping to the top of the lace before settling back up at her waist, letting him give this side, too, the attention it deserved.

By the time Azar pulled away from her breast, the combination of need and pleasure thrilled just under the surface of Seraphina's entire body. Her patience and control lost to the lust flowing through her with every heartbeat, she loosened the grip of her legs around his torso, expecting him to lower her to the ground.

Instead he shifted her higher, trailing hot, open-mouthed kisses over her abdomen until he reached the edge of her panties. Tongue swirling over the sensitive skin at the base of her belly, he instructed, *Put your feet on my shoulders.*

Too focused on how close his mouth was to where she wanted it, Seraphina didn't think before following his suggestion, slipping her feet in from under his arms and up to the front of his shoulders.

He stepped back out of the way of her bent knees, his hands easily holding her up against the sturdy tree at her back, her hips now level with his face. He pressed a kiss to the inside of her thigh, nuzzling closer until her knees fell open. His eyes flicked down to the wet fabric the movement had exposed before meeting hers.

His gaze didn't waver as he came closer, shifting her knees even wider apart. A smug glint appeared in his eyes when her hand nudged his head closer still. She braced the other on the tree, helping him hold her up so his attention could go where she wanted it. Needed it.

His teeth grazed the flesh of her inner thigh, and a moan that was half whine escaped her throat.

Whenever you're ready, he teased, laving the spot he'd barely bitten with his tongue.

Her fingers curled into the rough bark as she dematerialized the lace, leaving herself bare and open and oh so ready for his mouth.

His fingers curled too, digging into her sides, his eyes so focused on her that she writhed in his grip. Her impatience didn't sway him. Neither did the press of her hand tugging him closer. His tongue had the audacity to lick slowly over his bottom lip, so close but so far from where she wanted. And still, the motion nearly pushed her over the edge.

"Azar." *Come on.* "Please." The words came out a mix of exhale and telepathy and moan.

His eyes snapped up to meet hers, holding steady as finally he swept his tongue out in a long stroke over her, stopping just shy of her clit.

At her whimper, he asked, "Not what you wanted? I, for one, quite enjoyed that," he added, saying the words aloud obviously so his breath could torture her.

At her silence, he trailed his tongue along the edge of her opening, sending a shiver through her. Seraphina let her head fall back. Staring blindly up at the leaves, she gave herself over to another impossibly slow lick. The lust he'd stroked to an inferno left every nerve so sensitive, even the brush of her hair felt like a sensuous caress along the outsides of her breasts. Her muscles clenched, silently demanding more.

Azar lapped at her again, and her hips ground into the firm pressure. As if in warning, his thumbs swept over her sides and then his tongue swirled just as lightly around her clit, sending a pulse of pleasure through her core.

You can be as loud as you want, you know, he said. She would have laughed at the unintentional Broadway reference if not for the tip of his tongue finally pressing right where she needed, letting that waiting reservoir of satisfaction spill over and into her, his hands holding her steady as the swell carried her away.

He didn't move as her tremors settled, a coil of tension remaining in her core. Sensing or knowing or reading her mind that the orgasm still hadn't been enough, his tongue and lips worked over her in earnest now. Lapping, licking, sucking—the expert ministrations of his mouth caught her adrift and pushed her higher then higher still, until finally she cried out to the leaves as pleasure surged through her, leaving her gasping and limp against the tree.

Chapter 37

WITH SERAPHINA LOOSE-LIMBED AND SATISFIED, AT LEAST for now, Azar maneuvered her body into his arms, then lowered her to the ground a few steps away from the knotted roots. He undid the ties of her cloak as her body relaxed into the earth, her breathing still not quite settled.

Laying his own stretch of fabric near hers, he spread out beside her. His fingertips trailed over her torso, occasionally coaxing little quivers from her. With her nipples still tight but body languidly sprawled, eyes hooded with lingering desire, he changed his mind. *This* was what he would draw first.

Hand hovering above the blue-and-purple curls at the apex of her thighs, he asked, *More?*

No, she said, surprising him. His hand fell away as she rose up onto her elbows. "Your turn."

The simple words coalesced all his desire in a tight ball low in his abdomen. Despite it, he said, "You don't have to reciprocate."

She frowned, sitting up and absently flipping her hair forward on one side. It trailed over her breast, the other remaining unabashedly exposed. With her knees pressed together, legs bent modestly under her, and their verdant backdrop, she wouldn't have been out of place on the canvases of many great mortal artists.

Azar sat up as well, dragging his attention back up to her face.

"Can we establish as a base rule that if we're naked, or about to be naked, or doing anything sexual with one another, neither is obligated to do anything. Meaning anything we do is because we want to, not…" Her mouth pinched in distaste. "Politics."

"Definitely," he agreed, filing away the implication that this wouldn't be their last time enjoying one another's bodies.

That edge of frustration dropped from her shoulders. "So do you not want me to?" Mischief glinting in her eyes, she leaned back onto one hand, subtly lifting her breasts.

Though he still wore pants, the thrust of his erection was unmistakable. Nevertheless Azar leaned forward, cupping her jaw to capture her mouth. *Don't be ridiculous*, he said, the feel of her lips and tongue on his sparking insanely erotic images of that mouth settling over him.

A hand on his chest pressed him backward, ending the kiss. Seraphina licked her lips slowly, torturing him as she instructed, *Then lie down.*

Air streaming more quickly through his nostrils, Azar stretched back out like before, this time staring up at the vision beside him, committing everything about this moment to memory.

A fingertip trailed down his abs before both her hands came to the laces holding his pants in place. He grunted at the contact as her fingers worked to undo them. A deliberate skim of the back of her nails made his hips jerk and her lips curve. "You could make this go faster, you know."

He was nothing if not amenable.

Seraphina's smile dropped as the pants dissipated, revealing him fully. Desire flashed in her eyes, popping open her lips and even coloring her cheeks. Azar curled a hand around her calf, propping his other arm under his head.

She in turn curled her fingers around him, her thumb swiping away the bead of moisture at his tip. Loosely her hand moved down and up around his length, a faint promise of things to come. Then her index finger traveled with a touch more pressure down the underside of his cock.

Azar grit his teeth, fighting to stay still under her touch, let her explore however she wanted. She cut a knowing look his way as her hand stroked him firmly twice, three times…

Seraphina.

Her hand stilled, her eyebrows lifting as her head tilted, shifting the fall of her hair to expose both her breasts. *Do you want me to stop?*

His hand tightened involuntarily on her calf, and hers responded with matching pressure, prompting a low growl from his throat. *Absolutely not.*

Satisfaction flashed in her expression before she bent, the loose locks of her hair hiding her face from him, her free hand coming to rest on his hip. She pressed a delicate kiss to the tip, and Azar nearly saw stars. There was the slimmest chance he wouldn't survive this.

A flick of her tongue followed, accompanied by the downward stroke of her hand. Then her tongue swirled around the head of his shaft, and his breath hissed out from between his teeth.

With a frustrated huff she let go of him, straightening, and Azar bit back his protest. Deft motions braided her hair. He took the opportunity to reach for the taut peak of her breast, the touch making her squirm as she shot a rueful grin his way.

The braid completed, he silently begged her to continue. He might have questioned his ability to tolerate the deliberate teasing, but he certainly couldn't handle things stopping there.

Well he *could*, if she didn't want to keep going, but damn everything, he hoped that wasn't the case.

Azar was coiled so tightly, his muscles nearly trembled with the attempt to control himself as his erection jutted up to the sky. There was something incredibly satisfying about controlling that need. And something almost beautiful about the length of him, marbled with thin streaks of the gold from his eyes.

His fingers on her breast reminded that her own need wasn't so far from the surface, but Seraphina moved out of his reach. At the moment, she wanted to focus.

She straddled one of his legs, letting him feel the lingering wetness between her thighs as she considered what position might be comfortable enough to let her bring him the same pleasure he'd given her. For now, she slid lower down his leg, his other knee bending to give her room. So when she leaned forward, her mouth was precisely where she wanted. One hand braced on his upper thigh, her breasts skimming his leg.

Cupping him loosely, she rolled her eyes up to find him watching her. She held his gaze as her tongue licked slowly from his base up the length of him. At his side, his hand clenched into a fist, and his breath developed a ragged edge. She let her lips brush the tip of him once more before parting them to take that darker, more sensitive bit into her mouth, letting her exhale tease him as he'd teased her.

Azar's fist pounded the ground, but he didn't take his eyes off her. Her fingers encircled him more firmly as she repeated the swirl of her tongue, following it with light suction.

Sera—

Another flick of her tongue stole the rest of the thought. He twitched in her mouth, a jolt of his hips pressing him a touch deeper. She sucked at him again, working her hand in even strokes.

He growled, but she stopped, bringing her head up as she caught his thought. *Wait.*

A few steadying breaths later, he fixed her with that intent gaze, darkened by desire to the point that the gold flecks seemed to gleam. *I want to show you something.*

Seraphina started to straighten, but a concentrated push of power froze her in the crouch. It arrowed to her core, caressing the most sensitive parts of her, inside and out. She gasped, grinding into his leg even though it was his power, not the contact, spiking pleasure through her.

When that power receded, she was met with Azar's determined yet pleased expression. True, she'd only been with humans for centuries, but it wasn't like she'd never fooled around with dragons before, in mortal form at least. She didn't remember either of them being capable of anything like this.

You'll have to show me how to do that sometime, she said, managing to sound somewhat flippant though her muscles still quivered with that piercing need.

For now, though, she let him watch her tongue licking over him before taking him back into her mouth, dipping lower and lower over him with each stroke. A brush of power thrummed through her clit, and she moaned around him, making him groan in turn.

But if this was a contest to push the other over the edge, it was one she would win. Pulling back enough that only the tip of him remained in her mouth, Seraphina swirled her tongue in circles, adding a quick suck before changing directions. Her hand moved in smooth, slightly twisting strokes, speeding up along with her tongue as she reversed directions again.

Azar's power fluttered inside her then against her skin like he was losing focus. The muscles under her other hand tensed as his leg twitched, and her hips instinctually ground back into him. Still she maintained the pattern she'd found, sucking a couple times now between circles of her tongue. She glanced up his body to find his eyes still glued to her, and since that made her falter, she took him deeper with a hum that made those eyes shut with a deep groan.

Finally he gave himself over to her, letting his head fall back as his hips pumped in tiny jerking motions as if he couldn't help himself. She sucked at him with him still filling her mouth then resumed the circling pattern, interspersing it now with light flicks across his tip. Azar's breath caught, his body going taut with tension before the orgasm overtook him, a low growl growing into a full-throated groan of satisfaction that ended with him going limp beneath her.

Seraphina twisted off him, falling partially to the side onto the cloak. Pleased as she was at the fruits of her labor, so to speak, there was one little problem: his little trick had left her wound nearly as tightly as when they'd first arrived.

Azar wasn't human, however, and he recovered quickly. His hand tugging at the one that still rested on his thigh, he pulled her up until she straddled his waist. The knuckles of his other hand skimmed down her breast, pinching briefly before continuing down until his fingers slid along her slick opening. Two slipped easily inside as his thumb rested on the precise point demanding his attention. Seraphina braced on his ribs, her hips writhing in anticipation.

A lazy, contented smirk stretched Azar's lips, his fingers unmoving until a new whimper of frustration escaped her lips. Power swirled inside her then, spiraling her need tighter as she squirmed and quivered around his fingers. Her braid had come loose, strands of hair escaping to tease her skin.

She gasped as Azar swept his thumb across her clit, adding an extra flicker of power. It thrummed through her as her hips danced on his hand until the spiral burst, alighting all her nerves in a glorious rush of pleasure.

Chapter 38

S ERAPHINA COLLAPSED ATOP HIM, AND AZAR BRUSHED HER hair back from her face before wrapping her in his arms. Their lungs battled for the space between them until gradually their breathing settled into an easy rhythm.

Not long after, she rolled off him, one hand lingering on his chest before she sat up, the message clear. He rose as well, and they moved as one to dematerialize the cloaks they'd laid upon.

As she strode to the tree bearing the amulet, she wrapped herself in a knee-length white dress with a purple-and-blue vee accentuating her waist. They walked in silence to the exit, each step carrying them farther from the temporary peace they'd found by the stream, like they were marching off to a war. In a sense they were, or would be soon, and had been ever since he'd found her.

Could we extend our truce? he asked before she could pluck the charmed pendant from its branch.

Seraphina startled from her thoughts, turning back toward him. Reality seeped into her expression, replacing the contentment of moments before. *I don't want to fight you unless I have to.* A sigh escaped her lips. *Do I have to?*

Certainly not. He reached for her hand, and after a brief hesitation, her delicate fingers slid into his. *So I've been wanting to ask,* he added, this moment perhaps as good as any.

Hmm?

Can you extend your glamour to others?

Her brows pinched as she let him go. "Hold out your hand," she instructed aloud.

Azar did as she asked, and she considered the limb awhile. When nothing happened, she brought her hand close to his again. The colors of her fingernails alternated, but his hand remained unchanged. A light graze of her palm didn't produce results either.

Guess not. A small frown tugged at her lips as she twisted to reclaim the pendant he never wanted to touch again. She clasped it into place, tucking the stone beneath the neckline of her dress, and disappeared through the archway that would lead to her property in Canada.

Azar cast a parting glance at the unnaturally silent forest before following.

"Are you in the mood for anything specific?" Seraphina asked, already halfway to the large bed where the computer waited. "Food-wise," she clarified.

"Ser—"

She spun around, fear flickering in the depths of her eyes. "Don't."

"My apologies." Still he closed the physical distance between them, cupping her jaw. Only when his thumb swept along her cheek did he realize he didn't have the words.

And the words he suddenly wanted to say, needed her to know, she wouldn't welcome. Besides, it really was too soon.

In his silence she rose on tiptoes to brush his lips, then slipped away.

"You have a plan, don't you." The heaviness blanketing her confirmed it.

"Did you want to take a shower?" she skirted, engrossed in the device that connected her to everyone but him. "Or we could defrost some of the steaks."

"Why won't you talk to me?" He could help her refine her plan. After everything they'd been through, everything they'd just *done*, how was it she still didn't trust him enough to fill him in?

"Because I still want to save him!" she snapped, her eyes closing against the flood of her emotions. Her shoulders rose and fell with a measured breath, those seconds enough to find her strength, settle her voice. "I *wish* the glamour had worked on you just then, because I'd have my solution. Fake his death, get him away from the succubus, and we could all move on. But I can't!" Her head shook lightly. "With the funeral pyre, it wouldn't work anyway. It's literally not possible. Don't," she added when he lowered to the edge of the bed.

This time, however, he knew the thoughts behind the word, despite the amulet she wore. So his hand dropped to her leg, offering what wordless comfort he could.

"I know what you're going to say, that the maros has to happen for the power to transfer to a new zubir, but that's not true," she insisted, her eyes pleading for him to agree with her.

"If it were, his fate would never have been tied to that of the dragons in the first place."

He hadn't thought of that. Regardless the maros had to be completed. The dragons wouldn't accept her as their zubir any other way, and without belief, how could they be freed from the succubus's influence?

"I wish he didn't have to die," Azar said, meaning it. She scoffed, but he wouldn't be swayed. "The Zubir must die, but I do wish you could save your brother."

"Yeah, well," she said, deflating. "If wishes were horses…"

"Even beggars would ride," he murmured.

A tiny twitch of her lips shifted her mood through a flicker of humor to an exhausted resignation. "What do you want to eat?" she asked again.

"Whatever you've been missing. And…"

Her eyes rounded expectantly in his pause.

"Something sweet?" Desserts of all kinds were perhaps the thing he missed most since his time in the United Kingdom. Seraphina might not be sharing her plan with him, but he could tell they'd be returning home soon. Dragons could live well on meat alone, but that didn't mean they couldn't savor the fruits of humans' inventiveness.

The twitch of her lips was equally small, but a more genuine humor lit her face this time, tightened her cheeks. "Sure."

Her eyes drifted back to the computer, so with a parting slide of his fingers along her leg, Azar stood and headed for the shower. He helped himself to one of the towels stacked neatly on the shelves in the connecting alcove, dematerializing his clothes when he entered the glass stall. Only to be stymied by the complex series of knobs and levers.

He spun around, intending to call for Seraphina. And there she was, reclined against the headboard, in plain view of the shower. The plan of this suite was a fair bit more…intimate than he'd realized before. Only an opaque strip of glass around his midsection protected anyone in the shower stall from full view of someone on the bed.

Jealousy fluttered through him at the notion of her here with human males, only to be replaced by a spear of heat at the idea of her eyes on him while he washed. At any point, she could look up from her work, catch sight of him. Would that distract her from everything currently weighing her down?

Not if he couldn't even turn the water on. Wrapping the towel around his hips rather than wasting energy to create something he'd only dematerialize moments later, he stepped out and called, "Natalia."

Her head swung toward his voice, unfocused eyes landing on him. Her gaze sharpened as it trailed down his body. Satisfaction curled in his chest at the appreciation there.

Silently she slid off the bed and approached, detouring around him to step into the stall. She checked something, then pointed to the handle in the middle of the wall. "Pull up to turn on the water. If it's not hot enough for you, turn it up here," she added, tapping a circular control.

Her eyes flicked to the visible bedroom as she stepped back out, her cheeks pinkening. "I'll, uh, go work in the office. Give you some privacy."

"There's no need," he assured, holding back a smile.

She didn't, lips tugging up as her weight settled into one hip. "Bit of an exhibitionist streak, huh?"

He gave up the fight, his lips mirroring hers. "Look all you want." As far as he was concerned, she could touch all she wanted, too. But she wouldn't, even if she weren't preoccupied with setting her plans into motion. Not here, where the charmed pendant would prevent her from truly feeling it.

Still her body stretched toward him, as if any moment she'd rise up onto her toes for a kiss. Instead, she sighed, twisting around him on her way back to the bedroom. Computer in hand, she shot him a final glance that dipped down to his towel, then she disappeared from view. "Enjoy the shower," she called before the bedroom door clicked shut.

Chapter 39

ORE?" AZAR ASKED, STRETCHING OVER THE BACK OF THE couch to reach the bottle of wine on her kitchen counter. Remnants of the takeout she'd picked up lay scattered around them on the couch and the oversized ottoman they'd nudged within reach.

Seraphina silently raised her glass for the Sauvignon Gris she'd found in the wine cellar. Like the rest of the house, its racks lay mostly empty, except for a few special bottles patiently gathering dust. Azar resettled in their corner seat, one arm casually around her shoulders. The other lifted another cannolo to his lips.

She let the unusual white wash over her tongue as his eyes closed in response to the dessert. There were a couple chocolate-raspberry ones left, but Seraphina was stuffed. It was easy to let contentment suffuse this moment between them, but there was no ignoring the time ticking away.

Azar crumpled a napkin between his fingers, squeezing her shoulder lightly. He tipped his head down for a soft kiss that tasted of sweet ricotta. Even as he pulled back, the calm denial of their meal gave way to a more somber apprehension. Seraphina tried to wash it back with another large sip of wine. Predictably, that didn't work.

"So are you going to tell me your plan?" he asked quietly.

"I told you," she said with a sigh, letting herself have a few more moments pressed to his side. With the excuse of setting her wine glass down on the floor, she straightened away from him. "It really does boil down to showing up, letting my brother and all the dragons who can hear me know I'm there for the maros, then trying to kill him. And then killing—" She cut herself off before finishing with *your friends*. It wasn't entirely fair to keep blaming Azar for the actions of the others. He'd been manipulated, and when he'd realized the danger to her, he'd stepped up to intervene.

"You can't simply stroll through the sobran and up to the Zubir," Azar said, moving to the perpendicular side of the couch.

"With glamour, clothes from here to match the colors... No one there will recognize me or have reason to look beyond the surface. And I'll be bringing a special gift." Ridiculous as she found Nahash's hoarding of treasure, she could easily sacrifice some of her collection to fend off any lackeys who'd otherwise bar her way. "What do you think—a bar of gold?"

Her snark was in full force, but Azar didn't react to it. "The dragons at the sobran, they'll notice you. They'll feel your power."

"From what you said, there are enough of them there that I'll barely make a ripple."

"You don't understand." He shot up, running a hand through his hair as he stepped around their emptied containers of food.

Seraphina's hands wanted to smooth the disturbed locks back into place. Instead she settled deeper on the couch, slipping her fingers under her thighs.

"Your power—" Azar's head shook as he searched for words. "Believe me, they'll notice. It doesn't matter how many are around."

"Okay." She nodded in the face of his intensity. "So I'll use the amulet." It had been centuries. She could handle having it on her awhile longer.

"Wearing it will leave you too vulnerable. Even with me at your side, with hundreds of dragons around…"

It was a fair point. She wouldn't want to make her presence known before she was face-to-face with her brother, but there were many who would try to prevent that from happening, even if they didn't recognize her. "Well then, pockets. I'll keep my hand around the stone and let go whenever I need to. And—" She hesitated, standing to point out, "You won't be there."

Concern wrinkled around his eyes. "What are you talking about?"

"I doubt you have a literal price on your head, but Laisren and the others will be after you as much as me. Without glamour, you're too recognizable. I have to focus on what I have to do, not worry about—" She cut herself off, but he guessed where the thought was headed.

"Protecting me. Far cry from wanting me dead at least," he said with a wry frown.

Not much she could say to that. Of course she didn't want to see him hurt, and she couldn't be distracted with worry any more than she would have been with lust. When facing her brother, she would necessarily be alone. Like she would as zubir.

"I can protect myself, you know," Azar said softly.

"Not if they ambushed you. Do you know somewhere safe? Maybe away from any of the tribes." He'd be too conspicuous among the other tribes, maybe even mistaken for one of Nahash's envoys. Both the Drevan lands and the sobran weren't good options. "Or there's always Kansytura."

"You want me to hide?" Disbelief made his voice hoarse.

Ignoring the pang in her chest, Seraphina lifted her chin and straightened her shoulders. "I want you to do as you're told."

The ottoman between them was littered with leftovers and trash. Letting pragmatism rule, she bent to begin cleaning up. It all had to be taken care of before they left anyway.

Moving slowly, Azar's hands scooped up more of the containers. She really hadn't held back with the food, even though it wasn't quite their last meal. She had a few more things to take care of before confronting the fate she'd avoided.

Dumping the trash, she turned to face him from the little alcove of a kitchen. "There are only two ways this ends, you know. With me dead, or me as your zubir." He couldn't join her in the latter fate, and she refused to let him join her in the former. "Anything else was nothing more than a moment between time," she echoed, the words coming out smoothly despite the gnawing ache behind her breastbone.

Recognizing his own words, or perhaps simply giving in to the inevitable, Azar remained silent as he placed everything he'd gathered onto the countertop, his expression unreadable. Never had Seraphina wanted to intrude on another's thoughts more than now. Lucky him that the amulet prevented such invasions of privacy.

"If you have it," he said tonelessly, "you should choose something older to wear."

She turned away, moving back to the couch so she didn't have to face this version of him quite yet. "I didn't think dragons kept up with the latest fashions."

"Exactly. Knowing what the humans are wearing will mark you as someone who's been here recently, which would raise questions."

"Good point," she admitted, not for the first time. Azar had shown himself to be a useful asset, in these small ways of his. "Follow me."

For once fate—but definitely not *the* Fates—seemed to be on her side. This house was actually the perfect place to find something in an older style for her to wear.

Azar followed her through the archway beside the game table tucked into the corner, then to the left into a room she hadn't ever bothered naming. Regardless of its intended use, Seraphina had stuffed it full of storage containers, dressers, and most importantly wardrobes. She hadn't kept all the clothes and things she'd acquired over the years, donating much but holding on to her favorites. Over centuries, that piled up. Maybe that dragon instinct to hoard had come into play a bit. This room was stuffed full with memories, most kept in beautiful artisanal armoires.

Seraphina's palm lingered over one made of carved cedar. She opened it to search through the garment bags she'd periodically updated to keep everything safe. A more recent dress in blocks of neon caught her eye. "What do you think?" she goaded, giving her skin a luminescent green tinge and turning her hair bright orange. She marbled a glowing pink into her skin for extra oomph.

Azar had stalled by the door. Confusion shifted underneath that composed mask. "No dragons look like that."

"I know," Seraphina assured, dropping the neon look and replacing the dress. "I was kidding. I was thinking green or blue," she added, seized with a ridiculous need to fill their silence. "Something understated." The whole point was to be overlooked.

She skimmed over anything else with bright colors. "So you know," she said, moving to another row of wardrobes, set back to back with this one, "tomorrow we have to return to the Peran Estate."

It was risky, if Laisren expected the return and had it staked out. But if he or his lackeys were there, she'd kill them sooner. Not like the human justice system was something she had to worry about. It was a smarter call to conserve her energy for the maros first, but she wouldn't waste an opportunity if one presented itself.

"We could go tonight," Azar suggested.

Seraphina ignored an olive skirt suit a dear friend had hand-sewn for her, looking blindly through the wood in the direction of his voice. "Why?"

Was there a trap waiting back in Pennsylvania, after all?

"You like it there," he said guilelessly, his power growing nearer before he appeared in the makeshift aisle beside her.

"I do." She turned back to the clothes, safely sealed in their protective bags. "Too bad I have to sell it."

"Why?" he parroted.

Since this armoire was filled with ball gowns that had never been meant to be inconspicuous, she closed it and moved on to the next. "So no one can trace me back—" She spun toward him as her mind caught up to what she was saying.

His indifferent posture thawed, a glimmer of warmth returning to his eyes.

"I guess I don't have to sell it." Like she'd told him, there were only two options: either she'd be dead or she'd be zubir, with no need to keep hiding from other dragons. There was an odd freedom in that.

"I didn't see much of them, but the grounds looked beautiful."

"They are." She'd assumed they would spend this night back at Kansytura, using the burner phone to keep track of time but mostly enjoying each other while they could. Apparently those condoms she'd bought while out picking up their food had jinxed it.

Much as Seraphina hated to admit it, it was probably for the best. Whatever the outcome, Azar deserved to move on with his life. This distance between them would help that happen.

"Sure, all right," she said, unzipping a garment bag to find a mint-and-cobalt dress that would suit perfectly well. "We could wait out the night there. You still have that ID they gave you, right?"

Chapter 40

THEY LEFT ALMOST EVERYTHING BEHIND, READY AND WAIT-
ing in that in-between space with the portal. Seraphina
hadn't let him know when precisely she intended to enact her
plan, but whether she meant to return awhile or simply pick up
the supplies she'd need, the trip would be easy enough with her
network of portals. They didn't even seem to need charmed objects to carry one through. No wonder she had eluded so many
for so long.

Azar followed her through that cold mist sensation, appearing behind the couch in her private sitting room. Seraphina—or
was it Tia now?—started to step out of his way, but Azar wrapped
a hand over her mouth, his other arm around her waist. He
backed into the portal, stumbling against the solid wall.

Seraphina stiffened in his arms, straining against him.

"Hush," he whispered as softly as possible, his lip brushing
her ear. "Someone's here." He couldn't quite place the sound,
but they were certainly not in the manor alone.

Stilling, she nodded sharply, her breath trembling through her torso. Azar dropped his hand, keeping both arms loose around her in case she stumbled from the adrenaline or surprise. The unsteady beat of her inhales echoed in his ears until she turned around.

Her eyes flicked briefly to his before fixating on the wall behind him. Steadying herself with a palm casually braced on his chest, she rose on tiptoes to reach his ear, breathing, "Dragon?"

On instinct his head turned toward the bedroom door, and he flared out his power. His shoulders stooped as he shook his head. He'd scared her for nothing. "I'm sorry—"

"No." She still spoke quietly, only for his dragon ears, but moved the half a step away to lean on the back of the sofa. "Thank you for your caution," she added, her lips finding a tense curve though she remained pale. "At least that means they shouldn't be able to hear us."

A touch of humor lightened her expression when she glanced behind him again. "These portals still require power, so humans couldn't accidentally"—her fingers fluttered in the air—"fall through." With a calmer breath, she straightened from her perch. "We should go see who it is."

She strode confidently through the opening into the bedroom, but Azar caught up with a touch on her elbow. "I should go first," he said when she turned back.

Her jaw shifted, lips tightening with her frustration. He hated reminding her of the amulet, of the way it limited her powers. But despite her insistence that there could be nothing more between them than what already had been, he cared for her. Besides, of the two of them, he was in that moment both more powerful and more expendable.

They moved together toward the door, but after tapping her fingertips against it, she let him walk through first.

"Stairs?" he mouthed to her. The sporadic noises were faint, but they did seem to be coming from the lower floor.

Seraphina frowned her displeasure from the doorway but gestured to her right. For the first time between them, he led the way, creeping silently through the hallway then down the stairs. He peered below, but the dining room sat empty, and the mumbling sort of sound was further off. Seraphina followed only a step or so behind. Nevertheless, his reflexes should allow him to protect her from any human intruder.

They continued into the dining room, but Azar stopped when they reached the entrance to the butler's pantry. He huffed out his frustration, only slightly letting down his guard. "Naiara."

"Oh my—" She whirled on them with a large blade held at the ready. "Fuck!" she added upon seeing him.

"Naiara?" Seraphina repeated, coming around him. At least she remained within easy reach, not heading for the human.

"Tia? What the fuck." The knife-bearing arm drooped, though her eyes flicked to Azar. "What are you doing here?"

"What am *I* doing here?" She scoffed. "What are you doing? Who else is here?"

"No one, it's just—" Naiara smiled sheepishly, the green stud in her nose catching the light. It matched the new forest green and aqua of her hair. "No one was using it?" She headed for them, exposing the array of vegetables on the island she'd been using.

"Knife," Azar murmured, warning both the women in distinct ways.

Naiara didn't heed his caution, swinging it inexpertly through the air. "Scared I'm going to stab you with it?"

"No," Seraphina corrected with a sigh. "He's scared you're going to stab me."

That drew the human up short, still on the other side of the butler's pantry. And though she'd used it plenty already, the syllable took on an entirely different meaning when she repeated, "Fuck."

"You can't be here," Seraphina said the moment she and Naiara had lowered to the couch tucked into the corner of the informal dining room.

"Back up," the human ordered, with no filter or dissembling. "What are you doing back here? And what are you doing with *him*?"

"Naiara, seriously. Why are you here?"

She slumped, lips pursing in a frown. "I lost my job, okay? And when I couldn't make rent, I figured… No one's here. All this space sitting empty, and you were going to talk to the owner about me taking over your job anyway." She turned an accusatory stare on Seraphina. "Then again, you also said you left because of a family emergency. Yet here you are with the hottie TA who disappeared with you. Since you wouldn't let me stab him, I take it he didn't kidnap you."

Seraphina couldn't prevent a little huff of humor. She'd missed her friend. "I'm sorry about your job. Has anyone been by asking about either of us? Or the owner?"

"No, you weirdo. What the hell is going on?"

So maybe Laisren had realized Seraphina wasn't likely to come back here. Not for more than a few hours, anyway. How much would she need to share to convince Naiara to leave? Just because he hadn't yet shown up searching for clues—or weaknesses to exploit—didn't mean he wouldn't.

"So, Azar…" she started, knowing full well his dragon ears would easily be able to hear them from the kitchen the same way he'd heard Naiara singing under her breath from all the way upstairs. "We didn't know it at first, not until we spoke later that night, but he knows my brother."

The human's mood shifted instantly, and she placed a hand on Seraphina's knee. "I'm sorry. You never mentioned him before."

The question remained implied, but she answered it anyway. "We're estranged. Believe it or not, I'm the black sheep of the family."

"Hardcore delinquent like you?" Naiara deadpanned.

Seraphina chuckled. "Even I can make waves under the right circumstances. I've refused to do what's expected of me for a long time."

"And what, Azar is your new babysitter-slash-bodyguard?"

"Azar is…an ally." It was the truest description of their relationship. That she could say aloud in his presence, at least. He was an asset, a tool she was using to help her free the dragons. There could be nothing more between them than that.

Seraphina resettled on the couch, reaching for Naiara's hand. "Listen, that doesn't matter. You can't stay here. It's not safe. Let me help you out with rent money."

"What, is the place condemned? I'm not taking your money. When it starts falling down around me, I'll leave. Seriously, who am I hurting?"

"You." It came out more forcefully than she'd intended.

Her friend sobered, eyes narrowing. "What does that mean?"

Air rushed from Seraphina's lungs as she rose from the couch, pacing a few steps away before turning back to face Naiara. "Okay, look. You know how in all those action movies the hero tells someone, 'I can't tell you, because it'll put you in danger.' But inevitably fills them in, and equally inevitably their friend or lover or whoever gets captured by the bad guys to be tortured or killed? The bad guys are of course incompetent, so the hero shows up in the nick of time, saves their loved one, and everyone lives happily ever after?"

Naiara's brow quirked. "Where are you going with this."

"These bad guys *aren't* incompetent."

Naiara's tongue ran over her teeth with a little *tsk* as she took that in. Skepticism still colored her voice when she asked, "What does all this have to do with your family? And with lover boy in there?"

Seraphina bristled. "What do you mean by that?"

"Oh, please. Anyone with eyes could tell he's smitten." Naiara's head tilted, considering her.

"Our goals are aligned," Seraphina said when the human's lips parted to add something inevitably inopportune. "Look I get it," she redirected, "you need a place to stay. It can't be here, but I can give you money for a hotel until you find somewhere. Or for a deposit on a new place."

That got the human up off the couch. "This isn't you," she said quietly, all her attitude drained away.

The truth prickled against Seraphina's eyelids. "A lot has happened."

Naiara stalked toward her, concern bringing out the defiant

warrior side of her. "Then don't go back. Or—" She paused, deflating a little. "Call the police or something."

If only she could call someone, hand over responsibility for fixing the colossal mess Nahash had created. In this little metaphor, Seraphina was the one the dragons could call, the one with the power to fix it all. Hopefully.

And at least one of them had called her, as Azar's pulsing energy reminded. He was staying out of sight, but she could feel him pacing beyond the wall.

"I told you, I can't explain everything right now. What matters is you're not safe here."

"But the two of you are? Why would I leave if you're in danger here? We both know I'd be more help in a fight than he would." A little smirk tugged up the corner of Naiara's lips.

Seraphina's lips echoed it reflexively. "You totally would be."

If none of them had been what the humans considered supernatural, Naiara definitely would have been the fiercest of them. Seraphina returned to the couch, hugging her knees up to her chest as the soft cushions cradled her body. Naiara plopped beside her, throwing an arm around her shoulders.

"We aren't staying either. I have to sign some papers tomorrow, and then we'll be gone again." She reached out a hand, offering what comfort her touch could. "I'm sorry about your job."

Naiara shrugged, the movement awkwardly jostling through both their bodies.

"Look, it's complicated, but I have the money to help you. So let me, okay?"

Hazel eyes considered somberly for a prolonged moment before Naiara's head tipped, leaning in to Seraphina's. "Okay."

"Tia." Azar appeared in her line of sight, the concern in his eyes tightening the ache in her chest.

Naiara straightened. "Dude, way to ruin a moment. You sure he's one of the good guys?"

"Most days," Seraphina assured, not taking her eyes off the Drevan dragon who'd gone from nuisance to enemy to lover to ally. And now?

"You—sit," Naiara commanded, gesturing to Seraphina's other side.

Azar startled but took his ordered place, a hand brushing over Seraphina's arm where it was looped around her knees, the other cupping the back of her head.

Naiara squeezed her closer. "Whatever the fuck's going on, you can handle it," she murmured with enviable conviction. "The bad guys won't know what hit 'em."

Seraphina didn't speak, soaking in the certainty, the confidence. She'd returned here to take care of the technicalities, the estate's future in case she never came back. That and to pick up the last piece she needed to face her brother, or so she'd thought. Turned out, sitting in silence embraced by her friend, cocooned in that support and faith, was what she'd needed most.

Emotion had no place in the maros, or everything that would come after it. Seraphina would have to be ruthless. But in the solitude that would follow, she could hold on to this moment.

With a final squeeze, Naiara stood. "If you aren't leaving until tomorrow, you know what that means." An impish gleam had returned to her eyes.

Seraphina smiled back, her feet dropping to the floor. Despite Azar's bemused look, the women proclaimed together, "Movie night."

Chapter 41

WHICH DO YOU THINK WOULD MOST PLEASE THE ZUBIR?" Seraphina mused hours later, her tone betraying that she wasn't really asking as she examined the small velvet-lined drawers she'd removed from the dresser tucked into the corner. The jewels displayed atop her large bed were likely worth more among the mortals than Azar had ever seen at once, even when he'd served the British nobility in their finery. They paled in comparison to the Zubir's hoard.

After enjoying dinner and a recorded performance called a movie, they'd helped the human pack up her things. As she hadn't been there long, the time had been spent more on consuming bowls of ice cream. Much as he would have preferred to be the one holding Seraphina close, Azar had stepped out into the hallway. He didn't wander far, offering the two friends at least the illusion of privacy without leaving Seraphina entirely unprotected. The artwork lining the walls had been plenty to hold his attention.

Or it should have been. Instead, he kept returning to something she'd said. If she lost the maros, they were all doomed. But if she triumphed? She made it sound as if she'd be equally out of his reach.

He'd failed her on such a fundamental level. The tenuous truce and undeniable passion between them didn't change that. Would she ever truly trust him at her side?

Seraphina sighed now, stacking up the square drawers to replace them in the locked cabinet. Its twin sat on the opposite side of a large wardrobe, but rather than examine its contents, she rounded the bed and strode into the adjoining sitting room.

The distance she'd carved out between them prevented Azar from speaking. From his spot near the opening between the two rooms, he could easily see her approach the fireplace. She brushed her fingertips along one of the stones, and it popped open, revealing a deceptively large secret compartment. When she turned to him, a gold bar lay cradled in her palm, her fingers hidden by the soft fabric in which it had been wrapped. Was this what she hadn't wanted him to observe the first time he'd been up here, the night they met?

"I thought you were joking."

"I was." Her shoulders shifted in a gentle shrug, the bar remaining steady in her grip. "Seems like it'd be most effective." She frowned at the gold. "If a bit unwieldy. A collection of gold coins doesn't quite have the same impact, though."

"The Zubir should certainly be pleased with an offering like that." For a few moments, anyway. He was easily distractible. But Seraphina wouldn't need anything more than a moment.

She rewrapped the gold, tucking it back into the revealed compartment.

"If I am with you at the sobran, I can plant the seeds, let some know of your return to save us." One thing the Zubir hadn't yet found a way to do was to spy on their speech by intercepting telepathy.

"No," she said sharply. "It's too risky, and there's no need."

Do as you're told echoed in his head with her tone.

Seraphina dropped to the end of the angled couch, similar in style to the one directly below them in the living room, though a bit different in shape. She brought one knee up to her chest in an echo of her earlier pose, her arm curling about her leg as if to offer comfort. He would have been her comfort if she would have let him.

"You heard me talk about the lawyer coming tomorrow," she stated.

He wouldn't deny something they both knew to be true.

"I'll be signing paperwork naming you the primary heir to my Earthly possessions."

The implication speared through him, his feet carrying him forward a few steps before he caught the motion. "You won't fail."

"If I do, you can house many dragons on my properties, purchase or build more. Save them from his cruelty, maybe save us from extinction."

In his stunned silence, she added, "A backup plan is important."

"Listen to me." He stalked toward her, his hands rising as he crouched beside her. He cradled her face gently despite the roughness of his breath. "You will *not* fail." The fate of all dragons lay in the outcome, yet all that mattered to him in that moment was not losing her. It was selfish, and stupid, and undeniable.

Her hands came to his wrists to dislodge his grip, a haunting defeat deep in her eyes. "You need to be prepared either way."

Azar bowed his head, resettling the grip of their hands so his fingers were threaded with hers. He wouldn't change her mind with this worry. "Come outside with me," he suggested. Naiara was safely asleep, and wonderful as it had been for Seraphina to spend time with her friend, they'd come early for the grounds.

She nodded and stood in the same smooth motion, and soon they'd made it out onto the deck. Stars glinted in the inky sky, a plump moon shining over the acres of greenery.

Seraphina lay on one of the couches, the soft light glowing in her skin. Azar sat on one of the matching rectangles, allowing him to face her and the grounds rather than the house. Though glamour had turned her hair a pale blond, it remained silky under his touch. He'd expected her to object to the liberty of running his fingers through it, but she simply let her head fall toward him, meeting his gaze.

"What does it feel like?" he asked.

For all that they'd started out hardly able to find common ground, she understood exactly what he meant now. "A bit like holding hands while wearing thick winter gloves." A deep breath turned her head back up to the sky. "Still nice, just...not the same."

Was *nice* enough for him to move to the couch beside her, lean down and kiss her, let them both forget for a few moments more?

Before he could decide to act, Seraphina lurched up off the cushions, growling as much as her human form allowed. Azar zeroed in on the threat that had her hand ready to tear off the amulet. Hardly a breath later he stood between her and the two small figures on the porch railing, each not even the length of his palm. Seraphina's barely controlled rage with its undercurrent of fear pushed at his back.

"Your Highness," the one in a silver cap said, both bowing low to the railing. "We bring you a message, and an apology."

A third figure, bound nearly head to toe by thin vines, appeared between the two. There was something familiar about him despite the rage twisting his expression. Seraphina's sharp inhale was covered by the sound of the captive's spine snapping. His body fell limp.

The one in a mustard cap hobbled forward a couple steps. "Please know, we do not hold with Madern's actions," he said, eyes trained on Seraphina, who'd come around Azar enough to see the creatures. "We want no quarrel with one such as you."

"Is that your message?" she asked, only the breathiness of the final syllable giving away that she wasn't unaffected.

"No," the silver-capped one said. "This"—he kicked at the lifeless body, whose binds had begun browning—"was the apology." Though their faces were already wizened, the grooves in his deepened. "Koritza is dying. You haven't much time."

Chapter 42

"THAT'S IT, THEN," SERAPHINA SAID ONCE THE FRONT DOOR closed behind the lawyer. Since Naiara had already gone, she dropped the glamour she'd kept subtle enough that the older human had noted her "remarkable" resemblance to her "mother."

Azar hadn't strictly speaking needed to be present to be added to the paperwork, but it had been good for the lawyer to meet him. Although the man had pulled Seraphina aside, stammering only slightly over his words as he cautioned her not to give her "boyfriend" such nefarious motivation. She'd almost laughed, mostly at the grimace Azar tried to hide since human ears wouldn't have heard the exchange.

It was kind of the man to worry. Hopefully he wouldn't force an investigation if she died. She'd already written up instructions for Azar on contacting her trusted forger for a death certificate.

He'd been understandably grim ever since hearing the dream weavers' message. Both of them needed Koritza to survive as long as possible, practically speaking at least until after the maros. Though Seraphina had fond memories of the older dragon, for Azar, this loss would be deeply personal.

"You should go," she said, climbing the grand staircase in the entryway, because why the hell not? She'd used it far too rarely.

"Not yet," his determined voice said behind her.

She'd held him last night after the weavers left, though perhaps they'd held each other. Discussing plans, and eventually finding sleep only because they would both need their strength.

It didn't take long now to gather the gold and leave the mansion behind. Only moments more to change into the dress she'd selected, tucking the gold into one pocket and a thick pouch into the other, ready for the amulet.

Azar stood waiting with his satchel, filled with frozen cuts of meat she'd had to insist he take, if not for himself then for Koritza, who'd doubtless been sacrificing her share to younger dragons.

"It's time," Seraphina said. Glamour would be necessary to fool the other dragons, but she would remain herself for this goodbye.

"Not yet," Azar repeated, tugging her through the portal in the wall. His stance as rigid as his expression, he added, "Take it off."

She slipped the necklace off, removing the pendant from the chain to place it within the prepared pouch. It fell to the grass as Azar's lips met hers in a desperate kiss, crushing their mouths together. Her arms pulled him closer. *Please be careful,* she said as she savored the taste of him, the feel of his body pressed to hers.

His fingers wound into her hair, the furor of his lips easing into a kiss that felt like a goodbye. If they did see each other again, everything would have changed. Tears prickled behind her eyes as Seraphina let him go and stepped back. Azar's hands landed on her shoulders.

We could just pretend, you know, she said. *Ignore it all. Stay here and have a lot of sex.* Her head swung back to the portal that could take them through to Canada. "There's a whole box of condoms, right through there."

His thumbs brushed over her collar, lips tugging in regret. *But you really are the Savior of Dragons. You could never be that selfish. Even if I could,* he added with a sigh, his hands skimming down her arms as he took another step away.

She crouched to scoop up the pouch and settle it in her pocket. "What if it's a trap?" she asked aloud, her power flickering in and out as she tested the stone's position. They'd covered the possibility in depth last night. She wouldn't put it past Laisren to sacrifice an ally to get what he wanted, but Azar verifying the weavers' information posed the same risk as him going to Koritza's side, and really, there were no good reasons to postpone what Seraphina had to do.

"Listen to me." He waited until she met his gaze before continuing. "You're incredible, and you can do this," he stated as if they were indisputable facts.

"Let Koritza know I expect her there after the maros," she deflected, though she filed the words away, wrapping his certainty around her resolve.

With a humorless smile, Azar nodded. Traditionally, all the nettakim witnessed the ritual fights and convened the zoval soon after. If things were dire enough for the weavers to genuinely deliver such a message, Koritza wasn't likely to make the trip to the sobran at all.

Tacit agreement passed between them, and Azar stepped toward the portal that would lead him back to the Drevno. When using charmed objects from the zubiran tower, dragons could return only through the main portal in the sobran. But Rhea had placed no such limitations on this portal, which could open anywhere in Azhidar Zher.

Despite the temptation, Seraphina had never risked it.

"I'll see you soon," Azar said, though his eyes lingered as if burning the sight of her into his memory.

Seraphina slipped her hand into her pocket. "After the maros," she specified, holding his gaze until his chin dipped again. Words that needed to remain unsaid floated through her mind, but thankfully the amulet kept them unheard. There was no place for softness in what would come next.

After Azar disappeared, Seraphina returned to Earth and its mirrors so she could be sure of the glamour changing her to match the dress. Soon unfamiliar pale-green eyes stared back from her equally green face. Possibly her last time ever seeing her reflection, and it wasn't even her face looking back.

The misted magic of the portal back to Kansytura did little to calm the anticipation building under her skin. Seraphina paused before the archway that would take her back to the home she'd been forced to flee.

Now the fate of a species rested on her shoulders. Could she save the dragons without losing herself?

Only one way to find out.

Chapter 43

THE SOBRAN WAS CRAMMED WITH ACTIVITY, SO NO ONE PAID much attention to the green dragon slowly making her way to the ancient stone tower. Or maybe they did. Telepathy was one of the first powers the amulet stole. Just because no one commented on her presence aloud didn't mean they weren't commenting. This had always been true for the dragons, privacy much less foreign a concept for them since conversations usually couldn't be accidentally overheard.

Seraphina paused in her winding journey to breathe under the weight of power pushing at her in all directions. Azar had been right: it would take time to readjust to being surrounded by her own kind. Time she couldn't waste now.

Still she made mental notes about what she saw. The group of dragons grinding wheat into flour by hand was particularly absurd. It would be far more efficient to pop over to the humans and buy a bag. The mortals had taken their world; the dragons could take advantage of their industry. And was it even taking advantage if they paid for the goods they used? The heap of treasure glinting by the zubiran tower could purchase more flour than these poor souls could grind in a lifetime—and a dragon one, at that.

The ridiculous desire to fulfill every mortal stereotype by lying atop the mound of gold and jewels seized her, but Seraphina shook it away. It didn't exactly look comfortable, even if her hide could take it.

"What are you smiling at?" someone growled at her in Drakonazyk.

The smile Seraphina hadn't noticed dropped away, her shoulders hunching. "Apologies," she murmured, scurrying away from the striking jade dragon with enough cerulean marbled through his skin to rival mortal concepts of Neptune. Social media would lose it at the simplest portraits of her kind.

She forced that thought away, too. She had to stop thinking of everything in human terms, but how could she? She'd lived among them nearly twice as long as she had here. How farcical that the dragons' own rules made her the only one able to depose her brother and lead.

Or perhaps her familiarity with the mortal world presented an opportunity, if she survived. The portals limited how much they could take through, but why couldn't the dragons learn from the humans? Purchase the occasional supplies? Assuming their ability to do glamour returned.

And that Seraphina could rid them all of the succubus. And survive the maros.

Her fingers clenched around the twin weights of her offering and the amulet keeping her hidden, just another face in the multicolored crowd. Well, not exactly *twin* weights, the gold bar far heavier. So much so, she had to hold it aloft within the pocket so it wouldn't weigh down the dress too much as she walked. No need for an observant dragon to realize what she carried and try to take it for their own benefit. Seraphina wanted to be face-to-face with her brother before revealing her true identity, and according to Azar, a gift for Nahash's obnoxiously large treasure pile was the best way. Even if the ten-ounce bar she held was barely a splinter compared to that heap.

She skirted a group weaving clumsy baskets, adrenaline making itself known under the cold prickle and bite of others' powers. At the edge of the activity, maybe fifty steps remained between her and the zubiran tower. Deep breaths combatted the anxiety that made her mouth dry. Guards or friends or lackeys—whatever Nahash wanted to call them—would stop her before she reached the old stones where she'd spent much of her child-hood.

Not far behind the tower, the ground seemed to disappear, though she knew better. An enormous amphitheater had been carved into the rock walls of a relatively small valley. Or maybe the realm had been created with the amphitheater already in place, somewhere to gather the first dragons to inhabit this place. Refugees, technically.

"Where do you think you're going?" The voice jolted through her muscles. The Fates really were bitches.

"To see the Zubir," she said calmly, looking Egill in the face, nearly daring him to recognize her. It wasn't smart, but then neither was he. Even knowing Seraphina could do glamour, he didn't connect the body before him with the one from the cave. It probably helped he wasn't looking anywhere near her face. Would he recognize her when she killed him?

The bad guys won't know what hit 'em. Naiara's words twitched her lips, but despite the shot of relief, Seraphina kept a tight hold on her blank mask, burying the anger simmering inside her. Azar had put names to the faces etched into her memory, but she hadn't anticipated seeing any of them here.

She let Azar's words flow through her mind like a mantra, re-centering her. *You're incredible, and you can do this.* He hadn't meant facing her would-be rapist, but why not add that to her To Do list for the day?

She should have expected Laisren would have spies close to her brother, and if the jewels draped on Egill's chest today were any indication, he'd relished whatever the position required of him. If he stood between her and Nahash, she might have to adjust her plan. But if she had to get the Zubir's attention through violence rather than a gift, so be it.

"Why would the Zubir want to see you?" called a red dragon, joining Egill but standing apart from him, as if he, too, couldn't quite stomach the idea of being this close.

"I have an offering for him."

Egill smirked. "Give it here, then."

The red with enough hidden black that he wore clothing of that color—or did they swap clothing now?—cut him off with a sharp glance. Still he said, "We'll pass it along for you."

"Surely the Zubir wouldn't take kindly to you taking something of his," she countered coolly, the fingers of her left hand slipping to the edge of the pendant.

Egill stepped around her dramatically. "I don't see an offering, do you, Audoin?" A malicious grin split his face. "If you meant to offer him your body, I can assure you, the Zubir's not interested. So run along." He sneered, letting his eyes wander down her torso again. "Unless you have a gift for me?"

Audoin frowned at the vulgar suggestion but didn't soften. "Produce the gift, or get back to work."

Ignoring the part of her that wanted to drop the pretense and get this over with, Seraphina recalibrated. Strategy would serve her better than force, for now. "This gift is for zubiran eyes only," she said, backing away.

It was a gamble, but then so was her entire plan. Even Azar's information suggested her brother wasn't *always* at the tower. If he wasn't there now, he may never hear of the random dragon with hardly any power demanding to see him. Or maybe rumor would reach him days from now. Seraphina couldn't wait days, but she could conceal herself among the others for a while, re-consider her approach.

A harsh grip on her upper arm stalled her in her tracks. "I told you to stop." Irritation sparked in Audoin's eyes.

"I'm sorry, I must not have heard," Seraphina apologized, fanning those sparks into angry embers. She *hadn't* heard him, but the innocent comment implied the red didn't have enough power to reach her telepathically. It may not have been true, but he was manhandling—dragonhandling?—her, the stones in his many rings digging into her flesh. Knocking him down a peg or two wasn't entirely out of order.

"The Zubir doesn't like your games," he growled, dragging her along as his long legs ate up the ground, bringing them ever closer to the tower.

Her flesh bruised under his grip, but Seraphina waited si-lently to see her brother, searching the air for him. Even with the amulet, she felt his power growing closer. Muted, almost like it was buried at the bottom of an ocean, but still different enough that it stood out among the other dragons.

Or was it some kind of early imprinting that helped her recognize her kin? Her last living family member.

Don't think about that now.

He disappointed her, coming not from the air but on foot around the base of the tower. A female moved at his side.

Seraphina blinked repeatedly to avoid gaping at the succubus's beauty. There wasn't any single feature she could pin down as particularly alluring, but the sense that she'd never seen someone more striking was startling. Distracting enough that Seraphina's mind stopped whirling with all that had to be done.

Audoin dropped to his knees, bowing before the Zubir. His fingers brushed the back of Seraphina's calf, like he would have yanked her to the ground as well if she hadn't stepped forward.

The succubus pouted, her mouth a perfect moue, lips glistening in a way even glamour would have a hard time mimicking. Nahash, meanwhile, appeared more bored than irritated. His skin was tinged gray, or was she projecting? Hoping to see proof he wasn't himself, as if that could save either of them from what was to come.

"You forget yourself," her brother said. The first words he'd spoken to her since their father's death.

"A gift." Seraphina stopped within easy reach, pulling her right hand from her pocket.

Amusement sparked in Jadokari's eyes, interest finally waking Nahash. A mountain of gold in a land where it ultimately bought nothing, and still he sought more.

No recognition or even acknowledgment passed in Nahash's face when he lifted the bar from the cotton in which she'd wrapped it. Even the rich blue of the material didn't give him pause, despite her current pale coloring. "I will pardon your trespass." He looked up, frowning when he realized she still wasn't on her knees. "*This* time," he added with a touch of menace.

"It won't happen again," Seraphina murmured.

Nahash shifted his weight as if to leave, only her insolence keeping him here. It was now or never, but how could *this* be the moment? Wasn't there more that needed to pass between them?

"Punish her," Jadokari whispered in his ear, cementing Seraphina's resolve.

She pulled her left hand from her pocket, dropping all her glamour. Shock and hatred brought Nahash's eyes to life, but she spoke before he could act.

"I am Seraphina Ignatia, daughter of the last true zubir," she said aloud and telepathically to all the dragons who could hear her. Which was every single one at the sobran. No one ever explicitly compared their telepathic range, but Seraphina had always known hers to be on the higher end. At least in the literal sense, she had no problems making herself heard. Gasps and whispers began before she'd even finished.

"Fly fast to your tribes," she instructed, intentionally contradicting one of her brother's ridiculous rules. "Tell them I have returned. The maros takes place at dawn."

Chapter 44

A CONSTANT VIGIL SURROUNDED KORITZA, WHO LAY CALMLY on her favorite stretch of pale-gray stone, soaking in the sun and taking in the central Drevan lands. Behind her, a giant slab studded with stones as varied in shades of brown as all the Drevno glinted in the light. The scene wasn't much different from normal except for the anxiety pouring off the dragons. Two Radno guarded the penned livestock, but even those named for the tekkess were more focused on their Netta than confronting the zubiran envoys. The fights never changed much, though they did help with the general feeling of powerlessness among their tribe.

Azar hooked his leg around the tree where he hid, leaning forward to search the dragons for Laisren's co-conspirators. There was something ominous about the fact he hadn't spotted one yet. But then, they did like to huddle in their little clearing at the edge of the mountains. Azar gripped the bark tighter, his fingers snapping it off the trunk. He would have gone straight to that clearing if Seraphina hadn't wanted to confront those involved in her abduction herself.

Besides, there was a reason he was here. Azar palmed the satchel sitting at his hip. *I have meat,* he said. Soon enough, dragons would start picking up on the scent, despite the acrid smell of scorched carcasses in the air.

Koritza didn't budge, or respond.

Sera— Tasuna wanted you to have it.

The eyelid he could see lowered lethargically.

I don't know if you don't have the energy to answer, or the desire. He huffed out his shame, shutting his eyes against the image of his Netta fading. *I'm sorry.* She hadn't been thrilled when Azar had taken up with Laisren. *I trusted one dragon and distrusted another, and both times I was wrong.*

A quiet snort of amusement carried from Koritza's snout, though there was nothing amusing about his nearly catastrophic mistake.

Ignatius's daughter is back, Azar assured. However they'd gotten there, he didn't question Seraphina was the best thing for the dragons' future. That she would do her utmost to care for and protect all of them. *Soon, so soon you'll be receiving word from the sobran, but I'm telling you, she's back. Things will change. We need you to lead us through that change.*

Azar had been one of the last dragons hatched in centuries, but his parents couldn't have foreseen that. They'd taught him to hunt, to feed himself, but beyond that, they'd lost interest. Koritza hadn't stepped in as a surrogate parent, more like a surrogate presence. She'd encouraged his training, his growth, and sponsored his trip to the mortal realm, though he'd returned with enough saved to repay the investment. Later he'd realized he hadn't been a special case; she cared for all the Drevno, as a good netta should, intervening when and how she felt necessary. Much as Azar had as a youth appreciated her care for him, perspective allowed him to appreciate her care for each of them all the more. Whenever she died, he would grieve her, and he would be far from alone.

But if she passed before the maros, everything would be thrown into chaos. Perhaps Seraphina freeing them all from the succubus would grant Koritza the strength to live awhile yet. Even if not, the future of the dragons caught up in the tekkess had to be reason to hold on an additional several days. For that matter, Koritza deserved to pass secure with the knowledge the Drevno were on a better path.

Please, allow me to bring you this gift of meat, frozen as it is. Allow it to bolster you.

Are you quite finished? came the weary reply. *I will not fly to you, and you will not climb down from that tree to which you cling like a primate.*

Azar's lips curved. He should have known their Netta would have sensed him, no matter how weak.

I see you've grown more cautious. Or is that more afraid?

Both, perhaps. The dragons' extinction wasn't exactly imminent when he'd left, but it hadn't been that far off, either. There hadn't been much at all to lose before. Now there was not only the future of dragonkind but Seraphina herself. He loathed the idea of her being at the sobran alone, implementing a plan that despite all her strategizing and research still hinged on a guess.

Meanwhile her safety depended on how quickly dragons spread word of her return. If enough learned her identity, her brother couldn't assassinate her. It was a point of honor Seraphina had been certain he would adhere to. Azar's doubts about the Zubir's honor hadn't been allayed. And it would take time for the news to circulate.

Seraphina had held something back, however, merely ordering him to trust her.

Igantius's daughter was strong even as a child, Koritza commented. On the great slab, she heaved her body upright. *It takes more than strength to rule.*

The livestock grew restless, and soon the dragons did as well, noting the approaching flurry of wings.

She was wise to leave, less wise to return, Koritza continued.

Azar's mouth popped open, though he had the presence of mind to protest in thought, not making a sound other dragons would hear. *She returned to save us all.*

Consider perhaps, countered the spent voice of the Drevan Netta, *whether we should have saved ourselves.*

Chaos spread through the Drevno as news of the approaching messengers made its way through their web of telepathic reach. Dragons in human and their natural forms converged upon the central slab, appearing from within the forest, the direction of the bathing pool, or their scant few rows of traditional vines. Even the zubiran plants edged closer, startled by the rare sight. Few Drevno had standing permission from the Zubir to fly between the sobran and their tribe, and these weren't them, unless much had changed in his absence.

With everyone distracted, Azar swung down from the tree. He padded over the soft earth to hide within the ranks, keeping to their edges but gradually making his way closer to Koritza.

Fed up with the fights already breaking out among them as dragons argued over the significance of the news, jostling each other, taking old frustrations out on one another, Koritza roared her impatience. Disgruntled huffs were exchanged, but most settled, many of those in mortal form now shifting.

Azar found a seat behind a boulder close to Koritza's tail, wedging himself as close to the rock formation as possible. Impatience filled the air as the Drevan emissaries neared, waiting until they'd landed to announce their news.

The revelation transformed anticipation into hope and disbelief and even anger from those who felt abandoned by Seraphina's choice, who saw her actions as selfish the way he had mere weeks ago. Or perhaps among them were those who planned to end the zubiran line, their coup now at the very least delayed.

Quiet, their Netta's voice whispered through the assembled minds.

Heads swung around to face her, even Azar's neck craning though there was no way to see her from his position.

Stop gossiping. Gather the others. I expect you all to show this ancient ritual the respect it deserves.

It's a lie.

It's a trap!

Azar didn't recognize the first voice, but the second was Tapio, who'd have no reason to doubt Seraphina's return, having seen her firsthand. So, what, the plan now was to discredit the news?

How dare *you show your face here?*

Azar straightened from his crouch, facing the wave of hatred. With the boulders at his back, he had no space to shift, leaving him at a distinct disadvantage. *I did what I had to. What Laisren ordered was wrong.*

The magenta-streaked muzzle growled, baring sharp teeth. Azar steeled himself for the anger he deserved. Koios would never really hurt him.

Would he?

Chapter 45

THE RUSTLE OF WINGS HAD STARTED BEFORE NIGHTFALL, BUT even now with the sky losing its inky blackness to the hint of light that preceded dawn, no dragons ventured into the amphitheater that served as their true gathering spot. None except Seraphina, who had spent these hours stretched out on one of the stones of the lowest rung. With no more need to hide her identity, she'd replaced the mortal dress with a comfortable outfit in her own colors, keeping tight hold on the pouch that housed the amulet the entire time.

Rather than sleep, she'd spent the night centering herself, discarding distracting thoughts and fears. She might yet fail, but her plan seemed sound. If she couldn't save the dragons, perhaps she really had never been meant to lead in the first place. And if she lost, maybe the magic she'd misunderstood would infuse her brother with the strength he needed to do better. The Fates were tricky that way.

The crush of conversation up on the plateau above her dulled as the first hint of sunlight blossomed across the sky. Seraphina sat up, paused for one more deep breath to calm the prickle of gathering adrenaline, then stood, replacing her sweater and loose pants with a formal gown moments before the first figure appeared in the air above her.

Snippets of speculation danced through her mind, overwhelming the defenses meant to keep private conversations out of her thoughts. She was out of practice.

Seraphina unclenched her jaw, forcing another slow breath as dragons dropped to the stones stretching up around her. Hundreds of wings furled close to bodies, making room for others, as a multitude of eyes in a rainbow of colors sought her out. None of the dragons settled near her, the amphitheater intended for far more than the thousand or so dragons Azar had estimated to be alive today. Still most settled in clusters within their tribes.

Seraphina kept her gaze trained neutrally on the center of the grassy ellipse as pinpricks of resentment made themselves known through the cacophony. Among the dragons surrounding her, plenty were rooting for her to fail, some outright hoping for her death. It came as no surprise.

How many knew what Jadokari really was? How many simply hadn't cared?

Long minutes passed as the dragons streamed into the amphitheater. Seraphina fought the growing tension between her shoulders, forcing herself to keep the flow of air moving through her lungs even. She remained still, her posture impeccable, her expression neutral. All the openness recent decades among the humans had encouraged wouldn't be welcomed here. The same viciousness the dragons resented in her brother's rule was required of them both in the maros. No one thought too much about the paradox they cultivated. The zubir was more symbol than individual. No show of empathy or heartfelt pleas would change this crowd's loyalty, sway their sympathy. Only power mattered here.

And she had that in spades.

Seraphina slammed her mind closed to the racket around her, incinerating any lingering softness in the flames of her determination.

A lone shadow appeared and all movement around her ceased. Nahash descended in a lazy spiral. Seraphina's lip curled as he lowered himself to the ground for the lithe figure riding him to slip off. By the time he'd shifted to human form, she'd schooled her expression back to neutral.

Jadokari swept a pleased smile over their audience before turning to Seraphina. The impact of that gaze doused the fire in her gut, that indecipherable beauty whispering at the edges of Seraphina's shields, coaxing her to capitulate to the succubus's pleasure.

A delicate hand curled around Nahash's arm, crimson-tipped nails in stark contrast to his white tunic. The crisp material underscored the ashen cast to his skin.

Disgust and worry blended to extricate Seraphina from the succubus's mind games. Her fingers clenched around her secret weapon as she strode to meet the couple waiting regally for her approach.

A smug smile contorted Nahash's face, but this was one concession Seraphina was willing to make. Let him enjoy the perceived upper hand of her coming to him under the watchful eyes of their kind.

"Submit," he commanded when she stopped within easy reach, "and I'll make your death quick." His smirk kicked up a notch. "If not exactly painless."

"How lovely to see you too, brother." Noting their shared blood would do nothing to sway him, but it would remind the others: she was daughter to Ignatius Zmay, her claim to the role of zubir as strong as Nahash's, the maros's conclusion not in fact foregone.

Keeping her expression pleasant, Seraphina offered the velvet pouch she held to the succubus.

Nahash's smile slipped, his body shifting forward to shield the figure at his side. "A trick?"

"A *gift*," Seraphina corrected sharply. Her tone softened perhaps a bit more than she'd intended as she met Jadokari's eyes again. "For my brother's chosen mate."

Satisfaction gleamed in those hypnotic eyes, the simple motion of Jadokari accepting the pouch so elegant it sparked a deep yearning for the briefest touch.

Pity for Nahash saved Seraphina this time. No wonder he'd fallen under the creature's power.

Jadokari hefted the pouch before tipping it over her other palm, and a spike of adrenaline pushed the impact of the magical roofie further back. Seraphina's breath froze, the gleaming stone she'd worn for centuries seeming to drop to the luminescent surface in slow motion.

What if she'd been wrong and this didn't work? Even if Seraphina won the maros, would they ever be free of Jadokari?

Chapter 46

THE AMULET HIT SKIN AND ALL THE BODIES FILLING THE amphitheater inhaled at once, the whisper of breath pillowing the sharp sound of Nahash's disgusted roar as he sprang away from the succubus.

Jadokari bared pointed teeth in a face whose beauty had been stripped away. Rotted flesh and brittle skin stretched over the sharp protrusions of her skeleton, its proportions no longer quite right, as if certain bones had been elongated, others warped. The gleaming perfect locks of her hair had been transformed into a haze of damaged brown with a hint of moldy green that protruded around her head in what Naiara would have deemed a crazy case of bedhead.

The only touch of beauty that remained was her eyes, a gleaming red iris in a sea of black. That and the inarguably beautiful gown that now hung off her frame, the incongruity highlighting the disparity of Jadokari's true form from the visual they'd all been fed before. Her grotesque fingers spasmed around the stone that had once again proven its worth.

Nahash looked about ready to vomit, gaping at the creature he'd welcomed into his bed, and all their lives.

Amid the roar that had grown around her, Seraphina tipped her chin up, her unimpeachable posture no longer feeling like a false contortion. *Quiet*, she murmured in the minds of the dragons, and the second shock of her voice's reach made them obey.

"Leave, or die," she said aloud for Jadokari's benefit. It was a bluff, none of her research having revealed a way to kill succubi. But even if Nahash wouldn't act, the dragons would tear the decrepit body apart. Maybe that wouldn't kill her either, but it probably wouldn't be pleasant.

Jadokari hissed at Seraphina before adopting what was likely intended to be a seductive stance, her hip jutting to one side. Where the cutouts in the fabric had previously shown off the softly inviting expanse of her skin, now her ribcage protruded toward Nahash despite the portions rotted clear through, revealing glimpses of gooey gray organs.

He wasn't as generous as Seraphina, taking his true form a heartbeat before his talon slashed through the succubus's neck, swiping her head clear off. By the time it landed, its beauty had been restored. Somehow the effect wasn't the same as it bounced bluntly on the grass.

Relief washed over Seraphina as she stepped back from the headless figure with sludgy garnet welling at the clean edge of its neck. She shifted, stretching her wings under the sunlight of her home. Her fight technically hadn't even begun, but when the decapitated body crumpled to the ground, its fingers still clenched around the amulet, this first success felt like victory.

Before anyone could think to claim the stone for their own purposes, Seraphina released a burst of fire over the outstretched arm. All those years ago, Rhea had instructed that only a dragon's flame could obliterate the magic imbued within. No matter how the forthcoming fight turned out, Seraphina wouldn't need its protection again. She'd considered keeping it as a weapon, but there was no way to hold on to it during the maros. Destroying it was better than risking it falling into the wrong hands.

It took only seconds for the fire to burn itself out, the succubus's body remaining untouched by the heat. It deflated as its blood—or whatever the equivalent was—oozed into the ground. With no magic left to keep the corpse intact, the sludge also seeped through the holes dotting the flesh and into the rich cloth of the gown.

Disgust roiled through Seraphina's gut and through their audience. For the first time, she swept her gaze over the dragons she would soon be fighting to lead. Though she didn't let her eyes linger on the cluster of Drevno, Azar's form was nowhere to be seen. Which was as it should be. She was the one who'd instructed him to stay away. She couldn't worry about Laisren's attempts to retaliate while she fought her brother.

Still regret panged in her chest. Recorded history said the maros changed you. Maybe it was magic she hadn't appreciated, or simply the trauma of killing your kin. Either way, soon enough she'd be someone else entirely. Or dead. Did he realize that goodbye had been, effectively, their last?

Enough! Nahash roared in her mind, and Seraphina swung her head back around to him.

A petty part of her wondered how many others had heard him, how far his powers reached. With deliberate nonchalance she resettled to face him head on. Dragons weren't at their most elegant on the ground, but the rules of the maros were clear: only when they took to the sky did this battle begin.

Embarrassing me will be the last thing you do. This time she had no doubt the words had been meant for her alone.

You mean saving you? From the parasite you called a lover? she needled, letting her own words reach the others. Even now, did they realize the danger he'd allowed into Azhidar Zher? The threat he'd blithely welcomed?

You're pitiful, he growled in her mind. *You never had it in you to be zubir. Now I'll finally be rid of you.*

To the skies, then, brother.

His lips pulled back at the repeated reminder of their blood ties, his girth lowering to his back legs. Seraphina sprang into the air before he'd even pushed off the ground. Bodies below repositioned to better vantage points as she cleared the top of the amphitheater, Nahash's bigger wings easily bringing him up alongside her. Seraphina veered out of his path with a flick of flame ostensibly toward his tail, but really as a warning to the pair of figures sneaking greedily near the mound of riches.

Longing and grief throbbed in her heart as she took in the larger dragon, a blend of red, yellow, and black edging his wings. He'd always hated his coloring, considering it an impurity, glamouring it away back when he could. Back then the colors had almost glowed against the bright white he so preferred. Now there was that ashen cast to his scales, to the veins of black and yellow along his back. Had that glow she'd envied been glamour too?

Maybe he'd never been quite as powerful as she'd believed.

That couldn't matter now. Cockiness wouldn't help her win against his stronger wings, the longer reach of his talons. Impatience rolled in her mind, the dragons already growing restless with their little midair staring match. She may be fighting for them, but even so, they couldn't matter now, either.

What mattered was tearing apart the beast before her. What mattered was surviving. What mattered was making her first kill.

Chapter 47

NAHASH LUNGED FORWARD, TALONS ALREADY AIMED, AND again Seraphina dodged. She couldn't stay on the defensive.

She twisted up and out of his reach, getting her bearings above him for only a moment before dropping down to slash at his back. Her claw barely made a mark, but that wasn't the point. The first hit was hers.

Nahash roared his displeasure. The dragons below stayed ominously silent.

Seraphina took the opportunity to fly higher, stretching her wings and stoking the anger roiling within her. She'd thought Nahash had been duped, that perhaps it hadn't been his fault. And maybe he hadn't known the extent of the succubus's influence, how she'd sucked the dragons dry. But still, he'd done this to them, his rule fracturing the easy peace of her childhood—and of centuries before. Threatening their very lives.

A roar tore from her throat as she spun back around to the dragon following her ascent. He should have waited below, made her come to him. But strategy had never been Nahash's strong point. His neck extended, his jaw aiming for her tail. Seraphina whipped it across his face, following the petty strike with a burst of flame along his shoulder.

He recoiled from the heat, and she went in for the follow-up, her talons catching his underbelly near the shoulder joint.

A light burn across her foreleg revealed she hadn't managed it unscathed. Matching him injury for injury wouldn't work, his greater girth easily giving him the advantage there, too. She'd been so much younger when she'd run from the maros, so certain she would win. So certain she *could* be faced with that final choice of taking her brother's life. What if that had been nothing more than a trick of memory? Was hubris bred into their line? Nature seemed to favor him, even weakened as he was.

Behind you, whispered through her mind, snapping her out of her thoughts just in time for her to drop in a spiral descent. Seraphina pulled up short barely above the ground. Suddenly the dragons encircling her seemed more like weapons, extensions of her brother's will. Interfering in the maros was against the rules, but faced with the possibility of accepting her as zubir, would any of them play fair?

I knew you could hear me, Azar teased, pulling her back to the present once more. So he was here, and he was safe.

Focus, Seraphina, she admonished herself, soaring around the edge of the amphitheater in a wide ascent. Nature might have gifted her brother with greater size, but there was one trick she knew he didn't have. It felt like cheating, but if this was the advantage she'd been granted, she would sure as hell use it.

Nahash dove, his wings pressed tight along his side, the blood from his wound already dried atop his scales. Opening her mind to his, searching out his thoughts from the cacophony below, Seraphina swerved then once again propelled herself up.

Higher and higher she flew, away from all those minds with their internal monologues and endless conversations. Nahash redirected easily, following her up and away from them all.

Rage and hatred blurred the details of his intentions as he drew closer. He lilted left and disgust sharpened Seraphina's mind. Teeth bared, she didn't evade his telegraphed swoop down to his right, flying straight for him. Her jaw latched on the flesh a human would have called an armpit, her claws sinking into whatever they could reach. Her hind legs scrambled to find purchase on the tops of his, even as his own claws swept mercilessly along her sides.

Bitter blood pooled in her mouth, and she tore out of his grasp rather than swallow, burning it away with a belch of flame. His body shadowed hers, and Seraphina sped away, across the pit below toward the sand dunes beyond. She had to get above him. In the scramble of claws, neither had caught wing. Was he injured enough for her to take him down?

Running again? Nahash taunted.

She twisted mid-flight, redirecting up. Behind her an enormous freshwater lake beckoned. But even its pristine waters couldn't cool the revulsion burning within her. So many reasons she wasn't ready to lead, but there was no chance she'd be worse than this waste of flesh and bones. Of power.

Her teeth gnashed together. *Remember this?* she threw back, picking a few judiciously placed scales for a push of glamour. She almost laughed as sunlight bounced off the reflective patches, blinding him. He veered his head away, his eyes shutting reflexively. She dove. Claws shredded the gummy flesh of wing.

He yanked away, tearing her off-balance before she could dislodge her talons from the sticky mess. Seraphina fled upward, scrambling away before he could lash back out. His fangs scraped against her hind leg, a pointed tip tearing through flesh when she twisted out of his grasp. Better than letting him bite it off entirely.

Below them, dragons had scrambled to the top levels of the amphitheater, necks stretching toward them, a rumble of noises matching their telepathic cheers and jeers. As if this were entertainment, not life and death. Hers *and* theirs. She had to finish this, one way or the other.

Wings outstretched, she pointed her body down toward the fool who'd forced this on them both. Anger made him arrow for her as well. Petty triumph pulsed through her as she twisted her wing around his uninjured right one in the same maneuver she'd used to take down Azar.

Nahash's neck was longer, and he angled it back, snapping at her. She growled back, forcing their bodies into a descent that could easily have killed them both. Maybe it was what they both deserved.

She wouldn't give him the satisfaction.

Desperate, he lashed out with flame, but Seraphina didn't duck the heat like he'd wanted, her scales flaking painfully even as she sent her own fire back at him. Pulling his wing in closer to her body, she aimed for the stretch of grass where Jadokari's decaying corpse still lay. Vanity made her glamour the worst of her injuries into mere scratches. She wouldn't give the dragons below the satisfaction, either.

Don't you dare! Nahash roared as she dropped them beneath the edge of the amphitheater, the vocalization from his throat echoing off the stones.

Goodbye, brother, Seraphina thought, detangling her wing. With one more vicious twist of her body, her legs found purchase on his bulk, shoving him toward the ground as she lifted away. The silence was near perfect when his body hit, the dragons apparently too shocked to even think.

Nahash's head twitched up off the ground. She swooped down, landing beside the body that was healing even now. It wouldn't take much time for him to recover enough to attack once more.

Without even seconds to waste, Seraphina bent to the last of her kin. Blood dripped from her jaw as she tossed a massive chunk of his throat into the air as proof. It slipped down her own throat, scorching her with its significance. Fire cleansed her once again, making way for the roar that poured out the loathing overwhelming her every cell.

You did it, an awed voice she should have recognized whispered through her mind before the dragons lent their voices to her triumph.

Chapter 48

THE MOMENT SERAPHINA FLIPPED A PIECE OF HER BROTHER'S throat into the air, something changed. Maybe they didn't understand it, but all the dragons felt it, falling silent before a swell of recognition sounded through the amphitheater. That extra zing of power rushing through Azar's veins left him light-headed. Was it always like this? The transfer of power to a new zubir a rush of promise.

Seraphina had accomplished everything she'd set out to. Azar knew better now than to be surprised, but awe flooded his mind. She had saved the dragons.

The grief pouring off her was a steep price. He would do everything in his power to ensure she didn't have to pay it alone.

Silence, she commanded with an effortless murmur in their minds, and all the dragons in attendance obeyed. *Build the pyre. Bring me the Drevan Laisren. And anyone who touches the zubiran treasure—*

"I'm flattered," Laisren interrupted, striding out toward the carcasses and the elegant dragon who stood triumphant. "But there's no need to send for me."

Don't you dare move, their new Zubir snarled in Azar's mind. He hadn't even realized he'd been ready to pounce, to fly down and defend her the way he hadn't been able to before. He snorted his derision instead, claws scraping into ancient stone. If the dragons around him had any reaction to the dangerous drama playing out before them, he wasn't privy to their conversations.

And your friends? Seraphina prodded, her tone steady. *Are they here as well?*

Laisren folded his hands, the sleeves of his robe barely fluttering. The dragons never kept up with human fashion, and yet the basic floor-length tunic still marked him as old. Foolishly, Azar had once interpreted the choice of attire as a sign of wisdom.

"Come, now," Laisren said like a patient teacher. "Why don't you shift so all present can hear your words?"

The dragons hear me perfectly well, Seraphina countered. With a swift hop, she caged the Drevan in her claws, only then swinging her head around to catch sight of their witnesses. *Don't you?*

A startled silence greeted the challenge. Azar huffed his frustration, and a fresh roar erupted as they all admitted she could make herself heard to each one of them.

Hear me now, then. Her claw dug into the soil as she narrowed Laisren's cage. It was mostly for show, the spaces between her talons plenty big enough for him to slip through. But if he ran, his indulgent façade would be broken, and she would have reason to give chase.

Laisren broke our laws, she continued. *He and his pathetic little posse attacked a member of the zubiran line. Not only this*—her claw twisted in the ground, sending a spray of dirt up to batter the figure within—*but they used a dream weaver's magic to do it, too weak and scared despite their numbers and their treachery.*

"Lies!" Laisren shouted.

Her snarl startled him back into silence. *Tapio, Gonsal, Egill, Jillianne, Koios,* she listed. *Get them down here* now.

The dragons bristled on their rungs, inescapable eyes searching their ranks. Azar too swung his head around, peering over his shoulder at—empty space. *Koios...*

She'll kill me! came the panicked reply.

Azar scanned their ranks, but telepathy didn't work like sound. He didn't even know which direction to look. It had taken so long to talk Koios down from his justifiable anger that they'd nearly been late to the maros. Only the delay of dealing with the succubus had allowed them to slip up into the highest rung of the amphitheater. By the time they'd made it, Jadokari had already been decapitated, her gruesome body sprawled awkwardly away from her head.

Azar had convinced Koios to come forward, to face Seraphina and her mercy. Granted, he hadn't thought the meeting, Koios's apology, would be quite so public. And apparently Azar had underestimated how watching her slay their last zubir would impact his friend.

Would it in fact be better to wait? For Koios to slip quietly away for now and face her after the rush of grief and triumph and bloodlust faded?

No. Seraphina the dragon deserved to confront her attackers. And Seraphina the Zubir deserved to be obeyed.

Get down there. Bend your knee. Swear your allegiance. Running now will only make this worse.

Koios didn't respond this time, too far perhaps to hear Azar, or to be heard. A scuffle broke out midway down the rungs across from Azar's perch. Egill, confronted by some of the Radno he'd tried to escape into. Relief distracted Azar from the flight of his—former?—friend. These dragons were accepting Seraphina as their zubir. They were obeying.

For her part, Seraphina remained unflappable, not gawking at the confrontation the way so many of them were. Egill tried to launch away from the pack surrounding him, but unable to use his wings, he couldn't clear them. The Radno knocked him around with claw and wing and even head, bumping him further down the rungs. He tangled with an older Radan whose oranges and yellows blended vaguely like a flame with a touch of black shadow. The dragons around them snarled at the Drevan.

But Azar zeroed in on the figure with the magenta markings timidly zigzagging down toward the magnificent dragon who'd saved them. Koios dropped to the grass and shifted, falling to his knees without approaching any closer. Seraphina growled at him, her lips pulling back to expose her teeth. Koios flinched.

Mercy, please, Azar thought.

Amethyst eyes darkened with hatred found him though he hadn't meant to be heard. She snorted and refocused on the two figures before her, one pacing in his improvised cage, the other bowing, his terror beading at his temple.

As Egill was knocked to the ground at last, Laisren broke his silence. "Enough of this farce! Will you cower before this false zubir?"

Seraphina snarled, and he jerked back from her muzzle. *False?* she challenged. *I am the daughter of Ignatius Zmay. Everyone here watched me prevail in the maros. And you are nothing but a traitor.*

A swing of her head toward Egill, forced to face her, and he too shifted into human form. The rumble of warning had him dropping to his knees, though his head remained unbowed, his lip curling.

"Have you all forgotten?" Laisren recovered quickly, calling out to them once more. "There is another heir! One this pretender—who fled her duty for centuries—hasn't faced!"

Confusion settled over the dragons, dampening the protective anger that had riled them up.

Seraphina snorted, nonchalant humor coming through telepathically before she said, *The lost heir is a myth. But if you believe in fairytales, where is this missing heir? Among the Virno?* Her neck curved so she could look at the cluster of Viran dragons.

Not for the first time that day, the air around them seemed to freeze, none of the powerful lungs in the amphitheater disturbing it by drawing breath. Then the Viran Netta laid his head on his forelegs with the softer underside of his neck exposed to the air. One by one the Virno followed suit, the submissive gesture unmistakable.

No? Seraphina challenged, snapping her jaw at Egill's attempt to crawl away. *Among our other tribes, then? A secret descendant of the zubiran line?*

Patches of dragons adopted the same posture as the Virno, some of the stronger ones holding out, waiting to see if there was indeed another heir. Seraphina's sharp eyes took in the stragglers, but Azar watched them as well, making note. Eventually even they bent their necks to the new Zubir, every dragon in attendance yielding publicly to her rightful role.

That's what I thought. Seraphina turned back to the three figures before her.

Koios had followed the others, prostrating himself as close to the ground as he could, head turned to expose his neck inasmuch as it was possible in that form. In a disgusting habit picked up from his time among the humans centuries back, Egill spit at the ground. Hatred was plain now on Laisren's face.

Your delusions won't save you. Admit your crimes.

"You have no right—"

Seraphina's roar cut off Laisren's blustering. *Get up*, she instructed the dragons who hadn't moved from their subservient positions. *Bear witness.*

Azar was among the first to obey. Wings rustled as others repositioned themselves, the anxiety of waiting working itself out in the little discomfited gestures.

Well? The note of warning in the word was chilling. Azar had been truly ready to take his friend's place in an execution, but now, with even just the faint hint of what the dragons could be under a true zubir still adding an extra zing to his blood... With the possibility of a future at Seraphina's side...

"I helped." Koios's admission was muffled by the ground. Seraphina must have told him something privately because he rose back up to his knees, leaving his head bent. "Laisren, Tapio, Gonsal, and Egill used outside magic to weaken the daughter of

Ignatius Zmay. They captured her, tortured her with the help of more outside magic. The Radan Jillianne took part. Others were ready to take their turn, and I can't speak to what they would have chosen. But I helped."

A fresh roar filled the air. Claws scraped stone as dragons angled their bodies toward the three traitors. The others may have already run, escaping together to the human world or hiding somewhere in this one. Seraphina would no doubt track down every single one.

"My deepest apologies for the role I played," Koios continued when the disbelief and outrage quieted. "Even if these are to be my last moments, I pledge my allegiance to you, our rightful Zubir." His head touched the ground once more.

Then as a co-conspirator you will be sentenced, Seraphina decreed.

Azar's heart jumped to his throat, blocking the fires churning in his gut. Koios had made mistakes, but did he deserve to die? Could Azar let him?

Chapter 49

THE PATHETIC LITTLE FARCE SERAPHINA HAD BEEN FORCED to play out had given her time. Time for the bloodlust ignited by the maros to recede. Time for her animal instinct to relinquish its hold, ceding to her rational mind once more. Time for her to remember mercy. Particularly the mercy Koios had shown her.

It wasn't enough to absolve him, but the dragons had lost so many of their own to Nahash's whims. They would be losing more now to Seraphina's justice. But first, perhaps, her rule could start with clemency.

A century, she decided. It seemed a nice round number. *A century you'll serve here at the sobran. If you give me cause to doubt your allegiance, sworn here among our kind, you'll meet the same fate as the others.*

A fresh spurt of adrenaline spiked her heart rate before the next proclamation. Her first kill was fresh, but her next ones couldn't wait. She'd waited long enough already. *The others,* she repeated, picking up the thread of what she'd been saying, *whom I sentence now to death.*

A mix of disbelief and delight filtered in waves she couldn't quite separate into individual thoughts as the dragons trumpeted or roared their response.

Thank you, Azar said, his thought directed only to her, reaching her through the tumult.

His friend echoed the sentiment aloud. "Thank you, Hazhina. Thank you."

Choose your delegates! she commanded.

Tradition dictated a member of each tribe would participate in each execution, to strengthen their communal bonds. Usually one of the strongest aside from the nettakim themselves. Today it would be two. Multiple executions were rare, but nothing about this day was ordinary.

A red dragon with a magenta underbelly swooped down onto their de facto stage. Rather than stand at the ready, she shifted to mortal form and strode forward in an elaborate gown with a structured bodice and skirts that floated fluidly about her legs. Recognition stoked Seraphina's resolve.

"I will take Laisren's place!" Jillianne announced, quieting the whisper of dragon wings once more.

Cocking her head, Seraphina injected amusement into her tone. *And who will take yours?*

A vicious smile slashed across her face. "The coward you pardoned."

Koios jerked. *What? Mother, no...* he told the heartless Radan, believing their exchange private.

Whatever it takes! she snapped back at him, her smug expression unchanging.

Any guilt Seraphina used to feel for spying had burned up in the maros. *This is how you show your allegiance?* she challenged, her already thin patience waning. She was so ready to stop being on display, at least for a minute or two. Her injuries were starting to heal beneath the glamour, but the gashes had been deep. She needed rest.

Koios blanched, but his chin tipped up defiantly. "No," he said quietly. "I serve at the pleasure of the Zubir, not these traitors."

Jillianne finally spun to look at her son, but his eyes remained fixed on Seraphina. She dismissed him and relief nearly dropped him to the ground, his body sagging. He shook it off and ran, staying easily within sight but no longer spotlighted under the watchful eyes of their kind.

The Radan dropped to her knees, voluminous skirts pooling around her the way her blood would soon. The way Seraphina's had in the cave when she'd been strung up.

"Mercy," Jillianne gritted out, her neck bending so stiffly it barely inclined.

Three, then, Seraphina announced to the waiting dragons. *Three from each tribe for today's executions.* Now! she added, underscoring the order with a roar.

Bodies swept down from the rings around them, positioning themselves near the sentenced, standing at the ready. A dragon who betrayed their rules betrayed them all. The chosen representatives would tear them apart, literally. Gruesome, but maybe no more so than the two carcasses already on the field.

Only when all fifteen dragons had joined them did Seraphina pull her talons from the dirt around Laisren. The convicted three tried to communicate, their eyes flicking toward one another. Hardly surreptitious, but she was past caring.

Catching the eyes of each executioner in turn, she called on the brutal zubiran blood coursing in her veins to avenge the piece of her still cowering before the memories of that cave. *Make it hurt.*

Chapter 50

THE DRAGONS WASTED NO TIME BUILDING THE PYRE FOR Nahash's body. Seraphina stood at a window in the zubiran tower, watching them pull trees from the ground and settle them into a rough rectangle large enough for his corpse. They'd be done long before nightfall. Others had already cleaned up the four additional carcasses from the arena. As per tradition, the many chunks of the three traitors would be buried, their flesh turned to fertilizer. Redemption, of sorts, for their crimes. Or maybe further punishment. With today's double—or was that triple?—feature, those tasked with disposing of their remains would have an easier time, the gaping holes from the trunks used to build the pyre well suited for the task.

More dragons still stood guard now around the grotesque pile of treasure. One from each tribe again, at least until Seraphina could meet with the zoval in the morning.

The only dragon stupid enough to approach her after everything she'd done today landed on the roof of the tower, his magic easy to trace as he moved to the stairs. It didn't take him long to reach this level, traditionally the zovalan meeting room. Transformed into her brother's bedroom. Littered now with various knickknacks and jewels and even decadent chocolates from the human world. Sumptuous fabrics stained with his seed and a half-consumed carcass framed the bed.

"Most dragons know well enough not to approach the zubiran tower without invitation," she said, not even turning around when the Drevan finally crossed the threshold.

"My mistake, Your Majesty," he said, matching both her English and that she'd spoken aloud.

Telepathy took energy she simply didn't have to waste after this day that wouldn't end, and choosing modern English over Drakonazyk meant less chance they'd be understood if they were overheard.

Exhausted and hungry, she would have loved to be any-where else, alone, away from the dragons' magic and thoughts buffeting her. But this was her life now. She had no choice but to get reaccustomed, and fast. Soon enough she would go light the pyre, surrounded once more by the dragons who'd ostensibly accepted her as zubir but who wouldn't hesitate to go after her if she gave them any reason. She hadn't missed the way many hesitated to submit, waiting for the fairytale lost heir to show themselves.

"Why are you here, Azar?"

"Seraphina—"

The snap of her head in his direction cut off whatever he had planned to say. The concern lining his face cracked something in the shell she'd felt enclose her in response to everything she'd been forced to do. Had chosen to do.

Too bad the only thing left inside was wasteland.

"Are you all right?" he asked, stepping toward her though he stopped far short of making it even halfway into the room.

A bitter chuckle escaped her throat as she faced him, dropping her glamour. He jolted at the sight of the dried blood coating her face and throat, disappearing beneath her clothes. With glamour or without, she could feel it, the blood of her brother, of her captors. Materializing a clean outfit was easy enough, but only bathing could actually clean *her*. Literally if not metaphorically. Flying over to the vast lake beyond the dunes wasn't in the cards for tonight.

"I did what I came here to do," she said in answer to his question before resuming her position at the window. "Your mission was a success."

When he shuffled toward her, she added, "Go away, Azar. Return to the Drevno or to the mortals, whatever you like. Go live your life."

"The only place I want to be is at your side."

That made her turn back to him. Something had changed. She had to be really out of it not to notice immediately that his power had grown. "You're stronger. Or you were hiding your true ability all along."

A pleased smirk tugged up one side of his lips. "No. You did it, Seraphina. You saved us. Look." He held out his hand, cycling the skin in rough jerks through all the colors of the dragons. His smile dropped when she didn't react, and he shrugged. "It'll require some practice. It's all thanks to you." A thread of pity appeared as he added, "I know that doesn't change the price you had to pay. But I'm here, ready to help with everything that comes next."

"Was this always the plan, then? Ingratiate yourself so you could make a play for Shadow Zubir?"

Hurt flashed across features, the expression perfectly executed. "Of course not. I have no interest in being zubir, or playing at it. I care about you, Seraphina. I want to be with you. Mostly right now, I simply want to hold you."

"And I will not be fucked into submission!"

The snarl backed him up a few steps. He regained his balance quickly, finding a wide, battle-ready stance. "That was cruel."

The quiet observation pierced her composure better than any return accusation could have. Droplets welled deep within that wasteland. If she weren't zubir, maybe she would have sobbed all the chaos out within the illusion of safety his embrace could offer. If wishes were horses…

"It was," she admitted. "Maybe that's who the maros made me."

He sighed, his expression and his stance softening. "I don't think that's true." He approached, though he didn't make the mistake of reaching for her. "You don't have to do this alone."

"Of course I do!" she snapped, crossing away from the window, her lip curling at the bed in her periphery. Why couldn't her brother have just been strong enough to withstand the succubus? To lead like he'd been raised to.

"Tomorrow the zoval could very well challenge my sovereignty, try to enforce the hypocritical, misogynistic requirement to prove fertility. If I am to be zubir, I must do it alone so none of them can ever again question that a female could. I have to be unimpeachable. Merciful but vicious, my every move impacting the future of the dragons. Look at today." She shook her head, the difference in their years settling on her shoulders once more. "How many dragons are dead? How many more battles will I have to fight, tomorrow and the next day? My future has no room for you."

With a deep breath, she stuffed any lingering hint of emotion down until even the strongest telescope wouldn't have found it within whatever remained of her soul. Glamour once again hid the blood she wanted to scrape off her skin. "I don't care where you go, Azar. Before the pyre burns out, you will be gone from the sobran. And you won't return without permission." The implied threat smothered the air between them. "Now get out."

He hesitated briefly, a sharp nod preceding an equally sharp turn on his heel. Swift steps ran up the stairs. Only when the shadow of his wings hit her window did Seraphina crumple to the ground, a length of fabric stuffed into her mouth so none of the ears beyond these desecrated walls would hear her sobs.

She'd warned him—all she wanted from him was obedience. No matter how he'd thought there could be more, she didn't feel anything for him. She didn't even see the asset he could be, the one dragon she could be certain was trustworthy. But then, perhaps she didn't trust him as much as he had hoped. Had he built their attraction and mutual goals into something that wasn't there?

Or, perhaps, the maros had changed her after all. He was stronger now than he'd ever been, only a youngling when Nahash had ascended to become zubir. How had the older dragons not realized something was seriously wrong as their power was leeched away over the years? Had anyone else noticed their ability to do glamour had returned? How could anyone deny now that their rituals truly mattered, that the *zubiran* power defined that of all the dragons?

And since that was the case, perhaps all Azar could do was accept that the *maros did* blend the participating dragons into one victor. Seraphina could never be as cruel or negligent as her brother, but that also hadn't been quite her up in the tower. Nahash's paranoia had led him to place those he trusted as spies bullying the other dragons. Seraphina's seemed like it wouldn't allow her to trust anyone. Much less return the feelings he should have known better than to allow within himself. Perhaps, after all, this was the true reason none of the *zubiran* line ever chose a *bira* before the *maros*.

Whatever connection he'd thought they had didn't override a direct order from his new Zubir.

Someday he'd find comfort in the fact that she had, indeed, succeeded. Saved them. Because of her, he had a future. They all did, even if he had no idea what to do with his now.

Except leave.

Since he may not be allowed to return to the sobran for years, Azar landed beside Koios, who was overseeing the *zubiran* herd. Was the mercy she'd shown this one dragon proof that the Seraphina he knew wasn't too far gone, after all? At the very least, it proved she'd make a better zubir than her brother.

You were right, Koios greeted stonily. *She spared me, for the time being.*

She saved us, Azar responded. It seemed important to remind any dragon he could of a fact few seemed willing to acknowledge outright. He huffed a sigh out through his nostrils, frustration curling smoke up from his snout. *She banished me.*

Koios jolted, finally swinging his head around to look at him. *Who can decipher the mind of a female.*

Azar snorted his irritation. *Don't do that. She is not irrational or incapable, and being female doesn't make one so.*

Koios's head dipped down in acknowledgment, then he plopped into the grass. The day must have gotten to him, too.

Azar lowered to his haunches. *She has her reasons.* Even if he didn't understand or agree with them. *She'll make a good zubir.*

They didn't speak awhile, watching the herd munch on the grass on the other side of the large pen, wary of the predators nearby. The beasts startled at the shadows thrown by the bodies of three incoming dragons before Azar had even looked up.

A flicker of relief raised his spirits when the group landed. Even in the diminishing light of the setting sun, it was clear Koritza felt better than when last he'd seen her, her scales almost glimmering. That she'd abandoned the sling in which the others had been pulling her to take to the sky herself was also promising.

What news? she asked, flanked by the two who'd accompanied her on the slower path.

Seraphina Ignatia is the new zubir, Koios reported, back on his feet to show their Netta the deference she deserved.

So I gathered. She looked to Azar, the gesture needing no additional words.

Laisren, Jillianne, and Egill have been executed for treason, Koios continued. *And Jadokari is dead as well.*

Humor pulled at Koritza's lips, even in this form. *She's been busy.*

She saved us all, Azar felt compelled to add again.

The dragons flanking Koritza shifted uncomfortably. They hadn't seen it happen, but surely they felt the change running through their own veins?

And you two? Why aren't you at the pyre?

I'm doing as the Zubir ordered, Koios explained, his gaze turning briefly to the herd that had resumed their calm wandering.

I've been banished from the sobran. Azar shared his bit of news with only Koritza. When the two behind her took off, presumably at her order, he added, *It's good to see you feeling improved.*

The change in leadership has done me well. Do not be fooled. I fear the tekkess is not as far off as you would like. Although, some would prefer it sooner even now. A light snort accompanied her head swiveling like a sinuous headshake. *Shall I add your name to the formal list amid tomorrow's meeting? Doubtful our new Zubir would support her brother's lunacy.*

Before tonight, Azar would have been certain she would revert the stakes. She'd been so horrified upon learning of Nahash's slaughter of the Zeyno. Unfortunately… *She's changed. Perhaps wait for confirmation first. Then yes, if you find me worthy.*

Her head tipped, one golden-orange eye looking him over. *A netta and a zubir could never be joined.*

The knowing comment made Azar straighten. *It's not a concern. She's made that clear.* Perhaps this was what the Fates had intended all along. Seraphina as zubir, and Azar back in the running for the Drevan tekkess, though it would hopefully be years off yet. If she had returned to take up the responsibility she had been born into, how could he do any less by refusing to fight for the future of the Drevno?

Koritza's wings flared away from her body. *Give her time, young one. The day cannot have been easy on her.*

Without waiting for a response, Koritza took off for the pyre, her words sparking a corresponding flame of hope. Everything had happened so quickly since he and Seraphina had met. Azar could certainly be patient. And perhaps he wouldn't be returning to the Drevan lands quite yet.

Chapter 51

IT WASN'T GLAMOUR THAT MADE SERAPHINA'S SKIN LOOK flawless in the sunlight the next morning as the zoval convened. While the majority of the dragons had paid their respects at Nahash's pyre, someone had snuck into the tower, depositing a bar of lilac soap, a few skins of water, and some frozen cuts of beef. The soap had been taken from her bathroom at the Peran Estate, but even if it hadn't been, the thoughtfulness would have pointed to Azar. Easy enough to materialize strips of cloth to scrub herself clean, but the relief of washing away all that blood had been indescribable. And eating had helped her heal. Yesterday's violence had been necessary, but today dragonkind would start fresh.

"It's good to see you all," Seraphina said, meeting the eyes of each Netta. She added a little nod when she reached Koritza. The old dragon didn't look unwell, and her wisdom would be welcome here today.

The Radan, Viran, and Zeyan Nettakim exchanged looks at Seraphina's choice of speaking aloud. But the confidentiality of telepathy was hardly necessary for pleasantries, and most of the dragons had flown off home after the pyre had burned itself out. Besides, if the Nettakim considered their thoughts private, they may slip up. She might catch something important.

Seraphina wasn't a child, but she essentially had been the last time any of these dragons had seen her. None of them would trust her to lead, not even Koritza. Any one of them could challenge her plans for the future, including the Zeyan she didn't remember. The one who had slaughtered the competition under her brother's orders. Had he wanted to, or simply felt he had no choice?

"We have much to discuss," she added, taking a seat on the smooth ledge circling half the top of the zubiran tower. Nahash's debauchery meant they couldn't use the zovalan chamber below them. They could have met in the archive room several levels lower, but the musty scrolls were a reminder of the past that wouldn't help to take the dragons forward. The vantage point atop the tower also allowed Seraphina to track the goings-on below.

Perhaps it was her time among the mortals that made her take a particular pleasure in adding, "Please, make yourselves comfortable." With a gracious smile, she swept her hand out toward the stone roof. Taking the offered seat would leave all the Nettakim physically lower than her, but none of them would cross the imaginary boundary of joining her on the ledge.

So instead, none of them moved, standing in a circle that suddenly felt far more awkward and uncertain.

"Seraphina," Savitr, the Radan Netta, said, shuffling half a step forward.

Her smile dropped, and she speared him with a sharp look. If she didn't demand their deference from the start, she would never have their respect. "You want to try that again?"

His teeth gnashed together, but Kimin, the Viran, cut him off with a pale palm extended in a *pause* gesture. "Hazhina," he acquiesced. "After what happened with Nahash, the danger the dragons faced as a result of not following our traditions…"

Her fault for running, she caught from the Zeyan.

"You can understand why we must insist that we all"— Kimin cut a sharp look at the Radan, as if there'd been some communication Seraphina had missed—"learn from our mistakes. We must adhere to tradition. For all our sakes."

"And per tradition," Savitr picked up, "you are not yet zubir."

Seraphina gave herself the space of a breath to catch the thread of coherence within all the thoughts swirling in her head, shoving aside the sharp bite of fear. As long as she remained calm, she could set them straight. They needed her to lead, and she *would* be doing so alone.

"Aren't I?" she asked, standing again. "Do you not feel the difference in your own flesh? The dragons' power flows from me, including for each of you. Which is why, though you may have not realized it yet, your ability to perform glamour has returned." All of them were old enough to remember the power, even if they hadn't had it the last couple centuries. Nevertheless, Seraphina painted her skin in a rainbow of colors to emphasize the point.

All the males around her set their jaws. Koritza remained unreadable, her face impassive, her hands folded demurely at the waist.

Savitr crossed his arms across his broad chest, as if reminding Seraphina of his musculature would intimidate her into submission. As if she hadn't just taken down a dragon at least as big as him. "A female cannot be zubir without a bira, and her intended must be proven through breeding."

"It is tradition," Kimin contributed.

The Zeyan and Pretan Nettakim avoided her gaze.

Seraphina fought back the urge to burn them all to a crisp. It wasn't like she could do much lasting damage beyond singeing off their clothes, anyway. And no one needed to see that.

Sit, she commanded instead, keeping her tone quiet but steady.

"Seraphina—" Koritza tried to intervene, but Seraphina wasn't having it anymore.

"No. You want to talk about lessons learned? Then I will educate you all. *Sit,*" she repeated between gritted teeth. Frustration burning under her skin, she waited as they lowered to the not quite smooth stone, resettling their ridiculous old-fashioned robes and tunics beneath them.

"Let's talk about our history. Our one and only female zubir was brutally and repeatedly raped into submission because the males of the time were too weak and terrified to accept her rightful rule."

The Pretan's lip curled, revealing the light yellow of his gums. Savitr paled, but Kimin flushed, almost like their colors had seeped into each other. It would have been amusing if not for the fact they were challenging Seraphina's autonomy, her right and ability to lead.

Discussing the finer points of gender-based discrimination wouldn't help her get through to them, however. "Political motivations aside, I'm sure we can agree that something which happened *once* in our history doesn't count as a tradition, or else we must also accept Nahash's 'adjustments' to tekkessim. What happened back then was a travesty, an assault on the rightful zubir that will *not* be happening a second time."

"That's not for you to decide," the Zeyan protested. "This council holds sway."

"Watch yourself, Ninad," Koritza admonished.

"No." He started to rise, but a glance at Seraphina seemed to remind him of what she'd done the day before, and he settled back on his heels, his nostrils flaring. If he'd been in dragon form, smoke would probably have curled from the openings. "We cannot trade one tyrant for another."

Seraphina laughed bitterly. "You want tradition, Ninad? Then accept you have no choice. *I* triumphed in the maros." And she still had the wounds to prove it, though they were gradually healing even as they spoke. "In the name of tradition, I slaughtered the same dragon you all feared for centuries, and I am stronger than he ever was. Dragonkind's very existence, your future, depends on me. *Everything* is my decision." She tore her gaze from his resentful expression to take in all the other Nettakim as well. "Hear me when I say I will kill the first male who dares touch me without permission, and every single one thereafter."

She let those words sink in, standing strong in their startled silence.

Understand? she taunted in their minds.

Reuel, the Pretan, bent his dark head first. *Hazhina.*

With a blend of resentment and reluctance, the Viran, Zeyan, and Radan Nettakim echoed him. Koritza caught Seraphina's gaze—was that a hint of a smile?—before doing the same.

It was a superficial victory at best, but "fake it 'til you make it" was about the only strategy Seraphina had at this point. She turned her back on them and walked a few paces away where she lowered once more to the ledge. "Now that we've addressed the past, let's discuss the future."

Chapter 52

THE NETTAKIM SHUFFLED AROUND SO THEY FACED HER again. Even now, Koritza was the only one clever enough to have materialized a cushion for herself. Or was it that the old dragon was feeling the stress on her bones? Had it been left intact, the zovalan chamber would have been more comfortable for them all.

"The dragons could flourish, and your collective wisdom could help that happen. I welcome your input. To start, though I hope we have time before it becomes relevant"—her eyes flicked to Koritza—"tekkessim will return to their *traditional* format. Prospects can bow out, and the matchups will no longer be to the death." With a sigh, she caught the pistachio-green eyes of Ninad. "I am sorry for the great loss among the Zeyno."

The muscles in his throat worked before his head dipped in an abrupt acknowledgment.

"The herds will all be freed, but we need to discuss supplementing the food supply until they are replenished," Seraphina went on. At some point, they'd either have to jump on board with her plans or admit—at the very least to themselves—that they didn't truly care about the welfare of the dragons. "I'd like to find someone knowledgeable to weigh in on alternative options, such as bringing in rabbits from the mortal world, but that's a longer-term option."

They would have to be certain how introducing a new species would impact the ecological balance here, since the animals on Azhidar Zher were those of Earth millennia ago. Although if rabbits replicated more quickly than anticipated, the dragons certainly wouldn't have any problems hunting them down. A larger animal like antelope or even cattle would have been helpful, but transporting them through the portals would probably be too tricky.

"The treasure below will be divided in half," Seraphina continued.

Reuel opened his mouth to protest, but she held him off with a quick lift of her hand.

"Half will be further divided among the tribes, as equitably as possible. The other half will finance our other ventures, including simply purchasing meat from the humans for the time being. But we could do so much more."

Excitement for the possibilities she'd never quite allowed herself to consider bubbled in her chest. Though the old dragons before her might find her enthusiasm childish, Seraphina didn't hide it. "Agriculture, animal husbandry, viticulture—there is so much we can learn from the mortals. We could send volunteers to study and bring back skills that could benefit us all."

"Your obvious preference for them doesn't mean we need to emulate the humans," Savitr grumbled.

Seraphina swallowed her irritation this time. "No, we don't. But we can learn from them, benefit from their knowledge and inventions, and put it all to use for us. To replenish the herds, to cultivate the vines of the Drevno, to vary our diets—for our own enjoyment," she added, cutting off Ninad's question. "Art, literature, music… We are no less capable of these things than the humans, and we are no less deserving of the many bounties that realm has to offer. Why shouldn't we benefit from them?"

More cautious glances among the Nettakim seemed to indicate they were starting to see things her way.

"Our food supply is our first priority. But the future of dragonkind doesn't have to remain mired in the restrictions of our past."

We don't need her to barter with the humans, Savitr thought. *Take our share of the treasure and go our separate ways.*

He isn't wrong, Kimin added.

Neither is she, Koritza defended.

We've barely had a zubir these last years, Ninad contributed. *We don't need one now.*

Yet she is *zubir,* Reuel countered. *And her vision is interesting.*

"I will make one further concession to your love of tradition," Seraphina interrupted, though they wouldn't know she'd overheard their little chat. "All portal charms will immediately be returned here to the tower, to be recharged but also catalogued. Your tribes will surrender any unsanctioned powered objects as well."

Koritza smirked but quickly hid it. Savitr and Ninad shifted uncomfortably. The others seemed more resigned to obeying, or at least to keeping their intentions hidden.

Perhaps Seraphina would rethink the system for dragons visiting Earth in the future, but for now, returning to the old ways would restore some measure of order. Besides, they'd need all the portal charms to help supplement the food supply, as the small powered objects were required for dragons to return to Azhidar Zher. She wouldn't be sharing her network of direct portals, since those included links to Kansytura and Rhea's private chambers, both of which had to remain inviolate.

"I want what's best for all dragonkind. I am open to your feedback. Tell me your tribes' needs." Seraphina stood once more, and with perfect timing, the wind swept her hair and her skirts back. "But never forget that I am your Zubir. Any who dare disobey me *will* regret it."

Hours later the zoval dispersed with at least the start of a plan. Nearly everything they had discussed would take time to implement, but all the penned animals would be freed immediately. Hopefully it wouldn't take too long for their numbers to be replenished, but the dragons' appetite could easily decimate them. All the Nettakim had agreed it was in everyone's interest to encourage their tribes to hunt sparsely for now. Tomorrow Seraphina would start selecting and instructing dragons who would visit the mortal world to stock up on extra meat. Maybe they would ultimately purchase a farm or slaughterhouse to ensure their supply was fresher than what they'd find at the average butcher's.

Reuel had also suggested restoring some of the more personal heirlooms to the dragons who'd forfeited them to Nahash. Sorting the mountain of gold and jewels would be an immense task, and judging whose claims were legitimate would be yet another challenge. Still, it was a good idea, and those were problems for tomorrow.

Today, Seraphina had another council to face.

The High Council's chambers changed at the whim of the Fates, who took a perverse pleasure in reminding them all that their powers paled in respect to the trio's. When Seraphina had been introduced here, it had been like walking into the ocean, if the ocean could be lit from the inside until it shone like the most wondrous ever-shifting jewel. Today, the room was a black so deep it reflected the internal glows of the figures within, their own magic offering light that bounced repeatedly off the walls, creating a soft multicolored glow. Seraphina's reflection followed her as she strode down the excessive length of the room.

Not everyone had arrived yet, but those who had kept to themselves. The fury slumped on one chair, her crimson hair falling to her waist in luscious curls that somehow didn't snag on any of the hardware in her contemporary biker chic outfit. Rhea stood serenely across from her in a gown reminiscent of a cheerful garden, and the three Fates themselves clustered at the far end of the oval table. Their bodies transformed constantly, their androgynous forms cycling through a variety of shapes and sizes and colors. Seraphina had been baffled and dizzied by it the last time. Now, however, she could see the beauty in it, how the Fates represented the full breadth of mortal bodies, not choosing any one shape or quality as superior to the rest.

Rhea spoke first. "Seraphina." Worry creased briefly between her eyes, but in this chamber, they could not be friends. "Welcome."

"Challenged the gluttonous waste of dragon that came before you, did you?" Derision dripped from the fury's voice. "What a coup."

"I saved the dragons from the meddling of Jadokari," Seraphina corrected. "She's dead," she reported flatly. "And yes, so is Nahash."

The fury huffed. "No one here's going to cry about it."

"Much less do anything to help the dragons," Seraphina countered. She wasn't even sure who led the faction that included sirens, incubi, and succubi, but anyone on this council should have noticed something wasn't quite right with Nahash. The Fates had interfered over less, messing with anyone's life when it suited them. Maybe they hadn't cared to intervene, or maybe they were the ones to blame to begin with.

Rhea rounded the table, her movements elegant as ever but her concern now unmistakable. "Seraphina, perhaps we should—"

"Look at the baby Zubir," one of the Fates interrupted.

"Who knows it all," another added, as if the burden of a full sentence was too much effort for just one of them.

Pausing for a moment in a body far too reminiscent of Azar, the center one finished in his voice, "Except how to be happy."

Chapter 53

ESPITE THE IMPROVEMENT IN HER STRENGTH, KORITZA passed mere weeks after the ritual that changed everything. Azar lay on the edge of the half circle of Drevno surrounding her body, weighed down by regret he couldn't pinpoint. The glow had left her amber scales, ashen now even in the bright overhead sun. In her last days, she'd claimed she was ready, confident the Drevno would have a competent netta without losing all their strongest to the tekkess.

Though he hadn't officially been named, Azar had joined her and the prospects for training drills and final lessons. The future netta of the Drevno would have no obligation to adhere to Koritza's vision, but they all respected her enough to listen. Most of them hadn't moved from her side in her last hours, or since. Sometimes Azar thought he'd be perfectly fine never moving again, letting his body fade away here in this patch of grass, staring at her corpse. Despite her long life, seeing her like this now seemed a waste.

A particular tingle he hadn't felt in these last weeks made him lift his head for the first time in nearly two days.

The Zubir landed near the circle of grief, elegant and regal and even more beautiful than he remembered. Flanked by several others who'd flown in from the sobran, she took in all the dragons, her own sadness echoing theirs. Amethyst eyes seemed to linger a couple heartbeats longer on him than the rest. Or maybe time simply stopped when she looked at him.

When her gaze moved on, she appeared as indifferent as her recent silence had suggested, compassionate enough to share their grief but lacking any personal interest in him. Several of the Drevno shuffled away, clearing a path for their Zubir to approach Koritza. Azar laid his head back down.

In three days' time, the prospects and most of the Drevno would return to the sobran for the tekkess. He'd be joining them, whether their Zubir liked it or not. Officially, she could choose to take any prospect out of the running. Including ones she hadn't exiled. But Azar had to try. He had three days left to wrap his head around fighting to lead the Drevno, to find the fire to win.

The Zubir expressed her grief, her compassion, though her words were oddly muffled. Indecipherable, somehow, even though they tickled inside his mind. Since she spoke to them all uniformly, it hardly mattered.

In her time as zubir, Seraphina had already done so much good. The herds had been freed once more, and every tribe was receiving supplemental food from the human realm. Even the simple fact that every dragon was free to choose their own form had reinvigorated the Drevno, and presumably the other tribes as well.

The ridiculous attempts at craft and agriculture at the sobran had been halted, but everyone had been informed of the forthcoming opportunities to learn such skills and many more among the humans. The return of glamour had bolstered the outlook of all those who'd believed Earth to be off limits for them. A few of the Drevno were quite excited about the opportunity to study viticulture, to help their ancient vines truly thrive. Of course some would also have to study oenology, but the point was she had true vision for the dragons' future, and she was making it happen.

If Azar couldn't be a part of the change at her side, he would do his damnedest to contribute to the future of the Drevno. It would mean seeing Seraphina for zovalan meetings, but as long as they both focused on the needs of dragonkind, that would be fine, too. It may not look like the future he wanted, but Azar remained dedicated to his fellow dragons. Serving them as netta, if the Fates deemed him worthy, would make for a fine enough life. Certainly better than wasting the years pining for what could have been.

The following night, Azar's fingers fiddled with a scrap of folded paper as he stared blankly at a pale-peach wall. Another change Seraphina had implemented, supplying all the tribes with packages of white paper sheets and writing utensils. It may take a while for the dragons to find many uses for it, but it was certainly more convenient than cave walls or even the spelled, bound hides used for their official records. And though she likely hadn't realized it, it gave him the opportunity to escape into his drawings.

This particular sheet had been folded into a complicated pattern to form a sealed square, back when Azar had received it from Koios. No matter how Azar had tried to reform it along the existing creases, he hadn't been able to replicate the neat shape. He could have destroyed the note after reading it, but every so often he unfolded it to verify he hadn't misread the words within.

Meet me in Kansytura after sunset

—Tia

The sun had just begun to dip below the horizon when he'd landed at the sobran to come to the Peran Estate, where it was already full dark outside. Meanwhile, unless he'd been mistaken before, the sun never set in Kansytura. Leaning on the back of the couch in the private upstairs sitting room, Azar hesitated, despite the anticipation building with every heartbeat.

Why had Seraphina sent for him this way? Had she reconsidered? These last weeks had certainly demonstrated she was a capable leader, all on her own. Whatever she wanted to discuss, why not do it at home? Though perhaps she still struggled to feel at home at the sobran.

Was that why she'd signed the note as *Tia*? Or had it been, as he'd first assumed, to distinguish the request from one made by his Zubir? To give him a choice. Perhaps the signature had no more significance than assuring her anonymity, were it to be found or intercepted.

Whatever her reasoning, Azar couldn't deny the ache behind his breastbone, his need to see her. He would move forward with his life, if that was his only choice, but it would take far longer than a handful of weeks to approach anything resembling indifference when it came to Seraphina. If he could ever manage that at all.

When he stepped through the portal, she was already waiting, pacing before the semicircle of archways.

Twisting to face him mid-stride, she said, "You came."

The relief in those two words softened the tension in his shoulders. "Of course I came." He had a feeling he would always come when she called, no matter how many centuries passed.

"Will you walk with me?" Her head tipped toward the verdant sanctuary waiting behind her.

Azar nodded, not entirely trusting himself to speak. Not until he knew why she had asked him here.

Seraphina's slow steps led the way in the opposite direction from where they'd enjoyed each other's bodies. An intentional choice? That riverbank may have no physical trace of their time together, but it would be overflowing with memories. Did she want to avoid the reminder?

When they'd walked far enough that the portals were no longer visible, Seraphina stopped. "I'm sorry, Azar," she said, her expression giving nothing away. "For the way our last conversation went."

Azar caught up her hand, holding back the urge to pull her closer.

She squeezed as if on instinct but let go almost as quickly, stepping back. She clasped her hands before her. "You are of course free to come to the sobran whenever you wish, for the forthcoming tekkess and otherwise."

For all the turmoil within him, all the grief and heartache he'd seen in her the night of the maros, she appeared entirely calm now. Unperturbed, as if seeing him again had no real impact on her. And perhaps it didn't.

"Is that all you wanted to tell me?"

Her lips pinched before she cleared her expression once more. "Koritza didn't include your name among the prospects. Will you be participating?"

The answer depended on her, but since she refused to reveal her intentions, Azar forged ahead bluntly. This moment may very well be his last chance. "I won't surrender my responsibilities unto others, if they are indeed to be mine. But as netta, I could never be with you."

Was he flattering himself to think longing flashed in her eyes? "That isn't on the table," she said hoarsely. Her chin tipped up at the hint of vulnerability.

Azar seized on it. "Why not?" When she didn't respond, he took a step closer. Then another, until she had to look up to meet his gaze. "I would choose you, Seraphina."

Her breath caught, her eyes taking on a new sheen. Still her only response was an uneven shake of her head.

He hadn't put the words to it at first, mourning the loss of the dragon he'd come to know to the mysterious transformation of the maros without fully understanding why the loss shook him so. Yet even in this, Koritza had shown wisdom. The Seraphina he had known had found her way back from the desolate, emotionless edge on which she'd stood during their last conversation. Her determination and vision were already transforming the lives of the dragons, always tempered by her compassion for their needs. The personal apology only underscored that she remained precisely herself.

Closing the distance between them, Azar palmed her cheek. "I missed you," he murmured.

Once again her chin tipped up, but this time it was in welcome. Her hands came to his waist. Relief making him nearly dizzy, Azar bent to her lips. He nuzzled them softly, fingers sliding into her hair. Her lips parted and he succumbed to the taste of her, deepening the kiss, thrilling at the realization that she was kissing him back with equal need. She rose on tiptoes, pressing her body against his, her palm sliding up his chest. He would never get enough of her.

He would never get the chance.

With a whispered, "We can't," she pushed back against his torso and turned away, her steps taking her even further, her breathing ragged. "There is no future for us," she told the trees.

"There could be," Azar insisted. Whatever her practical objections, if she cared for him, they could find a way, overcome whatever obstacles there may be. "Perhaps not right away, but—"

She spun back on him, pain contorting her features. "You really want to go on to watch your children kill each other? To raise them knowing one day they'll have to?"

Understanding replaced the glimmer of hope he'd entertained, even as a part of him rejoiced that she'd considered raising children with him at all. There was so much heartache, so many complications, attached to being zubir. Or her bira. "Seraphina—"

"It doesn't matter." Severity wiped any trace of emotion from her expression, her shoulders pulling back. "I have to focus on dragonkind, on establishing myself as a reliable but independent leader. You should move on."

"I can wait."

Her chest jerked with her sharp inhale. But soon enough, it dropped along with her gaze, her head swiveling from side to side again. "It could take years." Her eyes rose to his, pleading with him to see reason. "Decades. You deserve a life."

"You're forgetting something," Azar pointed out, an odd calm settling over him. She hadn't proclaimed her feelings, and yet all her objections were practical in nature.

One lovely sapphire brow arched in challenge, her pride taking precedence over whatever else she was thinking. But Azar wasn't fazed. If she simply hadn't wanted to be with him, she would have said so. Which, quite logically, meant she did.

Azar's eyes were the only thing anchoring Seraphina to the ground as she scrambled to find the piece he claimed she'd forgotten in the whirlwind of obstacles and objections in her mind. There was so much she had to keep track of as zubir.

Since she couldn't find it, she waited.

"I'm not human, Seraphina," he said quietly, carefully, as if afraid the words would break her. "I won't wither away in years, or in decades. The promise of the centuries after will make them feel like barely a second."

The truth turned her brittle, afraid to take a breath for fear she really would shatter. She *had* forgotten. All those years among the mortals, watching them age and die—and live full lives in the span of mere moments of her existence—had skewed her sense of time.

"Tell me to wait, Seraphina."

In her silence, Azar once again closed the distance between them. His hands landed on the bare skin of her upper arms, infusing life back into the wizened interior beyond the shell that had begun flaking off as the dragons tentatively accepted her vision for the future.

Still she hadn't considered the possibility of Azar being anything more than someone from whom she could expect integrity on the sporadic occasions their paths would cross. Could she truly put a pin in the hint of happiness he offered? Waste years of his life before she would have the capacity to even examine her own feelings?

"Tell me the answer is *someday*," Azar insisted. "Say that you want that future with me, because we have the time to solve everything else. I love you. And if you'll but have me, I am yours."

He didn't move as she thought, the light pants of her breath sounding overly loud in the quiet of Kansytura. Since he'd found her, life had been a sprint. To hide, to escape, to save the dragons from the succubus, and her brother, and themselves. To prove herself worthy with every conversation and every decision since.

By giving her space to process, he was already proving their relationship didn't have to move at warp speed. They could take things slow, find snatches of time away to be together. Like now.

In sending her note, Seraphina had resigned herself to apologizing but ultimately saying goodbye. If he were to become the new netta of the Drevno, she would have found a way to deal with the longing that welled within her any time she saw him.

"You'd give up the tekkess?" she asked. There was more at stake for him than simply their relationship.

His lips tugged into a tiny smirk. "In a heartbeat." He skimmed his knuckles over her jaw. "I will always choose you."

Could it really be as simple as choosing him, too?

Azar bent his head as if to kiss her but stopped short. "Say yes to someday, Seraphina Ignatia."

A smile twitched her cheeks for the first time in weeks. Any hint of softness still threatened her legitimacy in the eyes of the dragons, always searching for proof a female zubir could never live up to the males who preceded her. To them, she must remain unshakeable, implacable, resolved.

Only Azar ever wanted to see the truth of her.

"Convince me," she murmured so close to him their lips brushed as she spoke, "that these stolen moments will be enough."

He dipped his head to make their contact a real kiss, flicking his tongue out before separating them. "The question is, am I enough for you?"

The hand that had been cupping her head fell lightly to her shoulder then skated down her arm as if he were about to pull away.

Seraphina grabbed hold of him before he could. "Of course you are." From his willingness to learn when he was wrong, to his somewhat naïve yet ultimately galvanizing ideals, to the way he cared for her needs as an individual rather than for her function. Eyes locked on his, she wrapped herself in the calm of a couple deep breaths before finally admitting, "You're more than I ever hoped for."

Chapter 54

I MISSED THIS," SERAPHINA SIGHED, SINKING DEEPER INTO THE hot water.

Azar nipped at her earlobe. "Indoor plumbing or me?" he teased, eliciting a chuckle.

"It's a tossup." It hadn't taken much convincing for her to agree to a detour to the Victoria house and the decadent soaking tub in her bedroom there. Having Azar's arms around her didn't hurt.

He hummed contemplatively, running his hands over her abdomen and her legs, anywhere he could reach. She shifted her hair over her right shoulder so nothing would separate them and leaned back against his torso. Without the amulet, the strands dried instantly. And nothing blocked the feel of Azar's skin or his power.

His hands separated in their wandering, one tracing swirls on her thigh, the other skimming a palm up to her ribcage. The latter wrapped around her in a snug one-armed hug. Seraphina's head fell back against his shoulder. His lips dropped to her neck as his fingers moved higher to run through the curls at the apex of her thighs. Those fingers dipped deeper and she gasped, jolting against the arm that held her securely against him.

With a low chuckle, he curled his fingers in the water, letting the shifting fluid caress her almost like the displaced surface teased her breasts. A flick of his power found her clit a moment before his knuckle circled it. Her hips writhed, needing to be closer, to encourage him along, but he simply tightened his hold around her torso, keeping her where he wanted. A finger slid languidly along her flesh, and Seraphina gave herself over to his whim.

The combination of his movements and her hips' kept the water lapping at her nipples. Azar supplemented it all with kisses on her shoulder and dancing touches of his power, until Seraphina's panting breaths bounced off the tiled walls of the bathroom.

Wait, she thought, unable to form the word aloud as the molten heat and vibrating tension warred at that edge of pleasure.

He stopped moving instantly, leaving his fingers exactly where they had been. The light remaining pressure at her entrance and on the tight bud was its own tormenting temptation, especially with the stiff length of him at her back.

With a shuddering breath, Seraphina found the words to explain why she'd stopped him. *I want you inside me.*

A growl escaped his throat. His hands found the outside of her hips, pressing into the flesh as he swiftly brought her up to her feet. With a quick kiss to the curve of her ass, he stood as well. He lifted her again, this time depositing her softly on the bathmat, joining her a moment later.

At the sight of him, thick and solid and oh so hard, with those beautiful touches of gold, Seraphina nearly forgot the point of getting out of the bath. Her tongue slipped out over her bottom lip.

Azar's fingers caught her chin, lifting her gaze to meet his. "Condoms," he murmured with a smug little smirk.

It was almost a shame to cover the length of him in latex, but if it meant she could finally fully feel him filling her, it was worth it. That first time, when she'd been wearing the amulet, hardly counted. And besides, it was so impossibly long ago.

With brisk movements, Seraphina grabbed the box she'd stashed the last time she'd been here and strode into the bedroom. She stalled a step short of the bed, but Azar's hand trailed down her spine, and soon the box landed on the comforter, the pair of them beside it. He made quick work of smoothing on a condom, then knelt between her legs. Propped on her elbows, Seraphina watched him take in the sight of her spread before him. One hand grasped her thigh, pushing it further from the other, displaying all of her to his eyes in the low light. He slid the back of one finger through her wetness, ending with the light scrape of his nail on her clit.

"Azar, please," she moaned, writhing closer to his touch.

His jaw tensed as he shifted forward, propping himself over her on one hand. Seraphina leveraged herself up to press their torsos together, wrapping her arms around him. She licked at a swirl of copper on his pec, then up the line of his throat to his jaw. A flare of power caressed everywhere their bodies were joined, and her head fell back on another gasp. Azar's responding groan suggested it hadn't been entirely intentional. But when he used his free hand to trace his tip up along one edge of her, then down the other, there was no doubt he was in full control.

Her hips bucked, trying to take him where she wanted him, but he anticipated the motion, slipping up to nudge the hyper-sensitized bundle. His name came out an exhaled plea, her eyes opening to find his gaze fixed on her face.

He slid his length along her, coating it in her wetness. *Say please, Hazhina.* Behind the thought, she caught, *Let me hear it again.*

This exhale was part chuckle. *Please,* she acquiesced, then tipped her mouth toward his ear and repeated, "Please."

A shudder worked itself through his torso, and he finally repositioned himself at her entrance. As if she needed more en-ticement, he swirled power around her nipples, teasing her almost to the point of pain, then finally, *finally* slid inside. All of her clenched around him, her knees coming up to frame his waist.

"Seraphina." He added a shallow pump to claim her atten-tion.

Hmmm? was all she managed.

His lips brushed her temple, the gentle flutter at odds with the force of the full thrust stretching her. His free hand skimmed up her side, the next slow thrust timed with his fingers rolling her nipple.

A whimper floated on the air. Had that been hers?

Continuing the slow, controlled slides out and in, he switched which arm kept them propped up off the bed. The change created enough space to let him tease the other nipple.

The heat of earlier had coated all of her, inside and out, leaving only that exquisite tension of balancing on that precipice. Seraphina's hips followed as he moved to withdraw again.

A low chuckle filled her ears and her mind. *In a rush?* he teased, stopping entirely. Her groan of protest only led to his knuckle lazily circling the taut peak of her breast. All those deep muscles trembling around him, Seraphina pulled herself higher to capture his mouth, nipping at his bottom lip.

Please, she whispered in his mind, slipping one of her own hands down to help things along.

He caught her wrist before she could reach between them, flexing his hips the tiniest bit.

"Azar." This time his name was mostly whine, swallowed up by his lips.

His responding growl rumbled through her, but he resumed that frustratingly slow, measured slide in and out. She pulled her hand from his grasp to grip his ass, and his rhythm stuttered. Finally he gave in, gradually picking up speed until he was thrusting hard and deep, filling her as she shattered.

His hips kept pumping, knocking her over smaller peaks as he joined her in the ecstasy of release.

Chapter 55

Two Years Later

THE RUSTLE OF WINGS STARTED BEFORE DAWN. SERAPHINA hadn't slept, anticipation jittering through her. As members of all five tribes streamed into the sobran, she uncurled from her spot atop the zubiran tower, straightening to keep a watchful eye. Nothing could go wrong today.

For most, this would be their first time seeing the new structure Seraphina had decided to build last year. As far as she knew, it was the first time in their history that all the tribes would come together for the hatching of a dragonlet not of the zubiran line. Even those hatchings had traditionally only been witnessed by the zoval, sometimes an additional advisor or two.

Historically, the five tribes only came together for the violent rituals that affected them all: the maros, tekkessim, and executions. It was past time for them to join together in celebration. If the Fates weren't feeling particularly cranky today, hopefully this hatching would commence a new tradition. As a species, they could be so much more than brutal and merciless. And arguably, nothing would impact all the dragons as much as the first new dragonlet in centuries.

The black egg with its peach and mauve splashes, easily the height of any of them in mortal form, was more precious than all the treasure of the dragons, in this world and that of the mortals. All the dragons living among the humans would return for the occasion. Except those who still hid from her, afraid of the price for their treachery. Today was not for such concerns.

As dawn colored the sky, Seraphina stretched then flew down to the new hatchery. Simple, for now, it was essentially a giant sloping roof. Massive curtains sectioned off the center where Willow watched over her egg. Eventually those would be replaced with sliding doors affording any mother-to-be even further privacy, but it would likely take a few more years for the dragons studying carpentry and construction to feel comfortable using the wheels and metal bits required to make that happen. They might not be able to transport large planks of wood or equipment through the portals, but the smaller useful parts would certainly be an option. Plus any small tools that could be charged from the sun, or solar-powered battery packs.

Seraphina had been somewhat overwhelmed by the enthusiasm of dragons wanting to become their tribe's delegates to the mortal world, despite the requirement of corresponding years of free labor for the benefit of them all. Dragons now studied carpentry, agriculture, construction, and so much more. Many were eager to learn new skills, or at the very least willing to do so for the sake of sponsored years among the humans.

Nowhere near as eager as they all were for this hatching. When she'd first learned of the pregnancy, Seraphina had spent weeks among the Pretno, talking to Willow. She refused to order the other dragon to have her child at the sobran. It had taken much honest conversation, sharing Seraphina's vision, the importance of allowing them all to celebrate this momentous occasion, to convince the pregnant dragon. That and the promise of privacy for all but these final minutes. Months later, Willow had appeared at the sobran, ready to lay the perfect little egg.

Quiet your thoughts, Seraphina commanded now, taking in the hundreds who had already arrived. *Let's not scare the little one.*

As more bodies streamed in, landing among the growing group behind her, Seraphina settled in for the wait. *Whenever you're ready, Willow.* Koios stood at the ready, in mortal form, to draw aside the curtains and reveal mother and child-to-be to them all. Though she might not quite call the other dragon a friend, the two had spent plenty more time talking over the last months. Seraphina was determined for Willow not to feel like a sideshow.

As she settled in for the wait, Azar landed at the edge of their group, his hide glimmering in the early sunlight. Though he spent most of his time among the humans nowadays, he'd also become known as one of her most trusted advisors. That confidence she'd glimpsed before had settled comfortably on his shoulders, his assuredness no longer rooted in untested naiveté. No one questioned his familiarity with the Zubir or how frequently he was seen at the sobran. Or at least, not within range of her.

Hi, beautiful, he murmured, keeping an appropriate distance. *Welcome back.*

Before she could say more, the curtains were parted and tied back. Willow and the egg whose heat was misting the dewy morning air stole everyone's attention. Unfazed at this point by the gawking, or doing a damn good job hiding it, Willow swished her tail outward, briefly displaying the full egg.

Brilliant idea as ever, Azar said, not taking his eyes away from the main event.

Here's hoping. Seraphina wouldn't relax until the dragonlet was fully hatched.

There'll be plenty to celebrate tonight.

The innuendo displaced some of her nerves with a lick of heat. Though Azar was essentially overseeing the dragons placed among the mortals, living primarily at the mansion with a handful—and yes, Naiara, who mostly considered her new roommates to be a bit odd—the two of them had made it a point to steal away for some privacy at least once a month. It wasn't much, but their hours together were a wonderful promise of what was to come. Sometimes they'd spend the time simply cuddling and talking, catching up on everything and anything that had happened since they'd last been alone. Other times they enjoyed the freedom of being the only two in Kansytura, especially since just about every property Seraphina owned was now filled with dragons, and they couldn't risk being overheard. A handful of times Seraphina had even returned to the mansion for a quick visit with her mortal friend, who skeptically accepted her explanation of "family obligations" keeping her from re-turning to the university.

The dragons were slowly accepting her as zubir, fewer and fewer challenging her authority as time went on. Some still remained unconvinced, despite the improving health of the herds and the renewed strength of them all. Even those who couldn't deny the drastic increase in their power ascribed that to the death of the succubus, conveniently forgetting how that had come about. And Seraphina wasn't naïve enough to believe those who had wanted her dead didn't still lurk in the shadows, biding their time.

Still, today's hatching should sway even more to accept her leadership, proving not only that the dragons would not die out, but also that a female zubir didn't have to breed to ensure the fertility of the rest.

Privately, Seraphina and Azar had come to the conclusion that the dragons' fertility had most likely been compromised by Jadokari, since succubi literally drew power from the seed of their victims. Ultimately, they would never know for sure.

A creaking noise forced her thoughts back to the present, her eyes zeroing in on the delicate crack that had appeared along the surface of the egg.

Everything will be fine, Azar assured, picking up on her nerves.

Seraphina didn't respond, close to cracking herself from the anticipation.

Someday we'll have one of these.

Her head swiveled toward him. He chuckled in her mind, outwardly unaffected, watching the main event.

One, she reminded. It was a conversation they'd had before. Until they could ensure the next maros would not lead to the slaughter of their children, they would simply rely on birth control to have only one heir. And even that was fairly far off for now.

Another crack in the eggshell demanded the attention it was due, revealing the wet tip of a little black muzzle. The dragonlet huffed the fluid from its nostrils, rocking in the egg. Willow uncurled her tail, giving her child the space to break free. The egg fell to its side, unmoving just long enough for Seraphina to have a mini heart attack. Then it rocked again, a larger crack zigzagging up around the side of the shell.

Soon enough the sweet warble of the dragonlet filled the air. Willow bent down to nudge aside the lingering bits of shell. The dragonlet's wet wings were still folded along its sides, squelching as the precious creature tried to straighten them.

Elation jabbed at Seraphina from all sides, but the dragons remained mindful of the little one, softly crooning their welcome.

Distracted by her awe, Seraphina only belatedly remembered to join them, vocalizing her pleasure—and relief—at finally meeting the newest dragon, who stumbled toward her mother.

You made this happen, Azar said, his gaze now firmly fixed on her amid the dragons' distraction.

She did, Seraphina corrected as Willow nuzzled the still slimy dragonlet.

Yes, but no. You saved a species, Seraphina, an entire world. You gave all of us this moment, a new life. He paused, his voice growing soft as he added, *In more ways than one.*

Seraphina sighed. She wasn't done, not with several of those who'd attacked her still eluding them, and other factions as looming threats with unknown members. Not while dragons still went hungry without the supplemental meat from the mortal world, the herds recovering but slowly.

Yet Azar was right, too, as he often proved to be. The joy around her, the dragons finally bonding around a happy occasion, was proof that thus far, she was succeeding. They would feast tonight on the influx of meat that came with the return of those living among the mortals. And tomorrow, the zoval would hear their reports, led of course by Azar himself. The dragons were building a brighter future, one challenge at a time.

Many around them had taken to the air to express their elation, but Azar plopped down onto his belly in the long grass, relaxing amid the pleasant chaos. Anticipation and a hint of pride radiated from him, but perhaps only to her eyes, so attuned now to the slightest change in his demeanor. When the others returned to the tribes or their assignments, he would remain. Together they would steal hours to celebrate this day, all that had been accomplished. The brief escapes to Kansytura never seemed long enough.

I know what you're thinking, he teased, aware now of her secret ability.

Her snort carried to his ears.

Two more days until I can be alone with you, he elaborated smugly.

A fresh lick of anticipation sparked through her at the undercurrent of promise in the words. A wave of longing followed it, but she couldn't risk moving closer to nestle at his side. *Soon*, she agreed, promising herself the same. Soon she would find a way for them to be together in truth. For now, she flared out her wings to work out some of the delicious tension thrumming through her.

Even centuries with you won't feel like enough, Azar claimed tenderly.

Then we'll have to make the best of them, she quipped, mirroring his position in the grass. As if drawn together magnetically, their tails curled toward each other despite the distance.

As you wish, he murmured meaningfully, no longer unaware of the contemporary mortal context.

With another little snort of amusement, Seraphina fell silent, soaking in the jubilation around them as she watched the dragon who'd upended her life. Who could have known that first night when he'd run at her side that they were running not away but toward this?

In that moment, happiness for them both—for all of the dragons—no longer felt out of reach. So maybe the Fates weren't *always* bitches.

Glossary

AZHIDAR ZHER: the realm of the dragons

BIRA: zubiran consort

DRAKONAZYK: the language of the dragons

DREVNO (ADJ: DREVAN): one of five dragon tribes, primarily a variety of browns in color

HAZHINA: (Your/Her) Majesty

KANSYTURA: small pocket realm created for Seraphina after she left Azhidar Zher; nothing lives here

MAROS: ritual fight among zubiran children after the zubir passes, to choose the next zubir

NETTA (PL: NETTAKIM): leader of a dragon tribe

PIRHA: derogatory term for a female dragon

PRETNO (ADJ: PRETAN): one of five dragon tribes, primarily black in color

RADNO (ADJ: RADAN): one of five dragon tribes, primarily a variety of reds in color

SOBRAN: central gathering area in Azhidar Zher, where the zubiran tower and the portal are located

TASUNA: (Your/Her) Highness

TEKKESS (PL: TEKKESSIM): ritual fight among select dragons of one tribe after their netta passes, to choose their next netta

VIRNO (ADJ: VIRAN): one of five dragon tribes, primarily white in color

ZEYNO (ADJ: ZEYAN): one of five dragon tribes, primarily a variety of greens in color

ZOVAL (ADJ: ZOVALAN): advisory dragon council consisting of all five nettakim

ZUBIR (PL: ZUBIRIM; ADJ: ZUBIRAN): sovereign, leader of all the dragons

Chapter 1

I SKRIMARA WAS A MYTH. SO SAID THE DRAGONS' NEWEST Zubir, mere moments after slaughtering her own brother. So therefore said all the dragons. After a lifetime of hiding in plain sight, of playing a weakling, Iskrimara had been among the first to prostrate herself in acceptance of Seraphina Ignatia's rule.

Months later, she couldn't stand it anymore. The dragons had moved on as if they'd forgotten the horror Ignatius's children had inflicted upon them these last centuries. True, the herds had been freed, and with supplemental food from the humans, none went hungry now. And the renewed power flowing through their veins couldn't be denied. Fixing what her own selfishness had wrought was the least Seraphina could do.

And some things could never be fixed. Lives lost would never be restored.

The zubiran vardjim had cost Iskrimara everything.

Yet even Ninad seemed keen to forget the bloodbath that had been forced upon the Zeyno. Her Netta capitulating to this erasure of all they'd lost was an insult Iskrimara couldn't bear. But it wasn't like she could melt into another tribe unnoticed.

So she bent her neck before the new Zubir, bowing to mask the fury roiling in her soul.

What Earth languages do you know? Seraphina asked.

None, Iskrimara admitted in the subservient tone that had been drilled into her as a youngling. *I hope that won't disqualify me.*

With no knowledge of the mortal realm, the only hope of escape Iskrimara had was the Zubir's new sponsorship program, complete with basic training in human life. The first step was enduring this mandatory interrogation. Then came life on Earth, acquiring skills ostensibly to benefit dragonkind.

And what is it you'd like to study? Seraphina probed.

Whatever would be most useful.

Not that Iskrimara would be returning to serve Seraphina's whims. Not when the whole scheme was funded with treasure stolen from their people.

I never dreamed I'd have a chance to visit Earth, she added to tip the scales in her favor. *I'm eager to learn.*

Because leaving meant time. Time to recruit others who remembered what the zubiran family had taken from them. Time to feel the truth of her own power, away from prying eyes. Time to plan.

And with time, Iskrimara would find a way to make her cousin pay.

This was it. The opportunity Oz had been waiting centuries for. A chance to return to Earth.

He hadn't even dreamed it could happen like this. All that stood in his way was convincing the new Zubir that he was strong enough to be useful to dragonkind. Lightning shot

through his thigh as he knelt in the line among the other hope-
fuls. But he'd been in more pain with less to gain.

The Zubir's skirts swished above the ground as she halted
in front of him. This one interrogation, and if he passed, he could
be gone from Azhidar Zher in a matter of weeks. The brutal
world of the dragons had little patience for those like him. But
Earth? A plethora of delights everywhere you looked.

Stand up, commanded the Zubir.

Oz's heart stuttered. *No, please.* He needed this, had been
yearning for it for decades that had stretched into centuries
which felt like eons.

Give me a chance, he begged privately. The others were already eying him surreptitiously. They'd all heard the order, but
they didn't need to witness the extent of his humiliation. *I can
be of use to the dragons. I swear it.*

I said stand, she repeated for all to hear.

But a quiet thought followed, for him alone. *There's no need
for you to be in such pain.*

Oz's head jerked back, his eyes claiming the audacity to
meet her gaze. The amethyst eyes that marked the zubiran line.

Her brow crooked.

He shook himself free from the shock and grit his teeth, his
muscles clenching in familiar pain as he rose to his feet, refusing to stumble before all those gathered. A true runt, with his
hindquarter damaged before hatching, he was accustomed to
fighting for any scrap of dignity, reminded every day that he
survived only on the mercy of his protector. He'd become an
expert at navigating her whims.

But he couldn't read the Zubir, certainly not from a brief
glance before dropping his gaze back to the ground. *This won't
disqualify me?*

Why should it? she responded, and the heart that had struggled to beat suddenly exploded in a rhythm of ecstasy and fear. A joy so potent it hurt.

Why do you want to go to Earth? the Zubir asked for all to hear, a standard question she asked of them all.

To learn from the humans. There was so much pleasure waiting at every turn, an ability to delight in life despite how short-lived the humans were. Such beauty in hedonism. Given the chance, he would indulge in any and every bit he could.

Do you speak any Earth languages? She was moving down the line of standard questions. But once again he heard extra words echo in his mind. *Just you wait until you see all they've invented. The whole world at your fingertips.*

Oz chanced another look up to her face. Though it remained largely impassive, he could have sworn a slight smile touched her eyes.

Then the meaning of her words registered, and Oz nearly fell back to his knees, ready to swear whatever allegiance she required. *Finally.*

At last, he would be free. Equal to any other dragon sent to Earth.

Want more of Iskrimara and Oz's story?

Read *Restored* as I write it by

supporting me on Patreon:

patreon.com/AriaGlazki

Exclusive Coloring Cards!

Get exclusive Defiant Dragonlet coloring cards
in the mail by supporting me on Patreon!

Acknowledgments

When starting this story, I absolutely never intended for it to become Fantasy (yes, with a capital *F*). I wanted to play around with dragons, sure. But inventing other realms and a language and a society was never part of the plan. Alas, such is the life of a "pantser"—the story goes where it wants, even if that later requires weeks of world-building for any of it to make sense.

I was quite fortunate, then, to meet someone who loves to play around in different worlds and figure out their rules while I was still drafting this book. Thank you, Jim, for being my sounding board on countless occasions, for your enthusiasm and support, for your patience along the way, and for all the many ways you improve my life. I'm pretty sure this story is the first thing you found interesting about me, and if so, writing it is the best decision I ever made. This book (and I) wouldn't be the same without you!

I am also endlessly grateful to my Patrons for their support, encouragement, and patience as I shared a very rough version.

Your faith helps keep me writing. Special shout out to my Super Supporters, Rachel and Irene!

Thank you as well to my cover designer, Danielle Fine, for creating not one but two stunning covers for this story. I so appreciate your help transforming the original cover into one that better reflects the final version, particularly with such a lightning-fast turnaround.

And though they should really take it for granted at this point, I must thank all the friends and family who continue to offer their support, for my writing, for my sanity, and for my life. These last years have been quite a struggle, and I would never have made it to this point—and finally brought this story into the world—without each of you.

About Aria

Aria Glazki's first kiss technically came from a bear cub. Though no fairytale transformation followed, she still believes magic can happen when the right people come together—if they don't get in their own way, that is. So now Aria writes heartfelt romances about hurt people healing as they build a love that lasts. Sometimes she adds a magical twist.

www.AriaGlazki.com